JOHN SANDFORD

"Grabs you by the throat and never lets go."
—Robert B. Parker

"Knows all there is to know about detonating the gut-level shocks of a good thriller."
—*New York Times Book Review*

"Creates a cracklingly authentic atmosphere, a you-are-there sense of place, a sharp and sympathetic feeling for the details of the police at work."
—*Los Angeles Times Book Review*

"Has created one of the most engaging (and iconoclastic) characters in contemporary fiction. His novel is an unbeatable recipe for a fast-paced, you-can't-put-this-book-down kind of read."
—*Detroit News*

"Whips his ingredients into a fresh and satisfying dish, the mark of a born storyteller. The result is a first-rate thriller."
—*San Diego Union-Tribune*

"Consistently avoids the routine or expected, with intelligence and surprising new wrinkles."
—*Washington Post Book World*

"Emotionally enriches his plot with some of the most persuasive personal relationships I've encountered in this genre for years, maybe decades."
—*Philadelphia Inquirer*

"Crafts the kind of trimmed-to-the-bone thriller that is hard to put down. A classic test of wills and wile."
—*Chicago Tribune*

TURN THE PAGE FOR MORE PRAISE...

RULES OF PREY

John Sandford's smash bestselling debut—introducing detective Lucas Davenport...

"Sleek and nasty . . . it's a big, scary, suspenseful read, and I loved every minute of it." —Stephen King

"A haunting, unforgettable, ice-blooded thriller." —Carl Hiaasen

"A surefire bestseller . . . scary . . . intriguing . . . unforgettable." —Chicago Tribune

SHADOW PREY

Lieutenant Davenport goes on a city-to-city search for a bizarre ritualistic killer...

"When it comes to portraying twisted minds, Sandford has no peers." —Associated Press

"Ice-pick chills . . . excruciatingly tense . . . a double-pumped roundhouse of a thriller." —Kirkus Reviews

"The pace is relentless . . . a classic." —Boston Globe

EYES OF PREY

Davenport risks his sanity to stalk the most brilliant and dangerous man he has ever known, a doctor named Michael Bekker...

"Relentlessly swift. Genuinely suspenseful . . . excellent." —Los Angeles Times

"His detective is one of the best hard-case cops on the crime scene today." —Houston Post

"Engrossing . . . one of the most horrible villains this side of Hannibal the Cannibal." —Richmond Times-Dispatch

SILENT PREY

Michael Bekker, the psychopath Davenport captured in Eyes of Prey, *escapes...*

"Sleek . . . superb!" —*St. Paul Pioneer Press*

"*Silent Prey* terrifies . . . just right for fans of *The Silence of the Lambs.*" —*Booklist*

"Readers will speed through the surprise twists . . . Sandford delivers." —*Publishers Weekly*

WINTER PREY

In the icy woods of rural Wisconsin, Davenport searches for a brutal killer known as the Iceman...

"Vastly entertaining . . . a furious climactic chase . . . one of the best *Preys* yet." —*Kirkus Reviews*

"The world's newest thrill master." —*Pittsburgh Press*

"An intense thriller with an unlikely killer." —*Playboy*

NIGHT PREY

Davenport faces a master thief who becomes obsessed with a beautiful woman—then carves her initials into his victims...

"One of the most engaging characters in contemporary fiction." —*Detroit News*

"There's action aplenty . . . Sandford is in top form." —*Minneapolis Star Tribune*

"*Night Prey* sizzles . . . positively chilling." —*St. Petersburg Times*

CONTINUED...

MIND PREY

Lucas Davenport tracks a vicious kidnapper who knows more about mind games than Lucas himself...

"His seventh, and best, outing in the acclaimed *Prey* suspense series."
—*People*

"Grip-you-by-the-throat thrills . . . impossible to put down."
—*Houston Chronicle*

"Sandford has always known how to twist his readers into knots and with *Mind Prey* he's in top form."
—*Chicago Tribune*

AND DON'T MISS JOHN SANDFORD'S THRILLING NOVELS OF STINGS AND SWINDLES...

THE EMPRESS FILE

Kidd and LuEllen are a pair of lovers and liars plotting the ultimate scam . . . until everything goes wrong...

"Impossible to resist."
—Carl Hiaasen

"Alfred Hitchcock would have been delighted."
—*Philadelphia Inquirer*

"The imaginative con scheme is clever . . . but the biggest thrills occur when events don't go as planned."
—*Library Journal*

THE FOOL'S RUN

Kidd and LuEllen return for a killer con in the high-tech world of industrial espionage...

"A gripping, ultramodern novel . . . fast-paced and suspenseful."
—*Chicago Tribune*

"Fast-paced action, high-intellect puzzle-solving, dandy characters . . . if you start guessing outcomes, you are fooled."
—*Minneapolis Star Tribune*

SUDDEN PREY

JOHN SANDFORD

BERKLEY BOOKS, NEW YORK

SUDDEN PREY

A Berkley Book / published by arrangement with
the author

PRINTING HISTORY
G. P. Putnam's Sons edition / May 1996
Berkley edition / May 1997

The Putnam Berkley World Wide Web site address is
http://www.berkley.com

ISBN: 0-425-15753-9

BERKLEY®
Berkley Books are published by The Berkley Publishing Group,
200 Madison Avenue, New York, New York 10016.
BERKLEY and the "B" design
are trademarks belonging to Berkley Publishing Corporation.

PRINTED IN THE UNITED STATES OF AMERICA

10 9 8 7 6 5 4 3 2 1

ONE

THROUGH THE SPEAKERS ABOVE HIS HEAD, LITTLE CHIL-dren sang in sweet voices, *O holy night, the stars are brightly shining, it is the night of the dear Savior's birth . . .*

The man who might kill Candy LaChaise stood in the cold and watched her through the glass doors. Sometimes he could see only the top of her head, and sometimes not even that, but he never lost track of her.

Candy, unaware, browsed through the lingerie, moving slowly from rack to rack. She wasn't really interested in un-derwear: her attention was fixed on the back of the store, the appliance department. She stopped, pulled out a black bustier, held it up, cocked her head like women do. Put it back, turned toward the doors.

The man who might kill her stepped back, out of sight.

A minivan pulled to the curb and a chunky woman in an orange parka hopped out and pushed back the van's side door. An avalanche of dumplinglike children spilled onto the side-walk. They were of both sexes, all blond, and of annual sizes: maybe four, five, six, seven, eight and nine years old. The van headed for a parking space, while the woman herded the kids toward the doors.

The man took a bottle from his pocket, stuck his tongue into the neck, tipped it up and faked a swallow or two. The woman hustled the kids past him, shielding them with her body, into the store and out of sight. That was what he wanted; he put the bottle away, and looked back through the doors.

THERE SHE WAS, STILL IN LINGERIE. HE LOOKED around, and cursed the season: the Christmas decorations, the dirty piles of hard, frozen snow along the streets, the wind that cut through his woolen gloves. His face was thin, unshaven, the skin stretched like parchment on a tambourine. Nicotine had stained his teeth as yellow as old ivory. He lit a Camel, and when he put the cigarette to his lips, his hands trembled with the cold. When he exhaled, the wind snatched away the smoke and the steam of his breath, and made him feel even colder than he was.

AN OILY BARITONE, A MAN WHO'D NEVER BE BING Crosby: . . . *Let nothing you dismaaay, Remember Christ our Sa-ay-vior was born on Christmas Day . . .*

He thought, "Christ, if I could only stop the music . . ."

From where he stood, he could see the golden spire atop the state capitol; under the December overcast it looked like a bad piece of brass. Fucking Minnesota. He put the bottle to his lips, and this time let a little of the wine trickle down his throat. The harsh grape-juice taste cut into his tongue, but there was no warmth in the alcohol.

What in the hell was she doing?

She'd cruised Sears Brand Central, taking her time, looking at refrigerators, buying nothing. Then she strolled through the ladies' wear department, where she'd looked at blouses. Then she walked back through Brand Central, checking the cellular telephones.

Again she walked away: he'd been inside at the time, and she'd almost trapped him in the television display. He hit the doors, went through, outside into the wind . . . but she'd swerved toward the lingerie. Had she spotted him? A TV salesman had. Picking up his ragged coat and rotten shoes, the salesman had posted himself near the Toshiba wide-screens, and was watching him like a hawk. Maybe she . . .

There. She was on her way out.

When Candy walked out of Sears, he didn't look at her. He saw her, but he didn't move his head. He simply stood against the outside wall, rocked on his heels, mumbled into his parka and took another nip of the MD 20-20.

CANDY NEVER REALLY SAW HIM, NOT THEN. SHE HALF-turned in his direction as she left the store, but her eyes skipped over him, like they might skip over a trash barrel or a fire hydrant. She *bopped* down the parking lot, not quite in a hurry, but not dawdling, either. Her step was light, athletic, confident, the step of a cheerful woman. She was pretty, in a thirty-something high-school cheerleader way, with natural blond hair, a round Wisconsin face and a clear Wisconsin complexion.

She walked halfway down the lot before she spotted the Chevy van and started toward it.

The man who might kill her, who still stood by the doors, said, "She just walked past her car."

A Republican state legislator in a wool Brooks Brothers overcoat heard the words and hurried into the store. No time for dialogue with a street schizo: you see them everywhere, mumbling into their wine-stained parkas.

"I think she's going for that van, dude."

•   •   •

CANDY LIKED COUNTRY MUSIC AND SHIRT POCKETS that had arrows at the corners. She liked line-dancing and drinking Grain Belt. She liked roadhouses on country black-top, pickup trucks and cowboy boots and small blue-eyed children and guns. When she got to the Chevy van, she took out a two-inch key ring filled with keys and began running them through the lock. She hit it on the twelfth one, and popped the door.

The van belonged to a slightly ragged Sears washing ma-chine salesman named Larry. The last time she'd seen Larry, he was standing next to a seven-hundred-dollar Kenmore washer with Quiet Pak and Automatic Temperature Control, repinning his name tag. He was about ten minutes late—late enough that she'd started to worry, as she browsed the blouses and underwear. Had the van broken down? That would be a major problem . . .

But then, there he was, breathing hard, face pink from the cold, leaning against the Kenmore. Larry was a wise guy, she knew, and she didn't care for wise guys. She knew he was a wise guy because a bumper sticker on the back of his van said, in large letters, *AGAINST ABORTION*? And below that, in smaller letters, *Then Don't Have One*. Abortion was not a topic for bumper-sticker humor.

THE MAN WHO MIGHT KILL HER MUMBLED INTO HIS parka: "She's in the van, she's moving."

The voice that spoke back to him was not God: "I got her."

Great thing about parkas: nobody could see the commo gear, the microphones and earplugs. "She's gonna do it," Del said. He put the bottle of Mogen David on the ground, carefully, so it wouldn't spill. He wouldn't need it again, but somebody might.

"Franklin says LaChaise and Cale just went into that pizza

joint behind the parking ramp," said the voice in his ear. "They went out the back of the ramp, through a hole in a hedge."

"Scoping it out, one last time. That's where they'll dump the van," Del said. "Get Davenport on the road."

"Franklin called him. He's on the way. He's got Sloan and Sherrill with him."

"All right," Del said, noncommittally. *Not all right*, he thought. Sherrill had been shot a little more than four months earlier. The slug had nicked an artery and she'd almost bled out before they got her to the hospital. Del had pinched the artery so hard that Sherrill had later joked that she felt fine, except for the massive bruise where Del had pinched her leg.

Putting Sherrill's face into this, so soon, might be too heavy, Del thought. Sometimes Davenport showed all the common sense of a . . . Del couldn't think of anything. A trout, maybe.

"There she goes," said the voice in his ear.

THE SALESMAN'S VAN STANK OF CIGAR SMOKE. CANDY'S nose wrinkled at the smell, but she wouldn't have to tolerate it for long. She eased the van out of the parking space, and checked the gas: half a tank, more than enough. She drove slowly up the block, to Dale, down Dale and onto I-94 toward Minneapolis. Georgie and Duane would be waiting at Ham's Pizza.

She looked at the speedometer: fifty-four. Perfect. Crooks mostly drove too fast. Dick said they didn't give a shit about the traffic laws or the other small stuff, and half the time they'd hit a bank, get away clean, then get caught because they were doing sixty-five in a fifty-five. She wouldn't make *that* mistake.

She tried to relax, checked all the mirrors. Nothing unusual. She took the P7 out of her coat pocket, slipped the magazine, pushed on the top shell with her thumb. She could tell by the pressure that she had a full clip.

Dick always made fun of the little bitty nine-millimeter shells, but she'd stick with them. The small gun felt right in her hand and the muzzle blast was easy to manage. The P7 held thirteen rounds. She could put nine or ten of the thirteen shots into the top of a Campbell's soup can at twenty-five feet, in less than seven seconds. A couple of times, she'd put all thirteen in.

Good shooting. Of course, soup-can lids didn't move. But on the two occasions when she'd been shooting for real, she felt no more pressure than when she'd been outside Dick's double-wide, banging away at soup-can lids. You didn't really line anything up, you kept both eyes open and looked across the front sights, tracking, and just at that little corner of time when the sight crossed a shirt pocket or a button or another good aim point, you'd take up the last sixteenth of an inch and . . .

Pop. Pop, pop.

Candy got a little hot just thinking about it.

DANNY KUPICEK HAD LONG BLACK HAIR THAT HIS WIFE cut at home, and it fell over his eyes and his oversized glasses so that he looked like a confused shoe clerk. That helped when he was working the dopers: dopers were afraid of anyone too hip. They trusted shoe clerks and insurance salesmen and guys wearing McDonald's hats. Danny looked like all of those. He pulled the city Dodge to the curb and Del climbed in and Kupicek took off, three hundred yards behind the Chevy van. Del put his hands over the heat vent.

"I gotta come up with a new persona for the wintertime," Del said. "Somebody who's got a warm coat."

"State legislator," Kupicek said. He'd been sitting in the car off the capitol grounds, keeping an eye on Candy's car.

He'd watched the politicians coming and going, and noticed how prosperous they seemed.

"Nah," Del said, shaking his head. "I wanna try somebody legit."

"Whatever, you gotta keep your head covered," said Kupicek. He wore heavy corduroy pants, a sweater over a button-down shirt, a wool watch cap and an open parka. "Fifty percent of all heat loss comes from the head."

"What do you think the hood is for?" Del asked, pointing over his shoulder.

"Too loose," Kupicek said, like he knew what he was talking about. He was nine cars behind Candy when they entered I-94, in the slow lane and two lanes to the right. "You need a stocking cap under there."

"Fuck a bunch of stocking caps. I need a desk job is what I need. Maybe I'll apply for a grant."

Kupicek looked at him, the yellow teeth and two-day stubble. "You ain't grant material," he said, frankly. "I'm grant material. Sherrill's grant material. Even Franklin is grant material. You, you ain't grant material."

"Fuck you and your wife and all your little children," Del said. He picked up Kupicek's handset. "Lucas, you there?"

Davenport came back instantly: "We're setting up in the Swann parking lot. Where is she?"

"Just passing Lexington," Del said.

"Stay with her. When she gets off at 280, let me know as soon as she's at the top of the ramp."

"Do that," Del said.

Kupicek was watching the van: "She's got some discipline. I don't think we touched fifty-six since we got on the road."

"She's a pro," Dell said.

"If it was me, I'd be so freaked, I'd be doing ninety. Course, maybe they're not gonna do it."

"They're gonna do it," Del said. He could feel it: they were gonna do it.

GEORGIE LACHAISE WAS A DARK WOMAN WITH BLUE eyes that looked out from under too-long, too-thick eyebrows. She had a fleshy French nose, full lips with the corners down-turned. She locked Duane Cale's eyes across the table and said, "Duane, you motherfucker, if you drive off, I'll find you and I'll shoot you in the fuckin' back. I promise you."

Duane leaned forward over the yellow Formica table, both hands wrapped around an oversized cup of Coke Classic. He had an unformed face, and hair that had never picked a color: one eyewitness might say he was blond, another would swear that he had brown hair. One would say apple-cheeked, another would say fox-faced. He seemed to change, even as you looked at him. He wore a camouflage army jacket over jeans and boots, with the collar turned up, and a Saints baseball hat.

"Oh, I'll do it," he said, "but it don't feel right. It just don't feel right. I mean, we did that one in Rice Lake, I was good there."

"You were perfect in Rice Lake," Georgie said. She thought, *You were so scared I thought we'd have to carry you out.* "This time, all you gotta do is drive."

"Okay, you see right there?" asked Duane, tapping the tabletop with the cup. "You said it your own self: I was perfect. This don't feel perfect, today. No sir. I mean, I'll do it if you say so, but I . . ."

Georgie cut him off. "I say so," she said bluntly. She glanced at her watch. "Candy'll be here in a minute. You get your asshole puckered up and get behind the wheel and every-thing'll go smooth. You know what to do. You only gotta drive two blocks. You'll be perfect."

"Well, okay . . ." His Adam's apple bobbed. Duane Cale

was too scared to spit and the Coca-Cola didn't seem to make a difference.

LUCAS DAVENPORT PEELED OFF HIS TOPCOAT AND THE gray Icelandic sweater. Sloan handed him the vest and Lucas shrugged into it, slapping the Velcro tabs into place, everything nice and snug, except if you took a shot in the armpit it'd go right through your heart and both lungs on the way out the opposite 'pit . . . Never turn sideways.

"Fuckin' cold," Sloan said. He was a narrow, sideways-looking man who today wore a rabbit-fur hat. "We live in fuckin' Russia. The Soviet fuckin' Union."

"Is no Soviet Union," Lucas said. They were in a drug-store parking lot, Lucas and Sloan and Sherrill, and had gotten out of the slightly warm car to put on the vests. A loitering civilian watched them as his dog, wearing a blue jacket, sniffed up an ice-bound curb.

"I know," Sloan said. "It moved here."

Lucas pulled the sweater back over his head, then slipped back into his topcoat. He was a tall man, dark-haired, dark-complected with ice-blue eyes. A scar trailed through one brow ridge and expired on his cheek, a white line like a scratch across his face. As his head popped through the sweater's neck hole, he was grinning at Sloan, an old friend: "Who was trying to start a departmental ski team?"

"Hey, you gotta do something in the middle of the . . ."

The radio broke in: "Lucas?"

Lucas picked up the handset: "Yeah."

"On the 280 ramp," Del said.

"Got it . . . you get that, Franklin?"

Franklin came back, his voice chilled. "I got it. I can see LaChaise and Cale, they're still sitting there. They look like they're arguing."

"Keep moving," Lucas said.

"I'm moving. I'm so fuckin' cold I'm afraid to stop."

"On University . . ." Del said.

"We better go," Sherrill said. Her face was pink with the cold, and nicely framed by her kinky black hair. She wore a black leather jacket with tight jeans and gym shoes, and furry white mittens that she'd bought in a sale from a cop catalog. The mittens were something a high school kid might wear, but had a trigger-finger slit, like hunting gloves. "She'll be picking them up."

"Yeah." Lucas nodded, and they climbed into the city car, Sloan in the driver's seat, Sherrill next to him, Lucas sprawled in the back.

"Here she comes," said Franklin, calling on the radio.

"Check your piece," Lucas said over the seat to Sherrill. He wasn't quite sure of her, what she'd do. He wanted to see. He slipped his own .45 out of his coat pocket, punched out the magazine, racked the shell out of the chamber, then went through the ritual of reloading. In the front seat, Sherrill was spinning the wheel on her .357.

As Sloan took the car through an easy U-turn and the three blocks toward the Midland Steel Federal Credit Union, Lucas looked out the window at the street, and felt the world begin to shift.

The shift always happened before a fight, a suddenly needle-sharp appreciation of image and texture, of the smell of other bodies, of cigarette tar and Juicy Fruit, gun oil, wet leather. If your mind could always work like this, he thought, if it could always operate on this level of realization, you would be a genius. Or mad. Or both.

Lucas remembered a stray thought from earlier in the day, picked up the handset and called dispatch.

"We need two squads on University," he said. "We're tracking a stolen Chevy van and we want a uniform stop as soon as possible."

He recited the tag number and license and the dispatcher confirmed it. "We've got a car on Riverside," the dispatcher said. "We'll start them that way."

CANDY PULLED THE VAN TO THE CURB OUTSIDE HAM'S Pizza. Georgie and Duane were waiting, and she slid over to the passenger seat, and popped the back door for Georgie as Duane got in the driver's seat.

"Everything okay?" Duane asked.

"Great, Duane," Candy said. She gave him her cheerleader smile.

Duane hungered for her, in his Duane-like way. They'd gone to school together, elementary through high school. They'd played on a jungle gym, smart Candy and not-so-smart Duane. She'd let him see her tits a couple of times— once down by Meyer's Creek, skinny-dipping with Dick, when Dick hadn't seen Duane coming, but Candy had. She was Dick's woman, all right, but wasn't above building extracurricular loyalty for a time when it might be needed.

"Drive," Georgie said from the back. And to Candy: "You set?"

"I'm set."

"This should be a good one," Georgie said.

"Should be great," Candy said. Ten o'clock on a payday morning. The paychecks were issued at eleven. The first employees would be sneaking out to cash their checks by eleven-oh-one. That'd be an hour too late.

"There's the nigger again," Duane said, distractedly.

A giant black man had come into Ham's before Candy had gotten there, ordered a slice, asked if he could pay with food stamps. When told that he couldn't, he'd reluctantly taken two crumpled dollar bills out of his pocket and pushed them across the counter.

"Food stamps," Georgia said in disgust. "He's one of

those screwballs. Look at him talk to himself.''

Franklin, shambling along the street, said, ''One block, fifteen seconds.''

DUANE SAID, ''THERE IT IS,'' AND HIS VOICE MAY HAVE trembled when he said it. Georgie and Candy turned away from the black man and looked down the street at the yellow brick building with the plastic sign, and the short stoop out front.

''Remember what I said, Duane. We'll be in there for one minute,'' Georgie said. She leaned forward and spoke softly into his ear, and when Duane tried to turn his head away, she caught his earlobe and tugged it back, pinched it between her nails. Duane flinched, and she said, ''If you drive away, one of us will hunt you down and kill you. If you drive, Duane, you're dead. Isn't that right, Candy?''

''That's right,'' Candy said, looking at him. She let some ice show, then switched to her God-Duane-I'd-Love-to-Fuck-You-But-I-Gotta-Be-True-to-Dickie look. ''But he won't drive. Duane's okay.'' She patted his thigh.

''Oh, I'll do it,'' Duane said. He looked like a trapped rat. ''I mean, I'll do it. I did it in Rice Lake, didn't I?''

He pulled the van to the curb and Georgie gave him a look, then the two women pulled nude nylon stockings over their faces and took the pistols out of their coat pockets.

''Let's go,'' Georgie said. She climbed out, and Candy followed a step behind; it passed through Georgie's mind that Candy looked radiant.

''I feel like I might pop one,'' Candy said to Georgie, as they climbed the four steps to the Credit Union door.

FRANKLIN WAS HALFWAY DOWN THE BLOCK WHEN they went inside and he said, ''The two women are inside. Pulled the nylons over their heads. It's going down.''

Five seconds later, Del and Kupicek stopped at the corner behind him, then eased forward so they could see the back of the Chevy van and Cale's head. They were forty yards away.

Sloan stopped at the next corner up, and eased forward until he could see the front of the truck. "You set?" Lucas asked. He cracked the back door.

"Yeah." Sloan nodded, looked almost sleepy and yawned. Tension.

"Let's go," Lucas said. And in the handset he said, "Go."

GEORGIE AND CANDY WENT IN HARD. VERY LARGE. very loud, screaming, masks, guns, Georgie first:

"On the wall," she screamed, "on the wall," and Candy behind her, vaulting to the top of the cash counter, screaming, the gun big in her hand, the hole at the muzzle looking for eyes. "On the wall . . ."

Four women employees and a single customer, a man in a black ski jacket and tinted eyeglasses, were inside the credit union. The woman closest to Candy looked like a carp, her mouth opening and closing, opening and closing, hands coming up, then waving, as though she could wave away a bullet. She wore a pink sweater with hand-darned blue flax blossoms in a line across the chest. Another woman curled up and turned away, looking back at them over her shoulder, and stepped against the back wall, next to a filing cabinet. She wouldn't look at Candy. A younger woman, a cashier, jumped back, yelped once, put her hands over her mouth, backed away, knocked a phone off a table, jumped again, froze. The fourth woman simply backed away, her hands at her shoulders.

Georgie said, rapid-fire, a vocal machine gun: "Easy, easy, everybody take it easy. Everybody shut up, shut up, shut up, and stand still. Stand still, everybody shut up . . . This is a holdup, shut up.''

They'd been inside for ten seconds. Candy dropped behind the counter and pulled a pillowcase out of her waistband and started dumping cash drawers.

"Not enough," she shouted over Georgie's chant. "Not enough, there's more somewhere."

Georgie picked out the woman with the best clothes, the woman with the flax blossoms, pointed her finger at her and shouted, "Where is it, where's the rest of it?"

The woman said, "No-no-no . . ."

Georgie pointed her pistol at the man in the ski jacket and said, "If you don't say, in one second I'm gonna blow his fuckin' head off, his fuckin' head."

Georgie was posed in a two-handed TV-cop position, the pistol pointing at jacket-man's head, never wavering. The flax-blossom woman looked around for somebody to help her, somebody to direct her, but there wasn't anybody. She sagged and said, "There's a box in the office."

Candy grabbed her, roughed her, shoved her toward the tiny cubicle in the back. The woman, scuttling ahead, pointed at a box on the floor in the footwell of the desk. Candy shoved her back toward the door, picked up the box, put it on the desk, and popped the top: stacks of currency, tens, twenties, fifties, hundreds.

"Got it," she shouted. She dumped it in the pillowcase.

"Let's go," Georgie shouted. "Let's go . . ."

Candy twisted the top of the pillowcase and threw it over her shoulder, like Santa Claus, and hustled around the cash counter toward the door. The man in the ski jacket had backed against the wall at a check-writing desk, his hands over his head, a twisted, trying-to-please smile on his face, his eyes frightened white spots behind the amber-tinted specs.

"What are you laughing at?" Candy screamed at him. "Are you laughing at us?"

The smile got broader, but he waved his fingers and said, "No, no, I'm not laughing . . ."

"Fuck you," she said, and she shot him in the face.

The blast in the small office was a bomb: the four women shrieked and went down. The man simply dropped, a spray of blood on the tan wall behind his head, and Georgie spun and said, "Go."

They were out the door in seconds . . .

"DO IT," DEL SAID, AND KUPICEK FLOORED IT.

Sloan was coming in from the front. Duane saw him coming, had no time to wonder. The car swerved and screeched to a stop three inches from the van's front bumper, wedging him to the curb. From behind, in a flash in his rearview mirror, he saw another car wedge in behind him. In the next half-second, the passenger door flew open and the big black pizza guy was there, and a gun pointed at the bridge of Duane's nose.

"Don't even fuckin' scratch," Franklin said, in his pleasant voice, which wasn't very pleasant. "Just sit tight." He reached across, flipped the shift lever into park, killed the engine, pulled the keys from the ignition and let them fall on the floor. "Just sit."

And then there were more guys, all on the passenger side of the car. But Duane, as interested as he was in the muzzle of Franklin's gun, turned to look at the door of the credit union.

He'd heard the shot: the sound was muffled, but there wasn't any doubt.

"Shit," said the black man. He said, loudly, "Watch it, watch it, we got a shot."

•   •   •

"GO," SCREAMED GEORGIE. SHE WAS SMILING, LIKE A South American revolutionary poster-girl, her dark hair whipping back, and she covered the inner door while Candy exploded through the outer door onto the stoop and then Georgie was through behind her and the van was right there.

And the cops.

They heard the shouting, though Candy never could isolate a word. She was aware of Georgie's gun coming up behind her and she felt her hand loosen on the bag and the bag falling off to the left, and her own gun coming up. She started squeezing the trigger before the gun was all the way up and she saw the thin slat-faced man, and his nose might have been about the size of a Campbell's soup-can lid and her pistol came up, came up . . .

LUCAS HEARD THE SHOT INSIDE AND HE WENT SIDEways and saw Franklin reflexively crouch. Off to the left, Sherrill was propped over the top of Kupicek's car, her pistol leveled at the door and Lucas thought, *Hope they don't look out the window* . . .

Then the door flew open and the two LaChaise women were on the stoop and their guns were coming up and he shouted, "No, don't, no, don't," and he heard Del yelling, and Candy LaChaise started firing and he saw Sherrill's gun bucking in her hand . . .

CANDY SAW THE MAN WITH THE YELLOW TEETH AND the black hole at the end of his pistol and the woman with the dark hair and maybe—if she had time—she thought, *Too late* . . .

She felt the bullets go through, several of them, was aware of the noise, of the flash, of the faces like wanted posters, all straining toward her, but no pain, just a jostling feel, like rays of light pushing through her chest . . . then her vision went, and she felt Georgie falling beside her. She was upside down, her feet on the stoop, her head on the sidewalk, and she waited for the light. The light would come, and behind it . . .

She was gone.

LUCAS WAS SHOUTING, "HOLD IT, HOLD IT," AND FIVE seconds after the two women burst from the credit union, there was no reason to fire his own weapon.

In the sudden silence, through the stink of the smokeless powder, somebody said, "Jesus H. Christ."

TWO

THE MINNEAPOLIS CITY HALL IS A RUDE PILE OF LIVERISH stone, damp in the summer, cold in the winter, ass-deep in cops, crooks, politicians, bureaucrats, favor-seekers, reporters, TV personalities and outraged taxpayers, none of whom were allowed to smoke inside the building.

The trail of illegal cigarette smoke followed Rose Marie Roux down the darkened marble halls from the chief's office to Homicide. The chief was a large woman, getting larger, her face going hound-dog with the pressure of the job and the passing of the years. She stopped outside homicide, took a drag on the cigarette, and blew smoke.

She could see Davenport inside, standing, hands in his pockets. He was wearing a blue wool suit, a white shirt with a long soft collar and what looked like an Hermès necktie— one of the anal numbers with eight million little horses prancing around. A political appointee, a deputy chief, his sideline software business made him worth, according to the latest rumors, maybe ten million dollars. He was talking to Sloan and Sherrill.

Sloan was thin, pasty-faced, serious, dressed all in brown and tan—he could lean against a wall and disappear. He could also make friends with anyone: he was the best interrogator on the force. Sloan hadn't taken his gun out that afternoon and was still on the job.

Sherrill, on the other hand, had fired all six shots from her revolver. She was still up, floating high on the release from the fear and ecstasy that sometimes came after a gunfight. Roux, in her few years on the street, before law school, had never drawn her pistol. She didn't like guns.

Roux watched the three of them, Lucas Davenport and his pals. Shook her head: maybe things were getting out of control. She dropped the cigarette on the floor, stepped on it and pushed through the door.

The three turned to look at her, and she looked at Lucas and tipped her head toward the hall. Lucas followed her back through the door, and shut the door against the inquiring ears of Sloan and Sherrill.

"The request for a uniform stop—when did you think of that?" Roux asked. Her words ricocheted down the marble halls, but there was nobody else to hear them.

Lucas leaned against the cool marble wall. He smiled quickly, the smile here and then gone. The smile made him look hard, even too hard: mean. He'd been working out, Roux thought. He went at it hard, from time to time, and when he'd really stripped himself down, he looked like a piece of belt leather. She could see the shape of his skull under his forehead skin.

"It seemed like a no-lose proposition," he said, his voice pitched low. They both knew what they were talking about.

She nodded. "Well, it worked. We released the voice tape from Dispatch and it's taking the heat off. You're gonna hear some firing-squad stuff from the *Star Tribune*, the editorial page. Questions about why they ever got inside—why you waited that long to move. But I don't think . . . no real trouble.''

"If we'd just taken them, it would have come to a couple of witnesses with bad records," Lucas said. "They'd be back on the street right now."

"I know, but the way it looks . . ." She sighed. "If the LaChaises hadn't shot this guy Farris, there'd be a lot more trouble."

"Big break for us, Farris was," Lucas said, flashing his grim smile again.

"I didn't mean it that way," Roux said, and she looked away. "Anyway, Farris is gonna make it."

"Yeah, a little synthetic cheekbone, splice up his jaw, give him a bunch of new teeth, graft on a piece of ear . . ."

"I'm trying to cover you," Roux said sharply.

"Sounds like you're giving us shit," Lucas snapped back. "The Rice Lake bank people looked at the movies from the credit union security cameras. There's no doubt—it was the LaChaises that did it over there. They looked the same with the panty hose, said the same things, acted the same way. And it was Candy LaChaise who killed the teller. We're waiting to hear back from Ladysmith and Cloquet, but it'll be the same."

Roux shook her head and said, "You picked a hard way to do it, though: a hard way to settle it."

"They came out, they opened up, we were all right there," Lucas said. "They fired first. That's not cop bullshit."

"I'm not criticizing," Roux said. "I'm just saying the papers are asking questions."

"Maybe you oughta tell the papers to go fuck themselves," Lucas said. The chief was a politician who had at one time thought she might be headed for the Senate. "That'd be a good political move right now, the way things are."

Roux took an old-fashioned silver cigarette case out of her

pocket, popped it open. "I'm not talking politics here, Lucas. I'm a little worried about what happened." She fumbled a cigarette out of the case, snapped the case shut. "There's a feel of . . . setup. Of taking the law in our own hands. We're okay, because Farris *was* shot and you made that call for a stop. But there were six or seven holes in Candy LaChaise. It's not like you weren't ready to do it."

"We were ready," Lucas agreed.

". . . So there could be another stink when the medical examiner's report comes out."

"Tell them to take their time writing the report," Lucas said. "You know the way things are: In a week or so, nobody'll care. And we're still a couple of months from the midwinter sweeps."

"Yeah, yeah. And the ME's cooperating. Still."

"The LaChaises started it," Lucas persisted. "And they were sport killers. Candy LaChaise shot people to see them die. Fuck 'em."

"Yeah, yeah," Roux said. She waved at him and started back toward the chief's office, shoulders slumped. "Send everybody home. We'll get the shooting board going tomorrow."

"You really pissed?" Lucas called after her.

"No. I'm just sorta . . . depressed. There've been too many bodies this year," she said. She stopped, flicked a lighter, touched off the fresh cigarette. The tip glowed like a firefly in the semidark. "Too many people are getting killed. You oughta think about that."

WEATHER KARKINNEN WAS DOING PAPERWORK IN THE study when Lucas got home. She heard him in the kitchen, and called down the hall, "In the study."

A moment later, he leaned in the door, a bottle of beer in his hand. "Hey."

"I tried to call you," she said.

Weather was a small, athletic woman with wide shoulders and close-cut blond hair. She had high cheekbones and eyes that were dark blue and slightly slanted in the Lapp-Finnish way. Her nose was a bit too large and a little crooked, as if she'd once lost a close fight. Not a pretty woman, exactly, but men tended to drift toward her at parties. "I saw a TV story on the shooting."

"What'd they say?" He unscrewed the beer cap and took a sip.

"Two women were shot and killed after a robbery. They say it's a controversial shooting." She was anxious, brushing hair out of her eyes.

Lucas shook his head. "You can't pay any attention to TV."

He was angry.

"Lucas . . ."

"What?" He was defensive, and didn't like it.

"You're really steamed," she said. "What happened?"

"Ah, I'm taking heat from the media. Everybody seems to worry about whether it was a fair fight. Why should the fight be fair? This isn't a game, it's law enforcement."

"Could you have taken them? Arrested them? Gone to trial, with the people at the other banks in Wisconsin?"

"No." He shook his head. "They were always masked, and always used stolen cars. There was a case down in River Falls, two years ago, where Candy LaChaise was busted for armed robbery. The guy she robbed, the car dealer, was mugged and killed two weeks later, before the trial. There weren't any witnesses and she had an alibi. The River Falls cops think her old nutcake pals helped her out."

"But it's not your job to kill them," Weather said.

"Hey," Lucas said. "I just showed up with a gun. What happened after that, that was their choice. Not mine."

She shook her head, still distressed. "I don't know," she said. "What you do frightens me, but not the way I thought it would." She crossed her arms and hugged herself, as she would if she were cold. "I'm not so worried about what somebody else might do to you, as what you might be doing to yourself."

"I told you . . ." Getting angrier now.

"Lucas," she interrupted. "I know how your mind works. TV said these people had been under surveillance for nine days. I can *feel* you manipulating them into a robbery. I don't know if *you* know, but I know it."

"Bullshit," he snapped, and he turned out of the doorway.

"Lucas . . ."

Halfway down the hall, the paperwork registered with him. She was doing wedding invitations. He turned around, went back.

"Jesus, I'm sorry, I'm not mad at you," he said. "Sometimes . . . I don't know, my grip is getting slippery."

She stood up and said, "Come here. Sit in the chair."

He sat, and she climbed on his lap. He was always amazed with how small she was, how small all the parts were. Small head, small hands, little fingers.

"You need something to lower your blood pressure," she said.

"That's what the beer's for," he said.

"As your doctor, I'm saying the beer's not enough," she said, snuggling in his lap.

"Yeah? What exactly would you prescribe . . . ?"

THREE

———◆◆◆———

CRAZY ANSEL BUTTERS WAITED FOR THE RUSH AND when it came, he said, "Here it comes."

Dexter Lamb was lying on the couch, one arm trailing on the floor: he was looking up at the spiderweb pattern of cracks on the pink plaster ceiling, and he said, "I told you, dude."

Lamb's old lady was in the kitchen, staring at the top of the plastic table, her voice low, slow, clogged, coming down: "Wish I was going . . . Goddamnit, Dexter, where'd you put the bag? I know you got some."

Ansel didn't hear her, didn't hear the complaints, the whining. Ansel was flying over a cocaine landscape, all the potentialities in his head—green hills, pretty women, red Mustangs, Labrador retrievers—were compressed into a ball of pleasure. His head lay on his shoulder, his long hair falling to the side, like lines of rain outside a window. Twenty minutes later, the dream was all gone, except for the crack afterburn that would arrive like a sack of Christmas coal.

But he had a few minutes yet, and he mumbled, "Dex, I got something to talk about." Lamb was working up another pipe, stopped, his eyes hazy from too many hits, too many days without sleep. "What chu want?"

His wife came out of the back into the kitchen, scratched her crotch through her thin cotton underpants and said, "Where'd you put the bag, Dex?"

"I need to find a guy," Ansel said, talking over her. "It's worth real money. A month's worth of smoke. And I need a crib somewhere close. TV, couple beds, like that."

"I can get you the crib," Lamb said. He jerked a thumb at his wife. "My brother-in-law's got some houses, sorta shitty, but you can live in one of them. You'd have to buy your own furniture, though. I know where you could get some, real cheap."

"That'd be okay, I guess."

Dex finished with the pipe and flicked his Bic, and just before hitting on the mouthpiece, asked, "Who's this guy you're lookin' for?"

"A cop. I'm looking for a cop."

Lamb's old lady, eyes big and black, cheeks sunken, a pale white scar, scratched her crotch again and asked, "What's his name?"

Butters looked at her. "That's what I need to know," he said.

BILL MARTIN CAME DOWN FROM THE UPPER PENINSULA, driving a Ford extended cab with rusted-out fenders and a fat V-8 tuned to perfection. He took the country roads across Wisconsin, stopped at a roadhouse for a beer and a couple of boiled eggs, stopped again for gasoline, talked to a gun dealer in Ashland.

The countryside was still iced in. Old snow showed the sheen of hard crust through the inky-green pines and bare gray broadleafs. Martin stopped often to get out and tramp around, to peer down from bridges, to check tracks in the snow. He didn't like this winter: there'd been good snow, followed by a sleet storm that covered everything with a quarter-inch of ice. The ice could kill off the grouse, just when the population was finally turning back up.

He looked for grouse sign, didn't find any. The season was too new for bear sign, but in another six weeks or eight weeks they'd be out, he thought, sleek and quick and powerful. A young male black bear could run down a horse from a standing start. Nothing quite cleared the sinuses like bumping into a big old hungry bear when you were out on snowshoes, armed with nothing but a plastic canteen and a plug of Copenhagen.

At two o'clock in the afternoon, heading south, he saw a coyote ripping at something in the foot-high yellow grass that broke through the snow beside a creek. Voles, maybe. He pulled the truck over, got out a Bausch and Lomb laser rangefinder and the AR-15. The rangefinder said 305 yards. He figured a nine-inch drop, maybe two inches of right-to-left drift. Using the front fender as a rest, he held a couple of inches over the coyote's shoulder and let go. The .223 caught the mutt a little low, and it jumped straight up into the air and then came down in a heap, unmoving.

"Gotcha," Martin muttered, baring his teeth. The shot felt good.

Martin crossed the St. Croix at Grantsburg, stopped to look at the river—the surface was beaten down with snowmobile trails—then made his way reluctantly out to I-35. The interstate highways were scars across the country, he thought: you couldn't get close enough to see anything. But they were good when you had to move. He paused a final time at an I-35 rest stop just north of the Cities, made a call and then drove the rest of the way in.

• • •

BUTTERS WAS WAITING OUTSIDE AN AMOCO STATION off I-94, an olive-drab duffel at his feet. Martin eased to the curb and Butters climbed in and said, "Straight ahead, back down the ramp."

Martin caught the traffic light and said, "How you been?"

"Tired," Butters said. His small eyes looked sleepy.

"You was tired last fall," said Martin. Martin had passed through Tennessee on one of his gun-selling trips, stopped and done some squirrel-hunting with Butters.

"I'm more tired now," Butters said. He looked into the back of the truck. "What'd you bring?"

"Three cold pistols, three Chinese AK semis, two modified AR-15s, a bow, a couple dozen arrows and my knife," Martin said.

"I don't think you'll need the bow," Butters said dryly.

"It's a comfort to me," Martin said. He was a rough-muscled, knob-headed outdoorsman with a dark reddish beard over a red-pocked face. "Where's this guy we gotta see?"

"Over in Minneapolis. Just outa downtown. By the dome."

Martin grinned his thin coyote-killing smile: "You been studying up on him?"

"Yeah, I have been."

They took I-94 to Minneapolis, got off at the Fifth Street exit, got a pizza downtown, then went back to Eleventh Avenue. Butters directed Martin to a stand-alone two-story brick building with a laundromat on the ground level and apartment above. The building was old, but well-kept: probably a neighborhood mom-and-pop grocery in the forties. Lights showed in the apartment windows.

"He owns the laundromat," Butters said. "The upstairs is one big apartment. He lives up there with his girlfriend." Butters looked up at the lights. "She must be there now, 'cause he's downtown. He runs his boys right to closing time. He got back here last night about two, and he brought a pizza with him.''

Martin looked at his watch, a black military-style Chronosport with luminescent hands. ''Got us about an hour, then.'' He looked back out the window at the building. There was just one door going up to the apartments. ''Where's the garage you were talking about?''

'' 'Round the side. There's a fire escape on the back, one of them drop-down ones, too high to get to. What he did last night was, he pulled into the garage—he's got a garage-door opener in his car—and the door come down. Then, a minute later, this light went on in the back of the apartment, so there must be an inside stairs. Then he come down through the back again, out through the garage, around the corner and into the laundromat. He was in the back, probably countin' out the machines.''

Martin nodded. ''Huh. Didn't use them front stairs?''

''Nope. Could be something goin' on there, so I didn't look.''

''All right. We take him at the garage?''

''Yeah. And we might as well eat the pizza. We only need the box, and Harp ain't gonna want any.''

They chatted easily, comfortable in the pickup smells of gasoline, straw, rust and oil. Then Martin, dabbing at his beard with a paper napkin, asked, ''What do you hear from Dick?''

''Ain't heard dick from Dick,'' Butters said. He didn't wait for Martin to laugh, because he wouldn't, although Butters had a sense that Martin sometimes enjoyed a little joshing. He said, ''Last time I talked to him direct, he sounded like he was . . . getting out there.''

Martin chewed, swallowed and said, ''Nothing wrong with being out there.''

''No, there ain't,'' Butters agreed. He was as far out there as anyone. "But if we're gonna be killing cops, we want the guy to have his feet on the ground."

"Why? You planning to walk away from this thing?"

Butters thought for a minute, then laughed, almost sadly, and shook his head. "I guess not."

"I thought about goin' up to Alaska, moving out in the woods," Martin said, after a moment of silence. "You know, when I got the call. But they'll get you even in Alaska. They'll track you down anywhere. I'm tired of it. I figure, it's time to do something. So when I heard from Dick, I thought I might as well come on down."

"I don't know about that, the politics," Butters said. "But I owe Dick. And I got to pay him now, 'cause I am gettin' awful tired."

Martin looked at him for a moment, then said, "When you're that kind of tired, there ain't no point of being scared of cops. Or anything else."

They chewed for another minute and then Butters said, "True." And a moment later said, "Did I tell you my dog died?"

"That'll make a man tired," Martin said.

LIKE THE SEVEN DWARVES, DAYMON HARP WHISTLED while he worked. And while he collected: unlike Snow White and her pals, Harp sold cocaine and speed at the semi-wholesale level, supplying a half-dozen reliable retailers who worked the clubs, bars and bowling alleys in Minneapolis and selected suburbs.

Harp had seven thousand dollars in his coat pocket and he was whistling a minuet from the Anna Magdelena Notebook when he turned the Lincoln onto Eleventh. A pale-haired kid with a pizza box was standing on the corner outside his laundromat, looking up at the apartments. The pizza box was the thing that snared him: Harp never thought to look for the delivery car.

Daymon turned the corner, pushed the button on the automatic garage door opener, saw the kid look down toward him as he pulled in, then killed the engine and got out. The kid was walking down the sidewalk with the pizza box flat on one hand and Daymon thought, *If that fucking Jas has gone and ordered out for a pizza when she's up there by herself...*

He was waiting for the kid, when Martin stepped up behind him and pressed a pistol to his ear: "Back in the garage."

Daymon jumped, but controlled it. He held his hands away from his sides and turned back to the garage. "Take it easy," he said. He didn't want the guy excited. He'd had a pistol in his ear before, and when caught in that condition, you definitely want to avoid excitement. He tried an implied threat: "You know who I am?"

"Daymon Harp, a jigaboo drug dealer," Martin said, and Harp thought, *Uh-oh.*

The kid with the pizza followed them inside, spotted the lighted button for the garage door opener, and pushed it. The door came down and Martin prodded Harp toward the stairs at the back.

"Take the position," Martin said.

Harp leaned against the wall, hands and feet spread wide. "Got no gun," he said. He looked sideways at Martin: "You're not cops."

"We'd be embarrassed if you was lying about the gun," Martin said. The younger guy patted him down, found the wad of cash and pulled it out. "Ooo," he said. "Thanks."

Harp kept his mouth shut.

"This is the deal," Martin said, as Butters tucked the money away. "We need some information from you. We don't want to hurt you. We will, if you get stupid, so it's best for you to go along."

"What do you want?" Daymon asked.

"To go upstairs," Butters said, in his soft Tennessee accent. Harp looked at him out of the corner of his eye: Butters had three dark-blue tears tattooed at the inner corner of his left eye, and Daymon Harp thought again, *Uh-oh*.

THEY CLIMBED THE STAIRS AS A TRIO, AND NOW THE southern boy had a pistol barrel prodding Daymon's spine, while the other focused on his temple. They all tensed while Daymon unlocked the door. A woman called down an interior hall, "Day? That you?"

Butters left them, padding silently down the hall, while Martin stayed with Harp. The woman came around a corner just as Butters got to it and she jumped, shocked, as Butters grabbed her by a wrist and showed her the gun. "Shut up," Butters said.

She shut up.

Five minutes later, Harp and the woman were duct-taped to kitchen chairs. The woman's hands were flat on her thighs, with loops of tape around her upper arms and body. She had a sock stuffed in her mouth, held in place with two or three more wraps of tape. Her terrified dark eyes flicked between Harp and whichever of the white men was in sight.

Martin and Butters checked the apartment. The landing outside the front door, Martin found when he opened it, was blocked by a pile of brown cardboard appliance boxes. The boxes made a practical burglar alarm and buffer, should the cops come, but still provided an escape route if one were needed.

Butters checked the two bedrooms and found nothing of interest but a collection of vinyl 33-rpm jazz records.

"Clear," Butters said, coming back to the front room.

Martin sat down in a third chair and, knee-to-knee with Harp, said, "You probably know people like us. Met us in the joint. We don't much care for black folks and we'd be happy to cut your throats and be done with it. But we can't, this time, 'cause we need you to introduce us to a friend of yours."

"Who?" Daymon Harp asked.

"The cop you're working with."

Harp tried to look surprised. "There's no cop."

"We know you gotta go through your routine, but we don't have a lot of time," Martin said. "So to show you our . . . mmm . . . sincerity . . ." He chose his words carefully, softly: "We're gonna cut on your girlfriend here."

"Motherfucker," Harp said, but it wasn't directed at Martin. It was simply an exclamation and Martin took it that way. The woman's eyes bulged and she rattled around in the chair, and Martin let her. Over his shoulder, he said, "Ansel? See if you can find a knife in the kitchen . . ."

There was no one standing in the street outside the laundromat, which was a good thing for Butters and Martin, because Harp wouldn't talk right away, and for one short moment, even with the gag, with the windows shut, in the middle of winter, even with that, you could hear Jasmine screaming.

THE MICHIGAN STATE PRISON SENT A SINGLE ESCORT with Dick LaChaise. LaChaise was four years into a nine-year sentence, and not considered an escape risk—with good behavior, he'd be out in a couple of years. They put him in leg irons and cuffs and LaChaise and Wayne O. Sand, the escort, flew into Eau Claire as the sun was going down, eight days after the shootings in Minneapolis.

During the flight, Wayne O. Sand read *The Last Mammoth*

by Margaret Allan, because he liked that prehistoric shit and magic and all. If he'd lived back then, he thought, he'd probably be a clan chief, or something. He'd be in shape, anyway.

LaChaise read a tattoo magazine called *Skin Art*. LaChaise had full sleeves: tattoos running up and down both arms, a comic-book fantasy of superwomen with football-sized tits and lionish hair tangled around his bunched-up weight-room muscles, interspersed with eagles, tigers, knives, a dragon. His arms carried four names: Candy and Georgie on the right, and Harley and Davidson on the left.

The sleeves had been done on the outside, by commercial tattoo artists. The work on his back and legs was being done on the inside. Prison work, with a sewing needle and ballpoint ink. Though the figures lacked the finish of the commercial jobs, there was a nasty raw power to them that LaChaise liked. An aesthetic judgment.

When the plane's wheels came down, LaChaise put the magazine away and looked at Sand: "How about a McDonald's? A couple of Big Macs?"

"Maybe, you don't fuck me around," Sand said, still in the book. Sand was a flabby man, an authoritarian little prison bureaucrat who'd be nice enough one day, and write you up the next, for doing nothing. He enjoyed his power, but wasn't nearly the worst of them. When they landed, Sand marched LaChaise off the plane, and chained him to the seat post in the back of a rental Ford.

"How about them McDonald's?" LaChaise asked.

Sand considered for a second, then said, "Nah. I wanna get a motel 'fore it's too late. There's a game tonight."

"Hey, c'mon . . ."

"Shut up," Sand said, with the casual curtness of a prison guard.

Sand dropped LaChaise at the Eau Claire County Jail for the night. The next morning, he put LaChaise back in the car and drove him through the frozen landscape to the Logan Funeral Home in Colfax. LaChaise's mother was waiting on the porch of the funeral home, along with Sandy Darling, Candy's sister. A sheriff's car was parked in the street, engine running. A deputy sat inside the car, reading a newspaper.

AMY LACHAISE WAS A ROUND, OILY-FACED COUNTRY woman with suspicious black eyes, close-cropped black hair and a pencil-thin mustache. She wore a black dress with a white collar under a blue nylon parka. A small hat from the 1930s sat nervously atop her head, with a crow's wing of black lace pulled down over her forehead.

Sandy Darling was her opposite: a small woman, slender, with a square chin and a thin, windburned face. Crow's-feet showed at the corners of her eyes, though she was only twenty-nine, four years younger than her sister, Candy. Like Candy, she was blond, but her hair was cut short, and she wore simple seed-pearl earrings. And while Candy had that pure Wisconsin milkmaid complexion, Sandy showed a scattering of freckles over her windburned nose and forehead. She wore a black wool coat over a long black dress, tight black leather gloves and fancy black cowboy boots with sterling silver toe guards. She carried a white cowboy hat.

When the rental car pulled up, Amy LaChaise started down the walk. Sandy Darling stayed on the porch, turning the cowboy hat in her hands. Wayne O. Sand popped the padlock on the seat-chain, got out, stood between Amy LaChaise and the car door and opened the door for LaChaise.

"That's my ma," LaChaise said to Sand, as he got out. LaChaise was a tall man, with heavy shoulders and deep-set black eyes, long hair and a beard over hollowed cheeks. He had fingers that were as thick and tough as hickory sticks. With a robe, he might have played the Prophet Jeremiah.

"Okay," Sand said. To Amy LaChaise: "I'll have to hold your purse."

The deputy sheriff had gotten out of his car, nodded to Sand, as Amy LaChaise handed over her purse. "Everything okay?" he asked.

"Yeah, sure." Sand drifted over to chat with him; La-Chaise wasn't going anywhere.

AMY LACHAISE PLANTED A DRY LIZARD'S KISS ON HER son's cheek and said, "They was shot down like dogs."

"I know, Mama," LaChaise said. He looked past her to Sandy Darling on the porch, and nodded curtly. To his mother he said, "They told me about it."

"They was set up," Amy said. She made a pecking motion with her nose, as if to emphasize her words. "That goddamn Duane Cale had something to do with it, 'cause he's just fine, talking like crazy. He'll tell them anything they want. All kinds of lies."

"Yeah, I know," LaChaise said. His mother was worried because Candy had given her money from some of the robberies.

"Well, what'cha gonna do?" Amy LaChaise demanded. "It was your sister and your wife . . ." She clutched at his arm, her fingers sharp and grasping, like buckthorn.

"I know, Mama," LaChaise said. "But there ain't much I can do right now." He lifted his hands so she could see the heavy cuffs.

"That's a fine thing," Amy LaChaise moaned, still clutching at him. "You just let it go and lay around your fat happy cell."

"You go on into the chapel," LaChaise said, with a harsh snap in his voice. "I want to take a look at 'em."

Amy LaChaise backed away a step. "Caskets are closed," she ventured.

"They can open them," LaChaise said, grimly.

Sandy Darling, still on the porch, watched the unhappy reunion, then turned and went inside.

LOGAN, THE FUNERAL DIRECTOR, WAS A SMALL, BALD-ing man, with a mustache that would have been tidy if it hadn't appeared moth-eaten. Although he was gray-faced, he had curiously lively, pink hands, which he dry-washed as he talked. "In a case like this, Mr. LaChaise," he said, looking nervously at LaChaise's handcuffs, "we can't be responsible for the results."

"Open the boxes," LaChaise said.

Logan, worried, cracked the lids and stepped back. Way back. LaChaise stepped up, raised them.

Candy, his wife.

She'd been shot several times through the body, out of sight under her burial dress, but one shot had gone almost straight through her nose. The nose had been rebuilt with some kind of putty. Other than that, she looked as sweet as she had the day he first saw her at the Wal-Mart. He looked at her for a full minute, and thought he might have shed a tear; but he didn't.

Georgie was worse. Georgie had been hit at least three times in the face. While the funeral home had sewed and patched and made up, there was no doubt that something was massively wrong with Georgie's skull. The body in the box looked no more like the living Georgie than did a plastic baby doll.

His sister.

He could remember that one good Christmas when they'd had the tree, he was nine or ten, she was three or four, and somebody had given her pajamas with feet in them. "Feet-sies," she called them. "I'm gonna put on my feetsies." Must have been twenty-five years gone by, and here she was, with a head like a football. Again he felt the impulse toward tears; again, nothing happened.

Logan, the funeral director, his face drained of blood, cleared his throat and said, "Mr. LaChaise?"

LaChaise nodded. "You did okay," he said, gruffly. "Where's the preacher?"

"He should be here. Any minute." Logan's hands flittered gratefully with the compliment, like sparrows at a bird feeder.

"I want to wait back here until the funeral starts," La-Chaise said. "I don't wanna talk to my mama no more'n I have to."

"I understand," the funeral director said. He did: he'd been dealing with old lady LaChaise since the bodies had been released by the Hennepin County Medical Examiner. "We'll move Candy and Georgie into the chapel. When Reverend Pyle arrives, I'll step back and notify you."

"That's good," LaChaise said. "You got a Coke machine here somewhere?"

"Well, there is a Coke box in the staff area," Logan said.

"I could use a Coke. I'd buy it."

"No, no, that's fine . . ."

LaChaise looked at the escort. "How about it, Wayne? I'll buy you one."

Sand drank fifteen caffeinated Diet Cokes a day and got headaches if he went without. LaChaise knew that. "Yeah," Sand said. "A Coke would be good."

"Then I'll make the arrangements," the funeral director said. "The Coke box is back through that door."

He pointed back through the Peace Room, as the staging area was called, to a door that said, simply, "Staff."

ON THE OTHER SIDE OF THE STAFF DOOR WAS A storage room full of broken-down shipping cartons for coffins, eight or ten large green awnings, folded, for funerals on rainy days, a forklift and a tool bench. The Coke box was just inside the door, an old-fashioned red top-opening cooler, with a dozen Coke Classic cans and a couple of white Diet Coke cans bathed in five inches of icy water.

"Get one of them Diets," Sand said, looking down into the water. He was watching his weight. LaChaise dipped into the cooler and got a regular Coke and a Diet, and when he turned back to the escort, Crazy Ansel Butters had stepped quietly out from behind the pile of awnings. He had a .22 pistol and he put it against Sand's head and said, "Don't fuckin' move."

Sand froze, then looked at LaChaise and said, "Don't hurt me, Dick."

"Gimme the keys," LaChaise said.

"You're making a mistake," Sand said. His eyes were rolling, and LaChaise thought he might faint.

"Give him the keys or *you'll* be making a mistake," Butters said. Butters had a voice like a bastard file skittering down a copper pipe.

Sand fumbled the keys out of his pocket and LaChaise stuck his hands out. When the cuffs came off, he rubbed his wrists, took the keys from Sand and opened the leg irons. "That deputy still out by his car?" he asked Butters.

"He was when I come in," Butters said. He slipped a Bull-dog .44 out of his coat pocket and handed it to LaChaise. "Here's your 'dog."

"Thanks." LaChaise took the gun and stuck it in his belt. "What're you driving?"

"Bill's truck. Around the side."

"Did Mama see you?"

"Shit no. Nobody seen me."

LaChaise stepped close to the escort, and turned him a bit, and said, "All right, Wayne, I'm gonna cuff your hands. Now you keep your mouth shut, 'cause if you start hollering before we get out of here, we'll have to come back and do something.''

''I won't say a thing,'' Sand said, trembling.

''You scared?'' LaChaise asked.

''Yeah, I am.''

''That's good; keep you from doing anything foolish,'' LaChaise said. He snapped the cuffs over Sand's hands, then said, ''Lay down.''

Sand got down awkwardly, and Butters stepped up behind him and threw a half-dozen turns of packaging tape around his ankles. When he was finished, LaChaise took the roll of tape, knelt with one knee in the middle of Sand's back, and took three more turns around his mouth. When he was finished, LaChaise looked up at Butters and said, ''Borrow me your knife.''

Sand squirmed under LaChaise's knee as Butters passed a black lock-back knife to LaChaise.

LaChaise grabbed a handful of Sand's hair and pried his head back and said, ''Shoulda bought me them Big Macs.''

He bounced Sand's head off the concrete floor once, twice, then said, ''You asshole.'' He pulled his head straight back, leaned to the side so he could see Sand's bulging eyes. ''You know how they cut a pig's throat?''

''We gotta move along,'' Butters said. ''We can't fuck around.'' Sand began thrashing and squealing through the tape.

LaChaise let him go for a minute, enjoying himself, then he cut Sand's throat from one ear to the other. As the purple blood poured out on the concrete, Sand thrashed, and LaChaise rode him with the knee. The thrashing stopped and Sand's one visible eye began to go opaque.

''Gotta go,'' Butters said.

''Fuckhead,'' LaChaise said. He dropped Sand's head,

wiped the blade on the back of Sand's coat, folded the knife as he stood up and handed it to Butters.

"Gonna be hell cleaning up the mess," Butters said, looking down at the body. "I hate to get blood on concrete."

"We'll send them some Lysol," LaChaise said. "Let's roll."

"Lysol don't work," Butters said, as they headed for the doors. "Nothing works. You always got the stain, and it stinks."

THEY WENT OUT THE SERVICE DRIVE ON THE BACK OF the funeral home, Butters with his thin peckerwood face and long sandy hair sitting in the driver's seat, while LaChaise sat on the floor in front of the passenger seat.

When they turned onto the street, LaChaise unfolded a bit and looked over the backseat, through the cab window, through the topper, and out the topper's rear window, down toward the funeral home. The deputy's car was still sitting in the street, unmoving. Nobody knew yet, but they probably didn't have more than a couple of minutes.

"Are we going up to the trailer?" LaChaise asked.

"Yeah."

"You been there?"

"Yeah. There's electricity for heat and the pump, and a shitter out back. You'll be okay for a day or two, until we get set in the Cities. Martin's down there today, waiting for some furniture to get there."

"You find a cop?"

"Yep. Talked to a guy last night, me and Martin did. We got us a cop the name of Andy Stadic. He's hooked up with a dope dealer named Harp. Harp took some pictures, and now we got the pictures."

"Good one." They crossed a river with a frozen waterfall, and were out of town. "How's Martin?"

"Like always. But that Elmore is a hinky sonofabitch. We told him we needed a place to stay, me 'n Bill, and I had to back him up against the wall before he said okay on the trailer."

"Fuck him," LaChaise said. "If he knew I was gonna be out there, he'd be peein' his pants."

"Gonna have to keep an eye on Sandy," Butters said.

LaChaise nodded. "Yeah. She's the dangerous one. We'll want to get out of the trailer soon as we can."

Butters looked sideways at him. "You and Sandy ever . . ."

"No." LaChaise grinned. "Woulda liked to."

"She's a goddamned wrangler," Butters agreed.

Butters drove them through a web of back roads, never hesitating. He'd driven the route a half-dozen times. Forty minutes after killing Sand, they made the trailer, without seeing another car.

LaChaise said: "Free."

"Loose, anyway," Butters said.

"That's close enough," LaChaise said. He unconsciously rubbed his wrists where the manacles had been.

LOGAN, THE FUNERAL DIRECTOR, RAN INTO THE chapel like a small, drunk tailback, knocked down a half-dozen metal folding chairs, staggered, nearly bowled over Amy LaChaise, struggled briefly with the door handle and was gone out the front door.

Sandy looked at Amy LaChaise across the closed caskets.

"What the hell was that?" Amy asked.

"I don't know," she said, but she felt suddenly cold.

Ten seconds later, the cop who'd been parked out front ran in the door with his pistol in a two-handed grip. He pointed the gun at Sandy, then at Amy, then swiveled around the room: "Hold it. Everybody hold it."

"What?" Amy asked. She clutched her purse to her chest.

Logan peeked out from behind the deputy. "Mr. LaChaise is gone."

Amy screeched, like a crow killing an owl, a sound both pleased and intolerable. "Praise the Lord."

"Shut up," the deputy screamed, pointing the pistol at her. "Where's the prison guy? Where's the prison guy?"

Logan poked a finger toward the back. "In there . . ."

"What's wrong with him?" Sandy asked.

The deputy ran through the door into the back, and Logan said, "Well, he's dead. LaChaise cut his throat."

Sandy closed her eyes: "Oh, no."

A HIGHWAY PATROLMAN ARRIVED FIVE MINUTES LATER. Then two more sheriff's deputies. The deputies split Amy LaChaise and Sandy, made them sit apart.

"And keep your mouths shut," one of the deputies said, a porky man with a name tag that said Graf.

LaChaise, Sandy thought, was at Elmore's daddy's trailer, out at the hill place. Had to be. That whole story about Martin and Butters needing a place to stay—it sounded like bullshit as soon as Elmore had told her about it.

But the problem was, she was Candy's sister, LaChaise's sister-in-law. She'd been present when LaChaise had escaped and murdered a man. And now LaChaise was up at a trailer owned by her senile father-in-law.

She'd seen LaChaise railroaded by the cops for conspiracy to commit murder: they'd do the same to her, and with a lot more evidence.

Sandy Darling sat and shivered, but not with the cold; sat and tried to figure a way out.

THE TRAILER WAS A BROKEN-DOWN AIRSTREAM, SIT-ting on the cold frozen snow like a shot silver bullet. Butters and LaChaise crunched through the sparse snow on four-wheel drive, then they got out of the truck into the cold and Butters unlocked the trailer. "I come by this morning and dropped off some groceries and turned on the heat . . . Can't nobody see you in here, but you might want to keep the light down at night," he said. "You don't have to worry about smoke. Everything's electric and it works. I turned the pump on and filled up the water heater, so you oughta be okay that way."

"You done really good, Ansel," LaChaise said.

"I owe you," Butters said. And he turned away from the compliment: "And there's a TV and a radio, but you can only get one channel—sort of—on the TV, and only two stations on the radio, but they're both country."

"That's fine," LaChaise said, looking around. Then he came back to Butters, his deep black eye fixing the other man like a bug: "Ansel, you ain't owed me for years, if you ever did. But I gotta know something for sure."

Butters glanced at him, then looked out the window over the sink: "Yeah?"

"Are you up for this?"

Ansel glanced at him again, and away: it was hard to get Crazy Ansel Butters to look directly at you, under any conditions. "Oh yeah. I'm very tired. You know what I mean? I'm very tired."

"You can't do nothin' crazy," LaChaise said.

"I won't, 'til the time comes. But I am getting close to my dying day."

The words came out with a formal stillness.

"Well, that's probably bullshit, Ansel," LaChaise said, but he said it gravely, without insult intended or taken.

Butters said, "I come off the interstate, down home, up an exit ramp at night, with pole lights overhead. And I seen an owl's shadow going up the ramp ahead of me—wings all spread, six or eight feet across, the shadow was. I could see every feather. Tell me that ain't a sign.''

"Maybe it's a sign, but I got a mission here," LaChaise said. "We all got a mission now."

"That's true," Butters said, nodding. "And I won't fuck you up."

"That's what I needed to know," LaChaise said.

FOUR

———⊶●⊷———

A CLERK NAMED ANNA MARIE KNOCKED ON LUCAS'S OF-
fice door, stuck her head inside, struggled for a moment with
her bubble gum and said, "Chief Lester said to tell you, you
know Dick LaChaise?"

"Dick?"

She paused for a quick snap of her gum: "Dick, who was
married to that one woman who got shot, and was brother to
the other one? Last week?"

Lucas had one hand over the phone mouthpiece and said,
"Yeah?"

"Well, he escaped in Wisconsin and killed a guy. A prison
guard. Chief Lester said you should come down to Homicide."

"I'll be down in two minutes," Lucas said.

A HEAVYSET PATROL COP, WITH A GRAY CREW CUT, WAS
walking down the hall when Lucas came out of the office.
He took Lucas's elbow and said, "Guy comes home from

work and he finds his girlfriend with her bags packed, waiting in the doorway.''

''Yeah?'' The cop was famous for his rotten jokes.

''The guy's amazed. He says, 'What's going on? What happened?' 'I'm leaving you,' says the girlfriend. 'What'd I do? Everything was okay this morning,' says the guy. 'Well,' says the girlfriend, 'I heard you were a pedophile.' And the guy looks at his girlfriend and says, 'Pedophile? Say, that's an awwwwfully big word for a ten-year-old . . . ' ''

''Get away from me, Hampsted,'' Lucas said, pushing him off; but he was laughing despite himself.

''Yeah, you'll be tellin' all your friends . . .''

LESTER WAS TALKING TO THE HOMICIDE LIEUTENANT, turned when Lucas came in, dropped his feet off the lieutenant's desk and said, ''Dick LaChaise cut the throat of a prison guard during the funeral of Candace and Georgia LaChaise, and vanished. About an hour ago.''

''Vanished?'' Lucas said.

''That's what the Dunn County sheriff said: vanished.''

''How'd he cut the guy's throat? Was there a fight?''

''I don't know the details,'' Lester said. ''There's a cluster-fuck going on at the funeral home. It's over in Colfax, ten, fifteen miles off I-94 between Eau Claire and Menomonie. Probably an hour and a half drive.''

''Hour, in a Porsche,'' the lieutenant said lazily.

''I think you ought to send one of your group over there,'' Lester said.

''Hell, I'll go,'' Lucas said. ''I'm sitting on my ass anyway. Do we have any paper on LaChaise?''

''Anderson's getting it now,'' Lester said. ''Anyway, the sheriff over there says LaChaise might be heading this way. LaChaise's mama says he's gonna get back at us for Candace and Georgia. 'Eye for an eye,' she says.''

Lucas looked at the lieutenant. "Can I take Sloan?"

"Sure. If you can find him."

Lucas picked up a half-pound of paper from Anderson, the department's computer jock, beeped Sloan, and when he called back, explained about LaChaise.

"You want to go?" Lucas asked.

"Let me get a parka. I'll meet you at your house."

LUCAS DIDN'T DRIVE THE PORSCHE MUCH DURING THE winter, but the day, though bitterly cold and sullenly gray, showed no sign of snow. The highway had the hard bone-dry feel that it sometimes got in midwinter.

"Are we in a hurry, I hope?" Sloan asked as they rolled north along the Mississippi.

"Yeah," Lucas said. As soon as they got on I-94 at Cretin, he called Dispatch and asked them to contact the Wisconsin highway patrol, to tell that he was coming through on an emergency run. They dropped on the interstate at noon, and at 12:20 crossed the St. Croix bridge into Wisconsin. Lucas put the snap-on red flasher in the window and dropped the hammer, cranking the Porsche out to one-twenty before dropping back to an even hundred.

The countryside looked as though it had been carved out of ice, hard sky, round hills, the creek lines marked by bare gray trees, snapped-off golden-yellow cornstalks sticking out of the snow, suburban homes and then isolated farmsteads showing plumes of straight-up gray wood smoke.

Sloan watched it roll by for a few minutes, then said, "I get to drive back."

DUNN COUNTY SHERIFF BILL LOCK WAS A FUSSY, OFFI-cious, bespectacled man, a little overweight, who, if he'd put on a fake white beard, would make an adequate department-store Santa. He met Lucas and Sloan among the coffins in the

Eternal Comfort Room at Logan's Funeral Home, where Logan had set up coffee and doughnuts for the cops.

"Come on and take a look," Lock said. "We'd appreciate it if one of our guys could talk to Duane Cale—you still got him over there in Hennepin County jail. He might have some ideas where they went."

"No problem," Lucas said. He dug out a card, scribbled a number on the back and handed it to Lock. "Ask for Ted, tell him I said to call, and what you want to do."

"Good enough." Lock walked them through the staging room, where the bodies of Georgie and Candy LaChaise were still waiting for a funeral. "You want to look?" he asked.

"No, thanks," Lucas said hastily. "So what happened?"

"Logan says LaChaise insisted that he open the coffins. They came back here and he opened them. Then LaChaise asked if there was a Coke machine around, and Logan told them where the machine was. That was one of the cooler things he did: he was so routine, taking his time with the bodies, saying good-bye, then asking for a Coke . . ."

Lock walked them through it, a couple other deputies standing around, watching. They wound up in the back room, next to the Coke box. Sand's body was still on the floor, in the middle of a drying puddle of blood. Sand looked small, white and not particularly tough, his head cocked up at an odd angle, his chin squarely on the floor, his nose off the ground.

"Logan figures he was gone for five minutes. When he came back to the staging room, there was nobody here. He looked into the back, and found this."

"Never saw LaChaise again?" Lucas asked.

"Never saw him again," Lock said, shaking his head. "Never heard any noise, nothing. Now we got the sonofabitch running around the countryside somewhere."

"He's long gone," Lucas said.

"Yeah, but we're doing a house-to-house check anyway," Lock said.

"He had to have help." Lucas walked around the body, squatted, and looked at Sand's hands as they stuck out of the cuffs. "There aren't any defensive cuts, so it wasn't like LaChaise pulled a shank on him." Lucas stood up and made a hand-washing motion. "If LaChaise was cuffed and wearing leg irons, there's no way he could have taken this guy without some kind of fight. There must've been somebody else here."

"Unless he'd cut a deal with Sand to turn him loose, and make it look like an escape—then double-crossed him."

"Huh. What'd he have to offer Sand? Candy and Georgie were dead, so the source of money had dried up . . ."

"We're checking with Michigan, see if Sand had any problems back there. Something to blackmail him with . . ."

"Nobody saw him walking away." Lucas made it a statement.

"Nope. Nobody saw nothing."

Sloan jumped in: "I heard his mother says he's coming after us."

"That's what she says," Lock said, nodding. "And she could be right. Dick is nuts."

"You know him?" Lucas asked.

"From when I was a kid," Lock said. "I used to run a trap line up the Red Cedar in the winter. The LaChaises lived down south of here on this broken-ass farm—Amy LaChaise is still out there. I used to see the LaChaise kids every now and then. Georgie and Dick. Their old man was a mean son-ofabitch, drunk, beat the shit out of the kids . . ."

"That's how it is with most psychos," said Sloan.

"Yeah, well, I wouldn't be surprised if somebody told me he'd been screwing Georgie, either. She always knew too much, there in school." Lock scratched his head, caught himself and slicked back his thinning hair. "The old man came after me once, said I was trespassing on his part of the river, and they didn't even live on the river."

"What happened?" Sloan asked.

"Hell, I was seventeen, I'd baled hay all summer, built fence in the fall and then ran the trap line. I was in shape, he was a fifty-year-old drunk: I kicked his ass," Lock said, grinning at them over Sand's body.

"Good for you," Sloan said.

"Not good for his kids, though—living with him," Lock said. "The whole goddamn bunch of them turned out crazier'n bedbugs."

"There's more? Besides Georgie and Dick?" Lucas asked.

"One more brother, Bill. He's dead," Lock said. "Ran himself into a bridge abutment up on County M, eight or ten years back. Dead drunk, middle of the night. There was a hog in the backseat. Also dead."

"A hog," said Sloan. He looked at Lucas, wondering if Lock was pulling their legs.

Lock, reading Sloan's mind, cracked a grin. "Yeah, he used to rustle hogs. Put them in the car, leave them off at friends' places. When he got five or six, he'd run them into St. Paul."

"Hogs," Sloan said, shaking his head sadly.

Lock said the only two people who'd showed up for the funeral were Amy LaChaise and Sandy Darling, Candy's sister. "They're both still sitting out there. They say they don't know what the heck happened."

"You believe them?" Sloan asked.

"Yeah, I sorta do," Lock said. "You might want to talk to them, though. See what you think."

AMY LACHAISE WAS A MEAN-EYED, FOULMOUTHED waste of time, defiant and quailing at the same time, snapping at them, then flinching away as though she'd been beaten after other attempts at defiance.

"You're gonna get it now," she crowed, peering at them from beneath the ludicrous hat-net. "You're the big shots going around killing people, thinking your shit don't stink; but you're gonna see. Dickie's coming for you."

SANDY DARLING WAS DIFFERENT.

She was a small woman, but came bigger than her size: her black dress was unconsciously dramatic, the silver-tipped black boots an oddly elegant country touch, both sensitive and tough.

She faced them squarely, her eyes looking into theirs, unflinching, her voice calm, but depressed.

Sandy had seen Lucas arrive with Sloan, had seen them talking with the sheriff. The big tough-looking guy wore what she recognized as an expensive suit, probably tailored. FBI? He looked like an FBI man from the movies. The other man, the thin one, was shifty-looking, and dressed all in shades of brown. They went in the back, where the dead guard was, and a few minutes later came back out, and talked to Amy LaChaise. She could hear Amy's crowing voice, but not the individual words.

After five minutes, the two men left Amy LaChaise and walked over to where she was sitting. She thought, *Hold on. Just hold on.*

"Mrs. Darling?" The big guy had blue eyes that looked right into her. When he smiled, just a small polite smile, she almost shivered, the smile was so hard. He reminded her of a Montana rancher she'd met once, when she'd gone out to pick up a couple of quarter horses; they'd had a hasty affair, one that she remembered with some pleasure.

The other guy, the shifty one, smiled, and he looked like Dagwood, like a nice guy.

"I'm Lucas Davenport from Minneapolis," the big guy said, "And this is Detective Sloan . . ."

She caught Lucas's name: Davenport. Wasn't he . . . ? "Did you shoot my sister?" she blurted.

"No." The big man shook his head. "Detective Sloan and I were at the credit union, but neither one of us fired a gun."

"But you set it up," she said.

"That's not the way we see it," Lucas said.

Sandy's head jerked, a nod: she understood. "Am I going to be arrested?"

"For what?" the thin man asked. He seemed really curious, almost surprised, and she found herself warming to him.

"Well, that's what I want to know. I came to the funeral, and now they won't let me go anywhere. I've got to ask before I go to the bathroom. Nobody'll talk to me."

"That's routine," the thin man said. "I know it's tiresome, but this is a serious thing. A man's been murdered."

The thin man—Sloan?—made it sound so reasonable. He went on. "We'll talk to the sheriff, see if we can get you some information on how much longer it'll be. I imagine you'll have to make a formal statement, but I'd think you'd be home for dinner."

"If you're not involved," Davenport said. She was sitting in a big chair, and he dropped into another one at a right angle to her. "If you've got anything to do with this, if you know where LaChaise is at, you better say so now," he said. "Get a lawyer, get a deal."

She shook her head, and a tear started down her cheek. "I don't know anything, I just came to say good-bye to Candy . . ."

Three things were going on in her head. When Lucas said, "Say so now," she thought, deep in her mind, *Oh, right*. At another level, she was so frightened she could hardly bear it. And in yet another place, she really was thinking about

Candy, dead in a coffin not ten yards away; and that started the tear down her cheek.

LUCAS SAW THE TEAR START, AND HE GLANCED AT Sloan. A wrinkle appeared between Sloan's eyes. "Take it easy," Sloan said gently. He leaned forward and touched her hand. "Listen. I really don't think you had anything to do with this, but sometimes, people know more than they think. Like, if you were Dick LaChaise, where would you go? You know him, and you both know this territory . . ."

They talked with her for another fifteen minutes, but nothing came of it. Sandy showed tears several times, but held her ground: she simply didn't know. She was a horse rancher, for God's sakes, a landowner, a taxpayer, a struggling businesswoman. She didn't know about outlaws: "Candy and I . . . she moved out of the house when I was in ninth grade and we didn't see her much after that. She was always running around with Dick, doing crazy stuff. I was afraid she'd wind up dead."

"What'd your folks do?" Sloan asked.

"My dad worked for the post office—he had a rural route out of Turtle Lake. They're both gone now."

"Sorry," Sloan said. "But you don't know anybody they might have run to?"

She shook her head: "No. I didn't have anything to do with that bunch. I didn't have time—I was always working."

"So how crazy is LaChaise?" Lucas asked. "His mother says he's gonna come after us."

Sandy flipped her cowboy hat in her hands, as though she was making an estimate. "Dick is . . . strange," she said, finally. "He's rough, he was good-looking at one time, although . . . not so much now. He was wild. He attracted all the wild guys in the Seed, you'd hear about crazy stunts on his bike, or sleeping on the yellow line. He really did sleep on the yellow line once—on Highway 64, outside a tavern. Dead drunk, of course.''

''Do you think he'll come after us?'' Lucas asked.

''Are you worried?'' asked Sandy, curiously. The big guy didn't look like he'd worry.

''Some,'' Lucas said. '' 'Cause I don't know enough about him. And his wife and his sister—excuse me for saying this, I know Candy was your sister—the things they did were nuts.''

Sandy nodded. ''That's from Dick,'' she said. ''Dick is . . . he's like an angry, mean little boy. He'll do the craziest stuff, but then, later, he'll be sorry for it. He once got drunk and beat up a friend, and when he sobered up, he beat himself up. He got a two-by-two and hit himself in the face with it until people stopped him and took him to the hospital.''

''Jesus,'' Sloan said, looking at Lucas, impressed.

''But he can be charming,'' Sandy said. ''And you can shame him out of stuff. Like a little boy. Unless he's drunk, then he's unstoppable.''

''You keep talking about drinking. Is he drunk a lot?''

''Oh, yeah,'' Sandy nodded. ''He's an alcoholic, no question. So are most of his friends. But Dick's not one of those guys who's drunk all the time—he'll go dry for a while, but then he'll go off on a toot and be crazy for two weeks.''

''Somebody cut this prison officer's throat while he was cuffed up and laying on the floor. You think LaChaise could do that?'' Lucas asked.

''He could if he was in one of his bad-boy moods,'' Sandy said. ''No question. I don't know if I'm getting this across— but when I say like a mean little boy, I mean just like that. He has tantrums, like fits. He scares everybody when he has one, because he's nuts, and because he's so strong. That's what's going on now: he's having one of his tantrums.''

''But a kid's tantrum only lasts a few minutes . . .''

"Well, Dick's can go on for a while. A week, or a couple of weeks."

"Is that how he came to get involved in this murder over in Michigan? A tantrum?"

"Oh, no, he wasn't involved in that," she said. "The cops framed him."

Lucas and Sloan both glanced away from her at the same moment, and she smiled, just a bit. "So you don't believe me—but they did," she said. "I testified at the trial. There was this guy named Frank Wyatt, who killed another guy named Larry Waters. The prosecution said that Waters stole some dope from Wyatt, and that Dick owned part of the dope—which he may have, I don't know. Anyway, the night that the dope was stolen, the prosecution said Dick and Wyatt got together at a tavern in Green Bay and talked about killing Waters."

"That was the conspiracy," Lucas said.

"Yes." Sandy nodded. "They had this informant. They let him off some dope charges for his testimony. He testified that he was at the tavern when Wyatt and Dick talked. Wyatt shot Waters the next day."

"And you say LaChaise wasn't at the tavern?" Sloan asked.

"I know he wasn't," Sandy said. " 'Cause he was at my place. I had a filly who broke a leg, shattered it. There was nothing we could do about it, the break couldn't be fixed, we had to put her down. I hate to do that; just hate it. Dick and Candy were in town, and I mentioned it to them. Dick said he'd take care of it, and he did. That was the night he was supposed to be in Green Bay. I had it written in ink on my income-tax calendar. In fact, Dick and Candy were there that whole week . . . But the jury didn't believe me. The prosecution said, 'She's his sister-in-law, she's just lying for him.' "

"Well." Lucas looked at Sloan again, who shrugged, and Lucas said, "We know it happens. You get some asshole—excuse me—who goes around wrecking people's lives, and you get a shot at him, and some cops'll take it."

"Sort of like you took with Candy and Georgie?" Sandy asked.

"We didn't cheat with Candy and Georgie," Lucas said, shaking his head. "They went to the credit union to rob it—nobody made them do it, or suggested that they do it. They did it on their own hook: we were just watching them."

She looked steadily at him, then nodded. "All right," she said. "If I was a cop, I'd have done the same thing."

THEY TALKED FOR A FEW MORE MINUTES, BUT NOTHING developed that would help. Lucas and Sloan said good-bye to the sheriff and headed for the car.

"What do you think about Sandy Darling?" Lucas asked as they skated down the sidewalk.

Sloan shook his head. "I don't know. She's a tough one, and she's no dummy. But she was scared."

"The cops scared her," Lucas said. "They were pushing her pretty hard."

"Not scared that way," Sloan said. Lucas tossed him the car keys and Sloan popped the driver's-side door. "She was scared like . . ."

They got in, and Sloan fired the car up, and after another moment, continued: ". . . she was scared like she was afraid she'd make a mistake. Like she was making up a story, and was afraid we'd break it down. If she isn't involved, she doesn't need a story. But I felt like she was working on one."

Lucas, staring out the window as they rolled through the small town, said, "Huh." And then, "You know, I kind of like her."

"I noticed," Sloan said. "That always makes them harder to arrest."

Lucas grinned, and Sloan let the car unwind down the snaky road toward the I-94.

"We better take a little care," Lucas said finally. "We'll get the word out, that we're looking for anybody asking about cops. And get some paper going on the guy, and his connections. Roust any assholes who might know him."

"I've never had any comebacks," Sloan said. "A few threats, nothing real."

"I've had a couple minor ones," Lucas said, nodding.

"That's what you get for sneaking around in the weeds all those years," Sloan said. Then: "Bet I beat your time going back."

"Let me get my seat belt on," Lucas said.

LACHAISE STRETCHED OUT ON A BED, A SOFT MATTRESS for the first time in four years, and breathed the freedom. Or looseness. Later, he made some coffee, some peanut-butter-and-Ritz-cracker sandwiches, listened to the radio. He heard five or six reports on his escape and the killing of Sand, excited country reporters with a real story. One said that police believed he might be on foot, and they were doing a house-by-house check in the town of Colfax.

That made him smile: they still didn't know how he'd gotten out.

He could hear the wind blowing outside the trailer, and after a while, he put on a coat and went outside and walked around. Took a leak in the freezing outhouse, then walked down to the edge of the woods and looked down a gully. Deer tracks, but nothing in sight. He could feel the cold, and he walked back to the trailer. The sun was nearly gone, a dim aspirin-sized pill trying to break through a screen of bare aspen.

He listened to the radio some more: the search in Colfax was done. The Dunn County sheriff said blah-blah-blah nothing.

Still, nightfall was a relief. With night came the sense that the search would slow down, that cops would be going home. He found a stack of army blankets and draped them across the windows to black them out. After turning on the lights, he walked once around the outside of the trailer, to make sure he didn't have any light leaks, came back inside, adjusted one of the blankets, and climbed back to the bed. The silence of the woods had been forgotten, submerged in his years in a cell, and for a while he couldn't sleep.

He did sleep, but when he heard the tires crunching on the snow, he was awake in an instant. He sat up and took the Bulldog off the floor. A moment later, he heard footsteps, and then the door rattled.

"Who is that?" he asked.

A woman's voice came back: "Sandy."

HER FACE WAS TIGHT, ANGRY. "YOU JERK," SHE SAID. HE was looking down at her, the gun pointed at her chest. Coldly furious, she ignored it. "I want you out of here. Now."

"Come in and shut the door, you're letting the cold in," he said. He backed away from her, but continued to look out over her head. "You didn't bring the cops?"

"No. I didn't bring the cops. But I want you out of here, Dick . . ."

"Tomorrow," he said. "We're heading for Mexico."

"At the funeral home, they said you were gunning for these cops that killed Candy and Georgie."

"Yeah, well . . ." He shrugged.

"Why'd you kill the prison guard?" she asked.

His eyes shifted, and she felt him gathering a reason, an

excuse: "He was the meanest sonofabitch on the floor. If you knew what he'd done . . ."

"But now they're looking for you for *murder*."

He shrugged: "That's what I was in for."

"But you didn't have anything to do with that," she said.

"Didn't make no difference to them," he said.

"My God, Dick, there *is* a difference . . ."

"You didn't know this guy," LaChaise said. "If you'd known what Sand put my friends through back in the joint . . ." He shook his head. "You couldn't blame us. No man oughta go through that."

He was talking about rape, she knew. She didn't buy it, but she wouldn't press him, either. She wanted to believe and if she pressed him, she was afraid she'd find out he was lying.

"Whatever," she said. "But now you've got to move. Martin was bragging about how good his truck is: If you leave tomorrow, you can be in Arizona the day after, driving straight through. You can be in Mexico the day after that, down on the Pacific Ocean."

"Yeah, we're figuring that out," LaChaise said, but again, his eyes shifted fractionally. "What happened at the funeral home?"

"The police kept us there for a couple of hours—and two detectives from Minneapolis talked to us—and then they took us down to Menomonie, to the courthouse. We had to sign statements, and then they let us go. A couple of deputies came around again, about dinnertime, and checked the house."

"They have a warrant?"

"No, but I let them in, I thought it was best," she said. "They looked around and left."

"What about Elmore?"

"Elmore was at work," Sandy said. "They already talked to him."

"Would Elmore turn us in?" LaChaise said.

"No. He's as scared as I am," Sandy said, and the anger suddenly leaped to the surface: "Why'd you do it, Dick? We've never done anything to you, and now you're dragging us down with you."

"We needed a place to ditch," LaChaise said defensively. "We didn't know what the situation would be. If the cops were right on our ass, we needed some place we could get out of sight in a hurry. I thought of this place."

"Well, I want you out," Sandy said. She poked a finger at him. "If you're not out, I'll have to take the chance and go to the police myself. When you get out, I'll come out here and wipe everything you've touched . . . and I hope to hell if you get caught, you'll have the decency to keep your mouth shut about this place."

"I won't get caught," LaChaise said. "I'm not going back inside. If I get killed, that's the way it is: but I'm not going back."

"But if you do get caught . . . you know, shot and you wake up in a hospital . . ."

"No way I'd tell them about this," LaChaise said, shaking his head. "No way."

"All right." She glanced at her watch. "I better get going, in case those deputies check back. I'll tell you something, though: one of the Minneapolis cops was this Davenport guy. The guy who's in charge of the group that killed Candy and Georgie."

"I know who he is," LaChaise said. "So?"

"He's awful hard," she said.

"I'm awful hard, too," LaChaise said.

She nodded: "I'm just telling you," she said.

When Sandy left, she walked head-down to her car, and sat inside for a moment before she started it. Now she *was* guilty of something, she thought. As a hardworking, taxpaying Republican rancher, she should be in favor of sending herself to prison for what she'd just done. But she wasn't. She'd do anything to stay out—the idea of a prison cell made her knees weak. If Dick had landed anywhere else, she'd have turned him in. But the trailer hideout would be impossible to explain, and she'd had the experience, in LaChaise's earlier trial, of seeing what vindictive cops could do.

Damn. She thought about the weapons in the hall closet back home, a .22, a deer rifle, a shotgun. She'd never considered anything like this before, but she could go home, get Elmore's deer rifle, come back out here . . .

Get Dick outside.

Boom.

She could dump his body in a cornfield somewhere, and nobody would know anything until spring. And if the coyotes got to him, probably not even then. She sighed. She couldn't do anything like that. She'd never wanted to hurt anyone in her life. But she wasn't going under. She'd swim for it.

WEATHER AND LUCAS ATE HANDMADE RAVIOLI FROM an Italian market while Lucas told her about the trip to Colfax. Weather said, ''Tell me that last part again. About the eye-for-an-eye.''

Lucas shrugged. ''We have to take a little care. The guy won't be running around for long, there're too many people looking for him. But everybody involved in the shooting . . . I've told them to keep an eye out.''

''You think he'd come here, looking for you?'' she asked.

''I don't think so,'' Lucas said. Then he said, ''I don't know. Maybe. He's nuts. We've got to take a little care, that's all.''

''That's why you've got the gun under your chair. A little care.''

Lucas stopped with a forkful of pasta halfway to his mouth. ''I'm sorry,'' he said. ''But it's no big deal—and it's just for a little while.''

FIVE

EARLY MORNING AT THE BLACK WATCH.

Andy Stadic pushed through the front door, took his gloves off and unbuttoned his overcoat as he walked around the bar and through the double swinging doors into the kitchen. Opening the coat freed up his weapon: not that he'd need it, but he did it by habit.

Stadic was short, bullet-headed, with close-cropped hair and suspicious, slightly bulging eyes. In the kitchen, he nodded to the cook, who was chopping onions into twenty pounds of raw burger, ignored the Chicano dishwasher, turned the corner past the pan rack and pushed through another set of doors.

The back room was cool, lit with overhead fluorescent, furnished with cartons of empty beer bottles, boxes of paper towels and toilet paper, cans of ketchup, sacks of potatoes— the whole room smelled of wet paper and potatoes and onions and a bit of cigar smoke.

Daymon Harp sat in one of two red plastic chairs at a rickety round table, chewing gum, his feet stretched out in front of him, crossed at the ankles. He wore a bomber jacket, faded Levi's and purple cowboy boots with sterling-silver toes.

"What'd you want?" Stadic asked, standing, hands in his pockets.

"We got a problem." Harp uncrossed his legs, put a foot on the second chair, and pushed it across the concrete floor at Stadic.

"I don't want to hear about problems," Stadic said.

"Can't be helped," Harp said.

"Man, I hate even seeing you," Stadic said. "If the shooflies walked in right now, I'd be all done. I'd be on the one-stop train to Stillwater."

"I couldn't help it. Sit down, goddamnit."

Stadic turned the chair and straddled it, his arms crossed on the back. "What?"

"Two guys showed up at my crib last night," Harp said. "Put some guns on me. They were looking for your name."

"My name?"

"Yeah. They knew I was working with a cop, but they didn't know your name."

"Jesus Christ, Harp . . ."

"They said they'd cut one finger off Jas every ten seconds until I came out with it, and had something to prove it by. They were gonna cut off two fingers just to show that they was tellin' the truth. And after they got all ten fingers, they said, they were gonna cut out her eyes and then cut her throat and then they were gonna start on me."

"You told them?" Stadic's voice rose in disbelief.

"Goddamn right I told them," Harp said. "They cut her pointer finger off right there, on a bread board. She was all tied up and gagged and flopping around, and they were like they was killed chickens or something . . . couple of goddamn mean crackers. I been in the joint with these motherfuckers before. They got little tears tattooed under their eyes, one for each man they killed, and when you start tattooing them on, you better be able to prove it to the rest of the crazies. This crackhead kid's got three of them and the fucker with the knife got two.''

''You coulda said anything,'' Stadic said.

Harp shook his head. ''They wanted proof. I had a little proof.''

Now Stadic was very quiet. ''What proof?''

''I had some pictures taken.''

''You motherfucker . . .'' Stadic stood up, kicked the chair aside, his hand moving toward his pistol. Harp held his hands up.

''It was from way back when, when I didn't know you. And I had Jas's motherfuckin' finger laying there like a dead shrimp, all curled up. What the hell was I supposed to do?''

''You coulda *tried* lying,'' Stadic shouted. His fingers twitched at the gun butt.

''You wasn't *there*,'' Harp said. ''You don't *know*.''

Stadic took a breath, as though he'd just topped a hill, turned in place, then said, ''So what'd they want with my name?''

''They need some information from you.''

''Tell me.'' He was nibbling nervously at a thumbnail, ripped off a piece of nail, spit it out, tasted blood. The nail was bleeding, and he sucked at it, the blood salty in his mouth.

''They want personnel files,'' Harp said. ''From the police department.''

LACHAISE HAD SPENT WHOLE DAYS THINKING ABOUT it, daydreaming it, when he was locked up: the requirements of the coming wars. Us against Them. They would need a base. In the countryside, somewhere. There'd be a series of

log cabins linked with storm sewer pipe, six feet underground
and more sewer pipe set into the hills as bunkers. Honda
generators for each cabin, with internal wells and septic fields.

Weapons: sniper rifles to keep the attackers off, heavy-duty
assault rifles for up close. Hidden land mines with remote
triggers. Armor-piercing rockets. He'd close his eyes and see
the assaults happening, the attackers falling back as they met
the sweeping fire from the web . . .

The attackers were a little less certain; some combination
of ATF agents and blacks from the Chicago ghettos, Indians,
Mexicans. Though that didn't seem to make a lot of sense,
sometimes; so sometimes, they were all ATF agents, dressed
in black uniforms and masks . . .

Daydreams.

THE REALITY WAS A COUPLE OF TRUCKS AND A RUN-
down house in a near-slum.

LaChaise and Butters drove down to the Cities in Elmore's
truck, with Martin trailing behind. They needed two vehicles,
they decided, at least for a while. Butters and Martin caught
Elmore in the barn, while Sandy was out riding, and squeezed
him for the truck keys.

"Just overnight," Butters said, standing too close. "Martin's got some warrants out on his car, if the cops check—
nothing serious, but we gotta have some kind of backup. We
won't do nothin' with it."

"Guys, I tell you, we're moving stuff today . . ." Elmore
stuttered. Martin and Butters scared Elmore. Martin, Elmore
thought, was a freak, a pent-up homosexual hillbilly crazy in
love with LaChaise. Butters had the flat eyes of a snapping
turtle, and was simply nuts.

Elmore tried to get out of it, but Martin put his hands in
Elmore's coat pocket, and when Elmore tried to wrench away,

Butters pushed him from the other side. Martin had the keys and said, ''We'll get them back to you, bud.''

THE HOUSE WAS A SHABBY TWO-STORY CLAPBOARD wreck on a side street in the area called Frogtown. The outside needed paint, the inside needed an exterminator. Half the basement was wet and the circuit box hanging over the damp concrete floor was a fire marshal's nightmare. Martin had brought in three Army-surplus beds, a dilapidated monkey-shit-yellow couch and two matching chairs, and a dinette set, all from Goodwill, and a brand-new twenty-seven-inch Sony color TV.

''Good place, if we don't burn to death,'' Martin said. The house smelled like wet plaster and fried eggs. ''That wiring down the basement is a marvel.''

''Hey, it's fine,'' LaChaise said, looking around.

No web of sewer pipe, no Honda generators. No land mines.

That evening, Butters sat in one of the broken-down easy chairs, his head back and his eyes closed. Martin sat cross-legged on the floor with his arrows, unscrewing the field points, replacing them with hundred-grain Thunderheads, a can of beer by one foot. He would occasionally look at LaChaise with a stare that was purely sexual.

''We're gonna do it,'' LaChaise said. He had a half-glass of bourbon in his hand. ''We've been talking for years. Talk talk talk. Now with Candy and Georgie shot to pieces, we're gonna do it.''

''Gonna be the end of us,'' Martin said. His beard was coppery red in the lamplight.

''Could be,'' LaChaise agreed. He scratched his own beard, nipped at the bourbon. ''Do you care?''

Martin worked for another minute, then said, ''Nah. I'm getting crowded. I'm ready.''

"You could go up north, up in the Yukon."

"Been there," Martin said. "The goddamn Canadians is a bunch of Communists. Even Alaska's better."

"Mexico . . ."

"I'm a goddamn American."

LaChaise nodded and said, "How about you, Ansel?"

Butters said, "I just want to get it over with."

"Well, we got to take our time, figure this out . . ."

"I mean, everything over with," Butters said. "I can take my time with *this*."

LaChaise nodded again. "It's the end for me, for sure. But I swear to God, I'm taking a bunch of these sonsofbitches with me."

Martin looked at him uncertainly, then nodded, and looked away. They worked together, comfortable but intent, like they did in hunting camps, thinking about it all, drinking a little, letting the feeling of the hunt flow through them, the camaraderie as they got the gear ready.

They checked the actions on their weapons for the twentieth time, loading and unloading the pistols, dry-firing at the TV; the good smell of Hoppe's solvent and gun oil, the talk of old times and old rides and the people they remembered, lots of them dead, now.

"If I lived," LaChaise continued, "I'd do nothing but sit in cells for the rest of my life anyhow. Besides . . ."

"Besides what?" Martin asked, looking up.

"Ah, nothin'," LaChaise said, but he thought, *Mexico*. He'd always planned to go, and hadn't ever been.

"It cranks me up, thinking about it," Butters said. His face was flushed with alcohol.

SANDY HAD BLOWN UP WHEN SHE'D COME BACK FROM her ride, and Elmore had told her about the truck. She jumped in her van and went after them, but they were gone. She got to the St. Croix, realized the futility of the chase, slowed, turned around and went back.

"What were you thinking about?" she shouted at Elmore. "You shoulda swallowed the keys."

That night, Elmore was in the kitchen making a pot of Rice-a-Roni with venison chunks, and she could smell the chemical odor of the stuff as she sat in front of the TV. She heard the rattling of the dishes, and finally, Elmore stood in the hallway behind her. She pretended to watch the sports.

He said, "We oughta talk to the cops."

"What?" She pushed herself out of her chair. She hadn't expected this.

Elmore's voice rose to a nervous warble: "If we stick with this, only two things can happen. We get killed, or we go to jail for murder. That's it: them two things."

"Too late," she said. "We gotta sit tight."

Tears came to his eyes, and one dribbled down a cheek, and Sandy suddenly didn't know what to do. She'd seen Elmore frightened, she'd seen him cower, she'd seen him avoid any serious responsibility, but she'd never seen him weep. "Are you okay?"

He turned his head toward her, the tears still running down her cheeks: "How'd this happen?" he said.

She'd thought about that: "My sister," she said. "The whole of this is because of Candy. And because of your dad's trailer. It's because of nothing that means anything . . ."

"We've got to go to the police."

"But what do we tell them? And why would they believe us?"

"Maybe they won't," he rasped. "But you saw all those guns and all that other shit that Martin had. How're they going to Mexico with all that shit? How are they gonna get across the border with it? And if they do get across, what are they going to use for money? They ain't going to Mexico. They're gonna pull some crazy stunt.''

''No—no,'' she said, shaking her head. ''They're out of here. Dick LaChaise is nobody's fool.''

''Dick LaChaise is fuckin' nuts,'' Elmore said. ''You want to know what's gonna happen? We got two or three more days, and then we'll be dead or in jail. Two or three more days, Sandy. No more horses, no more trail rides, no more going up to the store or running down to the Cities. We're going to jail. Forever.''

They stared at each other for a moment, then she said, almost whispering, ''But we can't get out. If we talked to the cops, what would we give them? We don't even know where Dick's at. And there're Seed guys all over the place—look what happened when that guy was going to testify against Candy. He got killed.''

''Maybe old John Shanks could tell us something,'' Elmore said. John Shanks was a criminal attorney who'd handled Candy's assault case. ''See if he can cut us a deal.''

''I don't know, El,'' Sandy said, shaking her head. ''This thing is all out of control. If they hadn't stayed in the trailer . . .''

''We can clean up the trailer.''

''Sure, but if we turn against them, they'll drag us in. How'd you like to be in the same prison with Butters and Martin?''

Elmore swallowed. He was not a brave man. ''We gotta do something.''

''I'm gonna walk down the driveway,'' Sandy said. ''I'll figure something out.''

SANDY PUT ON HER PARKA AND PACS, AND HER GLOVES, and stepped outside. The night was brutally cold and slapped at her skin like nettles; the wind was enough to snatch her breath away. She crunched down the frozen snow in the thin blue illumination of the yard light, thinking about it, worrying it. If she could only keep things under control. If only Dick would disappear. If only Elmore would hold on . . .

Elmore.

Sandy had never really loved Elmore, though she'd once been very fond of him; and still felt the fondness at times. But more often, she suffered with the fact that Elmore clearly loved her, and she could hardly bear to be around him.

Sandy had grown up with horses, though she'd never owned one until she was on her own. Her father, a country mailman, had always wanted to ride the range—and so they rode out of the county stables on weekends, almost every weekend from the time she was three until she was eighteen, three seasons of the year. Candy hadn't cared for it, and quit when she was in junior high; Sandy had never quit. Never would. She loved horses more than her father loved riding them. Walking down the drive, she could smell the sweet odor of the barn, manure and straw, though it was more than a quarter-mile away . . . She could never leave that; never risk it.

She'd gone to high school with Elmore, but never dated him. After graduation, she'd left for Eau Claire to study nursing, and two years later, came back to Turtle Lake, took a job with a local nursing home and started saving for the horse farm. When her parents died in a car accident—killed by a drunk—her half of the money had bought four hundred acres east of town.

Elmore had been working as a security guard in the Cities, and started hanging around. Sandy, lonely, had let him hang around. Made the mistake of letting him work around the ranch: he wasn't the brightest man, or the hardest worker, but she needed all the help she could get, working nights at the nursing home, days at the ranch. Made the mistake of sleeping with him, the second man she'd slept with.

Then Elmore had fallen off a stairwell and wrenched his back: the payoff, twenty-two thousand dollars, would buy some stock and a used Ford tractor. And there wasn't anybody else around. And she *was* fond of the man.

Sandy often walked down the drive when life got a little too unhappy, when Elmore got to be too much of a burden. The ranch, she'd thought, was the only thing she wanted in life, and she'd do anything to get it. When she'd gotten it—and when the breeding business actually started to pay off—she found that she needed something else. Somebody else. Even if it was just somebody to talk to as an equal, who'd understand the business, feel the way she did about horses.

Elmore was an emotional trap she couldn't find a way out of. There was the man in Montana; he was married now, but she thought about him all the time. With somebody like that . . .

She brushed the thought away. That's not who she had.

She turned, circling, crunching through the snow: prison for life. And she got around to the north, and saw the first slinky unfolding of the northern lights, watched as they pumped up to a shimmering curtain above the everlasting evergreens, and decided that she might have to talk to someone about Dick LaChaise.

"But not quite yet," she told Elmore when she was back inside. "Just a couple of more days—we let it ride. Maybe they'll take off. Anyway, we gotta build a story. Then maybe we talk to old John."

ANDY STADIC WENT INTO THE LAUNDROMAT AND SAT down. The place smelled of spilt Tide and ERA and dirty wash water, and the hot lint smell of the dryers.

A woman glanced at him once, and again. He was just

sitting there, a well-dressed white man, and had nothing to wash. She started to get nervous. He sat in one of the hard folding chairs and read a two-week-old copy of *People*. The woman finished folding her dry clothes, packed them in a pink plastic basket, and left. He was alone. He walked over to the door, turned the Open/Closed sign to Closed, and locked the door.

Stadic watched the windows. A blond-haired hippie strolled by, a kid who might have been the southern boy who'd jumped Daymon Harp. A minute later, a hawk-faced white man walked up to the door, stuck his head inside.

"You Stadic?"

"Yeah."

"Sit tight."

Damn right. He'd told them he wouldn't go anyplace private. He'd told them Harp would be watching.

Another minute passed, and then a bearded man came around the corner, Pioneer seed-corn hat pulled low over his eyes. He walked like a farmer, heavy and loose, and had a farmer's haircut, ears sticking out, red with the cold, and a razor trim on the back of his neck. The farmer took his time getting inside. Stadic recognized the eyes beneath the bill.

LaChaise.

"What the fuck do you think you're doing?" Stadic said. He wanted to get on top of the guy immediately.

"Shut up," LaChaise said. His voice was a tough baritone, and his eyes fixed on Stadic's.

"You don't tell me to shut up." Stadic was on his feet, squared off.

LaChaise put his hand in his pocket, and the pocket moved. He had a gun.

"Go for your gun," LaChaise said.

"What?" As soon as he said it, a temporizing word, uncertain, Stadic felt that he'd lost the edge.

"Gonna give me trouble, go for your gun, give me some real trouble. I already killed one cop, killing you won't be nothing."

"Jesus Christ . . ."

LaChaise was on top, knew it, and his hand came off the gun. "Where're the records?"

"You gotta be nuts, thinking I'd give you those things."

"I *am* nuts," LaChaise said. His hand was back on the gun. "You should know that. Now, where're the records?"

"I want to know what you're gonna do with them."

"We're gonna scare the shit out of a lot of people," LaChaise said. "We're gonna have them jumpin' through hoops like they was in a Russian circus. Now quit doggin' me around: either give them to me, or tell me you don't have them. You don't have them, I'm gone."

When they'd set up the meeting, by phone, LaChaise had said that if he didn't bring the papers, the next call would be to Internal Affairs.

Stadic let out a breath, shook his head. "Scare the shit out of them? That's all?"

"That's all," LaChaise said. He was lying and Stadic knew it. And LaChaise knew that he knew, and didn't care. "Gimme the goddamned papers."

"Jesus, LaChaise, *anything* else . . ."

"I'm outa here," LaChaise said, turning toward the doors.

"Wait a minute, wait a minute . . ." Stadic said, "I'm gonna stick my hand in my coat."

LaChaise's hand went back to his pistol and he nodded. Stadic took the papers out of his breast pocket and held them out at arm's length. LaChaise took them, didn't look, and backed away. "Better be the real thing," he said, and he turned to go.

"Wait," Stadic said. "I gotta know how to get in touch with you."

"We'll get in touch with you," LaChaise said.

"Think about it," Stadic said, his voice tight, urgent. "I want you outa here—or dead. I don't want you caught. Anything but that. If they figure out where you're at, and they're coming to get you . . . I oughta be able to call."

"Got no phone," LaChaise said. "We're trying to get one of them cellulars."

"Call me, soon as you get one," Stadic said. He took an index card from his pocket, groped for a pen, found one, scribbled the number. "I carry the phone all the time."

"I'll think about it," LaChaise said, taking the card.

"Do it," Stadic said. "Please."

Then LaChaise was gone, out the door, pulling the hat down over his eyes, around the corner. Harp came through the back door two minutes later.

"I think three is all of them," Harp said. "I saw the cracker on the street, then a pickup pulls up and this peckerwood gets out—he's new—and the pickup goes off; the driver was probably that other dude."

"Get the plates?"

"Yeah. I did."

"See anybody else? Anybody who looked like a cop?" Harp shook his head. "Just a couple of kids and some old whore."

LACHAISE FLIPPED THROUGH A COMPUTER PRINTOUT of the police department's insurance program. Some of it was gobbledygook, but buried in the tiny squares and rectangles were the names of all the insured, their addresses and phone numbers.

"Modern science," LaChaise said.

"What?" Martin turned to look at him.

"I'm reading a computer printout; I'm gonna get a cell phone," LaChaise said. "You go along and things get easier."

He started circling names on the printout.

SIX

WEATHER KARKINNEN WORE A WHITE TERRY-CLOTH robe, with a matching terry-cloth towel wrapping her hair. Through the back window she was a Vermeer figure in a stone house, quiet, pensive, slow-moving, soft with her bath, humming along with a Glenn Gould album.

She got a beer from the refrigerator, popped the top, found a glass and started pouring. The phone rang, and she stepped back and picked it up, propped it between her ear and her shoulder, and continued pouring.

"Yes, he is," she said.

Lucas was sitting in his old leather chair, eyes closed. He was working on a puzzle—a tactical exercise involving both a car chase and a robbery.

Lucas had once written strategy board games, had moved them to computers, then, pushed temporarily off the police force, had started a company doing computer simulations of police problems.

He'd made the change at just the right time: His training software did well. Now the company was run by a professional manager, and though Lucas still held the biggest chunk of the stock, he now worked mostly on conceptual problems. He was imagining a piece of software that spliced voice and data transmissions, that would layer a serious but confused problem beneath an exciting but superficial one, to teach new dispatchers to triage emergency calls.

Triage. The word had been used by the programmers putting together the simulation, and it had been rattling around his brain for a few days, a loose BB. The word had a nasty edge to it, like *cadaver*.

"Lucas?"

He jumped. Weather was in the doorway, a glass of dark beer in her hand. She'd brewed it herself in a carboy in the hall closet, from a kit that Lucas had bought her for her birthday.

"You've got a phone call . . ."

Lucas shook himself awake, heaved himself out of the chair. "Who is it?" he asked, yawning. He saw the beer. "Is that for me?"

"I don't know who it is. And get your own," she said.

"We sound like a TV commercial."

"You're the one who was snoring in the chair after dinner," she said.

"I was thinking," he said. He picked up the phone, ignoring her dainty snort. "Yeah?"

The man's voice was oily, a man who gave and took confidences like one-dollar poker chips. "This is Earl. Stupella. Down at the Blue Bull?"

"Yeah, Earl. What's happening?"

"You was in that shoot-out a week or so ago, in the papers. The credit union." He wasn't asking a question.

"Yeah?"

"So this chick came in here tonight and said she'd seen the husband of one of these girls, who like supposedly busted out of prison and killed somebody. It was like La Chase?''

Lucas was listening now. ''LaChaise,'' he said. ''That's right. Where'd she see him?''

''A laundromat down on Eleventh. She said she saw him going in and he talked to a guy in the window for a minute and then he left.''

''Huh. Who's the chick?'' Lucas asked.

''Don't tell her I talked to you,'' Stupella said.

''No problem.''

''Sally O'Donald. She lives somewhere up the line, by the cemetery, I think, but I don't know.''

''I know Sally,'' Lucas said. ''Anything else?''

''Nope. Sally said she didn't want to have nothing to do with LaChaise, so when she saw him, she turned right around and walked away.''

''When was all this?''

''Sally was in about an hour ago,'' Stupella said. ''She saw the guy this morning.''

''Good stuff, Earl. You'll get a note in the mail.''

''Thanks, dude.''

LUCAS DROPPED THE PHONE ON THE HOOK: LACHAISE. So he *was* here. And out in the open. Lucas stood staring at the phone for a second, then picked it up again.

''Going out?'' Weather asked from the hallway.

''Mmm, yeah. I think.'' He pushed a speed-dial button, listened to the beep-beep-boop of the phone.

Del answered on the second ring. ''What?''

''I hope that's not a bedside phone you're talking on.''

''What happened?'' Del asked.

''Nothing much. I thought we might go for a ride, if you're not doing anything.''

''You mean, go for a ride and get an ice cream? Or go for a ride and bring your gun?''

"The latter," Lucas said, glancing at Weather. She had a little rim of beer foam on her upper lip.

"Latter, my ass," Del said. "Give me ten minutes."

THE BACK STREETS WERE RUTS OF GNARLED ICE. THE EXplorer's heater barely kept up, and Del, who didn't like gloves, sat with his hands in his armpits. The good part was, the assholes and freaks got as cold as anyone else. On nights like this, there was no crime, except the odd domestic murder that probably would have happened anyway.

When the radio burped, Del picked it up: "Yeah."

"O'Donald is the third house on the left, right after you make the turn off Lake," the dispatcher said.

"All right. We'll get back."

Lucas cruised the house once, rattling the white Explorer down the ruts. The house showed lights in the back, where the kitchen usually was, and the dim blue glow of a television from a side window. "The thing is," Lucas said, "she has a terrible temper."

"And she's about the size of a fuckin' two-car garage," said Del. "Maybe we should shoot her before we talk to her."

"Just a flesh wound, to slow her down," Lucas agreed. "Or shoot her in the kneecap."

"We shot the last one in the kneecap."

"Oh yeah; well, that's out, then." Lucas parked and said, "Don't piss her off, huh? I don't want to be rolling around in the yard with her."

SALLY O'DONALD WAS IN A MOOD.

She stood on the other side of a locked glass storm door, her hair in pink curlers, her ample lips turned down in a scowl, her fists on her hips. She was wearing a threadbare plaid bathrobe and fuzzy beige slippers that looked like squashed rabbits.

"What do *you* assholes want, in the middle of the night?"

"Just talk, no problem," Lucas said. He was standing on the second step of the stoop, looking up at her.

"Last time I talked to that fuckin' Capslock, I thought I was gonna have to pull his nuts off," she said, not moving toward the door lock. She stared over Lucas's shoulder at Del.

Del shivered and said, "Sally, open the goddamn door, will you? We're freezing out here. Honest to God, all we want to do is talk."

She let them in after a while, and led them back to a television room so choked with smoke that it might have been a bowling alley. She moved a TV dinner tray out of the way, pointed at a corduroy-covered chair for Lucas and sat down in another. Del stood.

"We know you saw Dick LaChaise—you only told about a hundred people," Lucas said.

"I didn't tell no hundred people, I told about three," she said, squinting at him from her piggy eyes. "I'll figure out who it was, sooner or later. Pull his nuts off."

"Jesus, Sally," Del said. "Take it easy on the nuts stuff."

"We just want to know where you saw him, who he was with and what you know about him," Lucas said. "Our source says you used to hang out with him."

"Who is it? The source? I talk to you, you oughta give me something."

"You know I can't tell you that. I could ask sex to give your place a pass for a couple of months," Lucas said, adding, "if the information is decent."

She nodded, calculating. A two-month pass from sex added up. She said, "All right. I hung with the Seed, off and on, for maybe ten years? Up until—let's see—four or five years ago. They got me in the business to begin with, turned me out in Milwaukee. Dick was one of the bigger shots in the

Seeds when I first met him. He was maybe twenty-five back then, so he'd be what, forty?''

"Thirty-eight," Lucas said. "That's a long time ago."

"Yeah. I remember him especially because he thought he was Marlon Brando. He liked to wear those squashed fisherman hats, and gold chains and shit. I caught him practicing his smile once, in the can at this bar in Milwaukee."

"Practicing . . . ?"

"Yeah."

"I'm not getting a picture of a big leader, here," Lucas said.

"Oh, he was. Maybe a little too nuts, though. You know, most of the Seeds were sort of . . . criminal businessmen. A little dope, a little porn, a few whores. Bad, but not necessarily crazy. Dick . . . you heard about the sleeping on the yellow line?"

"Yeah, heard the story," Lucas said.

"I was there. He did. And he was asleep. And I once saw him try to ride a Harley up an oak tree . . ."

Lucas looked at Del and they both shrugged. "He killed this guard, cut his throat, pretty cold," Lucas said to O'Donald. "Does that sound like LaChaise?"

She thought for a moment, cocking her head, then said, "Well, ten years ago, he would've had to be pissed. But just cold like that . . ." She snapped her fingers. "I don't know."

"His old lady and Georgie LaChaise—they had a rep for stealing money and giving it to nut groups," Lucas said. "He had to have help in the escape. We thought maybe some of the nuts helped out."

"I didn't know his wife or his sister. The Seed had some serious goofballs around, though. Just before I left it was the blacks this and the Jews that and the politicians and media and cops and feminists and television and banks and insur-

ance companies and welfare and food stamps . . . the whole
pizza pie."

"Sounds like talk radio," Lucas said.

She laughed, an unpleasant gurgling sound, and her stomach bounced up and down. She pointed her finger at him.
"That's good."

"What was he doing at the laundromat?" Del asked.

"Talking to some guy," O'Donald said. "They was standing up, arguing with each other—that's when I came down
the street and saw him. He has a beard and he had a beard
when I knew him, but he didn't have a beard in the newspaper
picture."

"That was the last picture they had of him," Lucas said.
"He started growing the beard two or three months ago."

"How'd it look?" Del asked. He'd propped himself against
a chest of drawers. "Short and smooth? Special cut?"

"Bible prophet," she said. "Long and scraggly."

Lucas said, "Then what? After he was arguing with the
guy?"

"I didn't hang around. I don't need Dick LaChaise seeing
me and asking for a favor, if you know what I mean."

"You worried about freebies?" Del asked.

"I don't care about freebies," she said. She looked away,
her lips still moving, then she shook her head and said, "If
Dick is here, some of his old Seed buddies are probably
around, too. You really don't want to fuck with them."

"We did," Del said.

O'Donald nodded: "I read about it—that thing where you
guys killed his old lady and his sister."

"Yeah?" Del nodded.

"He's here to even the score on that," O'Donald said. "If
I were you guys, I'd move to another state."

Lucas looked at her. "You think he'd come after cops?"

"Davenport, have you been listening?" she asked impatiently. "Dick is a fuckin' fruitcake. You killed his woman and his sister. He's coming after you, all right. Eye for an eye."

She frowned suddenly, then said, "That guy he was talking to—at the laundromat. I think he was a cop."

Lucas said, "What?"

"I don't know who, but I recognized the attitude. You know how you can always tell a cop? I mean, except for Capslock here, he looks like a wino . . . Well, this guy was like that. A cop-cop."

"Would you recognize a mug shot?"

She shrugged: "Probably not. I didn't really look at him, I was sort of looking past him, at Dick. It was the way he stood that made me think cop."

Del looked down at Lucas and said, "That's not good."

"No. That's not good." Lucas looked back through the dark house, the smoke-browned wallpaper, the crumpled Chee-tos bags on the floor, the stink of a cat, and he said, half to himself, "Eye for an eye."

SEVEN

━━━◆◉◆━━━

MARTIN HAD BROUGHT A FOAM TARGET WITH HIM, A two-foot-square chunk of dense white plastic with concentric black circles around the bull's-eye. He'd nailed it to a wall beside the refrigerator, and was shooting arrows diagonally across the living room, into the kitchen. The shooting made a steady THUMM-whack from the bowstring vibration and the arrows punching into the target.

Form practice, he called it; he didn't care where the arrow went, if the form was correct. As it happened, the arrow always went into the bull's-eye.

LaChaise had been watching a game show. When it ended, he yawned, got to his feet and went to a window. The light had died. He looked out into the gloom, then let the curtains fall back and turned to the room. He cracked a smile and said, "Let's saddle up."

Martin was at full draw, and might not have heard. He held, released: THUMM-whack.

Butters had been playing with their new cell phone. They'd bought it from a dealer friend of Butters's, who'd bought it from one of his customers, a kid with a nose for cocaine.

"Good for two weeks," the dealer had promised. Butters had given him a thousand dollars for the phone, and the dealer had put the money in his jeans without counting it. "The kid's ma is a realtor. She's in Barbados on vacation, left him just enough money to buy food. The kid said his ma made fifty calls a day, so you can use it as much as you want; I wouldn't go calling Russia or nothing."

They'd used it twice, once to call Stadic, once to call a used-car salesman.

When LaChaise said "Saddle up," Butters put the phone down, opened the duffel by his foot, and took out two pistols. One was a tiny .380, the other a larger nine-millimeter. He popped the magazines on both of them, thumbed the shells out and restacked them. Then he took a long, thin hand-machined silencer out of the duffel and screwed it into the nine-millimeter: excellent. He unscrewed the silencer, picked up his camo jacket and dropped the silencer in the side pocket.

"Ready," he said simply. Butters had a thick blue vein that ran down his temple to his cheekbone: the vein was standing out in the thin light, like a scar.

"How about you?" LaChaise asked Martin.

Martin was at full draw again, focused on form: THUMM-whack. "Been ready," he said.

LaChaise parted the drapes with two fingers, looked out again. The streetlights were on and it was snowing. The snow had started at noon, just a few flakes at first, the weather forecasters saying it wasn't much. Now it was getting heavier. The closest streetlight looked like a candle.

LaChaise turned back into the room, stepped to a chair, and picked up three sheets of paper. The papers were Xerox copies of a newspaper article from the *Star Tribune*. He'd outlined the relevant copy with a pen:

*Officers Sherrill, Capslock, Franklin and Kupicek were
removed from active duty pending a hearing before a
weapons review board, a routine action always taken
after a line-of-duty shooting incident. Deputy Chief Davenport and Officer Sloan did not discharge their weapons and will continue on active duty.*

So Sherrill, Capslock, Franklin and Kupicek were the
shooters.

"What?" asked Martin. He opened his eyes and looked up
at LaChaise.

"Eye for an eye," LaChaise said.

"Absolutely," Martin said. He was pulling on his coat.
"So let's go."

MARTIN DROVE HIS TRUCK TO WEST END BUICK-
Oldsmobile. He'd called earlier, and asked for the salesman
by name: "I talked to you a couple of days ago about a '91
Pontiac, that black one . . ."

"The Firebird?" The salesman had sounded uncertain,
since he hadn't talked to anyone about the Firebird.

"Yeah, that's the one. You still got it?"

"Still looking for an owner," the salesman had said.
"There's a guy coming around tonight, but nobody's signed
anything yet."

Martin had grinned at the car-sales bullshit. "I'll come by
in an hour or so."

"I'll be looking for you," the salesman had promised.

Martin carried a Marine Corps combat knife with a five-
inch serrated blade. He'd bought it as a Christmas gift for
himself, through a U.S. Cavalry catalog, and carried it in a
sheath, on his belt. The knife was the only gift he'd gotten
in the past few years, except that LaChaise had given him a
bottle of Jim Beam the year before he went to prison.

Martin was thinking about the Jim Beam when he got to the Buick store. He parked across the street: he could see light from the windows, but the snow had continued to thicken, and the people on the other side of the glass were no more than occasional shadows.

He had ten minutes. He closed his eyes, settled in and thought about the other men he'd killed. Martin didn't worry about killing: he simply did it. When he was a kid, there was always something around the farm to be killed. Chickens, hogs, usually a heifer in the fall. And there was the hunting: squirrels, rabbits, raccoons, doves, grouse, deer, bear.

By the time he killed his first man, he didn't much think about it. The man, Harold Carter, was owed money by LaChaise, that LaChaise had borrowed to set up his motor-cycle parts store. Carter was talking about going to court. LaChaise wanted him to go away.

Martin killed Carter with a knife on the back steps of his own home, carried the body out to his truck and buried the man in the woods. Nothing to it; certainly not as hard as taking down a pig. A pig always knew what was coming, and fought it. Went squealing and twisting. Carter simply dropped.

His second killing had been no more trouble than the first. His third, if he did it right, should be the easiest yet, because he wouldn't have to deal with the body. Martin closed his eyes; if he were the type to sleep, he might have.

LACHAISE, DRIVING ELMORE'S TRUCK, DROPPED BUT-ters at the Rosedale Mall. Butters carried both pistols, the short .380 in his left jacket pocket, and the nine-millimeter, with the silencer already attached, in a Velcroed flap under his arm.

He cruised past TV Toys. A tall woman talked to a lone customer, and a thin balding man in a white shirt stood behind the counter. Butters stepped to a phone kiosk, found the paper in his pocket, and dialed the number of the store. He watched as the man in the white shirt picked up the phone.

"TV Toys, this is Walt."

"Yes, is Elaine there?"

"Just a moment."

The man in the white shirt called over to the tall woman, who smiled and said something to her customer and started toward the counter. Butters hung up and glanced at his watch.

Five-twenty. LaChaise should be getting to Capslock's place.

CAPSLOCK'S WIFE WAS A NURSE AT RAMSEY GENERAL Hospital, according to her insurance file. She finished her shift at three o'clock.

LaChaise stopped at a Tom Thumb store, bent his head against the storm, punched in her phone number—the insurance forms had everything: address, employer, home and office phones—and waited for an answer.

Like Butters, LaChaise carried two pistols with him, but revolvers rather than automatics. He didn't care about the noise he made, so he didn't have to worry about a silencer; and he liked the simplicity of a revolver. No safeties or feed problems to think about, no cocking anything, just point and shoot.

Cheryl Capslock answered on the fourth ring. "Hello?"

"Uh, Mrs. Capslock?" LaChaise tried to pitch his voice up, to sound boyish, cheerful. "Is Del in?"

"Not yet. Who is this?"

"Terry—I'm at the Amoco station on Snelling. Del wanted, uh, he wanted to talk to me and left a number. Could you tell him I'm around?"

"Okay, your name is Terry?"

"Yeah, T-E-R-R-Y, he's got the number."

"I'll tell him," Cheryl Capslock said.

MARTIN WALKED ACROSS THE STREET TO THE CAR LOT. The Firebird was in a display stand, forty feet from the main side window on the dealership. He walked once around the car, then again, then bent to look in the side window.

As he rounded the car the second time, he saw a salesman, in the lighted room, pulling on a coat. Martin took the knife out of the sheath and put it in the right side pocket of his coat. Ten seconds later, the salesman, shoulders humped against the snow, trotted out to the car. His coat hung open, showing a rayon necktie.

"She's a beaut," he said, tipping his head at the car.

"You're Mr. Sherrill?" asked Martin.

"Yeah, Mike Sherrill. Didn't we meet last week sometime?"

"Uh, no, not really . . . Listen, I can't see the mileage on this thing."

Sherrill was in his mid-thirties, a onetime athlete now running to fat and whiskey. A web of broken veins hung at the edges of his twice-broken nose, and his once-thick Viking hair had thinned to a blond frizz. "About fifty-five thousand actual. Let me pop the door for you."

Sherrill skated around the car, used a gloved hand to quickly brush the snow off the windshield, then fumbled at the locked keybox on the door. Martin looked past him at the dealership. Another salesman stood briefly at the window, looking out at the snow, then turned away.

"Okay, here we go," Sherrill said. He got the key out of the keybox and unlocked the car door.

Martin didn't mess around, didn't wait for the better moment. He stood to one side as Sherrill opened the door. When Sherrill stepped back, he moved close against the other man, put one hand on his back, and with the other, delivered the killing thrust, a brutal upward sweep, like a solar plexus jab.

The knife took Sherrill just below the breastbone, angling up, through the heart.

Sherrill gasped once, wiggled, started to go down, his eyes open, surprised, looking at Martin. Martin guided his falling body onto the car seat. He pushed Sherrill's head down, caught Sherrill's thrashing legs and pushed them up and inside. Sherrill was upside down in the car, his feet over the front seat, his head hanging beneath the steering wheel. His eyes were open, glazing. He tried to say something, and a blood bubble came out of his mouth.

"Thanks," Martin said.

Martin pushed down the door lock, slammed the door and walked away. There was nobody in the dealership window to see him go.

BUTTERS WAITED UNTIL THE MAN IN THE WHITE SHIRT had a customer and the woman was free. He walked into the store, his hand on the silenced pistol. At the back of the store, near the door to the storeroom, was a display for DirecTV. He headed that way, and Elaine Kupicek followed. She was a nice-looking woman, Butters thought, for a cop's wife.

"Can I help you?" She had a wide, mobile mouth and long skinny hands with short nails.

"I own a bar, down in St. Paul."

"Sure . . ."

"If I put in DirecTV, would I be able to get, like, the Green Bay games, even when there's no broadcast over here?"

"Oh, sure. You can get all the games . . ."

The man in the white shirt had moved with his customer to a computer display, where they were talking intently about TV cards for a Windows 95 machine.

"We have a brochure that shows the options . . ."

Butters looked at her, then put the fingers of his left hand to his lips. She stopped suddenly in midsentence, puzzled, and then he took the .380 out of his left pocket and pointed it at her.

"If you scream, I'll shoot. I promise."

"What . . ."

"Step in the back; this is a robbery."

He prodded her toward the door. She stepped backward toward it, caught the knob with her hand and her mouth opened and Butters said, conversationally, "Be quiet, please."

She went through, her eyes looking past Butters, searching for the man in the white shirt, but Butters prodded her further into the room, and then closed the door behind them.

"Don't hurt me," she said.

"I won't. I want you to sit down over there . . . just turn over there."

She turned to look at the chair next to a technician's desk: a brown paper lunch sack sat on the table, with a grease stain on one side. Her lunch sack, with a baloney sandwich and an orange. She stepped toward the desk and said, "Please don't."

"I won't," he promised, in his gentle southern accent. She turned back to the chair and when her head came around, he took the nine-millimeter out of the Velcroed flap in one swift, practiced motion, put it against the back of her head and pulled the trigger once.

Kupicek lurched forward and went down. Butters half-turned, and waited, listening. The shot had been as loud as a hand-clap, accompanied by the working of the bolt. Enough noise to attract attention in an ordinary room, but the door was closed.

He waited another two seconds, then stepped toward the door. Elaine Kupicek sprawled facedown, unmoving. Butters put the pistol back in the Velcroed flap, and the .380 decoy gun in his pocket.

When he opened the door, the man in the white shirt was still talking to the customer. Butters strolled out easily, hands in his pockets, got to the tiled corridor outside the store, looked both ways and then ambled off to the left.

LACHAISE CROSSED THE STREET IN THE SNOW, UP THE walk to the left-hand door of the town house. He carried the .44 in his right hand, and pushed the doorbell with his left. He stepped back, and a gust of snow hit him in the eyes. The gust came just as the door opened, and he wondered later if it was the snow in his eyes that was to blame . . .

A woman opened the inner door, then half-opened the storm door, a plain woman, half smiling: "Yes?"

"Mrs. Capslock?"

"Yes?"

He was coming around with the gun when Del loomed behind her: a shock, the sudden movement, the face, then Del's mouth opening . . .

Capslock swatted his wife and she went sideways and down, and Capslock screamed something. LaChaise's gun, halfway up, went off when Capslock screamed, and Capslock's arm was coming up. LaChaise's gun went off again and then Capslock had a gun, short and black with the small hole coming around at LaChaise's eyes, and LaChaise slammed the storm door shut as Capslock fired. Splinters of aluminum sliced at LaChaise's face and he backed away, firing the Bulldog again, aware that the door was falling apart, more slugs coming through at him.

The muzzle flashes were blinding, the distance only feet, then yards, but he was still standing and Capslock was standing: and then he was running, running toward the truck, and a slug plucked at his coat and a finger of fire tore through his side . . .

DEL FIRED FIVE TIMES, CUTTING UP THE DOOR, SMASH-ing the glass, then stopped, turned to Cheryl, saw the blood on her neck, dropped next to her, saw the wound, and her eyes opened and she struggled and he rolled her onto her side and she took a long, harsh, rattling breath.

"Hold on, hold on," he screamed, and he ran back to the phone and dialed 911 and shouted into it—was told later that he shouted. He remembered himself talking coldly, quietly, and so he listened to the tape and heard himself screaming . . .

LACHAISE WAS BLEEDING.

He drove the truck, looking at himself in the rearview mir-ror. Shrapnel cuts on the face, agony in his side. He was holding his side with his hand, and when he looked at his hand, it was wet with blood. "Motherfucker . . ." he groaned.

A spasm of fear seized his heart. Was he dying? Was this how it would end, with this pain, in the snow?

A cop car went screaming past, lights blazing, then another, then an ambulance. Hit somebody, he thought, with a thread of satisfaction. God, it hurt . . .

The man must have been Capslock himself; and he was fast with a gun, blindingly fast. And what had he screamed? He'd screamed *LaChaise* . . .

So they knew.

LaChaise looked into the rearview mirror.

He was bleeding . . .

EIGHT

LUCAS WAS ON THE WEST SIDE OF MINNEAPOLIS, PUSH-
ing the Explorer up an I-394 entrance ramp, when a dispatcher shouted, ''Somebody shot Capslock's wife,'' and a
second later, Del patched through: ''LaChaise shot Cheryl.''

''What?'' Lucas was on the ramp, moving faster. To his
right, an American flag as big as a bedsheet fluttered in the
gloom. ''Say that again.''

''LaChaise shot Cheryl . . .'' From behind Del's voice, Lucas could hear a jumble of noise: voices, highway sounds, a
siren. Del seemed to be out of breath, gasping at his radio.

''Where are you?'' Lucas asked.

''Ambulance. We're going into Hennepin.'' Now the
words were tumbling out, like a coke-fired rap. ''I saw him,
man. LaChaise. I shot at him. I don't know if I hit him or
not. He's gone.''

''What about Cheryl?''

''She's hit, she's hit . . .'' Del was shouting; several words
came through garbled, then he said, ''It's our wives, man;
he's going after the families. Eye for an eye . . .''

93

Weather.

She'd be in the clinic, doing minor patch-up work on post-op patients. The fear caught Lucas by the throat; Del said something else, but he missed it, and then Del was gone.

The dispatcher blurted, "We lost him, he closed down."

"I'm going to the U Hospitals. I want Sherrill, Franklin, Sloan and Kupicek on the line *now*," Lucas said. He fumbled a cellular phone out of an armrest box and punched the speed-dial button for Weather. A secretary answered, then transferred him to the clinic, where another secretary, bored, said Weather was busy with a patient.

"This is Deputy Chief Lucas Davenport of the Minneapolis Police Department and this is an emergency and I want her on the line *immediately*," Lucas shouted. *"GET HER."*

Then Franklin came back through Dispatch: he was in the office.

"Get your wife and kid and go someplace until we know what's happening," Lucas said.

"The kid's in school . . ."

"Just get them," Lucas said. "Have you seen Sloan?"

"I think I just saw him goin' in the can . . ."

"Tell him. Get his wife, get out someplace. Anywhere. Get lost, but stay in touch . . ."

"You think . . ."

"*Move it*, goddamnit." Lucas was stomping the gas pedal, trying to get more speed out of the Explorer.

Weather came up: "I'm on my way there," Lucas said. He took fifteen seconds to tell her what had happened: "Get out of the clinic and stay away from your office," he said. "Tell the secretary where you'll be. I'll stop and see her when I get there."

"Lucas, I've got things to do, I've got a guy with a skin cancer . . ."

"Fuck the clinic," he snapped, his voice a rasp. "Go

someplace where you're not supposed to be, and wait there. If the guy comes after you, he might start killing your patients, too. Everybody can wait an hour or two.''

"Lucas . . .''

"I don't have time to chat, goddamnit, just do it.'' He cut off a white-haired guy in a red Chevy Tahoe and could see the guy pounding the steering wheel as he went by.

Sherrill was working an ag assault in a bar off Hennepin, drunk college kids beating a black guy with bar stools until he stopped moving. He still wasn't moving, but he wasn't quite dead, either. Sherrill called, and Lucas gave her the word on Del.

"Oh, my God, I'm going over there,'' she said.

"No. Call Mike, tell him to take a walk. Tell him to go sit in a restaurant until you get to him. We want everybody where they shouldn't be until we figure out what's going on.''

Dispatch came back: "Del hit LaChaise—there's blood on the sidewalk, going out to where a truck was parked. All the hospitals know, we're covering the emergency rooms . . .''

Kupicek came up. He and his kid were at a peewee hockey match. "Call your wife, you all go out to eat somewhere on the department, catch a movie,'' Lucas said. "Check with me before you go home. Look in your rearview mirror, stay on the radio.''

"How's Del's wife?'' Kupicek asked.

"I don't know: we've got people on the way to Hennepin.''

"Keep me tuned, dude,'' Kupicek said.

Thirty seconds later, the dispatcher came back, and asked Lucas to switch over to a scrambled command frequency. "What?'' he asked.

"Oh, God.'' The dispatcher sounded as though she were weeping, a sound Lucas hadn't heard from Dispatch. "Roseville called: Danny's wife's been shot. She's dead. In the store at Rosedale.''

Lucas felt the anger rising, building toward a black frenzy: "Don't put this on the air, don't tell anyone outside the center . . . when did this happen?"

"The call came in at five-seventeen, but they think she might have been shot about five-twelve."

"When was Del?"

"About five-fifteen."

So there had to be more than one shooter. How many?

"Who'll tell Danny?" the dispatcher asked.

"I will," Lucas said. "Does Rose Marie know?"

"Lucy's on the way to her office."

Lucas called Kupicek back. "Danny, where are you?"

"Hennepin and Lake. Looking for a phone."

"Change of plans: We got Roseville with your wife, we need you at the emergency entrance to Hennepin General. Right now. You gotta light with you?"

"Yeah."

"Light it up and get it in there . . ."

"I got the kid."

"Bring him: he'll be okay."

When Kupicek was gone, Lucas got back to Dispatch: "Check Danny's file: he's got a sister named Louise Amdahl and they're tight. Get her down to Hennepin General. Send a car and tell them to move it, lights and sirens all the way."

And he thought about Sherrill and Weather. He punched up the phone again, caught Weather, told her about Kupicek's wife: "I'm not coming. But you gotta hide out and I'm not bullshitting you, Weather, I swear to God, you gotta get out of sight, someplace where I can get you. The guy could be in the hospital right now."

"I'm going," she said.

"Take care, please, please, take care," he said.

And he got Sherrill: "Did you reach Mike?"

"No, Lucas, they can't find him." Her voice was high,

scared. "He's supposed to be there, but they can't find him. I'm going there."

"I'm sending a squad."

"Lucas, you don't think . . . ?" Her marriage had been on the rocks for a while.

"We don't know what to think," Lucas said. Sherrill didn't know about Danny's wife. He didn't tell her. "Get on up there."

Back to Dispatch: "Two cars, get them up there. You gotta beat Sherrill up there . . ."

LUCAS WENT STRAIGHT THOUGH THE CITY TRAFFIC, not slowing for any light, green, yellow or red, his foot on the floor: driving the Explorer was like driving a hay wagon, but he beat Kupicek by two minutes, pulling in a car length behind Rose Marie Roux. The chief was pale, nearly speechless: She said, "This . . ." and then shook her head and they ran inside, Lucas banging the doors out of the way.

Del, covered with blood, stood in the hallway, talking to a doctor in scrubs: "Sometimes she gets stress headaches in the afternoon and she takes aspirin. That's all. Wait, she drinks Diet Coke, that's got caffeine. I don't know if she took any aspirin this afternoon . . ."

He saw them coming, Lucas and Rose Marie, and stepped toward them.

"He hit her hard," he said. He seemed unaware that tears were running down his seamed face: his voice was absolutely under control. "But if there aren't any complications, she'll make it."

"Aw, Jesus, Del," Lucas said. He tried to smile, but his face was desperately twisted.

"What happened?" Del said. He looked from one of them to the other. "What else happened?"

"Danny's wife's been shot; she's dead. And we can't find Mike Sherrill."

"The motherfuckers," Del rasped.

Then Danny Kupicek banged through the entryway, a kid tagging along behind, still in his hockey uniform, wearing white Nikes that looked about the size of battleships, a shock of blond hair down over his eyes. He seemed impressed by the inside of the hospital.

"Del," Kupicek said, "Jesus, how's Cheryl? Is she okay?"

"Danny . . ." said Lucas.

Ten minutes later, they found Mike Sherrill. Marcy Sherrill arrived just in time to see the cops gathering around the Firebird, and thrust through them just in time to see the door pop open, and look straight into her husband's open eyes, upside down, dead.

She turned, and one of the uniforms, a woman, wrapped her up, and a moment later she made a sound a bit like a howl, a bit like a croak, and then she fell down.

LACHAISE WAS THE FIRST TO GET BACK TO THE HOUSE. Martin had called from a pay phone and LaChaise sent him to get Butters.

"You bad?" Martin had asked, his voice low, controlled.

"I don't know, but I'm bleeding," LaChaise told him. "Hurts like hell."

"Can you breathe?"

"Yeah. I just don't want to," LaChaise said.

"Can you get in the house?"

"Think so. Yeah."

"Get inside. We'll be there in fifteen minutes."

LaChaise hurt, but not so bad that he couldn't make it to the house. That encouraged him. Except for the burning pain, which was localized, he didn't *feel* bad. There was no sense of anything loose inside, anything wrecked.

But when he got in the house, he found he couldn't get the jacket off by himself. When he lifted his arm, fire ran down his rib cage. He slumped on the living-room rug, and waited, staring at the ceiling.

Martin came in first, Butters, stamping snow off his sleeves, just behind him.

"Let's take a look," Martin said.

"You get yours?" LaChaise asked.

Martin nodded and Butters said, "Yep. How about you?"

"I got somebody, there were ambulances all over the place . . ."

They helped him sit up as they talked, and LaChaise told them about making the call, and then Del popping up behind his wife. "And the fucker recognized me . . . careful, there . . ."

They peeled the parka off, then the vest, then the flannel shirt, each progressively heavier with blood. His undershirt showed two small holes and a bloodstain the size of a dinner plate.

"Better cut that," Butters muttered.

"Yeah." Martin took out his knife, and the Jockey T-shirt split like tissue paper. "Roll up here, Dick . . ."

LaChaise tried to roll onto his left side and lift his arm; he was sweating heavily, and groaned again, "Goddamn, that hurts."

Martin and Butters were looking at the wound. "Don't look like too much," Butters said. "Don't see no bone."

"Yeah, but there's an in-and-out . . ."

"What?" LaChaise asked.

"You just got nicked, but there's a hole, in-and-out, besides the groove. Maybe cut you down to the ribs, that's the pain. The holes gotta be cleaned out. They'd be full of threads and shit from the coat."

"Get Sandy down here," LaChaise said. "Call her—no,

go get her. I don't know if she'd come on her own . . . She can do it, she used to be a nurse.''

Martin looked at Butters and nodded. ''That'd be best, she might have some equipment.''

''Some pills,'' Butters said.

''Get her,'' LaChaise moaned.

NINE

———◦◉◦———

THE SANDHURST WAS A YELLOW-BRICK SEMIRESIDEN-
tial hotel on the west edge of the business district. The building was three stories higher than anything else for two blocks
around, and easily covered. The clients were mostly itinerant
actors, directors, artists and museum bureaucrats, in town visiting the Guthrie Theater or the Walker Art Center.

Lucas and Sloan brought Weather in through the back,
down an alley blocked by unmarked cars. Two members of
the Emergency Response Team were on the roof with radios
and rifles.

". . . everything I've been trying to do," Weather was saying. Lucas's head was going up and down as he half-listened.
He scanned each face down the alley. His hand was in his
pocket and a .45 was in his hand. Sloan's wife was already
inside.

"It won't be long," Lucas said. "They can't last more than
a couple of days."

"Who? Who can't last?" Weather demanded, looking up

at him. "You don't even know who they are, except this LaChaise."

"We'll find out," Lucas said. "They're gonna pay, every fuckin' one of them." His voice left little doubt about it, and Weather recoiled, but Lucas had her arm and marched her toward the hotel.

"Let go of my arm," she said. "You're hurting me."

"Sorry." He let go, put his hand in the small of her back, and pushed her along.

The two hotel entries, front and back, met at the lobby: Franklin and Tom Black, Sherrill's former partner, sat behind a wide rosewood reception desk, shotguns across their thighs, out of sight. The largest cop on the force, a guy named Loring, read a paperback in one of the lobby's overstuffed chairs. He was wearing a pearl-gray suit and an ascot, and looked like a pro wrestler who'd made it small.

In the entry, a uniformed doorman turned and looked at them when he saw movement down the back hall. Andy Stadic raised a hand, and Lucas nodded at him and then they were around a corner and headed down toward the elevators.

"You know, anybody could find out where we are," Weather said.

"They can't get in," Lucas said. "And they can't see you."

"You said they were Seed people, and Seed people are supposed to be in these militias," Weather said. Weather was from northern Wisconsin, and knew about the Seed. "What if they brought one of those big fertilizer bombs outside?"

"No trucks are coming down this block," Lucas said. "We got the city digging up the streets right now, both sides."

"You can't hold it, Lucas," Weather said. "The press'll be here, television . . ."

Lucas shook his head: "They'll know you're here, but they won't get inside. If they try, we'll warn them once, then we'll put their asses in jail. We're not fucking around."

He took her up to the top floor, and down the hall to a small two-room suite with walls the color of cigar smoke; the rooms smelled like disinfectant and spray deodorant. Weather looked around and said, "This is awful."

"Two days. Three days, max," Lucas said. "I'd send you up to the cabin but they know about us, somehow, and I can't take the chance."

"I don't want to go to the cabin," she said. "I want to work."

"Yeah," Lucas said distractedly. "I gotta run . . ."

FOR TWO HOURS AFTER THE KILLINGS, ROSE MARIE Roux's office was like an airport waiting room, fifty people rolling through, all of them weighed down with their own importance, most looking for a shot on national television. The governor stopped, wanted a briefing; a dozen state legislators demanded time with her, along with all the city councilmen.

Lucas spent a half hour watching Sloan and another cop interrogate Duane Cale, who didn't know much about anything.

"But if Dick is here, I'd get my ass out of town," Cale said.

The interrogation wouldn't produce much, Lucas thought. He locked himself in his office with Franklin, away from the media and cops who wanted to talk about it. Sloan came in after a while, and started making calls. Then Del wandered in, his clothes still dappled with his wife's blood.

"How's Cheryl?" Lucas asked.

Del shook his head: "She's out of the operating room, asleep. They put her in intensive care, and won't let me in. She'll be there until tomorrow morning, at least."

"You oughta get some rest," Lucas said.

"Fuck that. What're you guys doing?"

"Talking to assholes . . ."

Between them, they called everyone they knew on the street who had a phone. Lucas tried Sally O'Donald a half-dozen times, and left word for her at bars along Lake Street.

A little more than two hours after the killings, Roux called:

"We're meeting with the mayor at his office. Ten minutes."

"Is this real?" Lucas asked.

"Yeah. This is the real one," Roux said.

A minute later, O'Donald called back.

"Can you come down and look at some pictures?" Lucas asked. "The guy you thought might be a cop?"

"I can't even remember in my head what he looked like," O'Donald said. "But I'll come down if you want."

"Talk to Ed O'Meara in Identification."

"Okay—but listen. I talked to my agent . . ."

"Your what?"

"My agent," O'Donald said, mildly embarrassed. "She said she might get five thousand dollars if I talked to *Hard Copy*."

"Goddamnit, Sally," Lucas said. "If you screw me and Del . . ."

"Shut up, shut up, shut up," O'Donald said. "I'm not going to screw anybody. What I want to know is, are you gonna take LaChaise off the street?"

"Yeah. Sooner or later."

"So if I talk, he won't be able to get at me?"

Lucas hesitated, then said, "Look, I'll be honest. If you talk, and then you bag outa here for a few days, he'll be gone. He won't last a week."

"That's what I wanted to know," O'Donald said.

"But you gotta tell me when you're going on," Lucas said.

"We'll put a guy on your house—in your house, maybe—just in case LaChaise comes looking."

"Jeez," she said. There was a minute's silence. "You put it that way . . . maybe I won't. I don't want to fuck with Dick."

"Either way, let me know," Lucas said. He glanced at his watch. The meeting was about to start. "Come in, talk to Ed . . ."

"Wait a minute, wait a minute. I thought of something else you might want to know."

"Yeah?"

"You ought to look at the ownership of that laundromat."

"Why don't you just tell me?" Lucas asked.

"I understand that it belongs to Daymon Harp." The name hung there, but Lucas didn't recognize it.

"Who's he?"

"Jeez, Davenport, you gotta get back on the streets a little more. He's a dealer. Pretty big time . . ."

"A Seed guy?"

"No, no, never. He's a black guy; good-looking guy. Ask Del. Del'll know who he is."

"Thanks, Sally."

"You talk to sex?"

"I'll talk to them tonight."

When he got off the phone, he said to Del, "Daymon Harp?"

"Dealer—semi-small-time. Careful. Reasonably smart. Came over from Milwaukee a few years back. Why?"

"Sally O'Donald says he owns the laundromat where she saw LaChaise."

Del frowned, shook his head. "I don't know what that means. I can't see Harp running with the Seed guys. That's the last combination I could imagine."

"Might be worth checking . . ."

Del looked at Sloan. "Want to run it down?"

Lucas interrupted. "Why don't you get cleaned up first? Sloan and Franklin can stay with the phones. When I get back, we'll all go down."

LUCAS WAS THE LAST ONE IN THE DOOR. THE MEETING included Roux, the mayor and a deputy mayor; Frank Lester, head of investigations; Barney Kittleson, head of patrol; Anita Segundo, the press liaison; and Lucas.

Rose Marie was talking to Segundo when Lucas eased through the door. She asked, "How bad?"

"CBS, NBC, ABC, CNN and one or two of the Fox cop shows all have people on the way. *Nightline* is doing a segment tonight. They're talking about LaChaise and his group being *militia*. Ever since the federal building was blown up in Oklahoma City, that's a hot topic."

"*Are* they militia?" the mayor asked. "Do these media guys know something?"

"The FBI says LaChaise was on the edge of things, but they don't show him really involved," Lester said. "He knew some of the Order people back in the eighties . . ."

"Didn't the Order kill that radio guy in Denver?" the mayor asked.

Lester nodded: "Yes. But the feds took them out a little while later. LaChaise was a big guy in the Seed, and some of the militia people from Michigan were involved in the Seed back when it was a biker gang. And later on, some of the Seed people got involved with Christian Identity—that's sort of an umbrella group. And we know LaChaise used to sell neo-Nazi stuff in his bike shop: *The Turner Diaries*, and all that. Some people think the Seed got its name from a right-winger who went on the radio and said it was too late to stop the movement, because there were Seeds everywhere. But that could be bullshit."

"We gotta nail that down," the mayor said, jabbing a finger at Roux. "If these are militia, we gotta start thinking in terms of bombs and heavy weapons."

Roux glanced at Lucas, scratched her head and said, "I don't think . . ."

She stopped, and the mayor's eyebrows went up. "Yeah?"

"I don't think that's much of a possibility, Stan. I think we're basically dealing with some goofs, with guns. Three guys, psychos, who maybe rode together in a biker gang. And maybe messed around on the edge of the Nazi stuff."

"Well, you're probably right," the mayor said. "But if they blow up the fuckin' First Bank, I don't want to be standing there with my dick in my hand, trying to explain why we didn't know what was coming."

Roux nodded. "That's one thing: we're gonna need a very tight public relations operation, or we're gonna get run over," she said. "We'll have cops gettin' paid off, we'll have reporters chasing witnesses . . ."

"The guy at Rosedale—the other clerk with Kupicek's wife, in the TV store—he's already signed up for *Nightline*," Segundo said.

The mayor was an olive-complected, bull-shouldered man, with fine curly black hair just starting to recede. He looked at his deputy, then at Roux: "Rose Marie, it's gonna be you and me."

"Sounds like a hit song from the fifties," the deputy said, "Rose Marie, it's you and me."

Everyone ignored him.

"We lay down the law about cops talking to the press: if you do it, you better get a lot of money, 'cause you won't be working here anymore," the mayor said. "We have four major press briefings every day: one early, to catch the morning shows; one just before noon; one just before five; and one at eight forty-five, to catch the late news. You'll have to coordinate with your investigators—we should have a bone to throw them at every press conference. Doesn't have to be real, but it has to be *satisfying* . . ."

The mayor went on for five minutes, laying out the handling of the press.

Then he turned to Lester and Lucas: "Lucas, I want you and your people totally off stage. We don't want any arguments about whether the response was provoked by the shootings at the bank."

"I didn't know that was still a question," Lester said.

"There isn't a question," the mayor said irritably. "But the media'll chew on any goddamned bone they can find. You gotta remember we're dealing with the entertainment industry. *Die Hard*, Oklahoma City, it's all the same. Now it's our turn to make the movie." He rapped on the table with his knuckles, still looking at Lester and Lucas: "We can only bullshit them for so long. We gotta catch these guys."

"We've got a procedure in emergencies," Roux said, and the mayor swiveled back to her. "We run two parallel investigations. Lucas and his bunch play the angles, and Frank runs the main sweep. Everybody coordinates through Anderson. He puts out a book every day on every little piece we get. Nobody hides anything from anybody."

"It works?" asked the mayor.

"So far," Lucas said.

"Then let's do that," the mayor said. "Do we have one single thing we can move on now? Anything?"

"Maybe one," said Lucas. He was thinking about the laundromat: a place to start.

SANDY DROVE WHILE BUTTERS LEANED AGAINST THE window on the passenger side. Elmore followed in Sandy's truck. Elmore hadn't wanted to go at first, and Butters agreed: Butters wanted Sandy, not her husband.

"I'm not going," Sandy had said.

Butters said, "I ain't got time to argue, Sandy. You're going." There was no doubt that she was going: he didn't bother to show her a gun, but it was there. Butters had an affable, southern-boy line of bullshit, but beneath it, he was as cold as Martin. When she went to get her coat, Butters went with her.

"Are you guarding me?" she asked.

"I'm making sure that you come along," Butters said. "I know you don't want to."

"You gonna tell me what happened? Who shot him?"

"No," Butters said. He'd told them that LaChaise had been shot in a fight. Sandy and Elmore had been feeding the stock, and hadn't seen any television.

When it was clear that Sandy was going, Elmore insisted that he go along too. Butters finally agreed, because he didn't want to waste time arguing: "But you come down in the van—Sandy goes with me," Butters said. "We're still gonna need both trucks for a while."

They stopped at the old folks' home, where Sandy still filled in when somebody was sick. A big first-aid kit in the nurse's office gave up bandages, needles and thread, razor blades and antiseptic. A large illegal bottle of Tylenol-3 was kept stashed in the bottom desk drawer, for the miscellaneous aches and pains of old age, and she emptied it. What else? Surgical scissors, a couple of Bic disposable razors, tape. Saline. There was a stock of sterile saline in the storeroom. She took five liters.

The nurses each had a personal drawer in a row of filing cabinets. Nobody bothered to lock them, and Sandy dug around in Marie Admont's drawer and found the bottle of penicillin pills. Marie had gotten them after a crazy old lady had raked her with her fingernails. Marie had only used a few of the pills, and a half-dozen remained in the bottle. Sandy took them.

THE DRIVE TO ST. PAUL SEEMED TO LAST FOREVER. THE dark strip through Wisconsin, then the winding road out to the interstate on the Minnesota side. Butters said a half-dozen words during the trip, Sandy four or five. Both were caught in their own thoughts.

Once in the Cities, Butters guided them down the interstate, then back into the narrow ice-clogged streets of Frogtown. They parked behind Martin's truck, and got out. Elmore parked behind them, and hurried through the snow, white-faced, and said, "I want to talk to Sandy. One minute. Before we go in there."

Butters said, "Get your asses in there, goddamnit."

"I'm going to talk to Elmore," Sandy said, her voice like the ice in the streets. "I'll get to Dick when I get to him."

"Listen . . ."

"Are you going to shoot me, Ansel? That'd help Dick a lot."

Butters backed off, and Sandy took Elmore twenty yards down the street. "What?"

Elmore was visibly trembling.

"I been listening to the radio," he rasped. "They been down here killing cops' families. That's all they're talking about on the radio, every station I could get. They killed two people and there's a third one might die. Everybody in the goddamned world is looking for them, Sandy."

Sandy looked at him, then turned and looked at Butters, who stood silently waiting. "Oh my God," she said.

"We got to get out," Elmore said.

"Let's go see Dick," Sandy said. "I'll work us out of here. But you're right. We've got to see John."

They walked down the driveway together, Butters lingering just out of earshot. Martin waited at the door.

"Come on in," he said to Sandy. He looked at Elmore and nodded, and Elmore looked away.

The house had one couch, a broken-down wreck in the living room. Martin had pulled the cushions off and thrown them on the floor, and LaChaise was lying on them, his head propped up with a pillow. Martin had covered him with a blanket, and LaChaise grinned at Sandy when she came in.

"How bad?" she asked.

"Not too bad," LaChaise said. "It's more like . . . it's gotta be cleaned up."

"Let me see," Sandy said. "I need a light."

They peeled the blanket off and LaChaise rolled onto his side. The pain had subsided somewhat, and he lifted his arm so she could see more clearly. At the same time, Butters took the shade off a table lamp, and held it like a torch over LaChaise.

Sandy looked at the wound for a moment. An open gash, at the back, became a bluish streak where the bullet had gone beneath the skin. A small round exit wound showed four inches below his nipple and over to the side. A trailing gash showed some rib meat. Sandy looked up at LaChaise. "You gotta go to a hospital," she said.

"Can't do that. You gotta fix it."

She looked at it again. In fact, she could fix it. "It'll hurt," she said.

"Atta girl," LaChaise said, and to Butters: "Told you so."

"I believed you," Butters said.

"What happened?" she asked. "How'd you get shot?"

"Argument over traveling money," LaChaise said. "The guy owed me . . ."

"Did you kill him?"

"No, I didn't kill him," LaChaise said, smiling faintly.

"Now, you want to fix me? This hurts like hell."

"You lying sonofabitch," Sandy said evenly. "You killed some cops' families. I oughta . . ."

Before she could finish, Martin backhanded her. His hand was like a leg of beef, and knocked her flat. For a second, she didn't know what had happened, and then dazed, ears ringing, heard LaChaise say, "Whoa, whoa . . ." Behind him, Elmore: "Goddamnit . . ."

She rolled, tried to sit up, and Martin was there, his face inches from hers: "Stop the bullshit. You fix him or I'll cut you into fuckin' fish bait." Across the room, Butters was smiling at Elmore, half expecting him to make a move, but Elmore swallowed and shut up.

Sandy got back to her feet, turned away from Martin without a word and said to LaChaise, "I brought you some pills. You should take a few before we start."

LaChaise looked at her, then at Martin, and grinned at Martin: "I wouldn't turn your back on her," he said.

LACHAISE TOOK THE PILLS WITH A SWALLOW OF water, and looked past Sandy at Elmore. "El, I hate to say this, but you better get back. I was recognized, and the cops'll probably be coming by again."

"I thought it'd be best if Sandy come back tonight," Elmore said.

"She's staying," Martin said bluntly. "Overnight, anyway. Until Dick's okay."

"What the hell am I supposed to tell the cops if they come?" Elmore demanded. "They'll want to know where she is."

"Tell 'em she went out to the store, then call us on my cell phone. She can be back in an hour," LaChaise said.

"Sandy . . ." Elmore couldn't say it, but she knew what he was thinking.

"Come on, El, let's get my stuff out of the truck," Sandy said. She nodded at LaChaise. "I'll get my stuff and kiss El good-bye."

"I'll help," Butters said.

"You can stand on the porch," said Sandy.

Outside, at the truck, Elmore whispered, "I'm sorry about that in there. I was gonna say something . . ." He scuffled at the snow with the toe of his boot. "We gotta get out."

"I know." She looked back at the house, at Butters standing there on the dark porch. "But I've got to get clear. If they killed cops' families, then they're dead men. I'll be back home tomorrow, and we'll figure something out."

"Sandy . . ." He stepped up to her, maybe to kiss her. She moved just an inch sideways and pecked him on the cheek.

"You go on; I'll be okay. Just wait 'til I get there, before you call John."

He didn't want to go, but he couldn't stay. He shifted his feet, looked up at the sky, shook his head, then started the low moaning that she'd seen earlier: he was weeping again.

"El, El, hold on," she said. "Come on, El . . ."

"Ah, Jesus," he said.

"I'll see you in the morning," she said.

As Elmore was starting the truck, Sandy walked back toward the house; Butters suddenly dropped off the porch and hurried past her, waving at Elmore. Elmore rolled down the driver's-side window and Butters came up, leaned close to Elmore, grinned and said, "You call the cops, we'll cut off her head."

THE BULLET HAD SIMPLY SLIPPED BENEATH THE SKIN and back out again, but the wound had to be opened and cleaned. Sandy cut through the skin, carefully, with a razor blade. Fresh blood trickled into the gash, but as soon as she had the entire pathway open, she flushed it with saline, then soaked a sterile gauze pad with more saline and dabbed it clean. At the bottom of the wound, there was a flash of white. Rib bone.

"Just touched a rib," she said to Martin.

"I see," he said, peering into the hole. He was interested in bullet wounds.

After a final wash, she repaired the razor cut with a long series of rolling stitches with black nylon thread, then painted the area around the wound with antiseptic. LaChaise wiggled a few times, but kept his mouth shut.

When she'd finished the stitching, Sandy's hands were red with blood. She went to the kitchen, washed, then returned to LaChaise and put a heavy bandage over the wound. She fixed the bandage in place with round-the-chest wraps of gauze, and then tape.

At the end of it, LaChaise sat up.

"Maybe you shouldn't move," she said.

He was feeling the pills, and smiled weakly and said, "Shit, I been hurt worse than this by sissies."

"That's the codeine. You're gonna hurt later on," Sandy said.

"I can live with it," he said. He got shakily to his feet and looked down at the bandaging job. "Jesus, good job. Really good job. You're a little honey," he said.

DEL AND LUCAS WERE ON THE WAY OUT OF THE BUILD-ing when Sloan caught up: "I'm coming," he said. "Keep you out of trouble."

All the way out to the laundromat, they argued about the shootings, and the response. Del said the season was open.

"Wouldn't be murder," Del said stubbornly. "I wouldn't just shoot them cold."

". . . and the thing is," Lucas continued, "you'd take all

of us down with you. We'd all go out to Stillwater together. Nobody'd believe it was just you."

An unwanted grin popped up on Del's face: "Hell, we know half the guys out there. Be like old home week."

Sloan said, "Lucas is right. I don't even think you should be riding with us. If you pop somebody now, after Cheryl, the media'd crucify us, and the grand jury'd be on us like a hot sweat: the politics would kill us."

"Well, who in the hell's side is everybody on?" Del asked. "What about Cheryl?"

"Don't ask that question," Lucas said. "The answer'll piss you off."

They were in Lucas's Explorer, Lucas driving, beating through the desolate streets to the near south side. Lights showed on the laundromat's second floor. Below them, behind the storefront windows of the laundromat, five women, all of them black, folded clothes, read magazines or sat and stared at the dirty pink plaster walls.

Lucas stopped in a bus zone on the corner, twenty yards up the street from the windows. "When I talked to Lonnie, he said if you go up the main stairway, you get to the top and there's a bunch of junk, cardboard boxes and stuff, all piled up. You can't get through to the door, not in a hurry, anyway," Del said, peering up at the second-story windows. "There's a back stairs that comes down inside the garage. But the garage door's locked, and you can't get through that."

"So you go up the stairs and make a lot of noise—kick the boxes out of the way, bang away on the door," Sloan said to Del. "We'll wait out back. If he opens up the front door, you call us; and if he runs, we'll be the net."

"All right," Del said, "but I think we might be barking up the wrong tree. I can't see Harp having anything to do with a bunch of . . ." He stopped in midsentence, pointed through the windshield. "Hey—look there."

A woman was walking toward them, half skating on the slippery sidewalk, holding what appeared to be a small white bakery sack. She passed under a streetlight and then into the brighter lights from the laundromat window.

"That's Jas Smith, Daymon's old lady," Del said.

Lucas said, "Let's take her. Maybe she'll invite us up."

"Yeah." Del and Sloan hopped out of the right side, while Lucas walked around the nose of the truck, converging on Jasmine. She was wearing a brimmed hat, and her head was down against the snow: she didn't see them coming until they were on top of her.

Then she jumped, and put her hand across her heart: "Goddamn, Capslock, give me some warning."

"Sorry . . ."

"If I was carrying a little piece or something, I might of shot you outa self-defense, popping out like that."

She looked at Lucas and Sloan, worried, and Del said, "This is Chief Davenport and Detective Sloan. We got something we need to talk to Daymon about. Not bust him; just talk."

"Whyn't you call him up?"

"Because we didn't want him hanging up on us," Sloan said pleasantly. "You hear about all those cops' husbands and wives getting shot today?"

"Everybody heard," she said.

"My wife was one of them," Del said. "She's in the hospital now, and she's hurting. We want you to know how serious this is—so why don't you just open up the garage and we'll go on up and talk to Daymon."

She looked from Del to Sloan to Lucas, and said, "He'd kick my ass if I done that. I mean, he'd kick me so bad."

Del looked at Lucas and nodded: he would.

"What happened to your hand?" Lucas asked. Jasmine

wasn't carrying a bakery sack; her hand was professionally wrapped in a huge white bandage.

She looked down at it, and her lip trembled: "Paper cutter," she said. "Cut my finger right off." She started to blubber. "It was just layin' there, and I knew it was off, and then the blood squirted out . . ."

Lucas said, "Jeez, that's too bad. Look, Daymon must have an unlisted number, right? Of course he does."

He nodded, and she nodded. He took a cellular phone out of his pocket.

"So why don't you dial him up, and tell him we're down here by the garage, and then he can go brush his teeth or whatever, and we can go on up."

"I'll try," she said, after a moment.

HARP LET THEM UP, UNHAPPY ABOUT IT. THE APART-ment smelled of marijuana, but nothing fresh, just old curtain-and-rug contacts, enough to get you started if you'd gone to college in the sixties. Harp was waiting for them in the kitchen, his butt against the edge of the table, his arms crossed over his chest. He looked at Jasmine as if she were at fault, and she said, "Honey, they snatched me right off the street, they knew you was up here . . ."

Del said, "That's right, Day; we were coming up, one way or another."

"What you want?" Harp grunted.

"You heard about the killings?"

"Didn't do it," Harp said.

Lucas felt a tingle: Harp was a little too tough. "We know you didn't do it personally, but we think you might have a connection," Lucas said. "Two of the people involved met down in your laundromat. We have a witness. We want to know why these two white assholes would come halfway across the country to meet in Daymon Harp's laundromat."

"You think I'd help them peckerwoods?" Harp asked indignantly. "I been inside with those motherfuckers. Daymon Harp ain't helping them no way, no place, no time."

"How'd you know they were peckerwoods?" Sloan asked. "We didn't say they were peckerwoods."

"They all over the TV," Harp said. "They're Seeds, right? I know all about it—you can't get nothin' but TV news. They canceled *Star Trek*."

"Who's your cop friend?" Lucas asked.

Harp's eyelid flickered, a quick twitch. "What kind of bullshit you talkin'?"

They pushed him for twenty minutes, but he wouldn't move. He knew nothing, saw nothing, had heard nothing. On the way out the door, Lucas said to Jasmine, "Take care of the hand."

OUTSIDE, THEY HURRIED ALONG TO THE TRUCK, blown by the breeze. Sloan said, "I don't know what he knows, but I think he's got a corner on something."

"I'll talk to Narcotics. We'll shut him down," Lucas said. He looked back up at the apartment lights. "Twenty-four hours, maybe he'll be ready."

Del shook his head: "He can't talk. Too many dead people, now. If he's got a connection, he'll do everything he can to bury it." He looked back at the apartment: "I'll bet you anything he books it."

LACHAISE HAD CALLED STADIC WITH THE NUMBER OF his new cell phone: Stadic had been in the office, and he scribbled it down, stuck the paper in his wallet.

Two hours later, the shit hit the fan. He tried calling the number, but there was no answer. Then he was swept up in the chaos of the response, and eventually found himself wearing a doorman's uniform, working the door at the hotel where the families were hidden. No time to call . . .

At ten o'clock the night of the attacks, the bank time and temperature sign down the block said −2°. Stadic traded his doorman's uniform for street clothes and hurried down the street to his car. The ferocity of the attacks had stunned him. Near panic, he'd spent the evening pacing in and out of the Sandhurst, wondering whether he should run for it. He had almost enough money . . .

But he realized, with a little thought, that it was too late. Cops' families had been attacked. That was worse than killing the cops themselves. If anyone found out that he'd been involved, there'd be no place to hide. If he were to be saved now, salvation would come in one form: the death of La-Chaise and all of his friends. Which wasn't impossible . . .

He sat in his car, took out his cellular phone, punched in his home number. Two calls on the answering machine. The first was Daymon Harp, who said two words: "Call me." The second call was nothing.

Stadic erased the tape, hung up, found LaChaise's number in his wallet and punched it in. The phone was answered on the first ring.

"Hello?" A man's voice, a southerner.

"Let me speak to Dick," Stadic said.

LaChaise came on a second later: "What?"

"You're fucked now. You can't walk a block without bumping into a cop."

"We can handle it. What we need is their location. We heard on the radio they were all being moved."

"They're at the Sandhurst Hotel in Minneapolis," Stadic said. "They're sequestered in interior rooms. There are cops all through the place. Snipers on the roof. The streets are being dug up outside, so you can't get a car close."

After a moment of silence, LaChaise said, "We'll think of something."

"No, you won't. There's no way in. And who got shot? One of you is hit, they found blood down Capslock's sidewalk."

"I got scratched," LaChaise said. "It's nothing. We need to know more about this hotel."

"There's no way in," Stadic said. "But there are some people outside you might be interested in—and I don't think there's a watch on them."

"Who's that?" LaChaise asked.

"You know Davenport?" Stadic asked. He looked down the street at the hotel. Another cop paraded the lobby, behind the glass doors, in the doorman's uniform. Stadic was due back in the uniform in the morning. "He runs the group that shot your women."

"We know Davenport. He's on the list," LaChaise said.

"He's got a daughter that almost nobody knows about, because he never married the mother," said Stadic. "She's not on any insurance forms."

"Where is she?"

"Down on Minnehaha Creek—that's in south Minneapolis. I got the address and phone number."

"Let me get a pencil . . ." LaChaise was back in a minute, and scribbled down the address. "Why're you doing this?" LaChaise asked.

" 'Cause I want you to finish and get out of here. You got three of them. You get Davenport's daughter, we set something up on Franklin, and you're outa here."

LaChaise said nothing, but Stadic could hear the hum of the open line. Then LaChaise said, "Sounds like bullshit."

"Listen, I just want you to get the fuck out of here," Stadic said. Then, "I gotta go. I'll call you about Franklin."

Stadic hung up, and dialed Harp's unlisted number. Harp picked it up on the first ring.

"What?" Stadic asked.

"Cops were here. Capslock and Davenport and another guy. Somebody saw you and LaChaise in the laundromat. They think I know something about LaChaise."

"Just hang on," Stadic said.

"I don't know, man. I'm thinking about taking a vacation."

Stadic thought a minute, then said, "Listen, how much trouble would it cause the business, if you were gone for a week?"

"Not much," Harp said. "I make a couple of big deliveries, we'd be all right. You think I should walk?"

"Yeah," Stadic said. "Go somewhere they wouldn't expect. Not Las Vegas. Not Miami."

"Puerto Rico?"

"That'd be the place," Stadic said. "They'd never think of it."

"Great pussy. No pussy like Puerto Rico pussy," Harp said.

"Forget the pussy. Just get your ass down there so Davenport can't get right on top of you. Take Jas."

"What for? She ain't doing me no good," Harp said. "She been weepin' around about this finger."

"You need a witness. There's some heavy shit coming down. You might want to prove that you weren't here. Take a credit card, and buy some stuff down there. Keep the receipts, so you can prove it."

"Yeah, okay. Good idea," Harp said.

"Stay in touch. Call my place, leave a hotel name on the tape. Nothing else, just the hotel name."

"We're outa here," Harp said, and he hung up.

Harp's disappearance would simplify things, Stadic

thought: one less problem to worry about. LaChaise would be gone in a week, and in two weeks, nobody would be coming back to Harp.

LUCAS CALLED A MEETING FOR TEN O'CLOCK: AT NINE-fifteen he shut himself in his office and closed his eyes, feet up on the desk, and worked parts of it out. At nine-thirty, he started going through LaChaise's file, everything that Harmon Anderson had managed to put together from Michigan, Wisconsin, Illinois and the FBI.

LaChaise's criminal career had begun when he was a teenager, with game-law violations in Wisconsin, followed by timber rustling off state forestlands—cutting and selling walnut trees out of the hardwood forests in the southern part of the state. He'd been convicted twice of taking deer out of season, and twice on the tree rustling.

Somewhere along the line he'd joined the Seed—called the Bad Seed at the time—a motorcycle club with ties to drug smuggling, pornography and prostitution. Then he'd apparently gone into business: he'd been convicted of failing to remit sales taxes to the state of Wisconsin, and the contents of a motorcycle shop had been seized.

A year later, operating another shop, he'd been closed again, and again, his motorcycle stock was seized, apparently to cover the remaining principal and outstanding interest on the late sales taxes from the first shop.

Two months after that, he was charged with underreporting his income for three years, but was acquitted. The next charges, illegal dumping of industrial waste, were filed in Michigan. Then there were charges of threatening a game warden, trespassing, two assaults that were apparently bar fights and two drunken driving convictions.

The murder count was weak, as Sandy Darling had said it was.

When Sandy Darling's name popped into his head, Lucas

dropped the file folder against his chest, thinking: if nothing turned up, he should make a quick run up to Darling's place. She wasn't all that far, and she knew LaChaise about as well as anyone alive. He had to be hiding somewhere . . .

He went back to the file: there was a sheaf of newspaper accounts of LaChaise's arrest and trial, and the reporters noted the difficulty of conviction—and the jubilation of the prosecutors and local lawmen when the guilty verdict came in.

A county sheriff was quoted as saying, "Sooner or later he was going to kill an honest citizen or a law enforcement officer. Putting Dick LaChaise in prison is a public service."

But the conviction smelled—and he thought of Sandy Darling again.

At nine-fifty, Del showed up, and in the next few minutes, Sloan, Franklin and Sherrill. Kupicek was out of it, for the time being: lost his shit, as Franklin put it, but he said the words with sympathy.

Sherrill was holding tighter than Lucas expected.

"I didn't think there was any feeling left, until I saw him dead," Sherrill said, slumped in her chair. Her face was dead-pale against her dark hair and eyes. "I served the papers on him two months ago, but Jesus, I didn't want him dead."

"You can handle it?" Lucas asked.

"Oh, yeah," she said. She was ten years older in five hours, Lucas thought. She had a little harsh wrinkle running from the left side of her nose to the corner of her mouth, and it was not a smile line. "Yeah, I'll tell you what: I'm in on this."

Lucas looked at her for a moment, then nodded and looked at the others. "I don't know what Del and Sloan have told you, but we think LaChaise and friends of LaChaise might be involved somehow with Daymon Harp, a dealer around town. We're gonna start pushing him. But what we need is to start working through Harmon's paper on LaChaise, and all the paper we can find on Daymon Harp, and see if we get any crossover. LaChaise had to have a good contact here, because they got a list of our relatives. And it's possible that the contact is a cop.''

"A cop," Sherrill said. She looked at Franklin, who shook his head once, as though he couldn't believe it.

"Could be," said Sloan.

"We need to chain LaChaise's known associates into the Cities, looking for *their* associates. There must be some. And we start busting ass. And I mean, like, tonight. One more thing: I want everybody to call each and every street contact you've got, and you tell them that there's big money for anyone who calls me with a location. Big money—ten grand. Ten grand, no questions asked, any way they want it.''

"Where's that coming from?" Franklin asked.

"Outa my pocket," Lucas said, looking across the desk at him. Lucas had the money, all right: they never talked about it, but they all knew it.

"Way to go," Del said. He looked at the others: "That's what'll get them. We'll buy the motherfuckers out.''

The phone rang on Lucas's desk.

ALTHOUGH COPS WERE EVERYWHERE AROUND THE HO-tel, there were still a few working the neighborhoods, doing the routine.

Barney's Old Time Malt Shoppe pulled in a lot of cops because Barney used to be one, before he retired, and because he rolled free coffee to any cops who stopped in, and always had a booth open. A single patrol car sat in Barney's lot. Stadic noted the number, 603, then cruised the place, peering through the windows. A tall, slender, pink-cheeked sergeant with pale hair and a much darker mustache: Arne Palin, two years behind Stadic at Central High.

Stadic pulled to the curb, kept an eye on the cops through the window. Harp had written down the plates on the truck LaChaise had taken to the laundromat for the meeting. Stadic took the piece of notepaper out of his pocket and called Dispatch on his handset: "Yeah, six-oh-three, run a Chevy S-10, Wisconsin Q-dash-H-O-R-S-E."

"Hang on . . ."

A moment later it came back: the truck was registered to an Elmore Darling, on a rural route in Turtle Lake, Wisconsin.

"Thanks for that . . ."

He looked through the window into Barney's. The cops inside hadn't heard their car number going out. He moved down the street, to a stop signal.

Now. One more call.

He brooded about the idea through the green light: the streets were empty, and he sat staring at nothing, the red-yellow-green bouncing unseen across his face. He knew the phone number, all right. If he had the guts . . . but then, it was hardly a matter of guts anymore. It was a matter of urgent necessity. And he'd already set it up.

If Davenport thought LaChaise was going after his daughter, LaChaise was a dead man: and that's what he needed. Dead men. Stadic pulled himself together and punched in the number. Christ, if they recognized his voice . . .

The phone rang once, then Davenport's voice said, "Yeah?"

"I don't want to say who this is—I don't want to get involved—but you gave me your card, once." He pitched his voice up, made it smooth, syrupy.

"OKAY," LUCAS SAID, AN EDGE OF IMPATIENCE IN HIS tone. He was staring at Sherrill, who was chewing on a cuticle. Lucas didn't need tips about loan sharks, cigarette smuggling, credit card dealing, dope factories.

"I live down by Richard Small and Jennifer Carey." The voice was curiously soft. "That's your little girl with Jennifer, right?"

There was a hard moment of silence, then Davenport said, "Jesus."

"There's been a truck driving around. I saw him twice when I was out walking my dog. Wisconsin plates. I thought I should call."

And the caller was gone.

Lucas exploded out of the chair and ran from the office and through the building to Dispatch. The other four, not understanding, went after him.

A PATROL CAR SQUATTED IN FRONT OF THE HOUSE, EX-haust curling up into the falling snow. Another was parked across the street, and the two cops from the car waited in the back of the house. Lucas arrived fifteen minutes after his dash to Dispatch, carrying his black wool overcoat and a briefcase. Del trailed a few steps behind, like a destitute bodyguard, watching the windows up and down the street. A cop met them at the door.

"We kept everybody away from the windows," the cop said. "There's been nothin' on the street. Nothin' moving."

"Good. And thanks. Keep an eye out," Lucas said.

Jennifer Carey and Richard Small waited for him in the dining room, the blinds pulled.

"Where's Sarah?" Lucas asked, without preamble.

"Upstairs, in bed," Jennifer said. She was still the willowy blonde, but with a few more wrinkles than when Sarah had been conceived. Lucas had wanted—had offered, in any case—to marry her, but though she'd wanted the baby, she hadn't cared for the prospects of marriage to Lucas. Now she and Small, a vice-president at TV3's parent corporation, had put together a family: Jennifer's daughter, his son. Jennifer looked past Lucas at Del, and a tiny smile caught her lips. "How're you doing, Del?"

Del shrugged. "Cheryl's gonna make it."

"What's the threat level?" Small asked. He was short, muscular, blunt, a onetime Navy pilot in Vietnam, and Lucas liked him.

"We don't know," Lucas said. "The call was weird, but we can't take any chances. You're gonna have to move."

"I can't quit working," Jennifer said. "This is too large."

Lucas said, "That pushes the threat quite a bit higher."

"We'll keep her behind security, inside the building," Small said. "We'll make sure she doesn't leave at any expected time. We can use different cars."

"That'll all help," Lucas said. "But we still haven't figured out their capability. We know there are several of them, and we've only got the ID on LaChaise. The other two—we just don't know."

Jennifer looked at Small. "Do you think you could get off?"

Small shook his head: "I'm not going anywhere; I gotta be here." He turned to Lucas. "How safe is this hotel you're putting people into?"

"Safe," Lucas said. "That'd be the best place. We don't really know how much these guys know about us. I don't know how they found out about Jen and Sarah . . ."

"Sloan's wife," Jennifer said.

Small and Lucas looked at her, and she said, "Sloan's wife. She'd take care of the kids—she loves kids. And she's in the hotel, right?"

Lucas nodded. "Give her a call."

Jen headed for the phone, and Lucas turned to Small: "If we can get you guys in the hotel tonight, we'd like to put a few guys in here . . . I'd be with them . . ."

"Use the house as a trap," Small said.

"Yeah."

Small nodded: "All right. So let's get the kids out."

Jennifer came back: "She says she'll be glad to take them."

Small said, "Pack a suitcase. You go with the kids for tonight. Lucas is gonna set up an ambush here . . . and I'm going to stick around. Make sure the cops don't steal anything."

Del looked him over. "You gotta gun someplace?"

Small nodded: "Yeah. I do. I don't like people fucking with my kids."

My kids . . .

Lucas never flinched, but as he stepped over to a telephone, he caught Jennifer's reflection in a windowpane. Behind his back, she'd brought a finger to her lips, and Small nodded. Lucas picked up the phone and called downtown: "Sherrill and Franklin are around somewhere," he said. "Get them on the line."

A high-pitched voice said something from back in the house, and Jennifer hurried that way. Lucas stepped into the hall, and saw Sarah standing halfway down the stairs in her fuzzy pink pajamas, rubbing her sleepy eyes. Lucas cleared his voice and said into the phone, "We're making some changes down here."

SARAH WOULD GROW UP TO BE TALL AND WILLOWY AND blond like her mother—like Lucas's mother—but with her father's tough smile and deep eyes. Jennifer let her go and she wandered over to Lucas and took his index finger in her hand, and when he dropped the phone back on the hook, said, "What's going on?"

Lucas squatted, so he could look straight into her eyes. "We have some problems. You have to stay at a hotel tonight. With Mom. And Mrs. Sloan will be there.''

"What kind of problems?"

"There are some really bad men . . .'' he was explaining when the phone rang. Small picked it up, then handed it to Lucas: "It's Chief Roux. I'll take Sarah,'' he said.

Lucas nodded. "Yeah," he said into the phone.

"*Nightline*'s coming on: watch it,'' Roux said. Her words came in a spate. "We picked up a thumbprint off that door in Roseville and damned if the FBI didn't come up with a name that fits. A man named Ansel Butters, from Tennessee, an old friend of LaChaise's. We've got a photo from Washington and we've released it, and it oughta be on *Nightline* in about a minute."

"Anything on Butters? Local contacts?''

"Not as far as I know, but Anderson's working the computers,'' Roux said. "Nothing happening down there?''

"Not yet,'' he said. "I'll go turn on the TV.''

"The word's out about the money you put on the street, the ten thousand,'' Roux said. "Channel Three has it, and if they've got it, everybody else will in an hour. I'm not sure it's a good precedent.''

"There aren't any precedents for this,'' Lucas said.

"All right. I hope it dredges something up,'' Roux said. "By the way, this Butters—his nickname is 'Crazy.' Crazy Ansel Butters.''

"That's what I want to hear,'' Lucas said.

LUCAS, DEL AND SMALL STOOD AROUND THE TELEVISION while Jennifer packed the kids: The regular *Nightline* host was on vacation, and an anonymous ABC newsman fronted the show. He started with "a significant bit of breaking news,'' and a black-and-white photograph of Ansel Butters filled the screen.

"If you have seen this man . . .''

A moment later, he launched into his prepared introduction, and said, "Minneapolis, a city crouched in shock and terror this wintry night," and all three of them—Lucas, Del and Small—said "Jesus" at the same time.

JENNIFER LEFT WITH THE KIDS IN A THREE-CAR CON-voy. Neighbors were wakened, and cops installed in corner houses. The snow stopped at midnight, and Lucas, Small and Del, trying to keep the house looking awake, watched on the weather radar as the snow squalls drifted off to the northeast and into Wisconsin.

At 12:30, which Small said was their usual time, they began turning off lights and killed the television. Moving cars were scarce. They sat behind the darkened windows and grew sleepy.

"Maybe it was just a bullshit call," Small said.

"Maybe, but we've got nothing else working," Lucas said. "Whoever it was had my card and my direct line. That says something."

"Maybe somebody's jerking you around," Del said.

Lucas yawned. "I don't think so. The guy knew something."

"I hope they come in," Del said fervently, in the dark. "I hope they come."

TEN

———◆———

WHILE LUCAS DASHED TO SMALL'S HOME, STADIC crossed the St. Croix at Taylors Falls and headed into the Wisconsin night on Highway 8. The going was slow: there were no lights, and at times, as he passed through the intermittent snow squalls, the highway virtually disappeared. A green sign—Turtle Lake 17—flicked past; and much later a John Deere sign, and then lights.

He was running on adrenaline now: only five hours since the attacks, and it seemed like a lifetime.

At Turtle Lake, he passed a hotel with a No Vacancy sign, and then the casino loomed out of the snow like an alcoholic hallucination. He turned into the lot and had to drive halfway to the back to find a parking space. The casinos were always full, even at midnight, even in a blizzard.

A uniformed security officer stood just inside the doors, eyes watchful. Stadic asked, "Where's the phone?" and the security man pointed down the length of the casino. "Outside any of the rest rooms," he said.

The first phone, mounted on the wall between the men's

and women's rest rooms, was occupied by a woman who appeared to be in crisis: she had a handkerchief in her hand and she twisted it and untwisted it as she cried into the phone. Stadic moved on, found another one. The noise from the slots might be a problem, he thought, but he needed the phone. He cupped his hand around the receiver and dialed the fire station.

A sleepy man answered. Stadic, watching the casino traffic, said, "This is Sergeant Manfred Hamm with the Minnesota Highway Patrol out of Taylors Falls, Minnesota. To whom am I speaking?"

The sleepy man said, "Uh, this is Jack, uh, Lane."

"Mr. Lane, you're with the Turtle Lake Fire Department?"

"Uh, yeah?"

"Would you by any chance cover a rural fire route, Mr. and Mrs. Elmore Darling?"

"Uh, yeah." Lane was waking up.

"Mr. Lane, we've got a problem here. Mrs. Darling has been involved in an automobile accident outside of Taylors Falls, and we need to send a man to speak to Mr. Darling. We don't know exactly where his house is, as all we have is a rural route address. Would you have a location on the Darling house?"

"Well, uh . . . Just a minute there."

Stadic heard the fireman talking to somebody, and a moment later he came back: "Sergeant Baker?"

"Sergeant Hamm," Stadic said.

"Oh, yeah, Hamm, sorry. The Darlings live at fire number twelve-eighty-nine. You stay on Highway 8, and you go a little more than a mile past the Highway 63 turnoff, and you'll see Kk going to the south. They're about a mile down that road . . . You'll see a red sign by the driveway, says, Township Almena and the number. Twelve-eighty-nine. Got that?"

"Yes, thank you," Stadic said, scribbling it down. "We'll send a man."

"Was, uh, the accident . . . ?"

"We're not allowed to say more until the next of kin are located," Stadic said formally. Then: "Thank you again."

THE SNOWFALL HAD EASED AS HE CREPT OUT KK, TRYing to stay in the middle of the road. Although the air was clear, the fresh snow flattened everything: he couldn't see the edge of the road, or where the ditches started. He crawled along, past the big rural mailboxes, hunting for the fire signs in the beam of a six-cell flashlight.

And he found it, just like the fireman had said he would.

The Darling house sat back from the road, and showed a sodium vapor yard light at the side of a three-car pole barn. The inverted mushroom shape of a satellite TV antenna sprouted at the side of the pole barn, pointing south. The house was two stories tall, white and neat. A white board fence led off into the dark and snow.

A fresh set of tire tracks led to the garage: with the snow coming down as it had been, there must have been a recent arrival. Stadic continued a half-mile down Kk to the next driveway, turned around and headed back.

LaChaise had given him a local phone number in the Cities, and another man had answered when he called. So at least two of them were down there—and after the fight, they were probably all three hanging together.

He wasn't sure what he'd find at this place: but if they were friends of LaChaise, they might know where he was . . . and they might know Stadic's name.

Just short of the Darlings' driveway, he turned off his headlights and eased along the road with the parking lights. He turned into the end of the driveway and, keeping his foot off the brake, killed the engine and rolled to a stop.

He had a shotgun in the back, on the floor. He picked it up, jacked a shell into the chamber, zipped his parka, put on his gloves and cracked the door. He'd forgotten the dome light: it flickered, and he quickly pulled the door shut. Watched. Nothing. He reached up, pushed the dome light switch all the way to the left, and tried the door again. No light. He got out, and headed down the drive, the shotgun in his hand.

A shaft of light fell on the snow outside the kitchen. Stadic did a quick-peek, one eye, just a half-second, past the edge of a yellowed pull-down shade. A gray-faced man in a plaid shirt and blue jeans, with a bare-neck farmer haircut, sat alone at a kitchen table. He was eating macaroni out of a Tupperware bowl, washing it down with a can of beer. He was watching CNN.

Stadic ducked under the window and, walking light-footed, testing the snow for crunch, continued past the house to a detached garage, and down the side of the garage to a window. He flicked his pocket flash just long enough to see the truck inside. He checked the plates: Q-HORSE2. So they had two vehicles. There were probably no more than two people inside the house, because that was the nominal capacity of the truck. And there was probably only one person inside, the one he could see, because the other truck was gone.

He stepped back to the house, checked the window again. The man—Elmore Darling?—was still there, eating. Stadic moved to the back door. The door opened onto a small three-season porch. He pulled open the aluminum storm door a half-inch at a time. Tried the inner door: the knob turned under his hand. Nobody locked anything in the country. Assholes. He opened the inner door as carefully as he had the storm door, a half-inch at a time, taking care not to let the shotgun rattle against the door frame.

Inside, on the porch, he was breathing hard from the tension, his breath curling like smoke in the dimly lit air. He could hear the TV, not the words, but the mutter. The porch smelled of grain and maybe, a bit, of horse shit: not unpleasant. Farm smells. The porch was almost as cold as the outside. He eased the storm door shut.

The door between the porch and the house had a window, covered with a pink curtain. He peeked, quickly: still eating. He'd have to move before Darling sensed him here, Stadic thought. He took a breath, reached out and tried the doorknob. Stiff.

All right. He backed away a step, lifted the shotgun to the present-arms position, cocked his leg.

Took a breath and kicked the doorknob.

The door flew open, the screws of the lock housing ripping out of the wood on the inside. Darling, a soup-spoon of macaroni halfway to his face, fell out of his chair and onto the linoleum floor, and tried to scramble to his feet.

Stadic, moving: "Freeze . . . Freeze." Stadic was on top of Darling, leaning toward him, the barrel of the shotgun following his face. Stadic shouted, "Police," and "Down on the floor, down on the floor . . ."

With his dark coat blowing around his ankles, the cold wind behind him, and the black gun, he looked like the figure of death. Darling flattened himself on the floor, his hands arched behind his head, shouting, "Don't, don't, don't."

SANDY SPENT AN HOUR WATCHING THE TV NEWS, THE crisis building in the newsrooms. Murder and terrorism experts arriving at the networks like boatloads of war refugees, looking for life on television. You could tell they liked it: liked the murder, liked the guns, liked having the expertise.

"Bunch of vultures," Butters said.

LaChaise and Butters and Martin were drunk. Martin simply got quieter and meaner: he'd stare at Sandy, drinking, stare some more. Butters tended to laugh and lurch around the house, and want to dance. LaChaise talked incessantly about the old days when they rode together with the Seed, and all the things the cops had done to him and his daddy.

"Nothing like what they did to my daddy," Butters said once. "He used to write some bad checks when me and momma got hungry, and they'd be all over him. Used to beat him up and make him cry. The goddamn sheriff there liked to see a man cry. I was gonna kill him when I got big enough, but somebody else did it first."

"So what finally happened?" Sandy asked. "To your old man?"

"Hung himself down the basement one day, right next to this big old rack of empty Ball jars. I come home from school and found him there, just twisting around. Did it with one of them pieces of plastic electric cable, had a hell of a time getting it unwrapped off his neck . . ."

The story angered LaChaise—topped him—and he walked around the house kicking doors down. Then he came back and said, "I don't want to hear no more about your daddy," and dropped into the one big chair and into himself, glowering at them, his disapproval rank in the air.

"Well, fuck you," Butters said, and Sandy felt like something could happen between them. But LaChaise grinned and said, "You, too," and that defused it.

Then *Nightline* came on, with the story about Butters, and they listened to the *Nightline* reporter list his life record.

"How'd they get that?" LaChaise roared, and he glared around the room, as though one of them had given Butters up. "Who'n the fuck is the traitor?"

And then it occurred to him. He swung, the bottle of Jim Beam still in his hand, to Sandy: "That fuckin' Elmore."

Sandy backed away, shook her head. "No. Not Elmore. I warned him to keep his mouth shut, and he said he would."

But she thought, *Maybe he did*. Maybe he got on a phone and gave them up to Old John.

"I might have touched something," Butters said calmly, and LaChaise swung around toward him.

"You had gloves," he said.

"Couldn't get the pistol out of my pocket with gloves, so I took them off. Tried to stay away from things, but . . . maybe I touched something. My fingerprints would ring bells with the cops."

LaChaise considered, then said, "Nah, it's that fuckin' Elmore, that's who it is."

"If it was Elmore, he would've given them Martin, too," Butters said. He was holding a bourbon bottle, and took a swig.

"He's right, Dick . . ." Sandy started, but LaChaise pointed at her, a thick forefinger in her face: "Shut up."

And he dropped back into his chair. After a moment he said, "I just fell apart. I saw the guy and I came apart."

Three people had gone out to kill, and only LaChaise had failed. He'd been brooding about it.

"There was no way you could know," Martin said finally. He was as drunk as Butters. "It would have happened to me or Ansel, too. You call, you make the check, who's to know that he's gonna walk in one second later?"

"No, it's my fault," LaChaise said. "I wasn't steady. I coulda took her. I coulda took them both. I coulda shot her, then shot him, let 'em watch each other die. She was right there, but I was gettin' fancy, then this cop pops up behind her. He was fast . . ."

"Lucky that shot caught you in the side, instead of square in the back," Butters said. They knew what he meant, but the word "back" seemed to hang in the air. LaChaise had been running when he was hit.

"I gotta get out of here," Sandy said. She stood up, but

LaChaise pushed himself out of the chair and said, "I told you to fuckin' shut up." And quick—quick as a whip—he caught her with an openhanded roundhouse, and knocked her to the floor, as Martin had earlier in the evening. Butters and Martin sat impassively, watching, as she struggled to her hands and knees.

She could taste blood in her mouth. She looked up at him and thought about getting a gun. She should have killed him the night she found out that he'd murdered the cop. She couldn't do it then. She could do it now.

"You gonna shut up?" LaChaise asked.

"Let me go home, Dick," she said. She wiped at her mouth with the back of her hand.

"Fuck that. You're staying here," he said.

But he didn't mention Elmore again that night.

ELMORE TOLD STADIC EVERYTHING HE KNEW, AND only lied in a few spots. "Sandy's not in it at all," he said. "They showed up, and there wasn't anything we could do. They got all the guns in the world."

"Who are the other guys?" Stadic asked.

"Martin, who's like this crazy queer from Michigan who walks around with a bow and arrow, and Ansel Butters. He's from Tennessee and he comes up and goes hunting with Martin."

"Is Butters a fag?" Stadic and Darling sat in wooden chairs, across the kitchen table from each other. The shotgun's barrel rested on the table, pointing at Darling's chest. Stadic had closed the outer door, and the house was getting warm again. The kitchen was a pleasant place, with just enough chintz and country pottery to make it homey. Darling had a nice wife, Stadic thought.

"No, Butters is straight, but he takes a lot of drugs," Darling said. "Martin, now, everybody says he's a fag and he's in love with Dick, but he never does anything homosexual or nothing . . . it's just a thing.''

"And that's all," Stadic said. "There's just the four."

"Just the three—you can't count Sandy," Elmore said. "I'd tell you where they were at, but I don't know. I mean, I kinda know . . ."

Darling was holding this one piece back, lying. He was an excellent liar, but Stadic was a professional interrogator. He wasn't sure that Darling was lying, but he also knew that he had no way to control the man. He couldn't take him with him, couldn't hold him. And if Darling got in touch with LaChaise, LaChaise would recognize Stadic's description. A problem.

He sat in the kitchen chair with the barrel of the gun pointing at Darling's chest.

"Tell me again," Stadic said. "You get off at Lexington . . ."

"And it must be about six blocks up the road. North. Then right. Just a little house."

"You didn't see the number or the street name."

"Nope. I was just following behind." He brightened. "But I'll tell you—my truck is on the street. So is Martin's. You could look for my truck, it's got a license plate says, Q-HORSE."

Stadic nodded. "So six or seven blocks."

"No more than that," Darling said. "We could find it. I'd go down there with you."

Stadic thought for another moment, then shook his head.

"Nah," he said.

"What, then?" Darling asked, his eyebrows going up as if mystified, a stupid smile on his face. Stadic shrugged, and pulled the trigger.

The 00s in the three-inch Magnum shell blew Elmore Darling completely off his kitchen chair.

• • •

SANDY HUDDLED IN THE BEDROOM, JUST TO BE AWAY from them.

LaChaise went to sleep in his chair, and Martin and Butters sat in the living room, the television turned down, talking quietly about the kills.

Martin said, "I had my hands on him and when the knife went in, he kind of rose up, and shook. Like when you cut the throat on a deer, they make that last little try to get goin' . . . you know?"

"Sure, they push up, try to get their feet under them . . ."

"Damn good time to get hurt," Martin said. "There's one old boy, Rob Harris over to Luce County, got down on a spike buck like that, stuck him in the throat with his knife, and that buck rose up and stuck one of them spikes right in Rob's eye. Blinded the eye."

"What happened to the buck?" Butters asked.

"Run off. Rob says it must've been a brisket hit 'cause there was blood all over hell," Martin said. "Probably out there to this day . . ."

"Yeah, well, this Sherrill dude sure ain't."

"Not when I get that close," Martin said. "When I get that close, the boy's a goner . . ."

They both turned and looked at LaChaise, thinking they might have given offense, but LaChaise was unconscious.

"This Kupicek, she never even twitched," Butters said. "Never even knew what hit her. One minute she's talking to me, the next minute, it's St. Peter."

"Silencer work good?"

Butters nodded. "Worked real good. All you hear is that ratchet sound, you know, maybe a little pop, but it's no more'n opening a can of soda."

"Wish I had me a silencer like that."

"If I were gonna do it again, I think I might do it as a

single-shot. You know, load one round, carry it cocked-and-locked over an empty clip. Then you wouldn't get the ratchet noise . . .''

They went on, working over the details, the TV turned down. Butters's face would come up every half hour or so. On the first newsbreak of the day, at five o'clock, TV3 produced a series of computer-morphed photos of both LaChaise and Butters, with a variety of hairstyles and facial hair.

"Oughta shave your head," Martin said. "That's the only thing they ain't got."

"Nah. Too late for me," Butters said. He looked at his watch. "Be daylight in a couple-three hours. I'm going out. Check this kid's house, the Davenport kid."

"Better wait for Dick," Martin said.

Butters shook his head as he stood up. "It's about fifty-fifty that it's an ambush," Butters said. "Better that only one of us goes; and Dick's hurt, and they don't know you yet."

"You sober?"

"As a judge."

Martin dropped his hands on his thighs, a light conclusive slap, and nodded. Butters said: "Help me load up."

"What're you takin'?" Martin asked.

Butters grinned: "One of everything."

LaChaise stirred in the chair, half-opened his eyes, shook his head and slept again.

"I better get going," Butters said. "Don't want to disturb Dick's beauty rest."

ELEVEN

━━━●◖●◗●━━━

DEL WAS IN THE HALLWAY, STRETCHED OUT ON THREE couch pillows. Small was in bed, still dressed but in stocking feet, alert. Every once in a while, he'd get out of bed and creep through the hallway, and whisper a question down to Lucas.

"Anything?"

"Nothing yet."

Lucas yawned, pushed a button on his watch to illuminate the face. Five forty-five. More than two hours to first light. He walked carefully back toward the bathroom, navigating by feel through the darker lumps of the furniture. The bathroom was for guests, for convenience: small, with a toilet and a sink, a tube of Crest and a rack of kids' toothbrushes for after-meal brushing. There was no exterior window. Lucas shut the door and turned on the light, winced at its brightness, splashed water in his face. His mouth tasted worse than his face looked; he rubbed a wormy inch of Crest over his teeth with his index finger, spat the green slime into the sink, and stood there, leaning over the sink, weight on his arms, watching the water.

There were all kinds of hints and pointers, but none of them solid. Not yet. But the case would go quickly, he thought. If he were alive, if Weather and Sarah and Jennifer and Small were all alive in a week, then it'd be done with.

It'd be done with even if they didn't stay around.

They could walk out now, catch a plane, fly to Tahiti—he had the money to do it a hundred times over—lie on the beach, and when they came back, it'd be done. The difference of a week.

And maybe they should.

But he liked the tightening feel of the hunt.

He didn't like what it had done to Cheryl Capslock or the others, the dead, but he did like the feel of chase, God help him.

He turned out the light, opened the door and went back to the living room.

DEL WAS AWAKE. HE SAID, "CHERYL COULDN'T FEEL much of anything after they got her out of surgery."

"She'll feel it today," Lucas said. He unconsciously touched a white tracheotomy scar on his throat.

"Yeah, that's what the docs said."

"They say anything about scars?" Lucas asked.

"She's gonna have some, but they shouldn't be too bad. What there is, she can wear her hair over."

"I know a plastic surgeon over at the U, friend of Weather's. If you need one."

They sat a while in the dark. Then Del said, "If she died, I don't know what I'd do."

"She'll be okay."

"Yeah." Then: "But that's not exactly what I meant. I mean, I never really thought of it until this afternoon. If she was gone, I'd be lost. I been on the streets so long, the whole world looks like it's fucked. Cheryl keeps me from going nuts. I *was* going nuts before I met her. I was a crazy motherfucker . . . I was such a good wino that I could've *become* one.''

''Made for each other,'' Lucas said, with a wry undertone cops affected when they were getting too close to sincerity.

''Yeah. Jesus, I want to kill that motherfucker . . .''

Then the handset:

''Lucas. Got one coming.'' A surveillance voice. Lucas grabbed the radio and stepped to the front door. He could see out the inset glass windows without being seen himself.

''White male in a pickup, moving slow. He's not delivering papers.''

''Can you see the plates?''

''I can't, but Tommy can, he's got the night scope . . . Tommy? He'll be there in a minute.''

''Right, I got him coming . . .''

''Lucas, he's coming up to the house now.''

Lucas could see the headlights on the snow, then the slowly moving pickup. ''Get the plate, get the plate.''

''He's going by, but he was looking. Jeff, what'd you think?''

''He was looking, all right.''

''We don't want to shoot a goddamn reporter, take it easy . . .''

Lucas said, ''Tommy, you got that plate?''

''Front plate's dirty, I can get CV. It's Minnesota . . .''

''Tommy, c'mon . . .''

''I got it, I got it . . .'' He read the license out, and Dispatch acknowledged. ''He's going around the corner . . .''

''Which way?''

''South. Wait a minute, he's stopping. He's stopping.''

''Dick, you guys get down here in the car,'' Lucas said into the handset. ''Come around the block from the back.''

"Didn't think it'd happen," Del said. He was wide awake, breathing hard.

"Take it easy," Lucas said.

Small called down the stairs: "What's happening?"

"Nothing," Lucas called back, and then Del led out through the front and down the sidewalk, moving with the wintertime short-step duckwalk of a man on ice.

Lucas still had the handset. Tommy: "He's getting something out of the back. He's got the dome light on and he's doing something in the back."

Lucas brought the radio up: "Everybody take it easy, he could have anything in there."

Dick came back: "We're coming in, we're coming around the corner."

Lucas said, "Let's go," and they started running, moving off the sidewalk into the snow, high-stepping. At the corner, they rounded an arbor vitae, and saw the truck fifty feet away, across the street, the door open now. The driver was turning toward them, he had something in his arms . . .

"Hold it," Lucas shouted. Del was sprinting ahead, and Tommy came in from the side, his long coat whipping around his legs, and Dick came in with the car . . .

BUTTERS HAD SPIRALED IN TOWARD THE HOUSE FROM A half-mile out, quartering the neighborhood, watching faces in the few cars he'd encountered, looking for lights, looking for motion. In the woods, he'd learned to look not for the animal, but the disturbance in the animal's wake. Deer sometimes sounded like they were wearing jackboots, pounding through the woods; squirrels made tree limbs jiggle and jerk in a way that wasn't the wind; even a snake, if it was big enough, parted the grass like a ship's prow cutting through water.

He watched for the odd motion; and saw none.

Still, there was something not right about this. He understood that the cop might think that the kid was safe, but why would he take the chance? Putting the kid in the hotel would have been the natural thing to do.

Butters saw nothing, but he smelled something: the kid felt like bear bait, a bucket of honey and oatmeal, meant to pull them in. They had to check, because the kid might be one of their last chances to really get even. And that, he thought, made the kid even better bait.

But he turned toward the house, spiraling, moving closer . . .

THE UNMARKED CAR CAUGHT THE TRUCK IN ITS HIGH beams, and the man turned, hearing Lucas's scream, saw the running men . . . put his back to the truck and said, "What? What?"

Del was twenty feet away and coming in, and the man raised his hands and Del almost popped him: almost . . .

"Freeze. Right where you are." Lucas behind Del, Tommy on the edge, the doors popping on the blocking car.

"What?" The guy was white-faced, shocked, his mouth dropping open. He stepped back away from the van.

There was movement in the van, and Tommy swiveled toward it, his shotgun raised. A blond head. Then a child's voice, tired and frightened: "Daddy?"

SPIRALING: AND CATCHING. DOWN A STREET THAT LED almost straight into the target house, a dark-night tableau. A car parked diagonally across the street, its headlights on a van. A man outside the van, his hands up. More men in the street.

"There you are," Butters said, with satisfaction. "I knew you were out there."

Lucas saw Butters's truck: noticed it mostly because it was identical to the truck they were standing next to.

Del was apologizing to the owner, who had just gotten home from his parents' farm, and trying to reassure the little girl, who was old enough to be frightened by the men who'd suddenly surrounded them.

The truck in the intersection paused for just a heartbeat, two heartbeats, then casually rolled on. The driver must have seen the commotion in the street, Lucas thought. "I've got a daughter just like you, who lives up the block," Lucas said to the little girl. "Do you know Sarah Davenport?"

The girl nodded without saying anything, but now the world was okay.

"Sure, she knows Sarah . . ." the father was saying, and Lucas made nice and forgot about the other truck.

And walking away, a shaky, white-faced Del said, "Jesus, I gotta ease off. I almost shot the guy. He didn't do a fuckin' thing, I just wanted to do it . . ."

STADIC THOUGHT ABOUT IT ALL THE WAY INTO THE Cities. He was exhausted from the day on duty, from the drive, from the killing. Through the thinning snow, he had flashes, almost visionlike in their clarity and intensity, of Elmore Darling sitting at the table in the instant before the gunshot. Darling was smiling, hopeful . . . afraid. He was alive. Then he wasn't. There was no transition, just a noise, and the smell of gunpowder and raw meat, and Elmore Darling wasn't there anymore.

The visions frightened Stadic: What was happening? Was he losing it? At the same time, his cop brain was working out the inevitable progression. He now knew where LaChaise and his friends were hiding. If he worked it right, if he came up with the right story, he could ambush them. He needed to draw them out of their house, unsuspecting.

He could set up outside the house, in the dark, next to their vehicles. Darling said the trucks would be on the street. Then he could prod them out. He could call and say that the cops had been tipped, that they were on the way. They'd have to run for it.

LaChaise was injured, so only Martin and Butters would be at full strength. He'd catch them as soon as they stepped out on the porch, before they could get the door shut, then he'd go in after the woman.

But how about the shotgun? Darling had been killed with 00s, maybe he ought to change to 000s? Or maybe just go with the pistol. If he was right there, real close, take them with the pistol and forget the shotgun. Of course, if LaChaise was really hurt, if he didn't come out, then he'd have to go in after him . . .

There'd be risk. He couldn't avoid it.

And how would he explain the sequence to the St. Paul cops? He could say he'd been tipped to the location by one of the local dopers, but he hadn't given it much credence. He'd gone to take a look, when he'd stumbled right into them . . .

But why would he go into the house? Why not fall back and call for an entry team?

Stadic chewed it over, worried it, all the way down to the Cities. If he was going to do it, he should stop down at his office and pick up a vest. But when he stopped at the office, the first thing he heard was people running in the hallways . . .

LUCAS STARED OUT THROUGH THE SLATS IN THE VENE-tian blinds. Still dark. "Not coming."

"So it was bullshit," Del said. He yawned.

"Maybe. Strange call, though," Lucas said, thinking about it. "Came straight into me. He had the number."

"We oughta leave a couple of guys here, just in case," Del said. "I gotta get down to Hennepin and see Cheryl."

"Yeah, take off," Lucas said.

Dispatch called: "Lucas?"

He picked up the handset. "Yes?"

"A woman called for you. Says she has some information and she wants the ten thousand."

"Patch her through."

"She hung up. She says her old man might hear her. But she gave her address. She says she wants you to take her out of her house, if her old man gets . . . she said, 'pissed.'" A dispatcher couldn't *say* "pissed," but she could quote "pissed."

"What's the address?" Lucas asked.

"It's over on the southeast side . . . you got a pencil?"

As Lucas took it down, Del asked, "You want me to come along?"

Lucas shook his head. "It's probably bullshit. Half the dopers in town will be calling, trying to fake us out. Go see Cheryl."

"They'll let me in pretty soon," Del said. The light on his watch face flickered in the dark. "I gotta be there when she wakes up."

"Keep an eye out," Lucas said. "The crazy fucks could be around the hospital."

LUCAS, BEGINNING TO FEEL THE WEIGHT OF ALL THE sleepless hours, looked at the house and wondered: called to a semi-slum duplex, in the early-morning darkness. An ambush?

"What do you think?" he asked.

"You wait here," the patrol cop said. "We'll go knock."

The two patrol cops, one tall and one even taller, were wearing heavy-duty armor, capable of defeating rifle bullets. Two more cops sat in the alley behind the house, covering the back door.

Lucas stood by the car, waiting, while the cops approached

the door. One of them peeked at a window, then suddenly broke back toward the door, and Lucas saw that it was opening. A woman, gaunt, black-haired, poked her head out and said something to the cops. The tall cop nodded, waved Lucas in, and then he and the taller cop went inside.

Lucas caught them just inside the door. The taller cop whispered, ''Her husband's in the back bedroom, and he keeps a gun on the floor next to the bed. We're invited in, so we can take him.''

Lucas nodded, and the two cops, walking softly as they could over the tattered carpet, eased down the hallway, with the woman a step behind them. At the last door, the lead cop gestured and the woman nodded, and the cop reached inside the dark room and flipped on the light. Lucas heard him say, ''Police,'' and then, ''Get the gun,'' and then, ''Hey, wake up. Wake up. Hey you, wake up.''

Then a man's voice, high and squeaky, ''What the fuck? What the fuck is going on?''

The woman walked back down the hall toward Lucas. She was five-six, and weighed, he thought, maybe ninety pounds, with cheekbones like Frisbees. She said, ''I heard you're putting up the money.''

''If your information is any good,'' he said.

The two patrol cops prodded her husband out into the hallway. Still mostly asleep, he was wearing stained Jockey shorts and a befuddled expression. His hands were cuffed behind his back.

''Oh, the information is good,'' the woman said to Lucas. Then, ''You remember me?''

Lucas looked at her for a moment, saw something familiar in the furry thickness of her dark brows, mentally put twenty-five pounds on her and said, ''Yeah. You used to work up at the Taco Bell, the one off Riverside. You were . . . let's see, you were hanging out with Sammy Cerdan and his band. You were what—you played with them. Bass?''

''Yeah, bass,'' she said, pleased that he remembered.

He was going to ask, ''What happened?'' but he knew.

Still smiling, a rickety smile that looked as though it might slide off her face onto the floor, she said, ''Yeah, yeah, good times.''

Her husband said, ''What the hell is going on? Who's this asshole?''

The tall cop said, ''He had a bag of shit under his mattress.''

He tossed a Baggie to Lucas: the stuff inside, enough to fill a teaspoon, looked like brown sugar.

''This is fuckin' illegal. I want to see a search warrant,'' the husband said.

''You shouldn't of hid the bag, Dex,'' the woman said to him. To Lucas, ''He never gave me nothin'. I'm boostin' shit out of Target all day and he never give me nothin'.''

''Kick you in the ass,'' Dexter shouted at her, and he struggled against the taller cop, and tried to kick at her. She dodged the kick and gave him the finger.

''Shut up,'' Lucas said to him. To the woman: ''Where are they?''

''My brother rented them a house, but he doesn't know who they are. The one guy, Butters? He was here asking about crooked cops and houses he could rent. As soon as I saw on TV, I knew that was him.''

''You cunt,'' her husband shouted.

Lucas turned to him and smiled: ''The next time you interrupt, I'm gonna pull your fuckin' face off.''

The husband shut up and the woman said, ''I want the money.''

''If this pans out, you'll get it. What's the address?''

''I want something else.''

"What?"

"When my mom took the kids, they kicked me off welfare."

"So?"

"So I want back on."

Lucas shrugged. "I'll ask. If you can show them the kids, then . . ."

"I don't want the kids back. I just want back on the roll," the woman said. "You gotta fix it."

"I'll ask, but I can't promise," Lucas said. "Now, where are they?"

"Over in Frogtown," she said. "I got the address written down."

"What about the cop?" Lucas asked. "Who'd you send him to?"

The woman shook her head. "We didn't know any cop. Dex just gave him names of some dopers who might know."

Lucas turned to her husband. "What dopers?"

"Fuck you," Dex said.

"Gonna give you some time to think about it," Lucas said, poking a finger in Dexter's face. "Down in the jail. For the shit." He held up the bag. "If you think about it fast enough, maybe you can buy out of the murder charge."

"Fuck that, I want a lawyer," Dex said.

"Take him," Lucas said to the patrolmen. To the woman: "Gimme the address."

LACHAISE WOKE UP SOBER BUT HUNG OVER. HE STOOD up, carefully, walked down to the bathroom, closed the door, found the light switch and flicked it on, took a leak, flushed the toilet.

He'd been sleeping in his jeans, T-shirt and socks. He pulled up the shirt to check the bandage on his ribs, looking in the cracked mirror over the sink, but saw no signs of blood, just the dried iodine compound. Best of all, he didn't feel seriously injured: he'd been hurt in bike accidents and fights, and he knew the coming-apart feeling of a bad injury. This just plain hurt.

The house was silent. He stepped back out of the bathroom, walked down the hall to the next room and pushed the door open. Sandy was curled on the bed, wrapped in a blanket.

"You asleep?" he asked quietly.

There was no response, but he thought she might be awake. He was about to ask again, when there was a noise in the hall. He stepped back, and saw Martin padding down the hallway, a .45 in his hand. When Martin saw LaChaise, his forehead wrinkled.

"You all right?" Martin asked.

"I'm sore, but I been a lot worse," LaChaise said. "Where's Ansel?"

"He went to see about that Davenport kid."

"Jesus Christ, that's my job," LaChaise said.

Martin's mouth jerked; he might have been trying to smile. "He figured you'd think that. But he thought it might be a trap and he figured, you know, you're the valuable one. You're the brains of the operation."

"Shoulda told me," LaChaise growled.

"You was drunk."

Sandy pushed herself up. Beneath the blanket, LaChaise noticed, she'd been wrapped in a parka. "What's going on?"

"Ansel went after the cop's kid," LaChaise said. He looked at her in the long coat, and said, "What's wrong with you? What's the parka for?"

"It's like a meat locker in here," she said, crossing her arms and shivering.

"Bullshit: she wants to be ready to run," Martin growled.

LaChaise turned to her: "You run, we'll cut your fuckin' throat. And if you *did* get away . . ." He dug in his shirt pocket, and came up with a stack of photographs. Two men sitting at a table, one black, one white. LaChaise riffled them at her like a deck of cards. "We got a cop on the string. The only way he gets out is if we get away, or we're all dead. If you get away from us, and go to the cops, he'll have to come after you, in case you know his name. Think about that: we've got a cop who'll kill you, and you don't know who it is." He put the photos back in his pocket.

Sandy shivered. "I'm not thinking about running," she said. "I'm just cold."

"Bullshit," Martin snorted.

"Whyn't you put some shoes on?" LaChaise said. "Let's go out."

"Go out?" she asked doubtfully. She looked toward a window: it was pitch black outside. Then she looked back at LaChaise. "Dick, you're hurt . . .♥

"Hell, it ain't that bad. There's no bleeding. And I can't be cooped up in here," LaChaise said. Despite the headache, he was almost cheerful.

"I'd rather stay here."

"Don't be an asshole," he snapped. "Let's go out and see what's cookin'. One of you can drive, I'll sit in the back."

WHILE SANDY AND MARTIN GOT READY, LACHAISE turned on the television, clicked around the channels and found nothing of interest but a weather forecast. The snow would diminish during the morning, and the sun might peek through in the afternoon. Big trouble was cranking up in the Southwest, but it was several days away.

"Cold," Martin grunted, coming back from his bedroom. He was wearing his camo parka.

"Better for us, since they plastered pictures of me and Butters all over hell," LaChaise said. "Less people on the street."

"Nothing must've happened with Ansel. They'd be going on all channels if he'd done something."

"Maybe backed off," LaChaise said. "Maybe nothin' there."

Martin looked at Sandy: "You ready?"

"I'm not sure about this," she said. "If somebody sees us . . ."

"We're just gonna ride around," LaChaise said. "Maybe go to a drive-through and get some Egg McMuffins or something."

"Gonna be light soon," Martin said.

BUTTERS GOT BACK TO THE HOUSE AND SAW THE SNOW-free spot where Martin's truck had been parked, and the tracks leading away. Hadn't been gone for more than a couple of minutes, he thought: wonder what's going on? He parked Sandy's truck over the same spot and went inside. A note in the middle of the entry floor said, "Cabin fever. Gone an hour. We'll check back."

Butters shook his head: Cabin fever wasn't a good enough reason to go out. Of course, he'd been out. Still. LaChaise had once saved his life, LaChaise was as solid a friend as Butters had ever known . . . but nobody had ever claimed that he was a genius.

WHEN LUCAS ARRIVED AT THE PARKING LOT OFF UNI-versity and Lexington, the St. Paul cops were putting together the entry team under a lieutenant named Allport. Four plain-clothes Minneapolis cops, all from homicide or vice, were standing around the lot, watching the St. Paul guys getting set.

Allport spotted Lucas and walked over to shake hands: "How're you doing?"

"Anything we can do to help?"

Allport shook his head. "We got it under control." He paused. "A couple of your guys were pretty itchy to go in with us."

"I'll keep them clear," Lucas said. "Maybe we could sit out on the perimeter."

Allport nodded: "Sure. We're a little thin on the ground 'cause we're moving fast. We want to get going before we have too many people on the street." He looked up into the sky, which seemed as dark as ever with snow clouds. But dawn was coming: you couldn't see it on the horizon, but there was more light around. "Why don't you take your guys up on the east side, up on Grotto. You'll be a block off the house, you can get down quick if something happens."

"You got it," Lucas said. "Thanks for letting us in."

"So let's go," Allport said.

Lucas rounded up the Minneapolis cops: "There'll be two squads on Grotto, which is a little thin. We'll want to spread out along the street. St. Paul will bring us in as soon as the entry team pops the place."

A sex cop named Lewiston said, "St. Paul don't have a lot of guys out here."

"There's a time problem," Lucas said. "They want to get going before they have too many civilians on the street."

Lewiston nodded, accepting the logic, but Stadic said, "I wish we were doing the entry. These fuckin' shitkickers . . ."

Lucas grinned and said, "Hey." Then: "We don't even know if it's anything. Could be bullshit."

The entry team left, followed by the other cops in squads and their personal cars, a morose procession down through the narrow streets of Frogtown, staying two blocks from the target, walking in the last block.

STADIC HUNG BACK AS THEY WALKED, HIS SHOTGUN under his arm. He'd been caught up in the rush around the office, when word got back that Davenport's source might have something. Now he was worried: if they got tight on the house, they just might pull some people out of it alive . . .

Davenport pushed on ahead, walking fast with two other Minneapolis cops. This was his first chance, and probably his last: Stadic stepped behind a dying elm, took his cellular from his pocket and pushed the speed-dial button.

"Yeah?" LaChaise answered in two seconds, as though he'd been holding the phone.

"Get out of there," Stadic rasped. "There's a St. Paul entry team coming in right now. Go out the back, go east, they're thin up there. Get out."

After a second of silence, LaChaise said, "We ain't there."

"What?"

"We're in the truck. Where're you at?"

"Old house in St. Paul, north of the freeway a few blocks . . . If that's your place, you stay away. I can't talk, I gotta go."

He heard LaChaise say "Shit" and then Stadic turned the phone off and hurried to catch the others.

BUTTERS HAD WALKED UP THE STAIRS TOWARD THE bathroom when he glanced out a back window and saw the man dart through the streetlight a block over. The motion was quick, but heavy. Not a jogger, a soldier. He knew instantly that the cops were at the door.

He was still wearing his camo parka. He ran light-footedly down the stairs to the hall, where Martin had stacked the weapons in an open hall closet, out of sight but easy to get to. Butters grabbed the AR-15, already loaded, and four loaded magazines. He jammed the mags in his pocket and jacked a shell into the chamber and kept going, right to the back door.

The rear of the house was still dark, and he listened for a

moment. He couldn't hear anything, but the door was the place they'd come. He turned back, crossed the house to the darker side away from the back door, went into Martin's bedroom, and tried a window. Jammed. He went to the next, turning the twist lock, lifting it. There was a vague tearing sound as old paint ripped away; the smell of it tickled his nose, but he had been quiet enough, he thought. The old-fashioned storm windows opened behind some kind of withered, leafless bush. He looked out, saw nobody, pushed open the storm window and peeked. Still nothing, too dark. He took a breath and snaked over the windowsill into the snow behind the hedge.

The snow crunched beneath his weight where dripping water from the eaves had stippled the surface with ice. He lay still for a moment, listening. Listening was critical in the dark: he'd spent weeks in tree stands, turning his head to the tweaks and rustles of the early morning, the deer moving back to bedding areas, the foxes and coyotes hunting voles, the wood ducks crunching through dried-out oak leaves, the trees defrosting themselves in the early sun, the grass springing up in the morning. Ansel Butters had heard corn grow; and now he heard footsteps in the snow, coming from the back, and then more, from the front.

Butters went down the side of the house, listening to the crunch of feet coming in: they wouldn't hear him, he decided. They were making too much noise on their own, city people in the snow, carrying heavy weapons. He went left, to the house next door, pressed himself against its weathered siding. Trying to see, trying to hear . . .

And here they came, through the backyard, three or four of them, he thought. Staying low, he moved to the corner of the house, then around it, to the east. He really had no choice about which way to go . . .

The loudspeaker came like a thunderbolt:

"Halt. By the house, freeze . . ."

And he thought, *Night scope*. Before the last words were out, he fixed on the position of the men coming up from the back.

He could sense the motion.

Butters ran sideways and fired a long, ripping burst across the group, thirty rounds pounding downrange, his face flashing in the muzzle flash like a wagon spoke in a strobe light.

The return fire was short of him, of where he had been. Moving all the time, he punched out the magazine and slammed in another, looking for muzzle flashes, squirting quick three- and four-shot bursts at them, more to suppress than to hit.

And still the return fire was short . . .

Then he was behind a garage; he sensed something in front of him and slowed just in time. He touched and then vaulted a four-foot chain-link fence, crossed a yard, went over the next fence, pushed through a hedge, scratching his face, took another fence, then another, heard garbage cans crashing behind him, screams, another burst of gunfire which went somewhere else, more screams.

He could hear himself breathing, gasping for air, trying to remember about how many shells would be left; he thought maybe six or eight, plus the third magazine in his pocket.

He felt good, he was moving, operating, he was on top of it.

Heading east.

THE LOUDSPEAKER AND THE GUNFIRE TOOK THEM BY surprise, Lucas and the other cops standing behind cars, talking quietly among themselves. They stiffened, turned, guns coming out, men crouching behind cars. Then radios began talking up and down the block, and Lucas, running to a St. Paul squad, said, "What? What?"

"Shit, one of them's out, he's maybe coming this way," a patrol sergeant said.

Lucas ran back toward his own people, touched them, "Watch it, watch it, he could be coming . . ."

Butters ran hard as he could, made it to the end of the block, passed between two houses, and in the dark space between them, ran almost headlong into a small tree. The blow knocked him down, but he held on to the rifle. Blood trickled into his mouth, and the sting told him that he'd cut his lip, probably badly. He crawled toward the street, gathered himself.

Across the way, he could hear people talking; more gathered behind him. He had no choice. He slapped the magazine once to make sure it was seated, and ran out into the street.

There: a cop—someone—dead ahead, behind a squad car, not much to see, turning toward him, crouching, hand coming up . . .

Butters, still running, fired a burst at the cop behind the car, saw him go down.

Another cop opened up from his right, then a third, and then he was hit: a stinging blow, as if somebody had struck his bare butt with a hickory switch. He knew what it was, and even as he returned the fire he passed through the line of cars, and cops were firing into each other as they tried to get him, men spilling themselves into the snow to get away from the bullets, others screaming . . .

And Butters ran.

A house, straight ahead, with lights on. And there was some pain now, more than an ache, more like a fire, in his thigh. He ran up four steps of the porch of the lighted house, to a stone-faced entry and an almost full-length glass pane in the front door. He fired a short burst at the glass, blew it out, and went through the door.

A man in pajamas stood at the bottom of a stairway; a woman stood at the top, looking down.

Butters pointed the gun at the woman and screamed at her: "Get down here."

And a kid yelled, "What? What's going on? Mom?"

LUCAS SAW HIM COMING, DOWN TO THE RIGHT. HE fired twice, thought he might have hit him once, but the man was very fast, and ran in an odd, broken, jerky two-step that made him hard to track, especially with the bad light. The man fired a burst and Lucas felt a hard, scratching rip at his hairline, not hard, like a slug, but ripping, like a frag. Then Butters went through the line of cops and Lucas could see muzzle flashes coming at him and he dropped, screaming, "Hold it, Jesus . . ."

And when the firing stopped, he lurched up on his elbows in time to see Butters sprint up the porch steps, and the muzzle flash from the gun as he went through the glass door . . .

"Around back, somebody around back," Lucas shouted.

Two St. Paul cops, frozen by the fire, broke toward the side of a nearby house, heading toward the back, and Lucas and another Minneapolis cop—Lewiston—moved in toward the porch.

"Take him?" Lewiston asked.

"Get in tight," Lucas said. "Let's . . ."

"You're hit," Lewiston said. "There's blood running out of your head."

"Just cut myself, I think," Lucas said. "You go right . . ."

BUTTERS POINTED THE AR-15 AT THE WOMAN ON THE stairs and screamed, "Get down here."

And then the kid called, "Mom?"

The woman shouted, "Jim, go back in your room. Jimmy . . ."

Butters couldn't think. His leg was on fire, and the man in the pajamas was frozen, the woman was yelling at the kid: a car rolled by outside and he turned, looked that way, couldn't see anything. The woman was shouting at the kid and Butters yelled at her, ''Get your ass down here, goddamnit, or I'll fuck your old man up . . .''

He pointed the gun at the pajama man and the woman came down the stairs, red-faced, terrified, watching his eyes. She wore a flannel nightgown, and something about it, the nightgown, the man's pajamas . . .

Then the kid came to the head of the stairs. He was wearing a T-shirt and Jockey shorts, skinny bare legs, and he looked frightened and his hair stood up where his head had been on a pillow.

And Butters remembered: the winter the cops came, and they got his mother and his old man out of bed, and Butters had come to the stairs in his shorts, just like this . . . He remembered the fear, and the guns the cops wore on their hips, and the way his old man seemed to crawl to them, because of the guns, and his mother's fear . . . They stank of it. He stank of it.

And all of this was exactly the same, but he had the gun.

''Don't hurt us,'' the woman said.

''Fuck this,'' Butters said.

He popped the magazine from the rifle, slapped in the third full one, checked to make sure that the half-empty one was ready, easy to reach in his pocket.

''You go back to bed, kid,'' he said.

He ran straight out the door, across the porch, at the two cop cars that were parked up the street to the right. There were two men close by, one left, one right, and the one to the right looked familiar and he decided to take that one.

He turned toward Lucas and raised the rifle, and saw Lucas's gun hand coming up but knew that he was a quarter-inch ahead . . .

STADIC WAS COMING UP THE MIDDLE, BUT WAS STILL thirty yards out, when Butters came through the door. Davenport and Lewiston were too close to the porch, and below it, to see Butters as he came through, but Stadic, back in the dark, had just enough time to set his feet and lift the shotgun.

Butters turned toward Davenport, the gun coming up. Davenport reacted in a fraction of a second, and maybe an entire lifetime, behind Butters. The shotgun reached out, a cylinder of flame, reached almost to Butters's face, it seemed.

And blew it off.

Butters went down like an empty sack.

THE COPS ALL AROUND FROZE, LIKE A STUCK VIDEOTAPE. After one second, they started moving again. Radios scratching the background. Everything, Stadic thought, moving in slow motion. Moving toward Butters, Davenport looking at him . . .

"Man," Davenport said. "He had me. You saved my ass."

And Davenport clapped him on the shoulder. Back in the furthest recess of his numbed mind, Stadic thought: *That's two.*

LUCAS CLAPPED THE WIDE-EYED STADIC ON THE SHOULder and then ran down the block toward the car where a cop had been hit. Lucas had seen him go down in the flash of fire from Butters, a fact stored in the back of his head until he could do something about it.

At that moment, a helicopter swept overhead, pivoted around in a tight circle, and they were bathed in light. A cameraman was sitting in the open door, filming the scene in the street.

Two St. Paul cops reached the downed man just as Lucas did. Lucas knelt: the man had been hit in the head, and the top of his skull was misshapen. There was blood out of his nose and ears, and his eyes were dilated, but still moving.

"Gotta take him, can't wait for an ambulance," Lucas shouted at one of the St. Paul cops. "Get him in the car . . ."

Together they picked up the wounded man and put him in the backseat of a squad; one of the St. Paul cops got in the back with the wounded man, and the driver took off, the back doors flapping like big ears as he turned the corner, followed by the lights from the chopper.

"Jesus Christ, get the fuckin' chopper out of here," Lucas yelled at another of the St. Paul cops, a sergeant. "Get them out of here."

The sergeant was leaning against the hood of a squad, and he suddenly turned, head down, and vomited into the street. Lucas started away, thinking now: the house. More people coming in? What happened down there?

Then the sergeant said, "We just never had a chance to say anything . . ."

"Yeah, yeah . . ." And he ran back down the street to the body of the shooter. Butters's face had been obliterated by the shotgun. He was gone.

All right—the house.

He stood, and stepped that way, and saw more running figures, cops, coming in. Another St. Paul lieutenant, a patrol officer, one he didn't recognize.

"What happened . . . ?"

"Got him, and we got one of your men shot. He's bad, he's on his way in."

"Jesus Christ."

"What happened at the house?"

"Jesus Christ, who got hit?" The lieutenant looked around crazily. "Who's hurt?"

"The house, the house," Lucas said. "What happened?"

"Empty. Nobody there. Guns," the lieutenant said.

"Shit."

The lieutenant ran down to the patrol sergeant, who'd stopped vomiting, and was standing shakily against the hood of the squad. "Who was it, Bill, who was it?"

LUCAS LOOKED DOWN AT BUTTERS. GONE.

He squatted, felt under Butters's butt. The dead man kept his wallet on the left. Lucas lifted it out, opened it, started riffling through the paper: a Tennessee driver's license, current. The picture was right.

Stadic came around the car, his eyes wide, staring at the dead man. "I hope I just, I hope I just . . ."

"You did perfect," Lucas said. Lewiston came up, and Lucas said, "You okay?"

"Fine. Freaked out."

"Why don't you run Andy into Ramsey?" Lucas suggested.

"I'm okay," Stadic said.

"You're tuning out," Lucas said. "You need to go sit somewhere, get your blood pressure down."

Stadic looked at him, a flat, confused stare, and then suddenly he nodded: "Yeah. Okay. Let's do it."

He used a sharp command voice, out of place, out of time. Lucas looked at the other cop: "Take him." And, as they walked away, "Hey: Thanks again."

LUCAS WENT BACK TO THE WALLET, LOOKING FOR ANY-thing: a scrap of paper with an address, a note, a name, but Butters carried almost nothing: a Mobil credit card, a Sears card, a Tennessee hunting license, the driver's license, an old black-and-white picture of a woman, wearing a dress from the '40s, and a more recent, color photograph of a Labrador retriever. Not much to work with.

The lieutenant ran up, said, "Dispatch is calling the FAA, they'll try to get these assholes out of here." They both looked up at the chopper, and then the lieutenant said, looking at Butters's body, "You know how lucky we are?"

"What?" Lucas looked up. His scalp had begun to hurt, as though somebody had pressed a hot wire against it.

"He was in that house," the lieutenant said, and Lucas turned to look.

A man, a woman and a kid were looking out through the shattered door, past a patrol cop who'd run up to see that everybody was okay. The woman kept pushing the kid back, but the kid wanted to see. "If he'd holed up in there, there wouldn't have been a goddamn thing we could do. We could've had some kind of nightmare out here."

"Yeah . . ." And Lucas suddenly laughed, all the tension of the last ten minutes slipping away. "But look what he did to your cars."

The lieutenant looked at the car, which showed a ragged line of holes starting in the front fender and running all the way to the back bumper. A couple of slugs had grooved the roof, the windows were gone. The lieutenant did a little Stan Laurel walk down the length of the car and said, "They hurt m' auto-mobile, Ollie."

"I guess. He didn't miss a single piece of sheet metal," Lucas said.

"Sure, it's a little rough," the lieutenant said, switching to a car salesman's voice. "But look at the tires: the tires are in A-1 condition."

They both laughed, shaking their heads. They laughed from relief, the lifting of the fear, the safety of the other cops and the people in the house.

Another chopper, TV3 this time, arriving late, swept over the house with its lights and beating blades and caught them standing over the body of Ansel Butters, looking at the car, laughing, unable to stop.

TWELVE

THE DAWN CAME LIKE A SHEET OF DULL STEEL PUSHED over the eastern horizon, cold, sullen and stupid. Fifteen cop cars blocked off the neighborhood, and yellow crime-scene tape wrapped the trail along which Butters had fled. A half-dozen cops were walking the route, looking for anything he might have thrown from his pockets—a piece of paper, a receipt, anything.

Tennessee cops had been to Butters's broken-down acreage since the night before, when his prints had been nailed down. They'd discovered what looked like a fresh grave in a decrepit apple orchard, opened it and found a Labrador retriever, shot once in the head.

"Old dog, had bones sticking out of his back, all gray on his muzzle," a Tennessee state cop told Lucas. "Probably shot him a couple of weeks ago. It's been cold enough that the body's still intact."

Lucas, standing in the street next to the shot-up cop car, was impatient with the dog information: "We need anything in the house that might point to associates," Lucas said.

"Any piece of paper, phone records, anything."

"We're tearing the place apart," the Tennessee cop said. "But when we saw the grave, we thought we had to do something about it."

"Screw the grave, we gotta find out where he's been and who he was hanging out with . . ."

"We're watching you on TV, we know you got a problem," the Tennessee cop said dryly. "We're turning over everything."

LUCAS RECOGNIZED THE TRUCK THE MOMENT HE SAW it: the truck that had slowed through the intersection. He couldn't be absolutely sure, but he was sure enough. Butters had been on his way in to Small's house. Whoever had called him had known, had saved Sarah's life, and probably Jennifer's and Small's and the boy's . . .

"Belongs to Elmore Darling," the St. Paul cops told him when he walked up. "Wisconsin cops are on the way out to his house."

"Goddamnit," Lucas said. The woman had suckered them. They'd had her, they'd let her go, and here was her truck.

The truck produced gas charge slips, maps, empty soda cans, and dozens of prints. The guns at the house had produced nothing but fragments of prints: they'd all been carefully polished with cleaning rags. There were a few good prints on a hunting bow, and more on some hunting arrows. The prints were on the way to the FBI.

St. Paul crime-scene guys had shrouded the truck's license plate from cameras, and asked the local media not to mention it, but the word was going to leak, and probably soon. If the Dunn County cops got to the Darlings' place soon enough, they might surprise them, and anyone staying with them. Lucas had to smother an impulse to run over to Wisconsin, to be in on the raid. The Wisconsin cops would do well enough without him.

As Lucas ran through the bits and pieces of paper coming out of the van, all carefully cased in Ziploc bags, Del wandered up.

"How's Cheryl?" Lucas asked.

"Hurtin'. They were giving her another sedative when I left. Christ, I heard about this, I couldn't believe it."

"It was interesting," Lucas said.

"What happened to your head?"

"Cut, somehow. Nothing much."

"You're bleeding like a stuck pig."

"Nah . . ." He wiped at his hair, and got fresh blood on the palm of his hand.

"Did you hear about the St. Paul cop that got shot? Waxman?" Del asked.

Lucas was trying to find a place to wipe the blood, stopped, and asked, "I didn't know his name . . . What?"

"Just came on the radio: he died."

"Ah, shit." Lucas looked down the street. Everywhere, the St. Paul cops were clustering. The word was getting out.

"Radio says they never got him to the table," Del said. "He was barely alive when he went in the door. They say he was gone thirty seconds later."

ROUX CAME THROUGH WITH THE ST. PAUL CHIEF AND found Lucas and Del eating cinnamon mini-doughnuts at the house. The guns from the closet had been carefully laid out on the living-room floor, waiting for a ride downtown.

"Jesus," Roux said to Lucas, shocked. "You were hit . . ."

"Naw, just cut." He pawed gently at his scalp. The cut was beginning to itch, and when he touched it, a burning sensation shot through his scalp, and he winced. "The bleeding's stopped . . ." He took his hand away and looked at it; blood dappled his fingertips.

"Lucas," she said, "I'm telling you, not asking you. Go get it fixed."

"Yeah . . ."

"Now," she said. Then, looking at the guns: "They brought an arsenal with them. We lucked out."

"Look, you gotta talk to the patrol people," Lucas said. "LaChaise is on the street, now. He'll be looking for a friend—old bikers, dopers, somebody like Dexter Lamb. In fact, we ought to stake out the Lamb place, they could turn up there."

"Yeah, yeah . . ."

"And you gotta get the patrol guys pushing the street people. Put some more money out there. The money worked. If we start running the assholes around, and there's some money in it, we'll find them."

Roux said, "*We'll* do that. *You* get your head fixed."

DEL DROVE LUCAS A FEW BLOCKS TO RAMSEY MEDICAL Center, where a doctor anesthetized, cleaned and stitched the scalp wound.

"Souvenir," the doctor said.

She handed Lucas a scrap of silver metal, like a fragment of Christmas-tree tinsel, but stiff—maybe a scrap of car aerial.

"How many stitches?" Lucas asked.

"Twelve or thirteen, I imagine," she said, sewing carefully.

Del was reading a two-year-old copy of *Golf Digest*, looking up every once in a while to see how it was going. When she finished, the doctor said "Okay," and tidied gauze and disinfectant-soaked cotton away into a steel basket, and then paused and asked, "Why were you laughing after you killed that man?"

"What?" Lucas didn't understand the question. Del dropped the top of the magazine and stared at the doctor.

"I saw it on television," she said. "You were standing there laughing, right over his body."

"I don't think so," Lucas said, trying to remember.

"I *saw* it," she snapped. "I thought it was pretty . . . distasteful, considering what just happened. So'd the anchorpeople: they said it was shocking."

"I don't know." Lucas shook his head, reached toward his scalp, which now felt dead, then dropped his hand. "I mean, I believe you—but I can't remember laughing about anything. Christ, we just finished carrying a shot cop down to a car."

"The cop died," Del said, putting the magazine down.

"And I didn't kill anyone," Lucas said. He hopped off the exam table where he'd been sitting, and loomed over the doctor.

"That's not what they're saying on television," the doctor said, giving no ground. She glanced at Del, pulled off her latex gloves with a *snap*!.

"Don't believe everything you see in the movies," Lucas said.

"This wasn't the movies—it was videotape, and I saw it," she insisted.

"The only difference between TV news and the movies," Del said, "is that movies don't lie about what they are."

"Oh, bullshit," the doctor said.

"If you operated on a cancer patient, and the patient died, and when you came out of the operating room, you saw a friend and smiled at him . . . if somebody took a picture of you, would that represent the way you felt about the patient dying?"

She studied him for a minute, then said, "No."

"I hope not," Lucas said. "I don't remember laughing.

Maybe I did. But that doesn't have anything to do with what happened."

ON THE WAY OUT, DEL SAID, WONDERINGLY, "ARE WE in trouble or something?"

"I don't know," Lucas said. They tracked through the endless hallways to the back, where they'd ditched the car away from the reporters in the lobby. "More and more, with TV, it's like we fell down the fuckin' rabbit hole."

ANDERSON CALLED: HE'D BEEN TRACKING THE VARIous investigations. "The Dunn County cops hit the Darling place. They found the husband . . . uh, Elmore Darling . . . was shot to death in the kitchen. His wife is missing. His truck is up there, so she's down here, somewhere, if she's still alive."

Lucas shook his head: "Huh. Family feud?"

"Hard to tell what's going on," Sloan said. "They got a charge slip from yesterday—from last night—at an Amoco station off I-94 over in St. Paul, so he was over there, probably at that house. And then he gets shot up there. There's no doubt he was shot in place, there's splatter all over the kitchen. Short range with a shotgun."

Lucas repeated the story to Del, who scratched his chin: "That don't compute."

Lucas said into the phone, "They're printing everything, right?"

"I guess. They've got their crime-scene guy up there."

"Be nice to know who all was in that house," Lucas said. "If Sandy Darling was there with the rest of them."

"I'll push them on it," Anderson said.

LACHAISE, MARTIN AND SANDY HAD BEEN HEADING back to the house with a bag of supermarket doughnuts and two quarts of milk, when Stadic had called and told them to get out.

"Shit." LaChaise was stunned. "They got us, they got the house."

"Maybe something happened with Ansel," Martin said slowly. "Maybe they spotted him scoutin' out the Davenport house, and followed him back."

He pulled the truck to the curb, reached out and poked the "power" button on the radio, got old-time rock 'n' roll, and started working down the buttons.

Sandy looked from one of them to the other: "Now what?"

"I'm trying to think," LaChaise said.

"Let me go back home," Sandy said.

"Fuck that," Martin said. To LaChaise: "We gotta get out of sight."

"How about the trailer? We could probably lay low in the trailer for a while."

"If they've got Elmore's truck, they'll bag Elmore for sure, and he'll tell them about the trailer," Martin said. "If they put any pressure on him, he'll talk his ass off."

He was still playing with the car buttons, and finally switched over to AM. They found a news station almost instantly, but no news—nothing but blather.

"Let's get turned around, and get out of here," LaChaise said finally. "If Stadic's right, we're too close."

"If he's right, we ought to hear something on the radio," Martin said.

But he swung the truck around, and they headed west toward Minneapolis. At that moment, a helicopter roared overhead, cutting diagonally across the city blocks, headed for Frogtown.

"Goddamnit," Martin said. "They're doing it."

LaChaise punched the radio buttons again, still found nothing. "Let's get over to Minneapolis. We can figure it out there."

"Maybe it wasn't Butters led them in—maybe it was Elmore," Martin said. "Maybe Butters is still out there."

LaChaise seized on the idea: "That's gotta be it." To Sandy: "You were talking about it last night, weren't you? Bailing out on us."

"No, we weren't," she lied.

"Don't give me that shit," he muttered; he poked spasmodically at the radio, and tripped over the news station again. This time, they were on the air locally:

". . . police are flooding the east side neighborhood around Dale on the possibility that one or more members of the gang escaped the house at the same time as Butters. Residents are asked to report unusual foot traffic through their streets, but not to approach anyone they may see. These men are armed and obviously dangerous . . ."

"C'mon," LaChaise said impatiently, "what happened?"

"They got Butters," Sandy said. "If they know he was one guy coming out of the house, they got him."

"Yeah, but is he dead or alive?"

". . . we've just gotten word from our reporter Tim Mead at Ramsey Medical Center that the St. Paul police officer wounded in the shoot-out has died. We still have no identification, and authorities say the officer won't be identified until next of kin can be found and notified, but our reporter at Ramsey says the officer definitely has died. With Butters's death, that brings to two the number of people killed in this latest clash between Twin Cities police officers and the LaChaise gang . . ."

LaChaise groaned: "Oh, goddamn, they killed Ansel. The sonsofbitches killed Ansel."

Martin: "We gotta get under cover. If they got the house, they'll get my prints. If they get my prints, sooner or later they'll get this truck. We don't have much time."

The highway was slippery with the snow, and LaChaise finally told Martin to get off and find someplace to park. "We gotta talk this out. We're in big fuckin' trouble. We lost our gear."

"You got your 'dog, I got my forty-five and the knife."

"We lost the heavy stuff," LaChaise said. He patted his pocket and said, "But I still got Harp's money."

"Dick, you gotta give this up and run for it," Sandy said. "Drop me off, I'll call the cops. I'll tell them I was kidnapped and you let me go. I'll tell them you're headed for Alaska or the Yukon, you can head for Mexico."

"Aw, that ain't gonna work," LaChaise said.

"The whole thing lasted one day, Dick," Sandy said, pressing him. "Now you're on the road, no guns, no transportation, no place to run to."

"But we do have some money," Martin said. "That can get us some guns. And I just thought where we might get a car and a place to hide."

MARTIN TOOK THEM INTO SOUTH MINNEAPOLIS, TO Harp's laundromat. The laundromat was empty: it was too early and too cold to think about washing laundry. They parked the truck in front of the garage doors, Martin got a claw hammer out of his toolbox, and all three of them walked around to the front. The door that led up the stairs was locked. Martin, with LaChaise blocking, popped the door with the hammer. The lock was old, and not meant to stop much. When Martin pushed the door shut, it caught again.

"Locks are different at the top," Martin said quietly. "Best you can buy. And it's a steel door. But if we can get him to open it, just a crack, there's nothing but a shitty little safety chain after that."

Martin led the way up the stairs. He'd told LaChaise about the pile of cardboard boxes at the top of the stairs. They moved and restacked them until they had a narrow passage to the door.

"Ready?" Martin had his .45 in his hand, and LaChaise drew his Bulldog.

"Try it," LaChaise said.

Martin banged on the door, then tried the doorbell next to it. And then banged some more.

"Open up, Harp," he shouted. "Minneapolis police, open up."

Silence.

Martin tried again. "Goddamnit, open the fuckin' door, Minneapolis police."

They could hear themselves breathing, but felt no vibration, no footfall, no bump or knock that might suggest somebody was home.

"He should be here, this time of day," Martin said.

"Maybe he can't hear us."

"He could hear us . . ." Martin put his ear to the door and stood that way, one hand up to silence LaChaise, for a full minute. Then he looked at LaChaise: "Shit, he's not here."

"We gotta get off the street," LaChaise said.

"I know, I know." Martin looked at the door, shook his head. "No way we're going through that. And the garage door will be locked. We could try pulling the fire escape down."

"The whole city would see us climbing up there," La-Chaise said. Then: "Run downstairs and see if there's any-body in the laundromat."

Martin nodded, trotted down the stairs, fought the jammed

door for a moment, then disappeared outside. A second later he was back. He shoved the door shut and called up, "Nobody."

LaChaise crushed one of the boxes, pushed others in front of the door, until he had a clear patch of wall.

"What're you doing?" Martin asked, hustling up the stairs.

"This," LaChaise said. He hit the wall with the claw side of the hammer. A square foot of old plaster cracked and sprayed out, showing the laths beneath.

"Jesus, sounds like dynamite," Martin said, looking back down the stairs.

"Nobody to hear us," LaChaise said. "And Harp don't come up this way, so he won't see it." He hit the wall again, a third time and a fourth. "Why don't you go down to the bottom and keep an eye out. This could take a few minutes."

LACHAISE BROKE A SIX-INCH HOLE THROUGH THE WALL, alternately beating it with the head of the hammer, smashing it, then digging the hole out with the claw. When the hole was big enough, he reached through and popped the locks on the door. They pushed inside, and found an empty apartment.

"Nobody around," Martin said, after a quick reconnaissance. "But his car's downstairs. The Continental. Maybe he ran out to the store."

"Give us some breathing space," LaChaise said. "We gotta be ready, though. Shouldn't cook nothin' until we got him."

Sandy had followed Martin through the apartment. The place had once been four tiny apartments, she thought, remodeled into one big one. A hallway divided the new unified apartment exactly in half—that would have been the old main entry hall.

The place *felt* empty. More than that. Vacated. She looked in the refrigerator: it was nearly bare. She stepped back down the hallway and looked into the master bedroom—she'd peeked in when they first entered, but this time, she pushed in and looked around. A small leather suitcase was lying empty at the end of the bed. The apartment was cold, she noticed. She went back to the living room and checked the thermostat. It was set at fifty-five.

She said, "I think they went on a trip."

"Huh?" LaChaise looked at her. "Why?"

"Well, there're holes in the closet where they took a whole bunch of clothes out at the same time. And there's a suitcase sitting on the floor like they decided to take a different one, but didn't put the first one back. And the thermostat's set at fifty-five, like you'd turn it down before you went some-where."

"Huh," said Martin, nodding. "It *feels* like they left."

Martin noticed the two telephone answering machines, sit-ting side by side. "He's got two answering machines," he said. "I wonder if he left a message."

He picked up one phone, and dialed the number posted on the other: the phone rang twice, then a man's voice said, "Leave a message." Nothing there. He hung up, picked up the second phone and dialed the first. And Harp's voice said, "We're outa here. Back on the twenty-sixth or so. I'll check the messages every day."

"He's gone," Martin said to LaChaise. "He says they're gone until the twenty-sixth."

LaChaise made him redial, listened to the message, then looked at Martin with a broad grin. "Goddamn. We landed on our feet," he said, when he'd hung up. He looked around the apartment: "This place is six times better than the other one. This is great. And we got a Continental. A fuckin' luxury car . . ." He started to laugh, and whacked Martin on the back. Even Martin managed to crack a smile.

●　●　●　●

ROUX AND THE MAYOR MET LUCAS IN ROUX'S OFFICE, and heard about the laughing incident.

"I didn't believe it was me, until I saw the tape," Lucas said. "I don't know why we were laughing. We just about had a goddamned disaster on our hands, and instead, it was all done with. I guess that's why." The explanation sounded lame.

"The St. Paul cop getting killed—that's not a disaster?" the mayor asked.

"We didn't know the cop was dead. And we thought we were going to get a whole goddamned family shot up. When Butters ran in there, when he blew through that door, I thought we were out of luck."

"The TV people are wondering why there weren't enough people out there in the first place. Enough to take him as soon as he showed," the mayor said.

"Normally, it would have been plenty. Except that he saw us coming and he had a machine gun. And he didn't care if he died. All that—that changes everything. We're lucky only one guy got killed; it could have been three or four. If he'd had some combat experience, he might've waited until the entry team was halfway into the house, and then took them on at close range."

"Anyway, that's all St. Paul's problem," Roux said. "And as far as Lucas is concerned, the laughing thing, I think I can clear it out."

The mayor's eyebrows went up. "How?"

Roux said, "You know Richard Small—TV3? He was on the stakeout last night. He wouldn't leave, and Lucas let him keep his shotgun. I talked to him this morning and he figures Lucas and Del are his war buddies now. I'll call him about the laughing incident, and why they were doing it—out of relief, or hysteria, and how unfair this is, some horseshit like that. He just about runs TV3. If he goes on the air with another perspective, we can turn it around. And he'll do it. When I talked to him this morning, he was still jacking shells in and out of the shotgun.''

The mayor looked from Lucas to Roux. ''Do it,'' he said, nodding. ''Emphasize the fairness thing, and how he'd be setting the record straight on his combat buddy.''

And to Lucas: ''You gotta keep your ass down and out of sight.''

''I'm trying,'' Lucas said.

HOMICIDE HAD BEEN TURNED INTO A WAR PLANS room: file cabinets and desks pushed into corners, two tables shoved together with a six-foot plastic map of the Twin Cities spread across it. Sherrill was there, wearing her .357 in a belt clip.

''You okay?'' Lucas asked.

''Yeah. We got the arrangements going on Mike. I'm all cried out.''

''We got one of them,'' Lucas said.

''Not the one I want, not yet,'' Sherrill said, shaking her head. ''We got Kupicek's guy. I want the third man, the one we don't know yet.''

Anderson wandered in, spotted Lucas, and stepped over: ''I got a lot of new paper, if you want it.''

They talked about the paper for fifteen minutes, what the Tennessee cops were doing, the Wisconsin cops, about the death of Elmore Darling. ''We've got more pictures of Sandra Darling, we'll put those out. But I don't know. I don't know if she's with this LaChaise, or we're gonna find her dead in a ditch somewhere.''

''She's with him,'' Sherrill said.

''Why do you think that?'' Lucas asked.

''I don't know. I just think she's with them. If they were going to kill them, why not kill both of them? I bet she's screwing LaChaise. Or maybe the second guy. I bet she helped set up the funeral home thing with the second guy . . ."

"Bonnie and Clyde," Lucas said.

"More like Dumber and Dumbest," said Sherrill.

LACHAISE, MARTIN AND SANDY DARLING WERE RIVETED by the images on the television. The pictures came up from a winter street, with a woman in a long wool coat and fur hat talking into a microphone.

". . . rushed the wounded officer to the hospital, but he died seconds after arrival. As that was going on, Chief Davenport and Lieutenant Selle were seen laughing as they stood over the body of the attacker . . ."

Her voice rolled on over a videotape, taken from a high angle, a uniformed cop and a guy in street clothes, standing over what looked like a pile of clothes in the street. Had to be Butters. And the cops were laughing, no doubt about it.

". . . police were refusing to disclose the identity of the officer or officers who actually shot Butters, saying that information would be available after LaChaise and his gang members are caught, but nobody has denied that Deputy Chief Lucas Davenport took part in the gunfight and was himself wounded. At the moment, a police spokeswoman said, the threat to the officers' families will not allow full disclosure . . ."

"Look at the fuckers," LaChaise said.

Martin frowned as the tape of Davenport and Selle was run again. The picture seemed wrong. "They don't look too happy," he said.

"They're laughing," LaChaise shouted at him. "They're laughing."

LaChaise paced in front of the TV, snarling at it, beating his hands together, palms open, the angry claps snapping into the room. He went to the window shades, looked down at the street, listening, then stalked back to the television.

"That cop who was laughing. They said it was Davenport, right? The guy on our list?"

As if to answer his question, the television reporter said, "The chain of events started last night, when Chief Davenport put a surveillance team on the home of his daughter by TV3 correspondent Jennifer Carey, who now lives with TV3 executive vice-president Richard Small . . ."

She went through the story, ending with the tape loop of Davenport and Selle laughing over Butters's body.

"We're gonna mow those fuckers down," LaChaise brayed at Martin.

Martin said, "Dick, we gotta take care. We can't go off half-cocked, if we want to get anything done."

LaChaise stalked around the apartment, kicking walls, then looked at Sandy: "Why'n the fuck don't you do something useful? Go cook something."

She got up, wordlessly, and went to the kitchen and started looking through the cupboards. She found canned food, but not much else. She dumped a couple of cans of Dinty Moore beef stew in a pot, put it on the stove and started a pot of coffee.

"If we're gonna stay here for more than a couple of hours, we'll need food," Sandy said, as she brought the stew out to the living room. The men were on the couch, still watching the television. As they ate, a TV3 television reporter was delivering a eulogy on the dead cop. He was cut off in mid-sentence. An anchorman came up, quivering with the urgency of his message.

"In Wisconsin, Dunn County sheriff's deputies raided the home of Dick LaChaise's sister-in-law and her husband, Sandy and Elmore Darling. According to first reports, Elmore

Darling was found shot to death in the kitchen of the couple's rural home, and his wife, Sandy, is missing.''

A five-year-old snapshot of Sandy Darling filled the screen. Sandy screamed, ''Elmore.''

LaChaise grinned. ''You put on a few pounds,'' he said, pointing at the picture.

She had her hands to her face: ''They killed Elmore.'' She looked from Martin to LaChaise. ''My God. They said Elmore's dead. They killed Elmore. Elmore's dead.''

''Could be bullshit,'' Martin said, his voice even, almost uninterested. ''They maybe got him in jail. Don't want anybody to know.''

''I don't think so,'' LaChaise said. The TV anchor was going on, then Martin said, ''Guess not.''

''No, no . . .'' Sandy said, riveted to the screen.

''You didn't much like him anyway,'' LaChaise said.

Tears started down her cheeks: ''I didn't want him dead. He wasn't supposed to die.''

LaChaise shrugged. ''Shit happens.''

Martin: ''I wonder if the cops killed him?'' His voice was flat, with no real emotion; he was only curious.

LaChaise thought for a minute, then said, ''Must've. Who else would do it?''

He looked at Sandy, who backed away from the TV and collapsed in a chair. ''Nobody was gonna kill Elmore,'' she said. And after a minute, ''Who'd kill Elmore?''

STADIC WAS WALKING DOWN THE HALL TO HIS APART-ment, shell-shocked, his mind running at two hundred miles an hour. He was digging for his keys when the cell phone chirped at him. He pulled it out of his pocket. ''Yeah.''

LaChaise, without preamble, asked, ''What happened to Butters? And Elmore?''

"Jesus Christ, where are you?" Stadic said, his voice hushed. "You know what's going on?"

"We're at a friend's," LaChaise said. "We seen it all on TV. Who killed Butters?"

"Davenport, of course. I told you . . ."

"We thought it might be him. What happened to Elmore?"

"I don't know about that. I thought you did it, when I heard."

"We didn't do it," LaChaise said. He pulled his lip. "Maybe the Wisconsin cops."

"Or the guys from Michigan," Stadic suggested. "There're a couple of Michigan guys running around over there. They are *very* pissed about this Sand guy, you cuttin' his throat."

"Yeah, well, that's what you get for working in the fuckin' joint," LaChaise said. "Try to find out who did it."

"Okay," Stadic said. "But listen—the wives up in the hotel . . . I hear they're getting antsy. They want out. Davenport's girlfriend is going back to the University of Minnesota hospital."

"What's her name? We never got any insurance on her."

" 'Cause they're not married and you didn't say what you wanted the information for. Her name is Weather Karkinnen and she's a doctor over there. In surgery."

"Who else? Who's leaving the hotel?"

"Jennifer Carey, the TV news reporter. She's the mother of Davenport's daughter . . . She's going back to work, but there'll be guards all over her and they've got locked security doors and stuff. She'd be hard to get at."

"All right. Find out about Elmore, if you can."

LaChaise hung up, pulled at his lip again, thinking. After a minute, Sandy said, "What?"

"Davenport killed Butters . . . and the women are gettin'

unhappy about being locked up. They may be going back to work.''

"Probably got guards all over the place,'' Martin said. "Tell you what: let's get Harp's car, and go on out to a supermarket and buy some food. Maybe dump the truck: hate to see it go, but I think we better.''

Sandy was sitting in the chair, folding into herself, not hearing any of it.

Elmore was dead.

The guilt was almost too much to bear.

THIRTEEN

━━━◦◉◦━━━

WEATHER KARKINNEN LAY ON THE HOTEL BED AND fumed: the television had gone into a news loop. The anchorpeople leaned into the cameras with the usual end-of-the-world intensity, but had nothing new to say. Weather looked at her watch: two o'clock.

Lucas had said he'd drop by at noon, then called to cancel. He told her about the laughing incident, which she hadn't yet seen when he called, but saw later. The television stations were showing it every twenty minutes or so, and it had been picked up by the national news channels.

Lucas said the laughter had been hysterical, or on that order. She only half-believed it. She'd lived with him long enough to feel the satisfaction he got from confrontation, and the deadlier the confrontation, the better. A death wish, maybe; sometimes when he talked about his world, she could barely recognize it as the same place she lived. They would drive across town, and she'd see good houses and nice gardens and kids on bikes. He'd see whores and dopers and pedophiles and retired cat burglars.

At first, it had been interesting. Later, she wondered how he could put up with it, the constant stench of the perverse, the lunatic, the out-of-control. Even later, she understood that he sought it out . . .

She looked at her watch again: two-oh-three. Screw it. She wasn't going to sit around anymore. This LaChaise might be extraordinarily bad, but he could hardly have an intelligence system that would tell him where she was—if he even knew to look for her, which she doubted.

And even if he *did* know where to look for her, once she was in a crowd, she'd be just one of a million and a half women wrapped in heavy winter coats, faces obscured by scarves. Then nobody could find her—not the FBI, not the Minneapolis cops, nobody—much less some backwoods gunman.

"All right," she said. She looked at her watch a third time. She'd had to delay a surgery scheduled that morning, but there was a staff meeting at four, and she could make that. And she could set up for tomorrow. The operation in the morning wasn't much—remove some cancerous skin, and patch the wound with a graft—but it would get her going again.

She found her sweater, pulled it over her head, and was checking her purse for money when the knock came at the door. She opened it, and instantly recognized the blonde in the hall, and the small girl with her.

The blonde smiled: "Hi. I'm Jennifer Carey . . ."

"I know who you are," Weather said, smiling back. "Lucas has talked about you. Come in. And hi, Sarah." She and Sarah were old friends.

Jennifer was tall, lanky, a surfer girl with degrees in economics and journalism. She noticed Weather's sweater: "Breaking out?"

"Definitely. I can't stand it here anymore," Weather said. "I'm going crazy."

"I'll give you a ride, if you want one," Jennifer said. "Unless you've got a car."

"Lucas brought me in, I'd like a ride. I understand you're working outside."

"Yeah. Sloan's wife is here, she's taking care of Sarah for me. But there's no point in letting Lucas have all the fun, chasing around with his gun."

"Daddy shot a man," Sarah said solemnly, looking up at Weather.

Weather sat on the bed so her eyes were level with Sarah's. "I don't think so, honey. I talked to him a couple of hours ago, and he said another policeman did the shooting."

"On TV, they said he did," Sarah said. Her wide eyes were the same mild blue as Lucas's eyes.

Weather said, "Well, I think they might be wrong on this one thing."

Jennifer, moving moodily across the room, dropped into a desk chair: "I understand you and Lucas are getting married. Pretty soon."

"That's the plan," Weather said.

"Good luck," Jennifer said. She was looking out the window at the street. "I . . . well, we talked about it, years ago. It wouldn't have worked, though. I hope it works with you guys. He's a good guy under the macho bullshit, and I would like to see him happy."

"That's interesting," Weather said. "Do you think that might be a problem? Happiness?"

Jennifer shook her head and turned back to Weather: "He has a very dark streak, a Catholic dark streak. And his job . . . I don't know how he stands it. I know what he does, because I've covered it, but I've got some distance. I mean,

I see burned-out newspeople all the time, and they are several steps back from what Lucas does.''

Weather nodded, and drifted toward the window herself. The sky and the day had the cold midwinter pre-storm look, a brooding somberness. "I know what you're saying—I was just lying here thinking about it," she said. "I can feel it in him. I can feel it in Del, too, almost as bad. I can feel it in Sloan, but with Sloan, it's mostly a job. With Lucas it's like . . . his existence.''

"That's the Catholic thing," Jennifer said. "It can be frightening. It's like, when he confronts a monster, he solves the problem by becoming a bigger monster . . . and after he wins, he changes back to Lucas the good guy." Then she blushed: "God, I shouldn't be talking this way to a guy's fiancée. I'm sorry.''

"No, no, no," Weather said. "I need it. I'm still trying to figure out what I'm getting into here." She looked at Sarah: "I would like a child before it's too late . . . just like this one.''

Sarah said, "I'm gonna be a TV reporter.''

Jennifer said, "Over my dead body. You should be a surgeon, like Dr. Karkinnen.''

"Did you cover the robbery at the credit union, where the women were killed?" Weather asked Jennifer.

"I didn't cover it, but I talked to all the people who did. I do mostly longer-term stories. We're working on a story now about police intelligence units.''

"What do you think? Some people have said it was an execution.''

"No, it wasn't. I'll buy the argument that nobody made them do it. But you know Lucas. He has a tendency to arrange things so they come out his way." She stopped again: "Jeez, I really sound like . . . I don't know, like I'm trying to scrag the guy.''

"That's okay—I know what you mean," Weather said. She picked up her coat, hat and mittens and smiled at Jennifer. "Ready to make the break?"

LUCAS WAS INFURIATED WHEN HE HEARD THAT Weather had left the hotel, and Jennifer had taken her out.

He tried to call the university, but was told Weather was in a meeting and couldn't be disturbed. He got Jennifer at TV3, shouted at her and she hung up. He called back, got her again, asked about Sarah.

"She's with Sloan's wife," Jennifer said. "She's fine. She's watching HBO and eating pizza."

"Listen, I want Weather back in that fuckin' hotel . . ."

"Hey, Lucas? You don't own her. If you call her with this attitude, you're gonna get the same answer from her as you're getting from me. Fuck you. Go away."

And she hung up.

LACHAISE SAID, "LISTEN: THEY'RE GONNA GET YOUR prints out of the house. Then they'll have all three of our faces. We've got to move before that happens."

Martin said, "They won't have any new pictures of me . . . but maybe we should change what we look like."

"Like what?"

Martin shrugged. "I don't know—you got that beard, and they show it on the tube as long. Maybe if you trimmed it, and cut it, and dyed your hair gray. Hell, with gray hair, we'd both look older than the hills."

LaChaise looked back toward the master bedroom: Sandy was in there, making up the beds, singing to herself while she did it. Not a happy song. A song like she was losing it, a song to herself, a singsong.

"Sandy could do it," LaChaise said.

"I think it'd be a good move," Martin said. "We could get out and scout around."

"Then let's do it." LaChaise nodded. "I want to get going again. Find this Weather. And Davenport himself. And the cops. Let's go after the cops."

SANDY AGREED THAT SHE COULD CHANGE THEIR HAIR color. She had a flatness about her that provoked LaChaise: "What's wrong with you?"

"When we got into this, Elmore said that in two or three days we'd all be dead. He wanted to go to the cops, and I talked him out of it."

Martin and LaChaise looked at each other, and then LaChaise said, "Why? Why'd you talk him out of it?"

"Because I thought I could still fix things. Get you out of here; pretend I didn't have anything to do with anything. Now they've got me on TV, and they'll have Martin pretty soon. Elmore was right: he's dead now and Butters is dead. Not even twenty-four hours yet. If Elmore was right, we've got another two days at the most. Then we'll all be dead."

She looked at LaChaise: "You want to be dead?"

Martin answered: "No big deal."

LaChaise said nothing at all for a moment, then poked a finger at her: "I don't want to hear this shit no more. You go on with Martin, and get the hair stuff."

"My picture . . ."

"You don't look like that picture—nobody'll know you," LaChaise said. "And we need the right stuff."

"I might want to make a couple of extra stops," Martin said. "They'll have my picture out there as soon as the prints come in. But if I get movin', I could tap a couple of friends for some decent weapons . . . guys I know from the shows. And we gotta dump the truck, sooner or later."

"We can do that tonight," LaChaise said. "Take the Continental, put the truck in the garage for now." He smacked his hands together. "Get a couple of ARs if you can . . ." LaChaise dug in his pocket for the money Butters had taken from Harp. "Couple thousand?"

"Better make it four," Martin said.

"Call me before you talk to anybody—I'll watch television for your face," LaChaise said. "And I might try Stadic again. See if he's heard anything."

THEY WENT TO A SNYDER'S DRUGSTORE, MARTIN STICK-ing close to her. Sandy already knew she was going to run for it, given the smallest opening: But Martin knew it too, she thought. They went through the store, and got bleach and coloring. Martin poked through a large industrial first-aid kit, and finally took it off the shelf. "Gonna have to change Dick's bandage sooner or later," he said in a low voice.

Just short of the cash register line, he bumped into a rack of commercial trail food and twirled it: he'd always kept some of the stuff around. As he was looking at the varieties, Sandy noticed a telephone by the pharmacy desk.

"Got a quarter? I'll call Dick."

"Yeah," Martin said absently. He dug in his pocket, handed her a quarter. She went to the pay phone, dropped the quarter, punched the number in: LaChaise answered.

"Anything?" she asked.

"Not a thing; same old bullshit," he said. "I'm gonna take a nap."

She hung up and saw the note on the bottom of the machine: 911—No charge. She looked at Martin. He'd just stepped into the cash register line, and his back was to her. She picked up the phone again, bit her lip and punched in the number.

A woman answered immediately.

"Is this an emergency?"

"Yes, I need to talk to Detective Davenport."

"I'm sorry, but this . . ."

"Please, please, please, I've got to talk to him, or they'll kill me."

"Are you in immediate danger?"

"No. Yes . . . I don't know."

"Just a minute, please."

Lucas was taking a nap in his office, stretched out on a plastic air mattress. The mattress was uncomfortable and cold, but the office was dark and quiet and he dropped off, slept for an hour and a half. The phone woke him up.

"Lucas, we've got a call coming in on 911. The woman wants to speak to you, but she's not sure whether she's in danger. She's calling from a Snyder's down on the south side. We're not sending anyone yet."

"Okay," Lucas said sleepily. "Put her on."

"You want us to stay on the line?"

"Sure . . . unless I say something."

The phone clicked once, and the dispatcher said, "Go ahead, ma'am. Chief Davenport is on the line."

"Hello?" Lucas said.

"Is this Detective Davenport?" A woman's voice, tentative, vaguely familiar.

He sat up. Could this be . . . ? "Yes, who's this?"

"This is Sandy Darling, I'm with Bill Martin and they're gonna kill me."

Jesus, Lucas thought. He prayed that the dispatcher was sending a squad. "If you stay where you are, you'll be safe . . ."

"No, no, Martin's right on top of me. I've got to talk to somebody, I've got to try to get away."

Her voice was a whispered croak: nothing fake about it.

"They're going after more guns," she continued. "They'll

kill anybody who gets close to them. They've got a policeman working with them. One of you.''

''What policeman?''

''Gotta go . . .''

''Just stay . . .''

''Can you get me a lawyer, let me talk to a lawyer? I haven't done anything, they just took me . . .''

''Absolutely. Absolutely,'' Lucas said. ''We can bring you in, give you all the legal help you need, all the protection you need. Just stay right where you're at . . .''

Sandy was afraid to turn around, afraid that Martin would be coming up behind with his knife. ''I can't,'' she said. ''I gotta go. Get me out.''

''Call back,'' Lucas said. ''Call us back. You don't even have to talk. Just dial the number, leave the phone off the hook, or just say, 'Sandy,' and we'll come and get you . . .''

''I gotta go . . .''

And she was gone.

''Hello? Hello?''

The dispatcher: ''She's gone, Lucas. I've got three cars coming in, we started them as soon as she said her name, but they're at least three or four minutes away.''

''Ah, Christ, ah, Christ. Listen: warn the squads that we took automatic weapons off Butters this morning, if they haven't already heard.''

''They know.''

''Get everything else you can, scramble it down there in case we get a chase going . . . How many people down in your office there know about this?''

''Just two.''

''Keep it that way. If we don't pick her up, and word gets around, she's dead.''

''Gotcha . . . Are you gonna talk to Chief Roux . . . about the cop thing?''

"Yeah. I'll talk to her."

Lucas hung up, rounded his desk and headed for the door, which almost hit him, opening inward: Anderson said, "Wup."

"I'm running," Lucas said.

"Only need a tenth of a second," Anderson said. "You know a guy named Buster Brown? Like in the shoes?"

Lucas tried to focus on the name. "Buster? Yeah, I do."

"He's trying to get you. Says it's urgent. Life-and-death about LaChaise." He handed Lucas a Post-it with a number on it. "He says he'll be there."

"Ah . . . All right." Lucas turned back to his desk, snatched up the phone, and began punching in numbers. "We've got some heavy stuff coming down," he said to Anderson. "Go get Lester, tell him to meet me at the chief's office. Right now . . . and hey, you got any gum? My mouth tastes like it's had a bird in it."

"No, but Lester's got some toothpaste in his desk drawer."

"I'll be up," Lucas said. The phone was answered on the first ring: "Hey, Buster? Lucas . . ."

REGINALD BROWN WAS A SCANNER FREAK. A TERMINAL diabetic, blind, a double amputee. He could be a pain in the ass, but sometimes he came up with nuggets of information: he knew most of the drug dealers in town by voice, from their cellular phone calls.

"Boy, do I have something for you. I think," Buster said.

"What happened?" Lucas asked.

"I heard some guys talking about you: just now, just a minute ago. I think it was this LaChaise guy. I got half the call on tape."

Lucas said, "Play it for me."

"Sure: Listen to this."

". . . need to know where this Weather is, and be good to know where Capslock's old lady is, her room number. And we need to know where Davenport is working, and Capslock, Sherrill, Sloan, Franklin and Kupicek. You know the list."

Long pause.

"That don't sound right; you better be tellin' the truth, or your name'll be on the list, motherfucker . . . Hey, listen to what I'm telling you . . . No, not you. Did you find out anything about Elmore?"

Another pause.

"That's what we thought. We'll look those boys up when we're done here . . . Now listen, we need that shit and we need it right now. We'll call back in . . . two hours. Two hours, got it?"

Pause.

"I don't know. And you let us worry about getting back to you. You might be pulling some bullshit. And if you are, you better think twice . . ."

Pause.

"Yeah, yeah. Two hours."

Lucas told him to play it again.

"I knew the names," Buster said, when it was done.

"A cellular call."

"Yeah, my end of it, anyway. Couldn't tell about the other end."

"Okay. Did you hear anything before what was on the tape?"

"Well, yeah. Something about how your girlfriend wasn't on the insurance."

"What?"

"That's what they said . . ."

"I'm sending a squad over," Lucas said. "They'll bring

you down here. I need to talk to you, face-to-face. Bring the tape with you. There'll be a payday in it.''

"You bet, chief," Buster said.

He hung up, thought a moment.

Had to be a cop. Or a civilian employee. If they'd gotten their information from insurance forms, they had to have access to inside computers. And the insurance did make sense: it would explain how they had located the spouses, which had been hard to figure.

He picked up the phone and called Roux.

"I understand you're on the way down here. Something good?" she asked.

"Not exactly. You might want to bring in the mayor."

He called Dispatch: "What happened?"

"We've got two squads at Snyder's. Nobody there. They remember her, though. They just missed them."

"Anybody get their vehicle?"

"No. We just got there, the guys are checking around . . ."

MARTIN AND SANDY GOT BACK IN THE CONTINENTAL and Martin said, "What'd Dick have to say?"

"He hasn't seen anything on the TV. He said he's going to take a nap."

"Getting shot can take it out of you," Martin said, as he eased the car into the street.

THE MAYOR LEANED ON THE WINDOWSILL, HANDS IN the pockets of his sport jacket, fists clenched, head down. Lester lounged in a side chair, looking almost as though he were sleeping. Roux turned back and forth in her swivel chair, her eyes on Lucas.

"Does anybody else know?" the mayor asked.

"Just Anderson. I told him the whole story, and asked him to check the computers, see if he could tell if anybody was messing with the insurance records. And he's running this Bill Martin name, to see if it pans out.''

"We gotta keep this one thing quiet, this insurance thing,'' the mayor said, shaking his finger at Roux and Lucas. "We gotta find this guy, if he exists, and nail him, before anybody else knows.''

"Man, I can hardly believe it,'' Roux said. "Maybe it's bullshit.''

"It's got a bad feel,'' Lucas said. "We've got one source who thought she saw a cop. Then Darling calls, and she says cop.''

Roux held up a finger and punched a number into her phone. She said, "This is Roux. Anything?'' She listened for a moment, then said, "Damnit. If anything happens, get back.''

She hung up and said, "Still nothing at the Snyders. We're sending some guys down to print the phone, make sure it was Darling. I can't imagine that . . .''

She was cut off by a knock at the door, and a half-second later, Anderson stuck his head in: "Lucas said if I got anything . . .''

"Yeah, come on in,'' Lucas said. "What'd you get?''

"Two things. You want the good news, or the bad news?''

"Good news,'' the mayor said. "We haven't had much.''

"We ran Bill Martin, conventional spelling, against Dick LaChaise, the Seed, Wisconsin and Michigan. We got a bunch of hits—he's pretty well known with the gang. He's a gun dealer, by the way. We're sending all the prints we took out of the house to the FBI, and they'll run them. We should know in ten minutes if we've got a match.''

"Excellent,'' Lucas said. To the mayor: "That'd be the third guy.''

"And it'd prove that you were talking to Sandy Darling,'' Anderson pointed out. "Not just some bullshit artist.''

"The bad news," Lucas said.

Anderson had a half-dozen sheets of paper in his hands, and he shuffled them nervously. "When did your source see the cop with LaChaise? In the laundromat?"

"Must've been . . . yesterday? In the early morning."

"Oh, God." He shuffled the paper some more, his mouth working. "Yesterday, somebody accessed the insurance files on everybody in your task force."

"Who was it?" asked Roux.

"We don't know," Anderson said. "They were accessed and printed out through Personnel, at six o'clock in the morning. There's nobody in Personnel at six o'clock."

"From what O'Donald said, the guy she saw was a street cop—not somebody from Personnel," said Lucas.

"So we got a cop with a source in Personnel," Roux said.

Lucas shook his head: "Something like this, you might get one bad guy, but not two. Unless . . . any of the women in Personnel married to a street cop?"

Anderson shrugged. "I can find out."

"Do that," Roux said grimly.

"But, uh . . ." Anderson seemed reluctant.

"What?" asked Lucas.

"Personnel has been raided a few times. You know that. Guys want to look at their files, want to look at test scores or salaries. There'd be more than a few guys around here who could get inside, and who probably know enough about computers to pull up the insurance records."

"But when you think about how many, I bet it wouldn't be *that* many," Lucas said. "So make a list. We'll show mugs to O'Donald."

"If there's a cop in on this, we're gonna get hurt," Roux groaned.

"But why would a cop line up with LaChaise? LaChaise is a goner," the mayor said.

"Blackmail," said Lucas. He looked at Anderson. "When you figure out the computer stuff, let's talk about who's got the shaky rep. Somebody LaChaise might get to."

"If it's a cop, he's dead," Roux said to the mayor.

The mayor pushed away from the windowsill. "I don't want to hear that," he said.

"I don't even want to think about it—but somebody would put him down, given the chance. I guarantee it."

THE CHIEF OF SURGERY TOOK WEATHER ASIDE AND asked, "Are you going to be okay?"

"Sure. I mean, heck, my own secretary can't track me down. I don't think some hillbilly gunman's gonna get me." She flashed a grin at him. "Don't worry about it, Loren. If I thought it'd be a problem, I wouldn't be here."

FOURTEEN

———◦◉◦———

LUCAS FOUND WEATHER AND ANOTHER WOMAN IN A thirteenth-floor laboratory, looking at skin grafts on a white rat. Weather was surprised when he poked his head in the door: "We need to talk," he said gruffly.

The other woman looked at Weather as though Weather should be insulted. But Weather nodded: "Sure . . ." And when they got out in the hall, she asked, "How mad are you? You look kind of white around the eyes."

"Don't joke about it," he said, his voice suddenly rasping. "We have a tape of a phone call and they were talking about you."

"About me?"

"Yeah. They want to get you, because you're with me. I'm out there busting my balls running these assholes down, and now I've got to spend a half hour looking for you because you've run off someplace . . ."

"Hey," she said sharply. "I did *not* run off. I went to a hospital, where I *work*."

"And told everybody you really didn't want to talk to me,

so when we get this phone call, I wind up having to ditch the investigation to find you.''

''I didn't ask you to do that,'' she said.

He stopped talking for a second, then said, ''Listen, just what the fuck do you think is gonna happen if one of these people shows up here with a machine gun? You think they're gonna ask for you, and take a number? Or you think maybe they'll shoot a couple of your friends to make the point, then ask where you're at. You're not just risking your life. You're risking theirs. There are already six people dead from this thing.''

''Eight,'' she said. ''Don't forget the two women at the credit union.''

MARTIN DROVE DOWN I-35W TO BURNSVILLE, THEN, BY memory, took them through a rat's-nest of suburban streets, and finally to a blue rambler, where a snow-packed driveway led to a double garage. Martin parked in the street. ''Hope he's home,'' Martin said, leaning across Sandy to look out the side window. ''He is, most days.''

''Want me to wait?'' she asked. She'd run, once Martin was out of sight.

''Better come along,'' Martin said.

''I was so scared in the store, that somebody would recognize me,'' Sandy said.

''I don't think Dave'll recognize you,'' Martin said. ''He doesn't watch much TV. And he's a little shy.''

Martin rang the doorbell, waited, rang it again and the door opened. Dave—Martin hadn't mentioned his last name—was an older man with thick glasses, wearing a Patagonia pullover. He pushed open the storm door, saw Sandy behind Martin and blushed.

''How y' doing, Dave?''

"Bill, come on in." Dave pushed the door wider. "You on a trip?"

"Yeah, I am—heading out to the Dakotas."

"You heard about the trouble we're having?" Dave glanced sideways at Sandy and blushed again.

"On the radio," Martin said.

Dave said, "And they want to take the guns away from the good people. I can't believe these guys in government." He shook his head.

Dave took them to the lower level, where a row of Remington gun safes lined one wall. He didn't have any ARs, AKs, ranch rifles or anything else that Martin was interested in, but he did have a rack of beautiful bolt-action hunting rifles—"Hunting's coming back in with the yuppies, I've been selling used Weatherbys like hotcakes. You see any Weatherby Mark V's in three hundred Mag or less, in good shape, think about me."

"I'll do that," Martin said. He was looking at another rack, short little rifles, and said, "What're all the Rugers for?"

Dave shrugged. "Just regular demand . . . jump-hunting deer. Can't hardly find them anymore."

"How much you get?"

"Upwards of four-fifty, for a good one," Dave said.

"Jeez, they only cost half of that, new."

"Well, they haven't made them for ten years. If Ruger doesn't come out with them again, I'll make a mint . . ."

They talked more guns for a while, Sandy standing silently behind them, and Martin finally bought two used .45s for seven hundred dollars.

"Wish I could help you more," Dave said, as they left.

To Sandy, Martin said, "Two more stops."

At the first stop, a sporting goods store, he bought four green-and-yellow boxes of .45 ammo, a Browning Mantis bow, two dozen Easton aluminum arrows, two dozen Thunderhead broadheads, an arrow rest, a fiber-optic sight, a release and a foam target like the one they'd left in the Frogtown house. They waited while the guy at the store cut the arrows to thirty and one-quarter inches, and seated inserts in the tips, so Martin could screw in the Thunderheads.

Martin looked at a Beretta over-and-under twenty-gauge while they waited, then sighed, put it back, and said, "Not today."

At the second stop, he bought six more boxes of .45 ammunition.

"Do you know where all the gun stores are?" Sandy asked.

"Most of them," he said. "Most of them from . . . well, from the Appalachians to the Rockies . . . and Salt Lake and Vegas and Reno. I don't know the coasts. Well, some in Florida, if that's a coast."

And a moment later, she asked, "Have you thought about getting out of this?"

Martin looked at her. "Have you?"

She shook her head: "No. I'm stuck with Dick, I guess. I just think we oughta move on. Mexico. I really don't want to die."

"Huh." Martin didn't relate well, but for the first time since she'd known him, he started to talk. "I'm like Butters," he said. "Running out of time. All the people like us are: they're coming to get us, there's no way we can win. We just make a stand, and go."

"Who's they?"

He shrugged. "The government—all of the government, the cops, the game wardens, the FBI, the ATF, all of them. And the media, the banks, liberals, whatever you want to call them. The Jews . . . They're all in it together. City people. They don't all *want* to do us harm—they just do."

"The blacks?"

"Ah, the blacks are more like . . . poker chips," Martin

said. "The government's just playing a game with the blacks. I mean, they might use the blacks to get us, but the blacks themselves won't get anything out of it. Never have, never will."

"That's pretty bleak," Sandy said.

"Yeah. Well, you know, the people who run things, they want power. And they get power by writing laws and making you depend on them. They can do anything they want to old people, because old people gotta have Social Security and Medicare and all that. And if you try to be independent, they get you with laws. Like Dick. No way he was ever gonna be able to run that bike shop. He screwed up one time with his taxes, and they came after him forever. Never let him go. Makes a man crazy."

"You think Dick is crazy?"

He grinned and said, "We're all crazy. You can't help it. I was thinking about it the other day—you know how you used to burn leaves in the fall? In all the small towns? And how good it smelled, the burning leaves in the air. Can't burn leaves anymore, because they won't let you. No reason for it, in the small towns anyway. You ain't polluting nothing . . . They just make the law to train you. I mean, it starts with the small stuff, and it goes all the way up to the big stuff, like lettin' the Mexicans in, so people like us can't get good jobs no more . . ."

Sandy nodded. "Okay."

"I used to love the smell of burning leaves in the autumn," Martin said, looking out the window at the snow.

SANDY GOT INTERESTED IN THE DISGUISES.

She got LaChaise to sit on a stool in the bathroom, ran her fingers through his thick, stiff hair. "Can't just layer over your natural color, 'cause it's too dark," she said, half to herself. She got the bleach and LaChaise said, "You sure about this?"

"I see it done all the time, up at Pearl's," she said, and she started working the bleach in. When she was done with his hair she said, "The bleach might be too harsh for your face . . . maybe you oughta shave."

"Try it," he said. She worked it in; the fumes were bad, but LaChaise, eyes closed, sat it out.

When she was finished, bleach had turned LaChaise's normally dark hair and beard to a thin, watery yellow, the color of corn silk. The delicate color contrasted oddly with the harsh contours of his face. "Holy shit, I look like some kind of fag," he said, staring at himself in the bathroom mirror. "Maybe I oughta leave it like this."

"Too weird," Martin said. "You want people to look away from you, not stare at you."

They did the color next, and when he looked again, LaChaise was impressed. With the gray beard, he looked as though he might be seventy. "Get your back humped, nobody'll give you a second look," Martin said.

LaChaise looked at Sandy: "You done really good," he said.

Sandy had been enjoying herself: now it went away, and under her breath, as she turned way, she said, "Fuck you."

LaChaise said to Martin, "Your turn."

ANDERSON HAD PHOTOS OF BILL MARTIN. "WE'LL PUT them out at the afternoon press conference," he said. "We've got a line on his truck and license tag, and we're putting that on the street right now."

"All right—have you seen Stadic?"

"Yeah, he was through here. We sent him home. I think he's kind of messed up."

"He's never shot anyone before," Lucas said. He yawned

and said, "He saved my bacon this morning . . . Jesus, I got to get some sleep."

"Go get it," Anderson said. "There's nothing going on . . . what happened with Weather and Jennifer?"

"Jen should be okay—they've got armed security at the station, and the kids are gone. But I want to find a couple of cops who'll stick by Weather on an off-duty basis. I'll pay them. She's getting bitchy, she won't stay put."

"You should have got her some knitting stuff," Anderson said. "You know, so she'd have something to do over there at the hotel."

"I don't think . . ." Lucas started. Then he looked at Anderson, whose face was resolutely stuck in neutral.

"I just don't want them hurt, that's all," Lucas said.

"Yeah, I know, you don't want them to take the risks you're taking . . . as much fun as they are."

Lucas looked sideways at him: "Whose side are you on?"

Anderson shrugged. "Theirs."

"A traitor to his sex," Lucas said, and he yawned again. "Listen, I'm gonna grab a few hours. If you need me, I'm at home."

"We'll call," Anderson said.

Lucas said, "Goddamn women."

LACHAISE STARTED LAUGHING WHEN HE SAW MARTIN, and made Martin link arms with him and shuffle around the apartment. Martin joined in, almost as though he'd stepped outside his dour personality.

"Don't quite look old," Sandy said. "You look old, but you move young."

"We need some practice," LaChaise said. And then, a spark in his eyes, "Let's go on out to this big fuckin' mall. What do they call it—the Mall of America?"

Sandy was appalled by the idea: "Dick, you're nuts."

His smile vanished. "You never fuckin' say that," he said.

She shut up: Dick, she thought, was losing it. Play to him, look for a chance. Try not to be in the way when the shooting started.

MARTIN TOOK THE TRUCK, AND SANDY AND LACHAISE followed behind in the Continental. Martin left the truck in a neighborhood north of the airport. He patted it once, like he might a horse, looked it over, then got in the Continental.

"Makes you want to cry," LaChaise said.

"Damn good truck," Martin said, looking back at it as they drove away. "You know, it was perfect, mechanically. New engine, new tranny—new about everything. I could go any-place, and nobody'd give it a second look. Good thing, too, when you're dealing guns."

"Where're we going?" Sandy asked, still behind the wheel.

"The mall," LaChaise said.

"We oughta take care of some business first," Martin said.

"Yeah? What's that?"

Martin had a map of the downtown area. "I want to go look up the hospital where they're taking these people . . . Hennepin General. Then I want to go over to this other one, where Davenport's old lady works. Just a recon, to see where it is."

"All right," LaChaise said. "I'm just glad to be out."

The first hospital, as it turned out, was only six or eight blocks from Harp's apartment. There were cop cars parked by the entrances.

"That'd be tough," Martin said.

"But we could get to it on foot, if we had to," LaChaise said. "If that big storm comes in . . ."

The other hospital was farther away, but easy to get to— straight down Eleventh to Washington, right, a couple of nat-

ural turns, across the river and up the hill past a building that
looked like it had been built from beer cans—and there it
was.

No cop cars.

"This one would be simpler," Martin said.

"But it's big," said LaChaise. "Finding her could be a
problem—even knowing for sure that she's in there could be
a problem."

"We could work it out," Martin said.

Sandy drove, listening; she was shocked by the coolness
of the discussion. They'd done robberies, she was sure: Candy
and Georgie hadn't started on their own. Still, she was reluctantly impressed by the cool appraisal of the targets.

"Now: out to this mall," LaChaise said. He stretched out
in back, favoring his side. The wound was tightening up.
"Feel like I'm being held together by banjo strings," he
grumbled. But he sat up as they approached the mall.

"Looks like Uncle Scrooge's money bin," he said.

"You ain't far wrong," Martin said.

Sandy found a parking spot in the ramp, and they went
inside. The mall was packed, but nobody gave them a second
look. And LaChaise was fascinated.

"Goddamnedest thing I ever seen," LaChaise said, as they
stopped outside the Camp Snoopy amusement park. A gang-
banger dragged by, looked them over—two old guys with
beards and long black coats. They looked like cartoons. The
gang-banger smirked, kept going.

LaChaise took them on a circuit of the mall, browsing
through the stores, checking out the women, dragging Sandy
along.

"We gotta get out of here," Sandy said, after the first circuit.

"We just got here," LaChaise said, enjoying himself.

"Dick, please . . ."

"Tell you what, let's catch a movie."

"We can see a movie back at the apartment, he's got HBO. Please."

"Then let's get a pizza, or something. God, is that cinnamon rolls I smell?"

The gang-banger went by again, this time from the other direction—they'd both made a circuit of the second level—but this time, after he passed, he turned and followed them.

There was something not quite right here, the banger thought. There was something wrong with the old guys, and the blond was nervous. Her nervousness gave the whole trio a sense of vulnerability. The feel of vulnerability brought him in, like a mosquito to bare flesh. Victims . . .

There may have been ten thousand people in the mall, but there were also dead spots. One of them was next to an automatic teller machine. The banger watched as the trio bought cinnamon rolls and Cokes, then sat on a bench next to the ATM.

Nobody real close. The banger put on a grin and wandered up, put his hand in his pocket and dropped the blade on a butterfly knife.

"How's it going, folks," he said to LaChaise. LaChaise bobbed his head, didn't look up, but the banger could see the smile. The victims usually smiled, at first, trying to pretend that the contact was friendly. "Whyn't you just give it up? A few bucks," the banger said.

Now LaChaise looked up at him, his voice soft. "If you don't go away, I'm gonna take that fuckin' blade and cut your nuts off."

The banger took a step back. "I oughta . . ."

"Fuck oughta. You want to do something, do it, pussy," LaChaise said. The banger looked at Martin, and the pale eyes fixed him like a bug.

The banger said, "Fuck you," and walked away.

"We gotta get out of here, Dick," Sandy pleaded.

"Felt kinda good," LaChaise said to Martin, and Martin's head bobbed. "Hey, c'mon; let's go see a movie."

"Dick, please . . ."

LaChaise pulled her close. "You shut up, huh? Quit whinin'. I haven't been outside in years, and goddamnit, I'm gonna enjoy myself one afternoon. Just one fuckin' afternoon, and you're coming along. So shut up."

LACHAISE COULDN'T FOLLOW THE MOVIE: BUILDINGS blew up, cars got wrecked, and the cops seemed to have antitank missiles. All bullshit. Martin fell asleep halfway through, although he was awake when it ended.

"Let's get out of here," LaChaise muttered.

On the way out, they passed an electronics store with a bank of TVs lit up along one wall. As they were passing, the chief of police came up: they knew her face from the hours of news. "Hold it," Martin said. They watched through the glass, and suddenly Martin's face came up.

"Shit," he said. "They got me."

"That means they got the truck," LaChaise said.

"We knew they would," Martin said.

LaChaise looked him over, then looked back at the TV, and said, "You know, nobody'd recognize you in a million years. Nobody."

Martin looked at Sandy, who looked at the TV picture, back to Martin, and nodded in reluctant agreement.

Martin watched until his picture disappeared, and then said, briskly, "Let's get a beer."

LaChaise nodded. "We can do better'n that. Let's find a bar." And he turned to Sandy and said, "Not a fuckin' word."

● ● ●

THEY FOUND A PLACE ACROSS FROM THE AIRPORT, A long, low, yellow log cabin with a Lite Beer sign in the window, showing a neon palm tree. The sign looked out over a pile of dirty snow, freshly scraped from the parking lot. Above the door, a beat-up electric sign said either Leonard's or Leopard's, but the light bulbs in the fourth letter had burned out, along with the neon tubes on one side. Seven or eight cars and a few pickups, all large, old and American, were nosed toward the front door. Inside, they found a country jukebox, tall booths, a couple of coin-op pool tables and an antisocial bartender.

The bartender was drying glasses when they walked in, and twenty people were scattered around the bars, mostly in clumps, with a few lonely singles. Two men circled the pool table, cigarettes hanging from their lips. They checked LaChaise and Martin for a long pulse, and then started circling again.

LaChaise said, "Hey, let's get some money in the jukebox, goddamnit. Sounds like a tomb in here." He held up his arms and wiggled his hips: "Something hot."

Martin muttered, "You're an old man."

LaChaise said, "Yeah, well . . . let's get a beer."

LaChaise got Waylon Jennings going on the jukebox, while Sandy found a booth. LaChaise slipped in beside her, and Martin across from them. A waitress stopped, and LaChaise ordered three bottles of Bud and two packages of Marlboros and gave the waitress a twenty.

When the beer came back, LaChaise shoved one at Sandy and said, "Drink it."

She didn't care for beer, but she took it, and looked out of the booth, thinking: Most ladies' rooms had telephones nearby. After a couple of beers, she'd have to pee. She could call . . .

She was trying to work it through when the waitress came

by again, and LaChaise ordered another round. She tried to tune in on the conversation: LaChaise and Martin started talking about some black dude in prison who spent all his time lifting weights.

". . . they thought something must've popped in his brain 'cause they found him layin' on this mat, nothing wrong with him except he was dead," LaChaise said. "Somebody said there was a hit on him and somebody stuck an ice pick in his ear."

"Sounds like bullshit," Martin said.

"That's what I say. How're you gonna stick an ice pick in the ear of a guy who can press four hundred pounds or whatever it was? I mean, and not make a mess out of it?"

Martin thought it over: "Well, you could spot for him, maybe. You're right there by his head if he's doin' presses, and when he finishes he sits up, and you're right there . . ."

LaChaise nodded. "Okay, that gets it in his ear, but how come there's no blood? That's the thing . . ."

Sandy closed her eyes. She was in a booth with two men trying to work out a way to kill a guy who'd wring your head off if the attempt failed—and how you'd do it with a weapon you'd have to sneak into the weight room.

Martin was tapping the table with the Bud bottle: "The suspicious thing is, he was found alone. How many times do you see the weight room empty?"

"Well . . ."

WHEN SHE OPENED HER EYES, SHE FOUND HERSELF looking into the face of a cowboy-looking guy sitting with three friends in a booth across the room. He was about her age; she glanced away, but a moment later, looked back. They made eye contact a couple of times, and she saw him say something to one of his friends, who glanced at Sandy and then said something back, and they both laughed. Nice laughs, more or less; nothing too dirty. Sandy looked away, and thought about Elmore. Dead somewhere: she should be making funeral arrangements.

Sandy didn't cry, as a matter of principle. Now a tear trickled down her cheek, and she turned away from the men to wipe it away.

"If I absolutely had to do one of those guys, I might think about getting a piece of steel cable, like a piece of that cable off the come-alongs in the welding shop . . ."

She made eye contact with the cowboy-looking guy again, and he winked, and she blushed and turned back to Martin, who was saying, ". . . two-hundred-grain Federal soft-points. Busted right through its shoulder and took out a piece of the lung . . ."

Talking about hunting, now.

More beer came, and LaChaise was getting louder as Martin slipped into a permanent, silent grin.

"Let's dance," LaChaise said suddenly, pushing at her with an elbow. She'd had three beers, the two men maybe six each.

She flinched away. "Dick, I don't think . . ."

LaChaise turned back to Martin and said, "You know, goddamnit, this is what I missed, sitting around in that fuckin' place. I miss going out to the cowboy joints."

LaChaise trailed off and looked up. The cowboy-looking guy, a Pabst in his hand, was leaning against the back of Martin's seat, looking at LaChaise. "Mind if I take the lady out for a dance?"

LaChaise looked at him for a minute, then at the beer bottle in front of him.

"Better not," he said.

Sandy smiled at the cowboy and said, "We're sort of having a talk here . . ."

"Ain't that, I just don't want him dancing with you," LaChaise said.

"Hey, no problem," the cowboy said, straightening up. Sandy realized he was as drunk as LaChaise, his long straw-colored hair falling over his forehead, his eyes vague and blue. "Wasn't looking for trouble, just looking for a dance."

"Look someplace else," LaChaise grunted.

"Well, I will," the cowboy said. "But it'd be a goddamn pleasanter thing if you were one fuckin' inch polite about it."

LaChaise looked up now, and smiled. "I don't feel like I gotta be polite with trash."

Talk in the bar suddenly turned off. Martin moved, just an inch or two, and Sandy froze, realizing that he was clearing his gun hand. The cowboy stepped back, to give LaChaise room to get out of the booth. "Come out here and say that, you ugly old dipshit," the cowboy said.

The bartender yelled, "Hey, none of that. None of that in here."

LaChaise spoke quietly to Martin, barely turning his head: "Barkeep."

"Yeah."

Then LaChaise slipped out of the booth, uncoiling, keeping his distance from the cowboy. Sandy said, "Dick, goddamn-it . . ." and LaChaise turned and pointed a finger at her and she shut up.

The cowboy said, "Here you are, old man, what've you got?"

The bartender yelled, "Not in here, goddamnit, I'll have the cops on you."

LaChaise said to the cowboy, "Fuck you, faggot mother-fucker, your faggot cowboy boots . . ."

The cowboy took a poke at him. He coiled his arm, pulled his shoulder back, uncoiled his arm: to LaChaise, the punch seemed to take a hundred years to get going. LaChaise brushed it with the back of his left hand, stepped inside, and with the heel of his right palm, smashed the cowboy under his nose. The cowboy went down and rolled, struggled to his hands and knees.

Sandy called, "Dick, stop now."

The bartender yelled, "That's all; I'm callin' the cops . . ."

Martin was out of the booth and he stepped toward the bartender as LaChaise circled to the right and kicked the cowboy in the ribs, nearly lifting him from the floor. The cowboy collapsed, groaning, and blood poured from his face. The other patrons were on their feet, and an older man yelled, "Hey, that's enough."

Sandy was out of the booth. "Dick . . ." she wailed.

LaChaise looked at the old man and said, "Fuck you." The cowboy was crawling on his stomach, a kind of military low-crawl, leaving a snail's track of purple blood, and LaChaise walked around and kicked him in the side of the head and the cowboy stopped crawling.

"Jesus Christ, you're gonna kill him," the old man yelled, and a few other men yelled, "Yeah . . ."

The bartender picked up the phone and Martin was suddenly there with his pistol: "Don't touch that dial."

LaChaise was walking around the cowboy, and the old man yelled, "Give him a break, for Christ's sake," and LaChaise pointed at him and said, "If you don't shut up, I'm gonna kick your ass."

And moving behind the cowboy, he kicked him in the crotch. Sandy caught his shirtsleeve: "Dick, c'mon, no more, Dick, please, please, let's go, he's hurt . . ."

"Get the fuck away from me," LaChaise growled.

Martin, his gun now hanging by his side, said, "She's right, man. We better get going."

The cowboy was not moving. He lay with one hand under his chest, the other thrown to the side. LaChaise said, "All right," and picked up one booted foot and stomped on the outstretched hand, the bones audibly crunching in the silent room. "Let's go."

On the way past the bar, he took a ten out of his pocket: "Four Buds to go: just crack the top."

And Martin said, "Don't nobody come running out to look at our tags, y' hear? I'd have to go and shoot you. So you just stay here inside and talk on the telephone, and don't get shot."

As they were going out the door, LaChaise with the four bottles of Bud, the old man shouted, "Crazy fuckers!"

SANDY HUDDLED IN THE BACK AS THEY TOOK I-494 west, then north up I-35W into town, LaChaise laughing aloud, Martin serious but pleased: "The hair was what done it," he said over and over. "He thought you was an old fuck, and he just sort of lobbed at you . . ."

They felt good, Sandy realized. This was what they liked.

"You know what we shoulda done with the truck? We shoulda driven it over to this Davenport's place, his house, and drove it right through the front of the place. Up the porch and right through the front, and left it there."

"Might be a lot of cops hanging around," Martin said, now a bit more sober. "And they could pick us up on the way . . ."

"Well, shit . . . we oughta do something."

Sandy said, "You oughta take the car and start driving. If you're careful, you could be in Mexico the day after tomorrow."

LaChaise said, "You know what? I bet if we tore up that apartment, I bet we'd find some more cash. I bet he's got a stash around somewhere. I can't believe a dealer wouldn't."

"Maybe in the car . . ." Martin said, and they started talking about money. Sandy sank back into her seat: at least they weren't talking about Davenport anymore.

A minute later, LaChaise said, "I think I got a leak in my side." Sandy sat up. "What?"

"It was itching, so I just reached in there to move the bandage, and got a little blood."

"Probably pulled a stitch in the fight," Martin said.

"So let's get back and take a look," LaChaise said. The ebullience left him, and, deflated, he stared morosely out the window. "Fuckin' place," he said.

FIFTEEN

———◀◉▶———

THEY'D SWEPT UP EVERYBODY THEY COULD FIND, RUN-
ning the dopers, dealers, bikers and gun freaks until you could
hardly find one on the streets.

"If they're holed up, I'd bet they've got a television,"
Lucas told his group. He was sitting behind his desk, his feet
on the top drawer, the others scattered around the small office.
"That's the first thing this kind of idiot gets: a TV. We could
use it to talk to Sandra Darling."

"What do we say?" Del asked. "We can't just come out
and tell her to run. They'd kill her."

"We make it a plea for information, stress how anyone
cooperating with LaChaise is going away for a long time. We
say, 'Just call 911, nobody'll know.' She'll know we're talking to her."

"Maybe get the shrinks into it," Sloan said. He was sitting
on a backwards chair, his chin on his folded arms. "You gotta
believe she's with them, at least semivoluntarily. Or started
out that way. She was at the funeral home when LaChaise
escaped . . ."

220

"And I don't think they would've taken her along if they thought they'd have to watch her every minute," Sherrill said, nodding at Sloan. She was slumped in a swivel chair. Her dead husband's parents were handling the funeral details, and she was torn between the hunt and the relatives.

Lucas sighed: "Listen, goddamnit. We need to push off in a different direction."

"What direction?" Franklin asked. "You show me the direction, I'll push."

Lucas dropped his feet out of the drawer. "We gotta find the cop. If we can shake him out, we'll have them."

"So . . ." Sherrill said.

"So we start pushing people out again—but this time, we want to know who on the force is dealing."

The others looked at each other, then Del said, "Dangerous."

Lucas nodded. "Yeah, but it's gonna get done, sooner or later. And right now, it's an angle nobody's working."

"So let's go," Franklin said.

"Everybody keep your goddamn heads up—and wear your vests. This is bad shit."

LUCAS TOLD LESTER, WHO SAID, "INTERNAL AFFAIRS are looking through a few things, but they're not on the street. You guys be careful."

Lucas nodded. "Del and I are gonna talk to Daymon Harp again, shake him pretty hard. He's been around for a while."

"You want somebody from drugs?"

Lucas shrugged. "We can handle it; and you're a little short right now."

"You could have Stadic," Lester said. "He's not carrying a gun until the board says okay."

"All right. He oughta know about Harp, anyway."

Lester said, "Take him. He's just been playing doorman up at the hotel . . ."

WHEN STADIC SAW LUCAS AND DEL WALKING TOWARD the front of the hotel, he caught the way their eyes picked him up and held him: and he thought, *They got me.* He took a step backwards, but realized he didn't have anyplace to run.

Lucas came up and asked, "How's it going?"

"Quiet," Stadic said. "The way I like it." To Lucas he said, "Your old lady came through again."

"Yeah, yeah . . ."

"Do you know a dealer named Daymon Harp?" Del asked.

Stadic thought, *Here it comes.* He said, "Yeah, I see him around. We took him down three or four years ago, he did two. Then we took him again last year, but we missed—he wasn't carrying, no money, no dope. Bad information."

Lucas nodded: "Good. We need somebody who knows him and his people. We're gonna go over and push him."

Stadic's eyebrows went up: "You want me to come?"

"That'd be good," Lucas said.

"Give me fifteen seconds to get out of this fuckin' doorman's suit," Stadic said. "You guys are answering my prayers."

They rode down in a plain gray city car, the heater running as hard as it could, and not quite keeping up. They passed a fender bender on Nicollet, slid through a stop sign at the next street. "Fuckin' Minnesota," Del said. "I'm moving to fuckin' Florida."

"I was reading a book by a guy down in Miami," Stadic said. "He says Florida's fuckin' fucked."

"The fuckhead's probably just trying to keep me out," Del grumbled.

"Both of you shut the fuck up," Lucas said. "You're giving me a fuckin' headache."

Del changed the conversation's direction: "You hear what's been happening over in St. Paul with the unmarked cars?"

"No."

"All their cars got these yellow bumper stickers, they said, 'Buckle Up, It's the Law.' "

"Yeah, I seen those," Stadic said.

"So the wiseasses over there have been peeling off the top of the stickers. Cut them in half with a razor, peel them right off. Now it says . . ."

"It's the Law," Lucas said, laughing.

"Not that anybody would drive a piece of shit like this except a cop," Del said. "What color you think this car is?"

After a minute, Lucas said, "Fuck gray," and they all laughed.

ALL OF SANDY'S STITCHES WERE INTACT, BUT LACHAISE'S wound showed some pink at the edges, and was leaking at one corner. "I'll rebandage it, but the best thing would be, if you just sat still for a while," Sandy told him.

As she worked, Martin nailed a piece of plywood over the hole in the hallway wall, next to the door. "Gonna get some goddamn junkies coming in, if we don't nail it up," he said.

When he was done, he stepped back inside, pulled the cardboard boxes up to the doorjamb, and closed the door.

A moment later, he was at the window; he saw the car pull up across from the laundromat.

"Cops," he said.

Sandy stood up, hand to her mouth. LaChaise rolled to his feet, started toward the window, but Martin waved him back: "Don't touch the curtain. They might look up."

LaChaise slowed, stepped carefully up to a narrow slot in the curtains, and saw the three men getting out of the car. All he could see was hats and coats, but the plain gray car was the key. They were cops, all right. They started across the street, talking, and the thin one laughed.

"They're laughing. They may be coming, but they don't know we're here," LaChaise said. He stepped quickly across the floor and killed the TV. "Down the back stairs. We can go out through the garage."

"No," Martin said, shaking his head. "We can't see out the back until we open the garage. If there're cops out there, they'd have us cold." He glanced at the window: "Man, I don't think they know we're here, but I don't think we can risk running, either."

"So let's set up and take them," LaChaise said. "Back to the stairs. Then we got a chance to run, anyway."

They padded quietly down the long central hallway, pushing Sandy in front of them. Sandy went to the bottom of the stairs, in the garage, while LaChaise and Martin stopped just below the level of the top steps. Martin crouched, and LaChaise stood on the step below him, LaChaise with his 'dog and Martin with a .45 in each hand.

"If they know we're here, an entry team'll try the garage door," LaChaise whispered. The garage door opener was plugged into an overhead outlet. LaChaise pointed at it with the gun barrel and said to Sandy, "Pull the plug."

Sandy pulled the plug.

"Let 'em get in a few feet. We want all of them in," Martin said. "If they don't know we're here, we have to take them all . . ."

DEL WENT AROUND BACK, TO WATCH THE GARAGE door. Lucas led Stadic up the stairs.

"Bunch of boxes at the top," Lucas said. "Supposed to be some sort of a barrier to keep the door from being rushed."

Stadic said, "I've seen that in a couple places. Whatever works."

At the top, they moved the cardboard boxes out of the way. On the right side of the door, a piece of plywood was crudely nailed onto the wall.

"Wonder what that is?" Lucas asked, looking at the board.

"Probably an extra barrier to keep people from busting through the wall," Stadic said. "The guy ain't taking any chances."

Lucas banged on the door. "Harp, open up."

Nothing.

"Awful quiet," Stadic said.

Lucas banged again. "Huh. Wonder if he booked."

"The way things are going . . ."

Lucas banged a third time. They waited for a few more seconds, Lucas looked at the lock, said, "No way," and they started back down the stairs.

INSIDE, SANDY WAS CROUCHED NEXT TO HARP'S CAR, her hands over her ears. After the third set of knocks, they heard what sounded like feet on the stairs. "I think they're going," Martin whispered.

"I can't fuckin' believe this," LaChaise whispered back. "I gotta go look."

Martin caught his arm. "Best not to. Sometimes, people feel it, when something moves."

LaChaise nodded, and they sat on the steps and listened.

ON THE STREET, LUCAS AND STADIC WALKED AROUND the corner and yelled down at Del. Del had been leaning against the brick wall by the garage door, and he pushed away from the wall and slouched back toward them. "Nothing?"

Lucas shook his head and they crossed the street to the car.

Stadic got in the back, and saw Sell-More Green walking down the street toward them. Sell-More worked for Harp, but he didn't know Stadic. Stadic made a quick calculation, and as Lucas cranked the car, patted Lucas on the shoulder and said, "Whoa," and pointed.

Lucas and Del looked where Stadic was pointing. A thin black man in an old parka and black sneaks was scuffling along, oblivious of them. "That's Sell-More Green," Stadic said. "He's one of Harp's dealers. Or he used to be."

Lucas said, "So let's ask him where Harp is."

They waited until Sell-More was passing the car, and then popped out, three doors opening at once, and Sell-More turned sideways and thought about running, but then just stopped, hands in his pockets. "What for?" he asked.

"How you doing?" Stadic asked.

"Hungry," Sell-More said. "Haven't ate in two days."

Lucas dug in a pocket, took out a small clip of bills, and pulled out a ten: "Where's the boss?"

Sell-More licked his bottom lip: "Who?"

"Daymon, for Christ's sakes," Lucas said.

"Oh, Daymon." Sell-More looked up at the apartment. "He said the cops was hassling him because of these white boys killing cops. So he went on a trip. With Jas-Min."

"You know where?"

"He said maybe Mexico. Someplace warm," Sell-More said. "Is that good for the ten?"

"You lyin'?" Lucas asked.

"No way," Sell-More said. He shivered. "If the boss was here, I'd be eating."

Lucas handed him the ten and said to Del, "Mexico."

Del looked around at the snow: "Wish I was with him."

Stadic nodded, happy with the story. If Davenport thought Harp was involved, he'd just keep coming back. He didn't want Davenport poking around Harp's operation: not now.

They'd taken a couple of steps away from Sell-More when Lucas stopped and said, "You wanna go for a hundred?"

Sell-More said, "What?"

"We're looking for cops who might be . . . dealing. If you want to ask around, get a name or two, it'd be worth some cash."

Stadic tensed: he hadn't planned on this. "Do I get the bread now?" Sell-More asked hopefully.

"Hell no," Lucas said. "When I get the names—and the names better be good."

Sell-More said, "That's pretty dangerous, what you want."

"Yeah, well, that ten won't last long," Lucas said. He took a card out of his pocket and handed it to Sell-More. "You get hungry again, get a name and call me. Nobody has to know about it."

Sell-More's eyes seemed to roll inward, and after a moment of silence, he looked from Lucas to Del to Stadic, and then he said, "I think I might know somebody."

LACHAISE LOOKED AT MARTIN: "THEY'RE GONE."

Martin nodded. "Yup."

"I can't believe it," LaChaise said. He looked down at Sandy and said, "We're good as gold."

Sandy nodded. She could still feel her heart thumping. The cops had hit the Frogtown house the day after the first shootings. She didn't know how they'd done it, but they'd killed Butters and they would have killed all of them, probably. Now they were knocking on the door of the new place. The whole thing was coming apart, just like Elmore had said it would. Elmore had never been bright: now he was looking like a prophet.

She didn't say any of that: instead, she thought, *Telephone.*

SIXTEEN

———◆———

LUCAS CHECKED ON HIS CREW: SLOAN AND SHERRILL were probing sources in the local biker groups. Del and Franklin were working independently, running more dopers. Anderson, who worked for Lester, was running lists of names though personnel, asking who might know enough to crack the personnel computers. Lucas stopped by his office: ''Anything?''

Anderson said, ''Your name keeps coming up.''

''I think we can eliminate that one,'' Lucas said.

Anderson yawned and said, ''Well, that leaves about sixty more, including everybody in your group, and I'm not finished running the roster.''

''Give me a list when you get it,'' Lucas said.

He also got a copy of Buster Brown's tape and carried it back to his office and listened to it again.

''. . . need to know where this Weather is, and be good to know where Capslock's old lady is, her room number. And we need to know where Davenport is working, and

*Capslock, Sherrill, Sloan, Franklin and Kupicek. You·
know the list.''*

Long pause.

*''That don't sound right; you better be tellin' the
truth, or your name'll be on the list, motherfucker...
Hey, listen to what I'm telling you... No, not you. Did
you find out anything about Elmore?''*

Another pause.

*''That's what we thought. We'll look those boys up
when we're done here... Now listen, we need that shit
and we need it right now. We'll call back in... two
hours. Two hours, got it?''*

Pause.

*''I don't know. And you let us worry about getting
back to you. You might be pulling some bullshit. And if
you are, you better think twice...''*

Pause.

''Yeah, yeah. Two hours.''

He rolled it back and listened for background sounds: he'd
seen a movie where they figured out where something was
by the sound of a train... but there was nothing. Buster
thought he could hear a television, but Lucas couldn't pick it
out of the tape noise. Then he thought, *What was that about
Elmore?*

LaChaise:

*Did you find out anything about Elmore?... That's what
we thought. We'll look those boys up when we're done
here...*

Huh. That sounded like they hadn't killed Elmore Darling.
That sounded like they thought they knew who had—and so
did the cop talking to them. Lucas puzzled through it: the cop
was telling them that Elmore had been killed by other cops,
probably the Michigan prison people, in revenge for the kill-

ing of Sand. That was absurd—but something a con might believe. But if the Michigan people hadn't killed Elmore, and LaChaise hadn't . . .

Lucas launched himself out of his chair and took a quick turn around his desk. Had to be the cop. But how had he known to kill Elmore? How had he known that Elmore was even involved? Was the cop that deep with LaChaise, that he'd know all of it? Had he been involved in the escape itself?

That didn't seem likely: the voices on the phone had been antagonistic.

So how did he know? They had enough pieces of the picture that he should be able to put it together. And when he found it, maybe the cop . . .

STADIC WAS FRANTICALLY TRYING TO LOCATE SELL-More. The junkie had said he might know somebody. And as one of Harp's dealers, *he might*. Harp and Stadic were careful in their rare meetings, always taking them well out of town. But money had to be moved, information had to be worked through, pictures had to be looked at. And with dopers, you could never tell: they were as likely to wake up in Chicago or Miami as at home, and somehow, somebody might have seen him, and Harp, and put two and two together.

Stadic hit all the spots, braced a few dealers with questions about cops, as cover. Davenport would probably shit if he found out that Stadic was covering the same ground as his own people, but that couldn't be helped.

Just after dark, he talked to a convenience store clerk who had sold Sell-More a doughnut not ten minutes earlier. Sell-More was walking, the clerk said. Stadic crisscrossed the side streets, and five minutes later found Sell-More wandering along a sidewalk, hands in his pockets, eyes glazed. Stadic pulled over, ran the window down: "Get in," he said.

Sell-More looked at him, then spoke slowly, a thin glimmer of intelligence: "I ain't got much."

"We want to talk to you anyway," Stadic said, the car grinding through the lumpy ice at the edge of the road. "Get in."

Sell-More shuffled around the car, got in the passenger side, slumped, then leaned forward and rubbed his hands in the air from the car's heater. "Fuckin' hungry," he said.

"You spent the money on dope?"

"I am a dope," Sell-More said. "What you want, anyway?"

"Where're your gloves?"

"Ain't got no gloves. Where're we going?"

"Just gonna drive around a minute, keep the heat going," Stadic said. "What'd you find out?"

Sell-More shrugged. "My man said that Daymon Harp's got a cop, 'cause every time somebody tries to edge in on Daymon, they get busted the next day. He says everybody knows that."

"That's it?"

"Dude gotta be in narcotics," Sell-More said.

Though he was driving, Stadic closed his eyes for a moment. He felt the world slipping out of control, like one of those nightmares where something goes wrong, and you can't ever get it quite right again. If a dumbass like Sell-More could figure this out, then other people could figure it out, too. He hadn't been given away by the name, but by the pattern. And if anyone looked at the pattern of arrests closely enough, they'd find Stadic's name.

"Hey, man . . ."

The tone in Sell-More's voice snapped his eyes open, and he found that he was drifting toward a parked Pontiac. He wrenched the car back to the middle of the street, missing the Pontiac by a foot.

"You okay?" Sell-More asked.

"Tired," Stadic said. He steadied himself. One thing at a time. When Harp got back, Stadic would have to move him out of town. Kill him? Probably not. The thing was, Harp maybe had stashed Stadic's name somewhere as an insurance policy, the same way he'd taken those pictures . . . Goddamn him.

Stadic slipped his hand inside his coat, found the cell phone. The cold lump of his pistol was next to it. "I need you to make a phone call," he said.

SHERRILL AND SLOAN HAD COME BACK, STILL IN THEIR parkas.

"Cold?"

"Yeah. Getting bad," Sherrill said. "Supposed to get warmer tomorrow, but they're talking about some big storm is getting wound up somewhere. Somebody's gonna get it in two or three days."

"Doesn't make it easier."

"Nobody on the streets," Sloan said. "You hear anything from Sell-More?"

"Not a thing." The phone rang, and Lucas picked it up.

Sell-More said, "This is the guy you give the ten dollars to."

Lucas grinned at Sloan and pointed at the phone: "Yeah? Sell-More?"

"I got a name for you."

Lucas leaned forward in the chair. "Who?"

"You said a hundred dollars."

"If you got a name."

After a five-second silence, Sell-More said one word: "Palin."

"Say that again?"

"Palin. Like, my Pal . . . in . . . trouble. Pal-in."

"Where'd you get this?" Lucas asked.

"Some homeboy down on Franklin."

"You come up here, ask for Davenport. If the name's anything, you got a hundred. And I want the name of the homeboy. That's another hundred."

"Don't leave," Sell-More said. "I'm on my way."

LUCAS DROPPED THE PHONE ON THE HOOK AND looked at Sloan. "Arne Palin?"

Sloan dropped his jaw in mock surprise. "Arne Palin? No way."

"Sell-More says Arne Palin," Lucas said.

"Arne's so goddamn straight he still doesn't say 'fuck' in front of women," Sherrill said.

Lucas scratched his head: "But he used to be a roaring drunk. You remember that, Sloan? He did some pretty wild shit, fifteen years ago."

"Yeah, cowboy shit. But jeez . . ." Sloan shook his head. "If you were gonna pick a name who didn't do it—I'd pick Palin. I don't think he's smart enough to think of doing it."

"Gotta be bullshit," Lucas agreed. "But I wonder where Sell-More got it?" He picked up the phone and called Anderson. "Is Arne Palin on your list?"

Anderson said, "Yeah. He's trying to transfer into personnel. They had him up there a few days. You got something?"

"Maybe. Check and see where he's been the last few days—when he's been on duty and so on. See if he was working that day O'Donald saw the guy at the laundromat."

"How close a check?" Anderson asked. He sounded tired.

"Close. We got the name off the street."

"Arne?"

"Yeah, I know. But check, huh?"

STADIC EASED THE CAR TO THE CURB. "OUT," HE SAID. "And you keep your mouth shut. You keep your mouth shut until Harp gets back, and you won't have to worry about gettin' high, not for a while. You be the man.''

"The man," Sell-More said, picking up on Stadic's fake jive. "I be the man.''

"That's right," Stadic said. He checked the rearview mirror: nothing in sight. He'd picked the darkest piece of ice-clogged street he could find. "You go on, now.''

Sell-More cracked the door and swiveled to clamber out. "And get you some gloves. Your hands are gonna freeze," Stadic said. He groped under his sweater for the stock of the old .38. "Do that," Sell-More said.

He was out, ready to slam the door, when Stadic called, "Hey. Wait a minute.''

Sell-More leaned forward to say, "Huh?" but never got the syllable out: As he leaned under the roof, Stadic shot him in the face, one quick shot, a bang and a flash, and Sell-More dropped straight down, banging his head on the doorsill as he fell, a wet snapping sound.

"Shit." Stadic stretched across the seat, and put the muzzle almost against the back of Sell-More's head, and pulled the trigger again. Sell-More's head popped up and down. "If you ain't dead, fuck ya," Stadic said, and he stretched out and caught the door handle and pulled the door shut.

He was in his own car with the murder weapon. He could feel his heart thumping: had to dump the gun. If he got a block away, no jury would convict him, unless he had the gun. But he couldn't ditch it too quick. They'd check close around the body, anyplace a gun might be thrown.

And he listened to the radio; the radio was routine, nothing more. Give it another block. Give it one more. Another one. No calls? He found another dark street, caught the black cut of a storm sewer, pulled up close, cracked the door, dumped the gun. Just before he closed the door, he heard an odd sound, and he hesitated.

What was it? His ears were still ringing from the shots, maybe he was hearing that. He rolled down the window, just an inch, and heard the sound again, over the noise of the wheels. And then he passed the end of the block, and looked down to the right. A group of kids on the sidewalk, with candles.

Carolers.

"Christ," he said. "Little fuckers oughta be in bed." And he went on.

SELL-MORE HADN'T SHOWN, AND DEL HAD COME AND gone—he'd be at the hospital, he said. Sherrill had left for the funeral home. Visitation night. Lucas and Sloan said they'd be along.

"You don't have to come," Sherrill said.

"Of course we have to," Lucas said. He patted her on the shoulder. "We'll be there."

When she was gone, Sloan said, "Why don't we pick up a burger and a beer before we go over?"

Lucas nodded: "All right." He was locking the door when they heard running footsteps. Anderson, white-faced, came around the corner: "It's Palin," he blurted.

"What?" Lucas looked at Sloan, then back to Anderson.

"I had Gina down at Dispatch running tapes, to nail down where Palin was when he was on duty. And night before last, he called in a Wisconsin plate. You won't believe . . ."

"Elmore Darling," Lucas said, snapping his fingers. "That's how he found Darling. Took the numbers off the plate when he talked to LaChaise, ran them, went over there and killed Darling."

"I think so," Anderson said, his oversized Adam's apple bobbing in his thin neck. "We never would have caught him if we hadn't run those old tapes."

"Arne Palin," Sloan said, shaking his head.

"Let's take him," Lucas said.

SEVENTEEN

LUCAS MET QUICKLY WITH ROUX AND LESTER, AND LESter got the Emergency Response Unit moving. Palin was at home: his precinct boss called him about emergency overtime. Palin said he'd be happy to work, and was told to stay close to the phone while they figured out a new schedule.

"LaChaise isn't with him. He couldn't be that far gone," Lucas said to Roux and Lester, as they walked out toward the doorway.

"We can't take the chance, we don't want anyone else killed. Let the ERU do the entry," Lester said. "If LaChaise isn't there, you get in there and see if you can crack Palin in a hurry. Maybe we can get LaChaise's location before he figures out that we've got Palin."

"Sloan's here, he can help with the interrogation," Lucas said. They turned a corner and saw Sloan waiting by the door, talking with Franklin. As they walked up, Stadic came in, stamped snow off his feet.

"You want to come?" Lucas asked Franklin.

"If you need the weight," Franklin said. He nodded at

Stadic, who nodded back. "I'm trying to sneak out to my house and pick up some clothes for my old lady."

"Do this one thing first," Lucas said. He turned to Stadic. "How about you? You look kind of fucked up."

"Yeah, I am," Stadic said, shaking his head.

"All right," Lucas said. He stuck a finger in Stadic's gut. "Get some sleep."

"But what's happening?" Stadic asked.

"We think one of our guys is talking to LaChaise," Lester said grimly.

Stadic's eyelids fluttered, and he said, "No way." And then, "Who?"

Lucas, Sloan and Franklin were already pushing through the door into the snow.

"Arne Palin," Roux said to Stadic, behind them.

"No way," Stadic said again.

"I gotta think he's right," Franklin said as they stepped out into the snow and the door closed. He looked up at the miserable sky, which was so close that he almost felt he could touch it. "I can't believe it's Arne Palin."

STADIC WENT DOWN TO HIS OFFICE: NOBODY HOME, just a bunch of empty desks. He kept a half-dozen white crosses stashed in a hole at the back of a desk drawer, where they couldn't be seen even if you emptied out the drawer. He popped one, as an eye-opener, took his phone out of his pocket and started to punch the speed dial, but stopped, frowned, thought about it and turned it off again. Cell phones are radios. He should stay off the air.

Then it occurred to him that LaChaise's calls on the cell phone could be traced. Shit. If they found the phone, and checked the billing, he'd be screwed. Stadic started to sweat. Christ, he had to get that cell phone. Had to.

He thought for a moment, then picked up a desk phone

and dialed LaChaise's number: as he dialed, the first of the amphetamine hit his bloodstream, and his mind seemed to clear out a bit.

LaChaise answered: "Yeah."

"I got a guy for you," Stadic said, without preamble.

"Which one?"

"Franklin. He and Davenport and a couple of other guys just left here, they're gonna raid a guy . . . nothing to do with you. But I heard Franklin say he had to sneak over to his house after this raid, to pick up some clothes for his wife. She's over at the hotel."

"When's he gonna get there?" LaChaise asked.

"This raid won't take long," Stadic said. "They'll probably hit this house in twenty minutes or so, and Franklin doesn't live too far away. I'd say, half hour to an hour, depending on what happens with the raid."

"Anybody watching his house?"

"No."

"Gimme the address," LaChaise said.

After he hung up, Stadic worked it through his quickening brain: wait in the snow across the street. If he saw LaChaise and Martin arrive, that was fine. If he didn't, he'd wait until Franklin showed. Franklin would pull out the other two. And when they moved in on him, to kill him, Stadic could come up from behind, and take them out.

Just as he'd planned it at the other house, but with one less guy to worry about. Had to get that cell phone, though.

Leaving the office, locking the door, he heard voices in the hall, and then Lester came around the corner with Lew Harrin, a homicide guy. He heard Lester say, "There's Stadic, let's get him," and then Lester called, "Hey, Andy."

Stadic turned as they came up. "Yeah?"

"We got a homicide down on Thirty-third, somebody ran over a guy laying in the street. The uniforms checked it out, say it looks like he was already dead, couple of bullets in the head. Run down there with Lew, see what's going on."

"Listen, I'm totally fucked . . ." Stadic began.

"Yeah, I know," Lester said. "We're all fried. We can't put you out front because you don't have a gun, but you can do this, this is just bullshit interviewing. Anyway, we hear the guy's a doper. Maybe you'll know him."

"Man, my head . . ."

"I don't want to hear it," Lester said. "Get your ass down there."

LACHAISE AND MARTIN SCRAMBLED TO GET READY FOR the attack on Franklin. Martin had field-stripped one of the .45s. He walked around finding his boots as he put it back together and reloaded. LaChaise pulled on his parka and said to Sandy, "I'm worried about you. You'd sell us out, just like your old man."

"C'mon, Dick," she said. "Don't scare me."

"You oughta be scared."

"I am scared," she said. "The police are going to kill us."

"Yeah, probably," he said, and he grinned at her.

Martin handed LaChaise a blued Colt .45 and a half-dozen magazines. "A little more firepower," he said. "I wish we had some goddamn heavier stuff. That AR'd be worth its weight in gold."

LaChaise broke his eyes away from Sandy. "These'll work," he said, stuffing them in his parka pocket. He turned back to Sandy. "I thought about taking you, but that won't work. We're gonna have to . . ."

"What?" she asked, suddenly sure that this was it: they were going to kill her.

LaChaise grinned at her. "Gonna have to tie you up a little."

"Dick, c'mon. I'm not going anywhere. I can't . . ."

"Bill and I have been talking: we think you will."

She looked at Martin, who nodded. "You will," he said.

"Down the garage," LaChaise said.

THEY'D FOUND A DOZEN PADLOCKS IN A KITCHEN drawer, of the kind Harp used as backup locks on his wash-ing-machine coin boxes. And from the garage, they got a chain. Martin brought an easy chair along, and a stack of magazines.

The lockup was quick, simple and almost foolproof: LaChaise, Sandy thought, probably learned it in prison. One end of the chain went snugly around her waist, and was pad-locked in place. The other end went around a support beam in the basement, and was padlocked there. She had just enough slack to sit down.

"You can try to get out," LaChaise said. "But don't hurt yourself trying, 'cause it won't do you no good."

"Dick, you don't have to do this," Sandy said, pleading. "I'd be here."

LaChaise looked at her hard: "Maybe . . . maybe we can have some fun when I get back."

"What?"

He said, "C'mon, Bill. We gotta move."

LUCAS KNEW FIVE MINUTES AFTER THEY TOOK ARNE Palin that they'd made a mistake.

They'd set up a few blocks away, pulled on the vests, ready for anything. The entry team went to the front door, knocked, and when Palin opened, pushed him back. Another team went through the back door at the same moment, breaking the lock. Palin, sputtering, stuttering, his wife screaming, watched as the team flowed through the house, from bedrooms to base-ment. Lucas, Sloan and Franklin moved in right behind the entry team. Palin had been patted down and pushed back on the couch with his wife. Palin was sputtering, angry, then dumbfounded.

"Nothing here," Franklin said. "Can I split?"

"Yeah, take off," Lucas said. "You coming back to the office?"

"Soon as I get the stuff to my old lady," Franklin said. He nodded at Palin. "Arne," he said, and he was gone.

"What the hell?" Palin asked Lucas. "What the hell?"

"Last night you called in a routine make on a Wisconsin pickup that belonged to an Elmore and Sandy Darling. Why'd you do that?"

Palin's wife looked at him, and Palin's mouth opened and shut, and then he turned his head, thought for a moment, then looked up at Lucas and said, "I never did that."

"We got you on tape, Arne."

"I never," Palin protested.

"Elmore Darling was shot to death last night and Sandy Darling is running, maybe, with LaChaise and these other nuts. We know you ran their tags . . ."

"You wanna fuckin' listen to me?" Palin screamed. He started to stand up but Lucas held a hand out toward his chest. He sat down again and shouted, "I didn't run no Wisconsin plates, and you ain't got it on tape because I never did it."

Sloan said, his soft act, "Arne, you might want to get a lawyer . . ."

"I don't need no fuckin' lawyer," Palin shouted, bouncing on the couch. "Bring the fuckin' tapes in here. Bring the fuckin' tapes in here."

Lucas looked at him for a long beat, then at his wife, who was weeping. "All right," he said. "Why don't you get your coat on? Let's go downtown and listen to the tapes, and see if we can figure out what's going on."

"I want to come, too," Palin's wife said.

Lucas nodded. "Sure, that'd be fine." He'd been about to

tell her to get her coat, as well. He didn't want anyone left behind, if they were talking to LaChaise.

STADIC LOOKED AT THE BODY OF SELL-MORE. SELL-More's head was bent against the curb, twisted hard to the right, and his legs had apparently been crushed by the car that hit him. There was no visible blood.

"Shit," he said to Harrin, the homicide cop. "I just talked to him, a few hours ago. Davenport's gonna freak out. This is LaChaise's work. Wonder what the hell's going on."

Lucas took the call from Stadic on the way back to the office: Sell-More? Why in the hell would somebody hit Sell-More? Because he was asking questions?

FRANKLIN LIVED IN NORTH MINNEAPOLIS, IN A SINGLE-story rambler in a neighborhood of mixed housing styles and ages. Across the street, a brick four-square looked across at him, while to his left, a white clapboard split-level crowded his driveway. Franklin drove slowly down toward his house, tired, feeling the day. There was a little drifting snow around, from the squalls that had come through during the night.

Maybe he ought to get the snowblower out and blast his driveway clean, before it got too deep, or run over too much by the paper delivery guy. He had an insulated jumpsuit in the front closet, along with some pacs; he could clean it out in ten minutes. But had he gassed up the snowblower?

LACHAISE AND MARTIN HAD CRUISED FRANKLIN'S house, then the side streets.

"If there's anybody around, they sure gotta be inside," Martin said. "Can't see shit out here."

"I been thinking about it," LaChaise said. "No point in both of us taking him on. So, you drop me up the block, where I can walk back. Then you find a place to park—you see that streetlight?''

LaChaise pointed at a streetlight on the corner two houses up from Franklin's.

''Yeah?''

''You park where you can see the light. If you can see it, then you can see his car lights when he shows up. As soon as you see him turn in, you come on down. I'll take him as soon as he gets out of his car.''

''What if he goes in the garage, stays in the car, drops the door without getting out?''

''Then I'll go right up next to his car window and fill him up from there,'' LaChaise said. ''That might even be easier.''

''Wish we had a goddamn AR,'' Martin said again.

''The 'dog'll do, and the forty-five.''

''You'll freeze out there . . .''

''Not that cold,'' LaChaise said. ''We'll wait for an hour. I can stand an hour.''

THEY'D BEEN WAITING TWENTY MINUTES WHEN FRANK-lin showed, Martin a block and a half down the street, La-Chaise ditched behind a fir tree across the street from the mouth of Franklin's driveway.

Four cars had passed in that time, and a woman in a parka and snowpants, walking, carrying a plastic grocery bag. She passed within six feet of LaChaise, and never suspected him. As she passed, LaChaise pointed the 'dog at the back of her head and said to himself, ''Pop.''

He had six shots in the 'dog. He thought about that for a minute. Martin had given him one of the .45s he'd bought from Dave. Now he took it out of his pocket, racked the slide to load and cock it and flipped the safety up.

·   ·   ·

WHEN FRANKLIN TURNED ONTO THE STREET, LACHAISE leaned forward, tense. The car was moving slow, and he had a feeling . . . yes. He clicked the safety down on the .45.

The garage door started up, a light on inside, and Franklin took a hard left into the driveway. The door was moving up quickly enough that Franklin could keep rolling into the garage. LaChaise unfolded from behind the fir, stumbled—his legs were cramped, he'd been kneeling too long—recovered, started to run after the car, stumbled again, caught himself and saw the car door swing open. But the stumbles had slowed him down . . .

FRANKLIN WAS A BIG MAN, BUT AGILE. HE SWUNG HIS feet out of the car and stood up, still thinking about the snowblower, and at that moment saw LaChaise running up the drive, knew who it was and said, ''Shit.''

LaChaise saw the big man turn toward him and saw his hand drop, and he flashed on Capslock making the same quick move. He was ready this time, and he pulled up and fired the first shot with the 'dog, into Franklin's chest from twenty feet, saw Franklin stagger back. He closed, walking, fired again at fifteen feet, then a third, a quick bang-bang-bang and then Franklin's hand came up and LaChaise jerked off a fourth shot and knew that it had gone wide to his right . . .

And then Franklin's gun was up and LaChaise saw the muzzle flash and he fired once with the .45 with his off hand; missed, he thought. Franklin fired again and LaChaise thought he felt the bullet zip through his beard and he was firing and Franklin fell down but he was still firing and LaChaise turned and ran . . .

Martin was there, skidding to a stop, the door opening. LaChaise piled through the passenger-side door and Martin took off, the back end slewing wildly once, twice, then straightening. LaChaise caught the door and slammed it, and looking back, saw Franklin on the floor of the garage . . .

"Got him," Martin said.

"I don't know," LaChaise said uncertainly. "He was this *big* motherfucker, and I kept shooting him and he kept bouncing around and he wouldn't go down . . ."

"You can shoot a guy in the heart, he can be good as dead, but he can go on pulling the trigger thirty seconds or a minute," Martin said. "That's what happened to them FBIs down in Miami. Those old boys were good as dead, but they kept on shooting, and they took the FBIs down with them."

"I don't know . . ." LaChaise said. He twisted to look back, but Franklin's place was gone in the night.

WHEN THE FIRST SLUG HIT, FRANKLIN FELT LIKE SOMEbody had smacked him in the breastbone with a T-ball bat. Same with the second one, and the third. Then he had his own weapon out, but the fourth shot caught his arm, and stung, as though somebody had hit him with a whip, or a limber stick, and turned him. He thought, *Don't be bad*, and he opened fire, knowing that he wasn't doing any good, his left arm on fire. Then another shot hit him in the chest and he fell down, slipping on the snow that had come off his car. He had no idea how many times he'd fired, or how many times he'd been shot at, but a slug ripped through his leg and he rolled, and now was hurting bad, but he kept his pistol pointing out toward the door, and kept it going . . .

And then it all stopped, and he was in silence. Out in the street, he saw LaChaise hurtle into a waiting car.

He said out loud, "What?" And he remembered, Christ, he probably was out of ammo. He automatically went for the second magazine with his left arm, and a tearing pain ran through his arm and shoulder.

"Ahhh . . ." He pushed himself up, and pain coursed through his left leg. He looked down, and saw blood pooling on the floor. Pushing with his right leg, he managed to flop across the driver's seat and grab the radio with his good hand.

"Help me," he groaned.

LESTER CAUGHT LUCAS JUST AS HE WALKED INTO THE OF-fice.

"Franklin's down. Two minutes ago. They hit him at his house," he shouted down the long marble hallway. "They're taking him to Hennepin."

"On the way," Lucas shouted back. "They're bringing in Palin, talk to him . . ."

Lucas ran through the snow to the medical center, down the street to the emergency entrance. No cops. A doctor was standing just inside the entrance, a couple of nurses were wrestling with a gurney.

"I'm a cop," Lucas said. "You got a . . ."

"Yeah, you're Davenport, I've seen you on TV. He's on the way," the doctor interrupted. "The paramedics got him, they're working on him."

"How bad?"

"He's shot in the arm and the leg. Sounds bad enough, but not critical. They say he took four rounds right in the middle of his vest."

Lucas flashed back to the street where they'd stopped to pull on the vests, so they could charge in on simple old Arne Palin. How did LaChaise—it had to be LaChaise—know to wait for Franklin?

Then he heard the sirens, and he and the doctor went out to meet the paramedics, and he stopped thinking about it.

EIGHTEEN

———◆◉◆———

LUCAS HURRIED THROUGH THE CROWD OF MEDIA IN the lobby, shaking his head, saying, "No, I'm sorry . . . the chief should be out in a minute, I'm really sorry I can't say anything."

Outside, he hurried, slipping and sliding, back toward City Hall. His office was dark, and he went up to Homicide, where he found Sloan, Del and Sherrill.

"How's Franklin?" Sloan asked, standing up. They all were beginning to fade.

"He's in surgery, but it's not critical," Lucas said. "Somebody said he might have some peripheral nerve damage in his arm. I'm not sure, but I think that means he might have some patches of skin where he can't feel anything."

"Could be worse," Del said.

"Where's his wife?" Sloan asked.

"She's at the hospital," Lucas said. "What happened with Palin?"

"We're keeping him around, in case you or the chief wants to talk to him. But it's not him," Sloan said.

"Tell me," Lucas said.

"Have you heard the tapes?"

"No."

"Well, if it's him," Sloan said, "he's disguising his voice. But why is he disguising his voice, when he gives his squad number? And even if you figure it's disguised, it sounds too much not-like him."

"Huh." Lucas nodded. "What was he doing earlier on the tape?"

"That's the other thing," Sherrill said. "I went down and listened to them, and he and Dobie Martinez cleared out a burglary report and then said they were going to stop for a cup of coffee, and they went off the air. Then ten minutes later, there's the request on the Darling car . . . then ten minutes after that, they come back on the air again, ready to go back to work."

"Shit," Lucas said. "Did you talk to Martinez?"

"Yeah. He remembers clearing the burglary, then stopping at Barney's. He says they were in there for fifteen or twenty minutes, that Arne never left him, and then they came back and started working again. He says they never called in any Wisconsin plates. So unless they're working together, the identification was bullshit."

"It's bullshit," Lucas said. "But I'd like to hear the tapes."

"I've got a copy on cassette, I'll get it," Sherrill said.

She stepped away, and Lucas said to Del, "Have you heard about Sell-More?"

"No, I just got here."

"Stadic called just about the time Franklin got shot. He was on a call down south. Sell-More was lying in the street with a couple of bullet holes in his head."

"Sonofabitch," Del said. "They used Sell-More to set up Palin."

"But I don't understand why," Lucas said. "It's gotta be a cop, and he's gotta know that it wouldn't hold up."

They all looked at each other, and then Sloan said, "Maybe he ain't the brightest."

"Bullshit. He's been leading us around by the nose," Lucas said. "Who's working the scene down at Franklin's?"

"Some of Lester's guys, I don't know who—Christ, people are all over the place."

"I want to talk to whoever it is . . ."

Lester came in, and they turned toward him, and a second later, Rose Marie Roux followed Lester through the door. She looked at Lucas and said, "Give me an idea."

Lucas said, "I got nothin' that we aren't already doing. He's gotta be holed up with a friend."

"We've shaken down every biker in the fuckin' city," Lester said. "The question is, who was a good enough friend that they'd put up with this shit? Maybe he's staying with . . . you know."

He didn't say it, but he meant, "the cop."

Lucas shook his head and said, "My brain isn't working right. I need to lie down for a while." Then he said to Roux, "There is one thing. We should talk to Sandy Darling. She's freaked out about lawyers, she thinks we're gunning for her with the rest of them . . ."

"So what do we say? Without giving her away?"

Lucas rubbed his chin. "Suppose we say that we had a source who has been useful, but now is apparently afraid and has gone into hiding. We're asking her to come back out, that we'll protect her and offer her immunity."

"I don't know about immunity," Roux said doubtfully. "What if she's deep into it, and she's just playing an angle?"

"All right, so we just say, 'Protect her.' I mean, there's three ways we can get them: we can take them on the street, we can find the cop who's pulling our dick or we can get

Darling to give them up. We're doing everything we can on the street, but we're getting nowhere with the cop . . .''

Roux nodded. ''All right. I'll put this out. They're using everything we give them, so it'll be on the air in ten minutes.''

Sherrill walked up, carrying a tape recorder, and said, ''Something else. What they're doing—they're not gonna back off. I think we've got to set up a combat team anywhere they might show. Everybody's house. The hotel's already covered. But maybe we should set up at the hospital to cover Franklin and Cheryl and whoever.''

Sloan said, ''And I don't think anybody ought to be running around loose.'' He looked at Lucas and said, ''Weather and Jennifer. Somebody is feeding these guys everything . . .''

Roux said, ''Lucas, get those goddamn women under control, will you? Can you do that?''

Lucas said, ''I'll talk to them.''

SHERRILL PLAYED THE TAPE, AND LUCAS LISTENED, EYES closed. The voice wasn't right: too smooth, too high-pitched: faked. Whoever it was would have fooled the Dispatch people, because the unit number was right and the request was routine.

''I think—I can't swear to it—but I think that's the guy who called me and warned me that Butters was cruising Jennifer and Sarah,'' Lucas said.

''Why?''

''I'll tell you why,'' Lucas said. ''Because that fuckin' LaChaise is blackmailing him, and he figures that if we take them alive, they'll deal him. And they probably will. So he's got to have them dead.''

LUCAS HEADED OUT TO TV3 IN A CITY CAR, MONITORING the radio, his cell phone in his pocket. This was like nothing he'd ever heard of: this was like a war. He didn't have the usual intervals of quiet, when he could sit and think about patterns, and the way the opponents were working. Puzzle pieces were slipping past him; he could feel it. Maybe if he got some sleep . . .

The TV3 lobby was locked. When he approached the glass doors, four men ranged behind two reception desks waved him off. He stood next to the glass, held up his ID. One of the men, large, in a heavy, dark suit, crossed the lobby to the door. Lucas realized that he was wearing a vest and carried a pistol on his hip. The man looked at the ID, looked at him, then turned the knob on the lock.

"I thought that was you," the man said, looking over Lucas's shoulder as Lucas came through.

"Who're you?"

"Thomason Security," the man said. "We're on all the doors."

Lucas nodded. "Good." Thomason was a heavy-duty security firm, used mostly for moving money at sports events and rock concerts, but also as a source of armed guards and bodyguards for celebrities. He asked for Jennifer.

"We'll call up," the man said. Lucas waited, leaning on a countertop. As the man called, he noticed that the other guard on his side of the lobby had a Winchester Defender twelve-gauge at his feet. Even better.

The first guard turned to Lucas and said, "Go on up. You know the way?"

"Yeah."

Jennifer met him at the elevators: "What's going on?"

"We've decided that we've got to pull everybody in tight—back at the hotel," Lucas said. "These guys are suicidal."

Jennifer shook her head: "I know, but you saw our security. There's no way they can get at me. I'm as safe here as

I'd be at the hotel. I've got to work; I'm on camera four hours a day. This is the biggest story of my life.''

"Look, goddamnit, we know they were coming after you guys . . .''

"That's all taken care of. They can't find out where the kids are, because nobody knows but you and me and Richard. And I'm safe in here," she said. "I'm sorry, but we've figured the risks. I'm staying here.''

He gave up. "All right. But I want to talk to Small. I want to make goddamn sure that you've got a tight communications link between here and City Hall, and the second something happens . . .''

WEATHER WAS WORSE.

When Lucas walked into the suite, Weather was talking with Sarah. When Lucas began the pitch, she picked Sarah up and held her on her lap.

"Listen, Weather . . .'' Sarah blocked Weather off, like some kind of psychic barricade. He couldn't operate with Sarah looking at him with his own blue eyes; couldn't sell. He couldn't touch Weather, and he needed to touch her to convince her, he thought.

"Lucas," she said, exasperated, when he finished. "Nobody can find me at the hospital. Nobody. People who work there can't find me, unless they have my schedule—and half the time they can't find me then. I've got jobs lined up all week. I just can't skip them because there are some lunatics running around out there.''

"The problem is, you're a lure," Lucas said. "You could bring a hell of a lot of trouble down on the heads of everybody around you. And now we know they've got a cop feeding them information . . .''

"Look," she said. "Let's do this. Let's tell everybody—everybody, including the police—that I'm in the hotel. We can sneak me in at night, and I'll go around and complain about being stuck there, so everybody knows I'm around. Then we'll sneak me out in the morning, and nobody'll know but the two of us.''

''Somebody'll know,'' Lucas said.

''Two or three people. You can use guys you're sure of.''

Lucas said, ''How about if you were interviewed on TV tonight—ten minutes from now, a half hour—in the hotel? About what it's like to be shut up here, and wait? So it'll be on TV?''

She nodded, ''If that will keep me on the job,'' she said.

''I'll call Jen and see if she can set it up,'' Lucas said. He made a quick circle of the room, coming back to the pair of them, picked up Sarah and bounced her. ''Want to see your mom?''

''She's breaking a major story,'' Sarah said solemnly.

''I think she could take a minute away to see her kid,'' Lucas said. ''Let's go talk to her.''

NINETEEN

❮❮◗◖❯❯

LACHAISE WAS MANIC: THEY'D SHOT THE COP, HE SAID,
his face alight, as though he expected Sandy to have a cele-
bration prepared.

"What d'ya think about that, huh? What d'ya think?"

Sandy, coldly furious, turned her face away until the chain
came off, and then stalked up the stairs, into the back bedroom, the one they said was hers, and slammed the door in
LaChaise's face. She said not a word. She'd felt like a dog
with the chain around her waist, and a mistreated dog at that.

She lay on the stripped-off bed for half an hour, thinking
about Elmore, thinking about horses, smelling the odd lingering body odors of strangers.

Horses. She got up, went out to the living room. LaChaise
and Martin were drinking, watching television. "I've got to
call a guy, to make sure he's feeding the stock," she said.

LaChaise shrugged. "Use the cell phone. It's in my coat
pocket. Don't talk more'n a minute or so, in case there's some
way they can trace it. And call from out here, where we can
hear you."

She nodded, went to his coat, dug around. She found the stack of photos, the photos of the cop, deep in one pocket. Ten of them, two men at a table, one black, one white. Which one was the cop?

She listened for a minute, then took two of the photos, the two that showed each of the faces best, and slipped them into her jeans pocket. She put the rest back, found the telephone, and went out to the hallway where the men could hear her.

Jack White. She knew the number, dialed in. Jack's wife answered:

"Sandy, where are you, we can't believe . . ."

"It's not what anybody thinks," she said. "I can't talk—but you've got to tell Jack to take care of the stock."

"He's already doing that, as soon as he heard about Elmore."

"Tell him he'll get paid; I swear, as soon as I can get out of this," Sandy said.

"He'd do it anyway."

"Gotta go . . . and thanks. I won't forget it."

She hung up and LaChaise said, "Still think you might get out of it, huh?"

"I'll put the phone back in your coat," she said coldly. She did, and went back to the bedroom, flopped on the bed.

Tried to think. Got up after a while and poked around the room: this was a guest bedroom, and had been used as storage. LaChaise had torn the place apart, looking for money, and found nothing of interest. She went to the window, lifted the blind and looked out. The snow had quit, and distant streetlights seemed to sparkle in the suddenly clear air. Must be an inch of snow, she thought. She leaned forward to peer at the ledge . . .

And thought: *Out the window.*

Bedsheets—but she didn't have any bedsheets. The bed had been folded and pushed against the wall when they got there. She could get sheets, there were sheets in a closet down the hall, that'd be natural enough: but that goddamn Martin would think about the sheets and the window.

She looked back out, then to her right. And the fire escape was there, one window down, at the end of the long hall. Ten feet, no more. The ledge was a foot wide . . . and snow-covered. The fall was twenty feet or more. Enough to kill her.

Still. The snow could be brushed away . . .

The window had a swivel lock, and she twisted it: after some resistance, it went. She tried the window. Didn't budge. She looked closely at it, but it didn't seem to be painted shut. She tried again, squatting to push up with stiff arms . . . and it gave, just an inch, but it'd go.

She looked back at the door. This would be a bad time, with both of the men drinking, both of them awake. As she thought it, LaChaise screamed from the front room.

"Motherfucker . . ."

The police?

Sandy pulled the window back down, locked it, pulled the shade and then quickly tiptoed to the door. Then she opened it and peered down the hall.

". . . can't get it right," LaChaise roared. "Why'd he wear a vest to go home . . ."

The television brought the news that Franklin wasn't dead—that he wasn't even in particularly dangerous condition, that he'd been saved by a bulletproof vest.

"What do I gotta do?" LaChaise shouted at Martin. "What the fuck do I gotta do?"

"You did right," Martin said. "You hit him four times in the chest, is what the news says."

But Martin's efforts to calm him down only made LaChaise angrier. Already full of beer, he got Harp's Johnnie Walker and started drinking it off, carrying a water tumbler full of ice cubes, pouring the whiskey over them, gulping it down like Coca-Cola. He paced as he drank, watching the television.

A blond newscaster from TV3—"She's the one we want to get," Martin said, "Davenport's woman"—reported that "Police are searching for an informant who provided critical information earlier this week, but who has disappeared. They ask that you call the department on the 911 line, as you did the last time, or any police line and ask for Chief Lucas Davenport. Police said they would offer the informant absolute protection from retaliation from Richard LaChaise or any of his accomplices."

"Yeah? How are you gonna do that?" LaChaise brayed at the screen. Then: "I'd like to fuck her," and then: "Who could be talking to them? We don't know anybody."

Sandy shrank back: she knew.

"Probably whoever told them about the house we was in," Martin said. "Ansel had to ask around, talking to a bunch of dopers. Somebody probably gave him up."

"Yeah . . . Goddamn, ol' Ansel. I miss that sonofabitch."

LaChaise's face crinkled, and Sandy thought he'd begun to weep. He turned abruptly, marched down the hall into Harp's stereo room and began tearing the vinyl record albums out of their covers and smashing them, three and four at a time.

Martin looked at Sandy, but showed no sign of disapproval—or approval, either. He showed nothing, she thought.

To the sound of the breaking records, Sandy went back to the bedroom and shut the door. Martin was nuts, but he was controlled. But the booze had pushed LaChaise over the edge, and the very air of the apartment carried the smell and taste of insanity, of the expectation that something crazy was about to happen.

She had to get out.

A moment later, she heard Martin's arrows start to whack into the target outside her door. Martin had put the target next to the window at the end of the main hall. If he pulled an arrow to the right, she thought, it'd go right through the window shade and glass, out over the fire escape and into the roof of the next building . . .

She was sitting on the bed when LaChaise stopped breaking records. A moment later, LaChaise and Martin were shouting at each other, and she heard the thumping of heavy bodies colliding in the front room. She ran to the door and down the hall again, and found Martin on the floor, on top of LaChaise, with a heavy arm around LaChaise's neck. LaChaise was facedown, and trying to get to his hands and knees.

"Let me up, you motherfucker," LaChaise roared.

"Can't do that; can't do that," Martin was saying urgently. "We need the goddamn TV . . ."

He saw Sandy and said, "Tried to kick in the TV."

"Fuckers don't do nothing but lie," LaChaise said, but he sounded calmer.

"But we need to see what they're saying, and what happens with the cops," Martin said.

After a moment of silence, LaChaise said, "Let me up. I won't kick it."

Martin nodded. "All right."

Martin stood up, between LaChaise and the television, and LaChaise grunted as he stood up, a tight grin: "You kicked my ass."

"You're drunk as a skunk."

"Well, that's true," LaChaise said. "But you're pretty fuckin' drunk yourself." Sandy moved away, stepping back toward the bedroom, but LaChaise turned and saw her and said, "What're you lookin' at?" and then, "Hey, wait a minute."

Sandy padded back toward the room, looking for a place to hide, and heard LaChaise say to Martin, "If I can't kick the TV, might as well jump me a little puss.''

Sandy turned around inside the bedroom: looking for a way out. There wasn't any. LaChaise came to the doorway and leaned in, and she said, ''Dick, don't.''

''Bullshit,'' he said.

''I won't fuckin' move. I'll lie there like a brick. And if I get a chance to kill you, I will.''

He stepped toward her and she thought he'd hit her. Instead, his eyes wavered, and he said, ''Fuck you,'' and staggered away.

She shut the door. Had to get out. Had to.

LUCAS AND SLOAN BROUGHT WEATHER INTO THE BACK of the hotel, while Sherrill and Del brought in Jennifer and a TV3 crew. Weather went to fix her hair and check makeup, and Jennifer, standing aside with Lucas, muttered, ''I wouldn't let Weather look at this Sherrill chick too long.''

''What?''

''Give me a break, Davenport. Never in your life would you fail to appreciate the young woman's qualities.''

''Well, I do appreciate them,'' Lucas said stiffly. He suddenly felt like an asshole, broke down and grinned. ''But I'd never do anything about it.''

Jennifer looked at him in an appraising way, and said, ''Maybe you really have changed.''

''Yeah, well . . .''

Weather came back out and they went down to the lobby for the interview, a two-minute no-brainer on the cops' families suffering from cabin fever, how it felt to be barricaded inside. Jennifer did another quick interview with Sloan's flustered wife, and then went out the back door with her protection.

''That should do it,'' Weather said, when they got back to her room.

"I hope so. I hope they're watching television," Lucas said. "Jen says they'll run the tape every time they do the updates."

"Are you still angry with me?" Weather asked. She sounded slow, depressed.

"No. I never was as much angry as I was . . . cranked up," Lucas said.

She patted the bed: "You need to get some sleep, I can see caffeine leaking out of your eyes."

"Maybe a few hours," he agreed.

SANDY COULD HEAR LACHAISE TALKING TO MARTIN, both of them still drinking. She got up twenty times to go to the window, to look at the ledge. Long way down. Higher than the hayloft in the barn. She'd lie on the bed, close her eyes, try to rest. Nothing worked.

Eventually, the talk in the living room stopped, and the television was turned off. She went to the window, looked out again. Then a sudden THUMM-whack outside her door. Martin was at it again, shooting the bow down the hall. He fired it twenty times, then quit.

The apartment was quiet for a half hour, an hour, the hands creeping around her watch. She went back to the door, listened, cracked it, looked out. If she could get sheets—or if she could just get out the door, for that matter. The men had been very drunk . . .

The hall light was on, and one more in the living room. A half-dozen arrows stuck out of the target at the end of the hall, five feet away. But nobody was moving. She went down the hall on her tiptoes: the door to the master bedroom was open, and in the half-light, she could see LaChaise sprawled across the king-sized bed.

Martin was wrapped in a blanket, lying on the floor by the

front door. She tiptoed down toward him and whispered, "Bill?"

He stirred, but his breathing remained even. She looked back down the hall toward the basement door. Martin's voice, thick with sleep, said, "The door's locked. I got the key in my pants."

She jumped: it was as though he'd snatched her thought from midair. "I wasn't going to the door. I was just making sure that Dick's sleeping it off," she said.

"Are you . . . ?" she was going to ask, *all right*? Before the words could get out of her mouth, he'd rolled and was pointing a pistol at her head. She stepped back and said, *"Please . . ."*

Drunk as he must be—he'd finished LaChaise's bottle of Johnnie Walker and a half-dozen more beers—his hand seemed absolutely steady. "You're gonna call the cops on us, aren't you?"

"No, honest to God . . ." She looked back at the bedroom; the black-and-white target loomed on the wall outside the door, next to the fire escape window.

"Are you gonna fuck him?"

Now, she thought, they were getting to the important is-sues. She crossed her arms: "Not if I can help it," she said, looking at the hole in the end of the pistol. "If Dick does it to me, I'd have to be unconscious or dead."

The hole at the end of the pistol seemed as large as a basketball hoop, and held between her eyes. He kept it there, kept it, and she closed her eyes . . .

"All right," he said. She opened her eyes and the pistol was pointing at the ceiling. He grinned at her, a wet, sleepy, evil grin, she thought. "Hope nobody down in the laundry heard me and Dick wrestling around."

My God, she thought, he's lying here thinking about it: Martin's turned on. Out loud she said, "They'd have been here, if anybody called the cops.'' Her eyes drifted toward the telephone: pick it up, 911, leave it off the hook, wait one minute . . .

Impossible. She could handle LaChaise, she thought, but Martin . . . Martin seemed to see everything.

The gun flashed back up and leveled at her forehead again, and Martin said, ''Bang.'' Then, ''Go on back to bed.''

LUCAS TRIED TO SLEEP, SNUGGLED AGAINST WEATHER. Though he felt as if he'd been awake for days, his internal clock still said it was too early. And the bed was wrong, not his, and the pillow was no good: it crooked his neck at a bad angle. But most of all, he couldn't stop his mind. He wasn't putting the puzzle together, he was simply reliving the whole long episode, without profit.

A few minutes after midnight, Weather finally spoke in the dark: ''You're vibrating,'' she said.

''Sorry.''

''You need the sleep.''

''I know,'' Lucas said. ''My brain's all clogged up.''

She half-rolled. Her voice was clear, and he realized she'd been lying awake: ''How much longer, before you get them?''

''Probably tomorrow, unless they just hide out. If they move, we'll get them. Tomorrow or the next day, I'd say.''

''What if they're running?''

''Their pictures have been on every TV in the country; they couldn't stop to get gas. They really can't go out in the open.''

After another moment of silence, Weather said, ''You think they'll be taken alive?''

''No.''

''You guys'll just shoot them?''

''It's not that—if they called up and said they wanted to

come in, and they told us where they were, and they came out with their hands over their heads . . . We'd take them. But it's not shaping up that way. The first guy, Butters, might as well have committed suicide. They figure they're dead. They've already written themselves off. And that's scarier'n hell.''

"Gotta be their parents . . . you know, who made them like that."

"Always is," Lucas said. "I've watched some kids grow up from little psychos into big psychos: it was always the parents that made them that way."

"If you could intervene early enough . . ."

Lucas shook his head: "Never work. Nobody spends as much time with the kids as their parents, even if their parents don't want them. And usually, nobody knows anything is wrong until the kid's already bent. Maybe you could set up an army of fascist social workers who'd go around to every house once a month and cross-examine every kid, but that'd probably be worse than what we've got. Look what happened with all these mass child-abuse things. They're all bullshit, and it's the social workers who've done it."

Another silence.

Then Weather said, "I don't believe that more violence is the way to solve the problem. I don't think shooting these people will do it."

Lucas said, "That's 'cause you're a doctor."

"Hmm?"

"Doctors think in terms of illness and cures. The problem is, when one of these guys gets sick, somebody else gets hurt. So we've got two problems, not one. First we've got to protect innocent people. Then we've got to do whatever we can with these guys—cure them or whatever. But first we've got to stop them."

"That doesn't seem to be what you're doing . . ." Then

she added, hastily, "Sometimes it doesn't, anyway."

"Yeah, I know. Sometimes we play it a little too much like a game. That's just a way to deal with it . . . but that's not the way it really is. It ain't football, even if TV thinks so."

They talked a bit longer, then Weather said, "I've got to get some sleep. I'm working in the morning."

Lucas kissed her good-night again, and lay on his back, watching the outside light trace feather patterns across the ceiling, and some time later, finally fell asleep.

SANDY MOVED THE WINDOW AN INCH AT A TIME, AND the cold air flooded in. That was a problem. Once she committed herself, she could hardly go back. The room would be cold, and if Martin or LaChaise came in, they'd know . . .

But she pushed the window up anyway. Then leaned out, brushed snow off the ledge with her hand. The ledge didn't seem too slippery, but she wouldn't be able to walk it with boots. She dropped to the bed, took off her boots and socks, put the socks in the boots and the boots in her parka pockets, the heels sticking out. Couldn't drop those . . .

She looked down. *I'm going to kill myself.*

She took a breath and stepped out on the ledge: and the shock of the cold on her feet almost pitched her off. She held to the inside of the window frame, then edged to her right. The ledge was plenty wide, almost as though it had been designed to get her to the fire escape. Probably had been, she thought.

She slid another step, and then another, refusing to look down again. She let go of the edge of the window frame, and now was balanced on nothing but her painfully chilled feet, the outside wall pushing against her back. She looked straight out, feeling more balanced that way. Two more steps. Two more.

Reaching out with her right hand, she groped for the steel of the fire escape. Another step. Christ, she was afraid to look to her right, another step, groping . . . and she felt it. Now she turned her head, saw it, grabbed the railing and stepped over to it.

She stopped to check the window above the fire escape. The shade was down, but there was a crack at the bottom between the shade and window frame, and she could see down the hall. In the semidark, Martin looked like an enormous cocoon, rolled up on the floor at the end of the hall.

She stepped over the railing onto the fire escape, breathing hard: she was excited and frightened to death. She took two steps down, onto the drop platform, and bounced gently, to see if that was enough to make it drop. It didn't move. She tried again, harder. Nothing. Hard, this time. There was a metallic clank to the left, but the platform stayed up.

This wasn't the way it was supposed to work, but in the dark, she couldn't see why the platform wasn't dropping. Something was stuck somewhere . . .

She thought about hanging from the bottom, and dropping. But even with a two-step platform drop, and the six feet she'd get by hanging, it'd be a twelve- or thirteen-foot drop onto an uncertain alley surface . . .

She'd break a leg.

But she thought about it, the cold in her feet growing to pain.

THEN SHE FELT THE VIBRATION.

She didn't know what it was, but she went to her knees under the window, and put her eye to the crack under the shade. Martin was on his feet, walking down the hall toward her room. He stopped at LaChaise's room, looked in, then went into the bathroom. Sandy took a breath—but Martin was back in three or four seconds, and now he was moving softly down the hall toward Sandy's door.

He stopped at her door, and she ducked, unable to watch, afraid he'd sense her eyes. She waited, then forced herself to look. Martin was at her door, one hand on her knob. Unmoving, listening.

Sandy's feet were burning: she had to move them, but she couldn't. She was afraid that he'd sense anything, any movement.

Then Martin left her door, came down the hall to the fire escape window, pulled arrows out of his target. Then he turned and went back down the hall, looked around once, put the arrows on a shelf and dropped back on the sleeping bag.

Sandy, still holding her breath, ducked below the window again, sat, lifted her feet off the fire escape and cradled them. They hurt, and for a while there was nothing in her world but her heartbeat and her feet. Had to move. She looked through the crack again. Martin was on the sleeping bag again, but awake, twitching. Twitching? She watched: Jesus, he was masturbating.

Now Sandy was breathing like a locomotive, great gouts of steam puffing out into the cold night air: her feet were freezing, the pain excruciating. She looked at the drop, looked at the ledge, and painfully stepped back over the rail onto the ledge.

Back to the bedroom. She moved faster going back, the pain pushing her. She caught the window ledge and crawled back through. Her feet felt as though she were walking on broken bottles, but she ignored them for the moment and focused on closing the window, carefully, not making a sound.

All right. The room was cold, but there was nothing she could do about that, not right away. She couldn't open the door: Martin might catch a draft. She pulled off her coat, took the boots out, sat on the bare bed, and used the inside of her coat sleeves to wipe her feet.

When they were dry, she touched them, ran her fingers along the soles. No feeling, but no blood, either. She put on her socks and lay back. If she were quiet . . .

Wait. She got on her hands and knees, crawled around the perimeter of the room, and found a hot air register. Open, closed? There was no heat coming out. She looked at the light, decided to risk it. She turned it on, just for a second, looked at the register—closed—and turned it off. Went back to the register, in the dark, and opened it as wide as the adjustment level allowed. Still no heat. The furnace wasn't running at the moment.

What else? The lock. She stepped to the window, twisted the lock, pulled the shade. The window ledge and fire escape would have footprints: nothing she could do about it. Hope for some wind.

She dropped back on the bed, wrapped herself in her parka, and tried to feel her feet. And tried to stave off the disappointment. Twenty feet . . . maybe she should have gone for it. Twenty feet.

NUDE EXCEPT FOR THE WHITE TAPE WRAP ON HIS wound, LaChaise walked out to the living room, looked at the TV, yawned, scratched himself and said, "What's on?"

Martin wouldn't look at him. He said, "That Weather woman was interviewed in the hotel. Didn't say where she was inside, but they got cops all over the place, with shotguns. Vests. Gas. Inside and outside, on the roof."

"Trying to scare us," LaChaise said.

Martin half-laughed and said, "Well, it's working." Still he wouldn't look, and LaChaise stepped over to the window and pulled the blind back an inch or two. Six o'clock in the morning and still dark.

"Sandy sleeping?"

"Yeah," Martin said. "You scared the shit out of her last night."

"Yeah?" He didn't care.

"We're gonna need some heavier gear if we're gonna keep going," Martin said, staring at the TV.

"What've you got in mind?"

"We can't get the hotel, and they're crazy if any of them are staying at home. We can't just hang out on the street, looking for them, 'cause they know what we look like . . ."

"Not with the hair." LaChaise touched his gray hair and beard.

"Well, we couldn't hang long—they're checking everybody."

"So where?"

"The hospital where Capslock's old lady is, and that other cop, Franklin."

"How do you know they're at the same place?"

"Saw it on TV."

"Goddamn. Glad I didn't kick it in," LaChaise said.

"Yeah. So we need some heavier gear."

"You know where to get it?"

"I know a guy. He's a problem, but we can work something out. We'd need Sandy. And we'd have to get moving."

"All right." LaChaise started toward the bathroom; halfway down the hall, he stopped and looked at Harp's record collection and said, "Jesus Christ, what happened to the records?"

"You got pissed off and broke them up."

"Christ, I must've been fucked." LaChaise bent and picked up half a record. *Sketches of Spain*, by Miles Davis. "Some kind of spic music," he said. He yawned again and flipped the broken record into the room, on top of all the other fragments, and went on down to the bathroom.

• • •

SANDY WAS DRESSED, WRAPPED IN THE PARKA, WHEN
LaChaise came to the door.

"Let's go," he said, rapping once.

"Where?"

"You gotta do something for us."

LACHAISE DROVE, WHILE MARTIN GAVE DIRECTIONS
from memory, out this street and down that highway, turn at
the lumber store with the red sign. They were somewhere
west of the city, around a lake. Dozens of ice-fishing shacks
were scattered over the frozen surface of the lake, and pickups
and snowmobiles were parked beside some of the shacks.

"The thing is," Martin said, "is that half his business is
illegal, 'cause he don't believe in gun controls . . . but I do
believe he'd shoot us down like dogs if he had a chance. If
he seen us coming." He looked at Sandy. "So you walk up
to his front door and ring the bell. I'll be right there, next to
the stoop."

"That's . . . I couldn't pull it off," Sandy said.

"Sure you can," Martin said. She remembered the night
before, his eyes over the sights of the pistol.

THE HOUSE WAS A BROWN-SHINGLED RAMBLER ON A
quiet, curving street. Lights showed from a front window and
the back of the house; the car clock said 7:30. Still dark
enough.

"Door latches on the right," Martin said. They continued
past the house, did a U-turn, dropped Martin and waited as
he walked away in the dark. After a minute or so, they started
back toward the house. "Quick beep, all the lights, then just
run up to the house with the bag in your hand," LaChaise
said.

They'd picked up a newspaper at a coin-op box, and

wrapped it in a plastic grocery bag they found in the backseat. "Don't fuck it up."

Sandy held on: just this thing, they said.

"Now," said LaChaise.

They pulled up to the house, stopped in the middle of the driveway. Sandy gave the horn a light beep, then hopped out of the car, carrying in the paper. At the same moment, Martin duck-walked down the front of the house, until he was directly beneath the stoop, on the right side of the door under the latch, but pressed to the side of the house.

Sandy saw a white-haired man come to what must be a kitchen window as she hurried up the driveway, shivering from the cold. The man was holding a mug of coffee, his forehead wrinkling at the sight of her. She hurried up the stoop and rang the doorbell. Martin's face was just beside her right pant leg, a .45 in his hand. The door opened, and the white-haired man pushed the storm door open a crack and said, "Yes?"

Sandy pulled the door open another foot, and Martin stood up and pushed his pistol at the man inside. "Don't move, Frank. Don't even think about moving."

"Oh, boy," the man said. He had a surprisingly soft, cultured voice, Sandy thought, for a gun dealer. He backed up, his hands in front of him. LaChaise was out of the car, and Martin pushed Frank into the house, Sandy following, and LaChaise coming up behind.

Inside, Martin said, "He'll have a three-fifty-seven under his sweater, back on his hip, Dick, if you want to get that . . ."

LaChaise patted the man, found the gun.

Martin went on, "And he might have an ankle piece . . ." LaChaise dropped to his knees, and the man said, "Left ankle," and LaChaise found a hammerless revolver.

"You dress like this to have coffee, I'd hate to see you

getting ready for trouble,'' LaChaise said, grinning at the man.

The man looked at him for a moment, then turned back to Martin. "What do you want?"

"Couple of special AKs, out of that safe in the basement. A couple of vests."

"You boys are dead, you know that?"

Martin nodded. "Yeah. Which is why maybe you shouldn't fight us. There's no percentage in it, 'cause we just don't give a fuck anymore."

The man nodded and said, "Down this way."

FRANK HAD THREE GUN SAFES IN THE BASEMENT, aligned along a wall with a workbench and a separate reloading bench. He reached for the combination dial on the middle safe, but Martin stopped him, made him recite the combination, and ordered Sandy to open it. He pressed his pistol to the back of the man's neck: "If anything happens—if there's a bang or a siren, or a phone line, you'll be dead."

"There's nothing," Frank said.

Martin said to LaChaise, "He's probably got a hand piece stashed behind something down here, where he can get it quick. Keep your gun pointed at him." And to Frank, he said, "I'm sorry about this, but you know what our problem is."

Sandy finished the combination, grasped the handle on the safe, turned her head away and tugged. The safe door opened easily; Martin said, "All right." Sandy almost didn't hear him: she'd seen the obsolete black dial telephone on the gun bench.

"You got him?" Martin asked LaChaise.

LaChaise moved a little sideways to Frank, and kept the gun pointed at his ear. Martin brushed past Sandy, reached into the safe and took out an AR-15. *"All right,"* he said, finding the custom selector switch. He quickly field-stripped it, found nothing wrong, put it together. There were three guns in the safe, and two dozen boxes of ammo. Martin took it all, stuffing the ammo boxes in his coat pockets until they were full, handing the rest to Sandy.

"And the vests," Martin said.

"Over in the corner closet," Frank said.

Martin walked across the basement to a closet with a sliding door, pushed it back, found a row of Kevlar vests in plastic sacks. He selected two of them, then glanced at Sandy, and took a third.

"I'm really sorry about this," Martin said. He handed the vests to Sandy, put his gun on Frank and prodded him toward the stairs. LaChaise went up ahead of them, so they could keep the white-haired man covered around corners.

Sandy fumbled one of the boxes of ammo, then another one. They hit the floor, and shells spewed out. "Oh, shit," she said.

"Goddamnit," Martin growled. "Get those . . ."

Sandy stooped, and began picking up the cartridges, stuffing them into her pockets, as the men climbed the stairs.

When they reached the top, and had started down the hall, Sandy darted to the telephone and dialed 911. The operator answered a second later, and she said, "This is Sandy Darling calling for Chief Davenport. We're here buying guns. They're gonna attack someplace. I'll leave the phone off the hook and try to keep them here . . ."

She placed the phone sideways across the top of the receiver and hurried up the stairs after LaChaise and Martin.

TWENTY

━━━◆◆◆━━━

LUCAS AND DEL WERE WAKING UP WITH DAY-OLD DAN-
ish and plastic foam cups of fake cappuccino when Dispatch
called.

"Woman called for you and identified herself as Sandy
Darling," the dispatcher said without preamble, excitement
under her steady voice. "Said they were buying guns and
they're gonna attack something, but she didn't say what or
when. She left the phone off the hook. We've got Minnetonka
started that way, but they've got almost nobody around: it'll
be a few minutes."

"Well, Jesus . . ." Lucas jumped up and grabbed his coat
as he spoke into the phone: "How long ago did she call?"

"Thirty-five seconds."

"Warn Minnetonka about the guns. Don't let some guy be
a hero, just seal off the streets around the address and bring
in a team, or whatever they do out there . . . If they need aid,
get Lester and see if we can ship some of our ERU guys out,
or maybe Hennepin County guys."

"Marie is doing that now, most of it. Are you going?"

"Yeah. Gimme the address . . ."

He scribbled it down and said, "Direct us in there: we'll be on the air in one minute."

He slammed the phone down and Del said, "What?" and Lucas said, "Darling called. She said they're buying guns and she left the phone off the hook." They were already running down the hallway.

LACHAISE AND MARTIN HAD ROLLED THE RIFLES UNDER their coats, and when Sandy came up from the basement, Martin asked, "Get it all?"

"I got most of it," she said, rattling the shells in her pockets. She felt herself flushing, and thought, Oh my God; Martin would figure it out. She said, "There's a lot more ammo down there. I think we missed most of it . . ."

"Forget it," Martin said. He turned away and said to Frank, "Here." He handed the white-haired man a wad of cash.

"This is not exactly a purchase," Frank said, tightly.

"Take the fuckin' money," Martin said impatiently. "I feel bad enough anyway. The cash comes off a drug dealer downtown, there's no tracing it, it's all clean. It'll more than cover the cost of the stuff."

"Still not right," Frank said. He took the money.

"I know," Martin said, almost gently. "But there's no help for it. Now walk us out to the car so you can wave good-bye."

They were in the car, rolling, and Frank went back to the house with his hands in his pockets. They turned the corner, headed down another side street, then out to the highway. As they sat at the intersection, waiting for the light, a dark sedan crossed the highway against the light, and flashed past, heading into the welter of streets they'd just left.

"Asshole," LaChaise muttered.

Sandy closed her eyes.

LUCAS PUSHED THE EXPLORER OUT I-394, HIS FOOT TO the floor, the car banging and creaking with the speed, Del braced in the passenger seat, cursing with every slip and bump. Dispatch said the owner of the phone was a guy named Frank Winter, no priors anywhere, but he was a registered federal firearms dealer.

"So she knew what she was talking about," Del said.

Ten minutes after they left City Hall, they found a phalanx of City of Minnetonka and Hennepin County cars blocking access to the subdivision. Lucas hung his badge out the window and a cop pointed at a group of men, some in uniform and some in plainclothes. Lucas parked and he and Del walked over.

The command cops looked up and one of them, in plainclothes, said, "Lucas," and Lucas nodded and said, "Gene, what's happening?"

"We got a couple of guys in the house across the street," the cop said. "There're lights on, but there's no cars out front. There's a set of tracks going up into the driveway, and then backing out. Pretty fresh. We've had this off-and-on snow and the guys say the tracks are crisp."

"Might have come and gone," a uniformed cop said.

"The question is, do we call ahead? Or do we just take the place?"

Lucas shrugged and grinned at him. "You da man."

"Yeah, right," the plainclothes cop said sourly. Then, "Fuck it. He's a firearms dealer, so he could have all kinds of shit in there . . . If we go bustin' in, we could have a fight. If we call ahead, what can they do? Can't get out."

He was thinking out loud. One of the Hennepin cops said,

"He can't flush the evidence down the toilet."

"Huh. All right. Let's call."

FRANK WINTER CAME OUT OF THE HOUSE WITH HIS hands over his head, and stood that way in the driveway, until an armored cop directed him down the middle of the street to a blocking car. Winter said on the phone that LaChaise, Martin and Darling had been there—had left only fifteen minutes earlier—but the house was now empty. When he got to the blocking car, where Lucas and Del were waiting with a group of uniformed cops, one of the uniforms turned Winter around and patted him down.

"He's wearing a vest," one of the cops said.

"Why the vest?" Del asked.

"In case one of you officers decided to shoot me," Winter said simply. "The woman called you in, didn't she?"

"What woman?"

"The one with Martin and his friend," Winter said. Then, "Do I need a lawyer?"

"Better give him his rights," Lucas said, and one of the cops recited the code. "You want one?"

"Yeah, I better," Winter said. "I was sitting there, thinking about calling you, when you called me."

"Why didn't you?" Lucas asked.

"Because I figured Martin would kill me, or LaChaise."

"What'd they get from you?" Del asked.

"A couple of pistols, an accurized seven-mil-Magnum Model 70 and a box of handloads and a whole bunch of AR-15 ammo. Martin's an Armalite freak: he's always reworking them. I'd be careful. I'd bet they've got modified with them."

"This Model 70," Lucas said. "Got a scope?"

"Yeah. A Leupold Vari-X III in 3.5 × 10."

"A sniper rifle."

"A varminter," said Winter.

"Yeah, if elk are varmints," Lucas said.

AN ENTRY TEAM SWEPT THE HOUSE. THE BASEMENT WAS an arsenal, but, as one of the cops said cheerfully, "Nothin' illegal about that."

Lucas was looking at a Model 70, a gray synthetic-stocked Winchester .300 Magnum with a Pentax scope. He turned the eyepiece down to two-power and sighted across the basement at a crosshairs target. Winter had opened the gun safes so the weapons could be inventoried, and they'd found fifty hand-guns, two dozen rifles and as many shotguns. Del was playing with a derringer, snapping it at a wall target, and Lucas was looking at the butt of the Model 70, when a plainclothes cop came halfway down the stairs and said, "We're sending Win-ter downtown. You got anything else you want to ask him?"

"Naw. I kind of think he's telling the truth," Lucas said.

"So do I, but he should have called us," the cop said. He grinned and said, "Now he claims he tried to call out, but his phone was screwed up and he was afraid to go out. Says he didn't know the phone was off the hook down here, just that it didn't work."

"Not bad, if he sticks to it," Lucas said.

The cop said, "We got guys walking the neighborhood, checking about the car." Winter had said LaChaise, Martin and Darling were in a big brown car, but he didn't notice what kind because he wasn't thinking about it. Maybe a Lin-coln or a Buick. The cop went on, "The media are swarming in."

"Jesus, that was quick," Del said.

"They're monitoring everything . . ."

"Can't let them know that there was a tip," Lucas said. "LaChaise'll know where it came from and he'll kill the woman."

"What'll I tell them? They'll want to know."

Lucas scratched his head, formulating the lie: "Tell them that Winter called us. Tell them that we used an entry team because we were concerned it might be some kind of ambush, and Winter was known to be a gun dealer with heavy weapons . . . Get that word out quick, so we don't get anybody speculating about tips . . . I'll get my chief to back us up, and we'll talk to Winter's lawyer about keeping Winter's mouth shut."

"All right." The cop nodded, and hurried back up the stairs.

Lucas turned to Del and said, "Look at this."

Del came over and Lucas knelt by the gun safe and said, "See the dust?"

There was a faint patina of dust on the floor of the middle safe, where Winter said he'd kept the stolen guns.

Del nodded. "Yeah?"

"Three guns were taken out of here. See? You can just barely see the outlines . . ." Lucas traced the dust outlines in the air, his finger a half-inch above them.

"Yeah?"

"Watch this . . ." He put the Model 70 in a rack-slot on the opposite end of the gun safe, and wiggled it in place. When he picked it up, he'd left in the dust an almost imperceptible outline of the gun butt.

"Doesn't look the same," Del said. "Too fat."

"But he said a Model 70 and this is a Model 70." He turned to the Minnetonka cop doing the inventory. "Give me one of those ARs, would you?"

The cop handed him an AR, a legal, unmodified rifle, and Lucas printed the butt in the dust next to the Model 70 imprint. The two prints were distinctly different—but the AR's print matched the dust shadows of the three stolen guns.

"They took the ARs out of here," Del said.

"And they're modified," Lucas said. "That's why he laid that rap on us about Martin modifying guns. He wanted us to know that they're running around with machine guns, but he didn't want to say they came from him."

"I'm getting pretty fuckin' tired of this machine gun shit," Del said.

"Let's get a photographer down here and see if we can get some shots of this," Lucas said, tapping the edge of the safe. "I don't know if we can get Winter or not. He's a smart guy. But maybe we can fuck with him a little."

"Why'd they come out for more guns? They've got guns."

"Because of Franklin," Lucas said. "If they'd shot Franklin with an AR, it would've gone through that vest like it was cheese." He took a slow turn around the basement, looking up at the ceiling: the ceiling was neat, just the way the rest of the basement was. Lucas's basement joists were full of cobwebs, which he had every intention of leaving alone.

"Say they took three ARs off Winter. And he says they took three vests. I'd say they're gonna make a suicide run."

"On what? The hotel?"

"Maybe," Lucas said, but then shook his head. "I really think it's gonna come somewhere else. They gotta figure that none of us are hanging around home, not after Franklin. They can't get at the hotel, we've made that pretty clear."

"They're gonna hit the hospital," Del said, suddenly white-faced. "They're going back in after Cheryl and Franklin, and Franklin's old lady's been over there . . . Shit, where's the telephone?"

STADIC HEARD ABOUT THE SCRAMBLE OUT TO MINNE-tonka, and called LaChaise, while LaChaise, Martin and Sandy were still driving back downtown.

"They're out there now," he said, with thin satisfaction. "They were about five minutes off your ass."

"What happened to Winter?" LaChaise asked, prompted by Martin.

"They're talking to him. The way I heard it, he's cooperating."

"Fucker must've called them the minute we were gone," LaChaise said. "They got the car?"

"I don't know," Stadic said.

"We better get out of sight."

"Yeah: and one more thing. Me and a half-dozen other guys are supposed to be on the way to Hennepin General. They think you might be on the way there."

"What? Why?"

"I don't know, but we're on the way over there. They talked to Winter, and he must've said something."

"I gotta think," LaChaise said. "Something's screwy."

STADIC SAT BEHIND A DESK IN THE EMERGENCY ROOM, a shotgun by his feet, while Lester and another cop named Davis talked about ways of blocking off the drive without being too conspicuous about it. Lucas and Del showed up, cold, damp, hurried.

"You get the new composites on the street?" Lucas asked Lester.

"Yeah, and we got the car out," Lester said. As they talked, they drifted toward a group of chairs a few feet from Stadic. "Big brown car. What the fuck does that mean? What we got to do is break out where they're hiding."

"Until we do that . . ."

Davenport went on talking but Stadic blanked. All he could think of was, Big Brown Car. And he thought, *Oh, shit, they're at Harp's.*

At noon, he was relieved of duty. He stopped at the office just long enough to pick up a pair of 8×50 naval binoculars, then drove down toward Harp's place. He stopped a block and a half away and put the glasses on the windows above the laundromat. He hadn't been watching for more than five minutes when he saw the blinds move—somebody looking out at the street.

All right, he had them again. Same deal? He could wait in the street until they came out—they'd be in the car, that'd be a problem. He could maybe park across the street, and wait: and when he saw the garage door going up, he could run over to the driver's side, blow it up from one foot away—press the muzzle of the shotgun against the glass and pull the trigger. That would take out the driver, then the other guy . . . He'd need his vest.

He chewed his thumbnail nervously. A lot could go wrong. There'd be questions, later, too. But he could talk those away. He kept thinking about the death of Sell-More, he'd say, and how Harp seemed to tie into it. He ran Harp's name on the computer and came up with a Lincoln . . . but why wouldn't he tell everybody at that point? Why would he go in by himself?

He tried to work it through, but his mind wasn't right: too tired. He drove past the apartment to a liquor store with a pay phone, and dialed LaChaise again.

"We're looking for a big brown car, a Lincoln or a Buick."

"That's it? No tags?"

"No tags. But they've got a new composite out on you—it won't be on TV until the late news, they want to see if you hit the hospital. But they say you've got gray hair, and gray beards, and you look like old men."

"That fuckin' Winter," LaChaise said. Then, "What's it like at the hospital. Security?"

"Tighter than a drum."

"Goddamnit . . ."

''If I was you, I'd think about packing up and getting out,'' Stadic said. ''Your time's running out.''

After a moment, LaChaise said, ''Maybe.''

Stadic could hear him breathing; five seconds, ten. Then Stadic said, ''Really?''

''We're talking about it,'' LaChaise said. ''Mexico.''

TWENTY-ONE

THE WHOLE DAY DRAGGED, THE HOURS SQUEEZING BY:
every cop in the department was on the street: there were
rumors that the local gangs were filling up the Chicago-bound
buses, just to get out of the pressure.

Lucas had run out of ideas, and spent half the day at the
hospital, with dwindling expectations.

Night came, but no LaChaise . . .

THE HOSPITAL WAS QUIET, DARK. NURSES PADDED
around in running shoes, answering calls from individual
rooms, pushing pills. Lucas, Del and a narcotics cop named
McKinney hung out in an office just off the main lobby.
There was no telling where LaChaise and Martin would try
to crack the place—if they tried at all—but from the lobby,
they could move quickly to either end of the building.

"Unless they come in by parachute," McKinney said.

"That'd be good," Del said. "You see that movie?"

"Yeah . . . actually, there've been a couple of them. There
was that one where the guy jumps out of the plane without a

'chute, you see that one? Grabs the guy in midair?''

''What's-his-name was in it, the kid, you know, the *Excellent Adventure* guy,'' Lucas said.

''Yeah, I saw that,'' said McKinney. ''That's what got me jumpin'.''

''Hey, you jump? Far out . . .''

They talked about skydiving until they wore it out, then Lucas went back down the hall and crawled into an empty bed. Del sat up with McKinney; when first light came, he put his gun away and went to sit with Cheryl until she woke.

"YOU WANT ME TO DRIVE?" MARTIN ASKED SANDY.

''No, I'm okay,'' she said.

''Watch your speed. We don't want to attract no cops,'' Martin said.

''Maybe we should of stopped in Des Moines,'' LaChaise said. ''This is a long fuckin' way.''

LaChaise had spent the trip in the backseat. Whenever they passed a highway patrolman—they'd seen three—he sprawled out of sight.

''Yeah, well, we're almost there,'' Martin said. ''See that glow out there? Way off, straight ahead? That's Kansas City.''

They'd made the decision late in the afternoon, LaChaise and Martin, and just after dark, LaChaise had walked back to the bedroom and said, ''Get your stuff ready.''

Sandy sat up. ''Where're we going?''

''Mexico.''

''Mexico? Dick, are you serious?'' She felt a quick beat of hope. If they made it out of town, they'd have some room. And someplace along the road, they'd forget about her for a while, and she'd walk away. A dusty little restaurant someplace, a small town out on the desert . . . she'd wait until they started eating, then she'd tell them she had to go to the ladies' room and then she'd walk out, leave a note on the car seat, hide until they were gone.

It was all there, in her mind's eye: and when they were gone—long gone—she'd turn herself in. Work it out.

A possibility.

But now Dick was complaining that they'd come too far? What was all that about?

She thought about it, a sinking feeling, and finally asked, "Why is Kansas City too far, Dick?" He didn't answer immediately. "Dick?"

"Because we don't want to drive in the daytime," Martin said. He looked at his watch. "It'll be light in another hour. We've got to find a motel."

Martin spotted an all-night supermarket on the outskirts of the city, and told Sandy to take the off ramp. LaChaise waited in the car with Sandy until Martin returned: he'd bought two loaves of bread, a couple of pounds of sandwich meat, and two big bars of dark green auto mechanic's soap.

"What's the soap for?" Sandy asked, peering into the bag.

"Whittlin'," Martin said, grinning at her.

LaChaise rented a room in a chain motel called the Red Roof Inn. LaChaise went in because he'd shaved just before they left the Cities, and Sandy had given him a neat trim. Wearing one of Harp's suits with a silk tie, he looked like a Republican. He paid cash for the room, two days, said he was alone, and asked that the maid be told not to wake him up.

"Been traveling all night," he said.

"No problem," said the woman behind the desk.

The room was on the back side of the motel, with two double beds and a TV. They slept, restlessly, until two o'clock, when Martin got up and ordered a pizza, Coke and coffee from a local pizza place. The stuff was delivered, no questions, and they ate silently. At four, with the sun slipping down in the west, they went back out to the car.

Martin said, "I'll drive."

"That's all right, I . . ."

"Get in the back and shut up," LaChaise said.

"What's going on?" Sandy asked. LaChaise grabbed her by the jacket and jerked her forward, until his face was only an inch from hers: she could smell the cheese and onions from the pizza.

"Change of plans. Now get in the fuckin' car."

She got in the car. "Dick, what're you going to do? Dick . . . ?"

"We're gonna rob another goddamned credit union, is what we're gonna do," LaChaise said.

LUCAS WAS AT THE HOSPITAL BECAUSE HE COULDN'T think of any better place to be: they now hadn't heard from LaChaise for thirty-six hours. Del, Sloan, Sherrill came and went and returned. They were running out of conversational gambits, sitting in dark rooms, out of sight, waiting . . .

Lester called. "Lucas: LaChaise, Martin and Darling just hit a credit union in Kansas City. Not more than an hour ago—four twenty-five."

"Kansas City?" The news came like a punch, left him unsteady. "Are they sure?"

"Yeah, they say there's no doubt. We're getting a video-tape relayed through TV3. The Kansas City cops gave it to everybody in sight."

"How soon will you have the tape?"

"Ten or fifteen minutes, I guess. TV3's putting it on the air soon as they get it. We're gonna tape it off them."

Lucas hung up and looked at Sherrill and Sloan: "You ain't gonna believe it," he said.

THE ROBBERY WAS SMOOTH, PROFESSIONAL. MARTIN was in first with an AR-15. He was shouting the moment he came through the door, leveling the rifle, pointing at people.

LaChaise pushed Sandy Darling through the door behind Martin, then vaulted up on the counter. There were only two customers in the place, and three people behind the counter. LaChaise looted the cash drawers, said something to one of the younger women, smacked her on the ass with the palm of his hand and crossed through the counter gate. The camera, taking in the whole office, showed Sandy Darling pressed against the wall, her hands over her ears.

"They ain't no cherries," Del said. They were in homicide, fifteen guys and four women standing around a small TV.

"You've seen it before," Lucas said. "It's the same god-damn robbery that we broke up, all over again."

"Except for the grenade," Sherrill said.

As they were backing out the door, Martin gave a little speech. "We want everybody into the manager's office, on the floor, behind the desk. We're gonna roll a hand grenade in here . . . now I don't want to scare anyone, 'cause they're nothing like you see in movies. There'll just be a little pop. You'll be fine if you're behind the desk . . ."

Martin held up what looked like a grenade, and the office staff and customers jammed into the manager's office, out of sight. Martin called, "Here we go," and rolled the grenade into the room, and disappeared. The grenade turned out to be a hand-carved lump of green soap that didn't look too much like a grenade, when you looked at it close.

"No plates," Lucas grunted, watching. "They didn't want anybody to run out and see the car and get the plates."

"Darling didn't look too happy to be there. No gun, she looked scared, they had to push her in and out," Sloan said.

"They got eight grand," said somebody else.

"So he says to this chick," Lester began, and then corrected himself, ". . . this woman, the teller, he says, 'You oughta make it to Acapulco sometime, honey.' "

"Sounds like bullshit," said Del.

"I don't know," Lester said. "He's the kind of guy who'd say something like that." He looked around the room: "I wish we'd taken him here, goddamnit."

LATE THAT NIGHT, SANDY SAT IN THE BACKSEAT, UN-moving, wide awake, not quite believing it. The lights of Des Moines were fading in the rear window. They were headed back to Minneapolis, ahead of what the all-night stations were saying was a major storm coming up from the Southwest. Already blizzard conditions in Nebraska.

They'd be in the Cities by dawn, back in the apartment. The whole thing had been a game, to loosen up the targets.

"A stroke of fuckin' genius," LaChaise said, pounding Martin on the back. "I just wish we had someplace to spend the cash."

TWENTY-TWO

———◀◉▶———

LUCAS SAT AWAKE, TRYING TO MAKE SENSE OF IT. IF LaChaise and Martin were on a suicide run—and it had appeared that way from the beginning—what had changed their minds? They couldn't believe that escape was as simple as running to Mexico. The Mexicans would ship them back to the States as quickly as they were found; or kill them.

Maybe it was simpler than he was making it: maybe their nerve failed.

He got up, hands in his pockets, and stared out the window across his snow-covered lawn. In the distance, on the other side of the Mississippi, he could see Christmas lights red, green and white along somebody's roofline. A silent night.

And he was restless. He hadn't wanted Weather to come back to the house—one more night in the hotel, he'd said, just until we find their trail again—but she'd insisted. She wanted to sleep in her own bed. She was in it now, and sleeping soundly.

Lucas was sitting up with a pistol and a twelve-gauge Wingmaster pump. He looked at a clock: four in the morning.

He picked up a TV remote, pointed at a small TV in the corner of the room, and called up the aviation weather service. All day, the weather forecasters had been talking about a huge low-pressure system that was pinwheeling up from the southern Rockies. Snow had overrun all of the southwestern and south-central parts of the state, and now the weather radar showed it edging into the metro area.

If they were coming back, he thought—if this thing was no more than a shuck—and if they'd fallen behind the snow line, they might be stalled for a day. If they'd stayed ahead of it, they'd be coming into town about now.

Nobody thought they'd be coming back. The network TV people were getting out of town as fast as they could pack up and find space on an outgoing plane. Nobody wanted to be stuck out in flyover country the week before Christmas, not with a big storm coming.

The cops were the same way: going home, filing for overtime. Lucas called Kansas City cops, and the Missouri and Kansas highway patrols every hour, looking for even the faintest sniff of LaChaise. Nobody had gotten one: they'd vanished.

Just as if they'd taken country roads east and north, instead of west and south, where the search was focused, Lucas thought. He looked out the window again, then self-consciously went and closed the wooden blinds.

After killing the TV, he wandered through the dark house, moving by touch, listening, trailing the shotgun. He checked the security system, got a drink of water and went back to the living room where he dropped on a couch. In a few minutes, he eased into a fitful sleep, the .45 in a belly holster, the shotgun on the coffee table.

THEY STAYED AHEAD OF THE SNOW.

They drove through southern Iowa in the crackling cold,

millions of stars but no moon, following the red and yellow lights of the freighter trucks heading into Des Moines, and after Des Moines, up toward Minneapolis-St. Paul. They stopped once at a gas station, the bare-faced LaChaise pumping the gas and paying a sleepy attendant, the hood of his parka covering his head, a scarf shrouding his neck.

"Colder'n a witch's left tit," the attendant said. He looked at a thermometer in the window. "Six below. You want some Heat to put in the gas?"

"Yeah, that'd be good," LaChaise said. A compact television sat in a corner, turned to CNN. As the attendant was ringing up the sale, a security-camera videotape came up, replaying the Kansas City robbery.

"What's that shit?" LaChaise asked.

The attendant glanced at the TV. "Ah, it's them assholes that were up in the Cities. They're making a run for Mexico."

"Good," LaChaise said.

"Wisht I was going with them," the attendant said, and he counted out the change.

As they continued up I-35, the nighttime radio stations came and went, playing Christmas music. Clouds began to move in, like dark arrows overhead; the stars winked out.

"Christmas, four days," Sandy said, sadness in her voice.

"Don't mean a fuckin' thing to me," LaChaise said. "My old man drank up our Christmases."

"You must of had a few," Sandy said.

LaChaise sat silent for a moment, then said, "Maybe a couple." He thought about his sister and her feetsie pajamas.

Martin said, "We had a couple of good ones, when my old man was alive. He got me a fire engine, once."

"What happened to him?" Sandy asked.

"He died," Martin said. "Throat cancer."

"Jeez, that's awful," Sandy said. "I'm sorry."

"Hard way to go," Martin said. "Then it was me and my

ma, and we didn't have no Christmases after that.''

LaChaise didn't like the subject matter and fiddled with the radio: the scanner locked on ''O Holy Night.''

''I know this song; my old man used to sing it,'' Martin said.

And he sang along in a creditable baritone,

O holy night, the stars are brightly shining, this is the night of the birth of Our Lord.

Sandy and LaChaise, astonished, glanced at each other: then Sandy looked out the windows, at the thin snowflakes now streaking past, and felt like she was a long way from anywhere.

They drove in silence for a long time, and Sandy slept off and on. She woke with the sense that it was much later, sat up, and looked out. They'd slowed: the snow was now coming at the front of the car like a tornado funnel, but they were passing through a bridge of light.

''Where are we?'' she asked.

''Just south of the Cities,'' Martin said. ''We'll be in town in twenty minutes.''

''Lots of snow.''

''Started hard about ten minutes ago,'' Martin said. He looked at LaChaise.

''What do you think?''

''Let's do it. Get back, drop Sandy and do it.'' He looked out the window. ''This storm is perfect. We won't get a better shot than this.''

''What?'' Sandy asked.

LaChaise looked back over the seat. ''We're gonna take the hospital.''

LACHAISE CAME TO HIM IN A DREAM. LUCAS WAS ON THE couch, struggling to wake up, but he couldn't. He was too tired, and whenever he tried to open his eyes, he'd immediately fall back into a deep sleep—and then struggle out again. He *had* to wake up, because LaChaise and Martin and Darling were sneaking through the garage, coming up to the kitchen door, guns in their hands, laughing, while Lucas struggled to wake . . .

"Lucas. Lucas . . ."

He bolted up, and Weather jumped back. "Whoa," he said. "Sorry."

"That's okay. You wanted me to wake you . . ."

"Time to go?"

She was dressed in slacks and a long-sleeved blouse, operating clothes, and was carrying a plastic bag with one of her simple black Donna Karan suits from Saks. Faculty meetings. "Pretty soon. I'll put some coffee on. It's snowing like crazy out there."

MARTIN SKETCHED OUT THE LAYOUT OF THE EIGHTH Street entry of the Hennepin County Medical Center, from the earlier recon.

"Two doors: the main emergency room is locked. We could fake that we're hurt, and they'd let us in, but there'll be a bunch of people there . . ." He tapped the second door. "This one leads back to the main lobby, right past the emergency room—the emergency room is off to the left, down this hall. There's a guard desk just inside. If we was hurt, he'd let us in, I seen hurt people come in that door. But we'd have to take him out . . ."

"No problem."

". . . Then we go on down the hall and the elevators are over to the left. We want the second-floor surgical care . . ."

They worked through it: get the room numbers at the front desk, get up, hit the place, get out.

Martin said, "It's six blocks or so: if we really got in trouble, we could run back here in five minutes, on foot. That snow'd help: can't see shit in the snow, not until dawn. We got almost two hours yet.''

"Let's do it.''

Sandy didn't want to hear about it. She paced in the bedroom, stared at the walls: but not dumbly. Her mind was a torrent, a jumble of suppositions and possibilities. She looked at the window and thought, *I should have jumped.*

In the front room, Martin and LaChaise geared up—each with two pistols and an AR-15, each wearing a bulletproof vest. "Wish I could take the bow,'' Martin said.

"Makes no sense,'' LaChaise grunted.

"What about Sandy?'' Martin asked, dropping his voice. "Chain her up again?''

"If we don't, she'll split,'' LaChaise said.

"Which wouldn't be that terrible, if she didn't tip off the cops.''

"She would,'' LaChaise said. "She's been thinking about how to get out—how to save her ass.''

Martin nodded. "Yeah. Well. We could do her.''

LaChaise said, "Yeah, we could.''

"Can't take her with us,'' Martin said.

LaChaise pulled on his long winter coat, slipped his arm out of one sleeve, and held the AR-15 beneath it. "How do I look?'' he asked Martin.

"Okay, as long as you're a little ways off.''

"Huh.'' LaChaise turned the weapon in his hands, looked back toward the bedroom and said, "If you want to do her, you could. Or we could just chain her up again.''

Martin thought for a minute, and said, "If we do this right—if we faked them out—we could be coming back. We might need her.''

"So we chain her up,'' LaChaise said.

"Well—unless you really want to do her.''

· · ·

LACHAISE CAME INTO THE BEDROOM AND SAID, "WE'RE gonna have to chain you up again."

"Dick, for God's sakes . . ."

"Hey, shut up. Listen. We can't let you go to the cops. And you would. So we're gonna chain you up. It's either that, or . . ." He shrugged.

"You shoot me."

"Probably wouldn't shoot you," he said.

The way he said it chilled her. Probably wouldn't shoot her. Probably kill her with a knife, she thought. Martin liked the knife.

"So put your coat on . . ."

She put her coat on, afraid to say anything at all. She was standing on a knife edge. She went ahead of LaChaise, down the stairs, where Martin was waiting like Old Man Death. He was holding the chain.

"Sorry about this," he said, but he didn't sound sorry.

They'd put the chair back next to the post, and they chained her into it again, snapping the padlocks. "You'll be okay," LaChaise said.

"What if you don't come back?" she blurted.

He said, "You better hope we do—you'd have to get pretty damn skinny to get out of that chain." He grinned at his own wit, then said, "We'll leave the keys over on the steps."

He dropped the keys on the steps, far out of reach, and then they got in the car, ran the garage door up, backed out, and dropped the door, Sandy disappearing behind it.

"Glad we didn't do her," LaChaise said.

"Yeah?"

"When we do her, I want to fuck her first. She always sorta treated me like I wasn't . . . good enough."

LUCAS FOLLOWED WEATHER TO A PARKING RAMP A block from the University Hospitals, a slippery slog through the heavy, wet snow. On the way, he checked with Del, who was staying at the hospital, to see if he was awake yet.

"Just barely," Del said. "I'm thinking about brushing my teeth."

"Cheryl's still asleep?"

"Like a baby."

"I'm heading into the office," Lucas said. "I'll walk over later."

"Is it snowing yet?"

"Look out the window," Lucas said. "It's gonna be a nightmare."

Lucas followed Weather into the parking ramp, waited until she'd parked her car, then drove her back out of the ramp to the hospital entrance, and saw her as far as the front desk.

"This is a little ridiculous," she said.

"I'll feel funny about it when I hear LaChaise is dead," he said.

Inside, he said, "Call me before you head home." She waved a hand as she headed toward the elevators, turned the corner out of sight.

Lucas headed back to the car. He'd had the shotgun between the seats, and now he put it on the floor in front of the backseats, out of sight. He had to use the wipers to clear the window, and he horsed the Explorer out of the parking circle and headed toward the office.

TWENTY-THREE

LACHAISE LOOKED AT MARTIN: "THIS IS IT, DUDE."

Martin nodded. "Could be."

"We could drive north up to Canada, run out of the snow, head west . . ."

Martin said, "The Canadians got computers at the border. We'd set them off like a skyrocket."

LaChaise was silent for a minute: "Probably couldn't get out of the snow anyway." They slowed at a cross street, and a single orange plow truck, its blade raised off the roadway, went banging by: "Look at that asshole. Doing nothing, probably getting overtime." LaChaise's mouth was running: "You scared?"

Martin seemed to think for a minute. "No," he said.

"Tense?"

"I'm . . . thinking."

"Somebody ought to," LaChaise joked.

"We gotta be ready to ditch the car," he said. "I don't think we'll get in and out without running into somebody—we can take them if we're fast enough, that won't be a prob-

lem, but in maybe two or three minutes, we'll have cops coming in from the outside, ready for us. If we've got them hot
on our trail, you go left and I'll go right. But remember, they
can track us: try to stay in the street where you can. That'll
slow them down . . .''

"That's just if we have trouble."

"Yeah."

LUCAS CROSSED THE MISSISSIPPI ON THE WASHING-
ton Avenue bridge, rolled through a couple of turns in Cedar-
Riverside and eased the Explorer into the loop. He could
make thirty miles an hour, but even in four-wheel drive, the
truck's wheels kept breaking loose. The driver's-side windshield wiper, which had never worked right, left a frozen
streak just at his eye level. He had the radio going, and the
morning show guy on 'CCO said there'd be a foot of snow
on the ground when the storm ended.

*"We've got school closings all over southwest and east-
central Minnesota, and the Minneapolis and St. Paul
systems will be making a call in the next ten minutes.
The governor'll probably shut down state government,
since he does it every time somebody sees a snowflake
. . . don't get me started on that, though . . ."*

A cop car was pulling out of the driveway at the medical
center when LaChaise and Martin arrived. They coasted to
the curb and sat for two minutes, letting the cop get well clear,
then Martin said, "You're the hurt one. Pull your hat down."

"I'm good," LaChaise said. He was breathing through his
mouth again, gulping air. "My fuckin' heart feels like it's
gonna explode."

Martin took the car into the emergency entrance drive:
"You won't notice when we get inside."

"This is a fuckin' war, man," LaChaise said. "This is like fuckin' 'Nam."

"Especially the snow," Martin said.

MARTIN STOPPED OUTSIDE THE FIRST OF THE TWO doors and left the car running. If they made it back, it'd be quicker. If they didn't, who cared what happened to the car?

LaChaise got out of the driver's side, and limped toward the door to the lobby. Martin ran around the front of the car and caught him, slipped an arm around him, and they hobbled to the entrance. The door was open, all right, and just like Martin said, a security guard was looking at them from a phone-booth-sized security room just inside the entrance.

"Little help," Martin grunted at the guard. "He's hurt."

The guard didn't even hesitate, but went out a small door on the side of the room into a hall and walked up to them and said, "What's the . . ."

And saw the guns.

"Turn around," Martin said quietly, pointing the AR-15 at the guard's chest. "We don't want to hurt you."

"Aw, shit."

"Yeah, shit," LaChaise said. "Turn around."

The guard wavered and then said, "Naw. Fuck you."

"Fuck me?" Too quickly to see, Martin struck the guard in the face with the butt of the eight-pound rifle, a horizontal stroke that caught the man in the forehead with the force of a small sledge. The guard jerked back into the wall and slid to the floor.

"Go," Martin said, but LaChaise was already moving, heading down the hall to the lobby.

Visiting hours didn't start until midmorning, so only seven people turned to look at them when they walked into the lobby: a woman and two children; two young men who sat together; a teenaged girl who curled on a chair, reading a romance novel; and the woman behind the reception desk, who said, "Great God Almighty."

They did it like a bank job: LaChaise faced the people waiting in the lobby chairs, and made his little speech: "Don't anybody move . . ."

Martin focused on the woman behind the counter: "We want the room numbers for Capslock and Franklin in surgical care. If you don't give them to us quick, we'll kill you."

"Yes, sir." She called up the names on the computers and read off the room numbers. LaChaise could see them over her shoulder.

"Where are those numbers? When we get off the elevators."

"You turn to your right going down the hall . . ." She drew a line on the desk with her index finger. Martin nodded.

"All right, come out of there, and sit with these other people," Martin said. "Keep your hands where I can see them."

They'd been inside for a little more than a minute.

LaChaise pushed the elevator call button as the woman walked from behind the desk. Martin motioned her toward a chair, and as she went past him, struck her with the gun butt as he had the security guard. The butt hit the woman in the nose, which shattered, and she went down with a chopped-off shriek. The teenaged girl yelped at the same instant, but choked it off, a hand over her mouth. The two young men watched them with flat eyes that said they'd seen guns before.

"Anybody calls the cops, we come down here and waste them," LaChaise snarled. "And you know we will."

The elevator car arrived and LaChaise and Martin backed inside. As the door closed, they heard people running.

THE TWO MEN RAN FOR THE DOOR WHILE THE WOMAN tried to gather up her kids and start moving. She was screaming, "Help us, help us . . ."

The teenaged girl stepped to a wall-mounted fire alarm and pulled the handle down.

Inside the elevator, the alarm went off like a bomb. LaChaise freaked: "Holy shit . . ." and kicked the doors.

"Hang on, we'll be there in one second," Martin said. But it took longer than that, eight or ten seconds, with the alarm screaming the whole time.

DEL WAS BRUSHING HIS TEETH IN A REST ROOM WHEN the alarm went off. He spat once, caught his pistol in his right hand and his radio in the left, ran toward the door with white foam dripping down his chin and said into the radio, "Lucas? Lucas?"

Lucas came right back. "Yeah?"

Del was in the hall, running toward his wife's room. "Something's happening here, there's some kind of alarm."

"Be there in one minute," Lucas said. "I'm right straight down on Washington."

"Get some more guys coming . . ."

FRANKLIN WAS ASLEEP WHEN THE ALARM WENT OFF, but it shook him awake and he pushed himself up, reached for the bedside table and pulled his pistol out. He could hear people in the hallways, the night nurses, he thought. But the alarm made too much sense to him. They were coming, he thought, just like Davenport said they might, and there weren't any cops between himself and the door. He'd have to do it alone . . .

And then Del yelled, "Franklin, I'm in Cheryl's room, you awake?"

And he yelled back, "Yeah, I'm up now."

"Can you get to the door?"

"Yeah."

Franklin pulled the IV from his arm and more or less fell

off the bed onto his good side, winced at the impact, and low-crawled to the doorway. Two nurses were standing in the hall, looking up and down it, and he shouted at them: ''Get out of sight. Get out of sight.''

They saw the gun in his hand, froze for a second, then scurried into a doorway. Del peeked from the doorway across the hall two doors down. ''Maybe it's not . . .'' he shouted.

But as he said it, LaChaise peeked from his end of the hall. His face was clean-shaven but unmistakable, as was the hard black form of his rifle. Del snapped a shot, missing, and Franklin jerked one off and thought it'd probably gone into the ceiling. Then LaChaise was out of sight for a second, and the next second, the muzzle of the rifle came around the corner and began chattering down the hall, a ferocious up-close pounding followed by a hail of plaster from the walls, the bits and pieces of .223 slugs zipping past like bees, the sound of shattering glass, and then the quick hollow boom of Del's automatic.

With plaster pouring on him like rain, Franklin peeked down the hall, saw movement and fired three quick shots. Somebody screamed, ''No,'' a yelp, the sound of a man hit. Then the machine gun opened up again, and more plaster rained down, and the door above his head exploded in plastic and chipboard splinters.

Del, across the hallway, heard the man scream ''No,'' and thought that Franklin had hit one of them. Franklin fired three more times and Del popped back out and fired three evenly spaced shots: Franklin was working a revolver, and he'd need time to reload. There was now so much dust in the hallway that Del could barely see the end of it. Then there was movement again and he jerked his head back and the walls came apart again and something slashed at his throat. He touched it, he could feel something sticking out. A bone? A piece of his jawbone? Shocked, he turned and looked at Cheryl, whom he'd rolled off the bed onto the floor. She was looking at him and began screaming and crawling forward, toward him.

He was hurt, but he didn't feel hurt: he popped out the door and fired another half-dozen shots down the hall, then snapped on an empty chamber.

Franklin came in with two shots: Del groped for another magazine, dropped the empty out of the gun butt, and slapped the next one in and jacked a shell into the chamber. Cheryl was on top of him, trying to hold him, and he was trying to push her away, get back to the door.

Franklin was yelling, and dimly, he heard, "Hold it, hold it. I think they're gone."

Del looked down the hall, but saw nothing. Then Cheryl was screaming something he couldn't make out, fear in her eyes, and she grabbed at his throat.

MARTIN WAS HIT. THE SLUG, A LUCKY SHOT, WENT through the inside part of his thigh, just below his testicles, catching mostly skin. There was a big artery there, he knew, and he pulled back and ripped open his pants leg. His leg showed a raw open wound but no heavy pulse of blood. He was bleeding, all right, but wouldn't bleed to death—not in the next minute or so. LaChaise was screaming at him, "You hit? You hit?" as he slammed another magazine into the AR.

"Yeah, I'm hit. This is no good, man."

LaChaise jumped into the hallway, fully exposed, like in the cop and cowboy shows, and blew the entire thirty-shot magazine down the halls, playing it like a hose. Martin had gone to the elevators. He pushed the "down" button and the doors slid back: "Let's go!"

"One more," LaChaise screamed. He poured another magazine down the hall, then skipped across the hallway and piled into the elevator and the doors closed and they started down.

"Maybe somebody waiting," LaChaise said. He shoved

his last magazine into his rifle. The wells around his eyes were white, his nostrils wide as he gasped for breath: "How bad is it?"

"Bad enough, but I ain't gonna die from it," Martin grunted. "Watch the doors," LaChaise said, and they leveled their rifles at the opening elevator doors. Nobody.

The lobby was deserted and they ran out toward the hall that would lead to the car.

They'd been inside for little more than a minute.

LUCAS SKIDDED TO A STOP IN THE PARKING LOT, ON the opposite side of the building from the emergency room entrance. Del's wife was screaming on the radio: "Del's hurt, Del's hurt . . . they're going away, but Del's hurt . . ."

Lucas had everything on the street headed for the hospital, and Dispatch said more guys were running down from City Hall. They'd be there in a minute, in thirty seconds . . . He jammed the truck into park and got the shotgun off the seat and ran toward the lobby doors. As he ran up, he saw the elevators open, and LaChaise and Martin lurched out, Martin hobbling.

They turned the other way, not seeing him, heading down a hall that would lead to the emergency room exit. He was behind them, sixty or eighty feet away, on the wrong side of the hospital. He pulled at the door and nearly fell down: locked.

Without thinking, he backed up a step, pointed the shotgun at LaChaise's back through the glass and fired. The glass exploded, and he pumped and fired through the hole, and pumped again, was aware that somebody was screaming, and then the glass panes ten feet to his left blew out and he could see the flash of a machine gun rolling toward him. He went down and automatically ducked his head, and the shattering glass ripped at his coat and pants.

When the long play of the machine gun passed, he got to his knees and fired two more shots as quickly as he could, got no response and stood up.

The hall opposite him was empty. There was a sudden, keen local silence, as though he had suddenly gone deaf. Then the sound of sirens faded in, and he stepped through the holes in the glass doors and ran across the lobby.

He ducked behind the wall at the reception desk, and saw a woman with a bleeding face looking at him from the floor where she'd crawled for cover. He waited, listening, then hurried down the hall, ready to take someone at the corner . . .

Another body, the security guard, breathing but blowing bubbles of blood. There was a double blood-trail, going out the door, one stopping five feet from the curb, the other going all the way to the curb. They had a car, but they were gone.

A cop car skidded into the lot, and Lucas stepped out with his hands up, waved, groped for his radio and said, "They're on the streets . . . look for the brown car, the big brown car. They're not more than fifteen seconds out of the lot. They got machine guns, they're hit . . ."

A doctor was running down the hall toward him. He glanced at Lucas, then bent over the security guard and shouted back toward the emergency room: "We need a cart, get a goddamn cart."

Lucas said, "There's another one by the reception desk."

The doctor screamed, "We need two carts . . ."

As the cops broke out of the incoming car, Lucas turned and ran back to the lobby. The elevator doors were open, the floor a pool of crimson blood. There was only one puddle, he noticed, with two footprints in it. The other man hadn't been hit yet, so he'd got him with the shotgun.

He pushed two, rode up, and when the doors started to open, he yelled, "Davenport coming in."

He could hear a woman shouting, and he hurried around

the corner toward Del's room. Del was on the floor, with Franklin and Cheryl, both in hospital gowns, bent over him. A nurse was hurrying down the hall with a cart.

"How bad?" Lucas yelled as he came up.

"He's not gonna be as pretty as he used to be," Franklin said grimly.

Lucas knelt beside Cheryl and Del looked up at him: a splinter of Formica, thin as a knife, and about the width of a pencil, was sticking through Del's neck, inside the lines of his jaw. He looked at Lucas and shook his head, his eyes wobbling.

Cheryl turned to the nurses and shouted, "Hurry," and to Lucas, in a calmer voice, "It goes all the way through, up in the roof of his mouth."

"Jesus, let's get him . . ."

The nurses came up and Lucas picked Del up and laid him on the cart. "Down to the ER," one of the nurses said. The other one pointed at Cheryl: "And you've got to lie back down, you can't be up . . ." And at Franklin: "You too . . ." She pushed Cheryl toward the bed behind them.

Franklin said, "You get them?"

"They made it out, but we got guys coming in all over the place."

"Shit."

"I hit one of them and you guys hit one. We've got one blood trail going in and out of the elevator, and another one starting in the lobby." Lucas started to tremble with the adrenaline.

"Good," Franklin said, and he began to shake as well. He looked down at the wreckage of the hallway, and said to Lucas, "You know what it was like in here?"

"What?"

"It was like one of those scenes in *Star Wars* where the Storm Troopers are shooting about a million shots at the good guys and never hit anything. I mean, more shit went up and down the hall . . .''

Lucas looked at him, covered with plaster dust, and said, ''You know, you might want to sit down.''

Franklin rubbed his chest, looked at Cheryl, now flat on her back and deathly pale, and said, ''Yeah, I might.''

TWENTY-FOUR

---◆◆◆---

MARTIN WAS RUNNING, STAGGERING, TURNING THE
corner into the hall that would take him out past the emergency room, past the body on the floor, LaChaise a step behind, when the world blew up again, and a hail of glass and
lead blew past them.

LaChaise screamed, but Martin could sense him still moving, then another shot pounded past them and LaChaise
turned and opened up with the machine gun and Martin went
through the door out onto the sidewalk, half expecting to die
there.

But the car was waiting, idling peacefully. A woman was
a half-block away, walking toward them carrying a bag. She
stopped, suddenly, when she saw them, but Martin was already around the car; he threw the gun in the backseat and
climbed inside. LaChaise piled in the passenger side and they
rolled out of the lot, the passenger side door flopping open,
then slamming as they slewed in a circle and headed south.

"Hurt bad . . ." LaChaise moaned. "My fuckin' legs . . ."

"Fire alarm," Martin said. He had one hand clamped over

the wound in his leg, and he could feel the blood seeping between his fingers. "Sonsofbitches set off the fire alarm."

"How bad are you hit?" LaChaise asked, then moaned again as they bounced over a curb and around a corner. The streets were empty.

"I'm bleeding heavy," Martin said. "Christ . . . Hang on."

Martin was trying to turn into the side street that led to the garage. But he was moving too fast, and driving with one hand, and they hit a curb again, ran through a small bare tree, bounced off the parking strip and back into the street. La-Chaise, groaning, reached over Martin's head to the sun flap and pushed the button on the garage-door opener. Across the street, the door started up, and Martin horsed the car inside.

Sandy Darling was there with the chain, her eyes wide as she moved behind the steel post, and Martin reached up and jabbed the garage-door opener again and the door started down.

They had not been gone more than ten minutes, and were now no more than a minute and a half out of the hospital. Martin pushed his door open and climbed out, leaving the rifle behind, clutching his thigh, trying to stop the flow of blood.

LaChaise was out, got the padlock keys. "Hurt," he said. "Get your first-aid shit . . . we're hurt."

"What happened?" Sandy asked, as LaChaise popped open the padlock at her waist.

"Fucked up," LaChaise said. "They were waiting."

"Are they coming?"

"Don't know," LaChaise said. "Let's get upstairs . . ."

THE TWO MEN PULLED OFF THEIR OUTER CLOTHES IN the living room. Martin's leg looked like somebody had carved out a golf ball–sized chunk of meat with a dull hunting knife: the wound was circular, ragged, choked with blood and chopped flesh, with pieces of thread from his pants mixed in the gore. Sandy handed him a heavy gauze wound pad and said, "Clamp that over the hole . . . let me look at Dick."

All of LaChaise's wounds were in the back of his legs, the back of his arms and the back of his head, and most were superficial cuts from glass. When he first took off his pants and shirt, he appeared to be shredded. But blood was actively flowing from only one wound, and when Sandy dabbed at the rest of him, she said, "I don't think you're too bad. Get to a hospital, and you won't die."

"Kiss my ass," LaChaise groaned. "Wipe it up or something."

"On the other hand," she said, looking at the one wound that was bleeding, "you've got a bullet hole in the back of your arm." She rolled his arm, and found a lump under the skin near the front. "And that's the bullet, I think."

"Cut it out," LaChaise said.

"It's pretty deep."

"I don't give a fuck, cut it out."

"Dick, I'd just hurt you worse."

"All right, all right . . ."

Martin stretched out on the floor and lay silent and motionless as she poured a glass of water over the wound, probed at it, shook her head and said, "All I can do is put some more pads over it and bind it up. You need a doctor. You're going to get infected."

Martin's stomach heaved and she realized he was laughing: hysterical, she thought. Then again, maybe he thought it was funny. "Infection'll take a couple days. We ain't got a couple days." He looked at LaChaise. "We gotta keep moving, boy."

"I'm really fuckin' hurtin', man."

"They'll wonder where we went, and sooner or later, they'll kick their way in here. If we're gonna do any more damage, we gotta move." He looked at the windows. "Before light."

LaChaise groaned, but got to his hands and knees, looked sideways at Sandy and said, "Tape me up where you can."

"I don't have that much tape."

"Well, get the worst ones," he said. To Martin: "That fuckin' shotgun. Somebody had a fuckin' shotgun and he had me dead, but that first shot missed. That fuckin' glass was like a hurricane . . . Second shot hit me in the vest."

Sandy said, "I'll get a towel."

As she ran back to the bathroom LaChaise crawled across the floor to the bulletproof vest he'd taken off. A ragged pattern of pellet holes punctured the nylon back panel. "Probably shooting triple-ought," he said. "Christ, if he'd been a little worse shot and a little high, I wouldn't have a head."

Martin was on the phone, dialing.

"Surgery, please . . . Thanks." Then, after a moment, "This is Chief Davenport, is my wife Weather there?" He listened as LaChaise watched, then said, "No, that's okay. Tell her to call when she gets done, okay?"

"She's not his fuckin' wife," LaChaise said, when Martin hung up. "Was she there?"

"She's scrubbing for surgery."

"That's where we're going, then," LaChaise said. "That motherfucker Davenport set the whole thing up. I wouldn't be surprised if that was him up in the hallway. Jesus, that was something . . ."

SANDY CAME BACK FROM THE BATHROOM, AND OVER-heard the last part of the conversation. "Where're you going?"

"Hospital where Davenport's old lady works," LaChaise said.

"You gonna let me go?"

"Something like that," LaChaise said, and he grinned at her. Her heart lurched: they were going to kill her.

"Turn over," she said. She dabbed his back with the wet towel, cleaning him up as best she could, isolating the biggest cuts, pulling a few pieces of glass out of his back and legs. "I can't patch the ones under your hair," she said.

"Just get the rest."

Martin had slid over to his travel bag, got a pair of camo jeans out, and pulled them on as he sat on the floor. "We wait an hour, and then we head out: if we go right straight across to Washington Avenue . . ."

"Around that curve and down that ramp and across the bridge and the hospital's right there," LaChaise finished, remembering the recon.

"Five minutes from here," Martin said. He pulled on his boots and looked at Sandy. "You about done with him?"

"About as much as I can do," Sandy said.

"We could use some coffee and eggs," Martin said. He found the TV remote and clicked it on. An announcer was barking something into the screen, and he fumbled a minute to get the sound up. ". . . just a few minutes ago. They have been positively identified as . . ."

"I better get the rifles, in case they show up," LaChaise said. He stood carefully, groaned and started down the hall. "Coffee and eggs," he said to Sandy. "Toast."

Sandy followed him down the hall and stepped into the kitchen. LaChaise went on, and she glanced back at Martin. He'd picked up his bow, but he was watching the television. Sandy stepped into the kitchen. She hadn't done this because she suspected that the cops would kill anyone with LaChaise: but now she had no choice. She took the phone off the hook, punched in 911. When it was answered, she said, quietly, "Sandy Darling. They're here."

She put the receiver down beside the phone, leaving the

line open, and started banging around in the cupboard, looking for a frying pan. LaChaise came by a minute later, carrying an AR under his arm. He was pushing shells into a magazine as he walked, and he continued by into the living room. "Where'd you put your rifle?" he asked Martin.

"Aw, shit, it's probably on the floor in the backseat," Martin said. "I just threw it . . ."

He stopped, suddenly, at the sound: breaking glass down the stairs, then pounding feet. "They're here," Martin said. He pointed a pistol at the door, and LaChaise ran to the window and looked out. "Nothing on the street."

A man screamed through the door: "LaChaise, they know you're here, they're coming . . ." The screaming continued for a moment but they couldn't make it out, and the feet pounded back down the stairs.

"Aw, shit, aw, shit," Martin yelled. "Down the back . . ."

TWENTY-FIVE

———◦◦◦———

STADIC WAS UP, DRESSED BUT STILL GROGGY—HE WAS A
hundred hours behind on his sleep, he thought—and thinking
about breakfast cereal when he heard the screaming on the
radio.

He threw on a parka and gloves, grabbed his gun, and ran
for his car. He was five minutes from downtown: he made it
in four. The parking lot outside the medical center looked like
a used car lot, cops coming in from everywhere in their own
cars. Light racks lit up the snowstorm.

He paused, looking at the chaos, then went on by, and took
a turn down Eleventh. Yes: Lights shone down from Harp's
apartment. Damnit: He went around the block, got a shotgun
out of the trunk and loaded it. If he could flush them, unsuspecting, he could finish it. Dispatch said both men were hurt.

He decided to wait a few minutes: if they'd been shot,
maybe the woman would be going out for medical supplies.
He could take her at the door, and then go right on in. Otherwise, the place was a fort.

• • •

A DOCTOR CAME DOWN THE HALL TO THE PHONES AND said, "Are you Davenport?"

"Yeah." Lucas was on the phone with Roux. He said, "Hang on," and looked at the doctor.

"We got a picture, you might want to look at it."

"OKAY." OUT THE WINDOW, HE COULD SEE THE MEDIA vehicles piling up down the street. Cameramen orbited the building, their lights like little suns illuminating the night. "Gotta go, they got an X ray on Del," he said to Roux.

"I'll be there in fifteen minutes," she said.

Lucas followed the doctor back into the emergency room, where two other doctors were looking at an X ray clipped to a lighted glass. Lucas could see the outline of the Formica where it pierced Del's face.

"He got lucky," the doctor said, tapping the film. "It just penetrated into the base of the tongue. Didn't quite make it through: we were afraid that it had penetrated the pal . . . the roof of the mouth, but it didn't. It's just sort of jammed in there. We'll get it cleaned out."

"No damage?"

"He's gonna hurt like hell, but in a couple weeks, he'll be fine. He's gonna need a plastic guy on his neck, though. The thing looks nasty."

"How about his wife?"

Cheryl had ripped some IV tubes loose when she'd crawled across to her husband, and had been bleeding. "That's nothing," the doctor said. "She's fine."

"God bless," Lucas said. "And Franklin?"

"He's okay."

TWENTY-FIVE MINUTES AFTER THE FIREFIGHT, LUCAS was talking to a patrol captain, trying to figure out why they hadn't found the car: "Christ, they were no more than thirty seconds ahead of you guys."

The captain was getting a little hot: "Look, a fuckin' mouse couldn't have gotten out of here on its hands and knees. We're looking at every car parked in the loop, they must be in a parking garage, somewhere. We'll get them . . ."

Lucas was staring over his shoulder, his eyes defocused. He said, "Stay put," and put his handset to his mouth and said, "I need a run on Daymon Harp. That's first name D-A-Y-M-O-N, last name H-A-R-P. I need to know what he drives."

The captain looked at him curiously; five seconds later, Dispatch came back, a different voice. "Lucas, Sandy Darling just called. She's left the phone off the hook, she says they're there . . ."

"On Eleventh Avenue?" Lucas asked.

"Yeah . . . how'd you know?"

Then the other dispatcher: "Lucas, he's got a 1994 Lincoln . . ."

"A brown one," Lucas said.

"Yes."

"All right," Lucas said, and he felt the rush, the lift that came at the end of a hunt. "I want to do this right. They're at Harp's apartment on Eleventh, it's a two-story, they're up above a laundromat. There's a front stairs and a garage on the side. I want somebody down there now, and we'll need an ERU team . . ."

Behind him, the patrol captain broke for his car. He shouted back, "I'll get some guys moving."

AGAIN, STADIC HEARD THE SUDDEN RUSH ON THE RA-dio. And the phrase, "Down on Eleventh."

He knew immediately what it was. He grabbed his phone,

punched in Harp's number. Busy. Christ. He couldn't allow a siege: there'd be survivors.

The apartment would be surrounded, there'd be helicopters overhead . . . when it came to outright suicide, LaChaise and the other crazy fucker might change their minds. And once they were out, and behind bars, they'd deal him.

The fear clawed at him, propelled him out of the car door. He ran up the side street past the garage, around the corner, kicked in the glass on the bottom floor door and ran up the stairs. At the top, facing the pile of cardboard boxes, he screamed: "LaChaise, they know you're here. They're coming now. Right now. You've got less than a minute. They've got Harp's car, they've got Harp's car. You hear me? Harp's car, they got it."

And he ran back down, seeing in his mind's eye a cop car pulling up from across the street, leveling a shotgun at him, the questions . . .

The street was empty. Hell, the radio traffic hadn't started more than a minute ago. He ran back around the corner, jumped in his car, started it and rolled away.

And as he went, he noticed the utter silence of the night, the quiet in the snow. Every siren in town had been killed. But every cop car in town was rolling toward him.

He punched the car down the street, one block, two, and stopped: when the first cars came in, he wanted to be with them.

The first car came in as he thought, gliding in silence toward the laundromat on the corner.

TWENTY-SIX

———◆◆◆———

LACHAISE RAN TOWARD THE BACK DOOR, SAW SANDY IN the kitchen, grabbed her, and she screamed, ''Let me get my coat, my coat . . .''

LaChaise ran back to the front room, grabbed his own coat and Sandy's. Martin had his bow in his hand, six arrows in the bow-quiver, a fistful more in the other hand, his coat gaping open. He hobbled after them as LaChaise hit the stairs and Sandy followed, pulling on the coat.

When Martin reached the bottom of the stairs, the garage door was halfway up. He heard LaChaise scream, ''Aw, shit . . .'' and LaChaise's rifle came up and began the stroboscopic flash and stutter, and then LaChaise, with Sandy a foot behind, was out in the snow.

Martin was ten feet behind. He looked left: a cop car, windows shattered, sideways in the street. LaChaise was already running to the right.

''This way, this way . . .'' LaChaise was screaming at him. Martin caught up and they turned the corner and Martin said, ''Give me the rifle.''

"What?" LaChaise's face was white, antic, the skin stretched around his eyes. Sandy was running away from them, down the street. *Let her go.*

"I won't make it. I can't move, my leg's fucked, I pulled something loose again," Martin said. He fumbled at his waistband. "Take my pistol," he said, handing it to La-Chaise. "You got yours. That'll be enough. Grab a car, get moving . . ."

"Christ," LaChaise said. He tossed Martin the rifle, fumbled two spare magazines out of his pocket, passed them over, then caught Martin around the neck in a bear hug, held him for a half-second, said, "I'm going for Davenport's woman. I'll probably be seeing you in a while," then turned and ran after Sandy.

Martin went back to the corner and peeked. Fifty yards down the street, a cop was behind a car door, looking at him. He fired a burst, then pulled back and hobbled away, across the street, a thin trickle of pink in the snow where he passed.

He could hear the sirens now, coming in from everywhere.

LUCAS AND AN OUT-OF-UNIFORM PATROL COP NAMED Bunne rode toward Eleventh in Lucas's Explorer. Bunne wore a baseball jacket, the first thing he'd seen when he'd run out of a locker room before heading down to the hospital on foot. They were six blocks from Harp's: one minute. A half-minute after they left the hospital, they got the choked call on the radios, almost unintelligible over the panicked, harsh, into-the-mike breathing, "We got fire, we're shot, we're taking fire, Dick's shot, for Christ's sake, get help."

"Goddamn," Bunne said. Lucas had been following the patrol captain. Now he put the Explorer on the wrong side of the slippery street and they roared along, side by side, sirens everywhere. At the same time, he was shouting, "Where'd they go, you dumb shit?"

The cop came back, as though he'd heard, "They're on Eleventh, they're on Eleventh heading toward the Metrodome, they're on foot."

"Ten seconds," Lucas said.

Bunne drew his pistol and braced himself, white-faced, but at the same time showing Lucas a shaky grin: "This stuff scares the shit out of me," he said.

Lucas, focused on the driving, said, "The snow isn't that bad, it's the fuckin' night that's killing us."

"Nah, it's the fuckin' snow," Bunne said.

A red car, a small Ford, pulled out of a side street and Lucas nearly hit it. The Ford jumped a curve and piled up on a street sign, and they went by, the ultra-pale face of a red-headed kid peering at them through the glass. "Lawsuit," Bunne said, and they went around the corner, on the outside, and then they were on Eleventh on top of Harp's place, the patrol captain fifteen yards behind them. A squad was parked sideways in the intersection. A cop ran toward them, as Lucas and the patrol captain, in the other car, slid to a stop. The cop was pointing back past them: "They're on foot," he hollered. "We gotta get a perimeter up. They're not more'n a minute ahead. You must've come right past them . . ."

Lucas got out of the car and another plainclothes guy, Stadic, joined them, carrying a shotgun. Lucas got his own shotgun out of the car and tossed it to Bunne and said, "Let's go."

The three of them started off, and then another cop ran up behind, carrying another shotgun, and the four of them went off into the snow. The last cop, in uniform, said, "Charlie said they crossed the street . . ."

Lucas led the way, said, "Don't bunch," and the others self-consciously spread out. Lucas said, "Everybody got a vest?" Stadic and the uniform cop said yes; Bunne shook his head, he was bareheaded, barehanded, and wearing penny loafers. "Go back and get a vest," Lucas said.

"Fuck that, I'm coming," Bunne said. Lucas opened his mouth to object, but Bunne pointed at the ground ahead of them: "Look at that. Blood trail."

They all stopped and Stadic said, "He's right," and they all looked down the street toward a row of old brown brick apartment houses. "This is them," Bunne said, pointing at the fresh tracks in the snow. "See the different sizes of holes . . . that's the woman, this one guy is dragging his leg, that's the blood trail."

"Can't see shit; it'll be light in an hour," the uniform cop said, looking around. He was nervous, nibbling at his brushy black mustache. "Got snow on my glasses . . ."

They pushed into the snow, past the apartment houses and small businesses, a Dairy Queen, a jumble of parking lots and fences, the occasional hedge, Dumpsters behind buildings, all good cover: following the blood which appeared as ragged, occasional sprinkles in the snow, black in the dim light. As they moved up under a streetlight, Lucas said into his handset, "We're tracking them . . ." and gave the position.

No way they could get out of the neighborhood, he thought, but there was an excellent possibility that they'd take a house somewhere, and they'd have a siege. "Better get a hostage team down here," he said. "They could hole up . . ."

At that minute there was a sharp slap and Bunne said, "Oh, Christ," and fell down. Lucas screamed "Shooter," and they scattered. But they could see nothing, and hear nothing but sirens, the traffic on the highway and the peculiar hushed purring of the snow.

The uniform was screaming, "Where is he? Which way, which way?"

Lucas put the radio back up and shouted, "Man down, get a goddamn ambulance up here." He scrabbled crabwise to

Bunne and asked, "How bad?" while Stadic was shouting, "Over to your left . . ."

Bunne said, "Man, hurts . . . Can't breathe . . ."

Lucas unzipped the baseball jacket coat and found a torrent of blood pouring from a chest wound, and more, sticky and red, in the back. The hole in the coat looked more like a cut than a bullet puncture. Lucas pressed his palm against the chest wound and looked back in the street, and saw it lying against a car. A fuckin' arrow? No sound, no muzzle flash . . .

"He's shooting a bow," Lucas shouted at the others. "He's shooting a bow, you won't hear it, watch it, he's shooting a bow, stay out of the streetlights."

One of the cops yelled, "What the fuck is this? What the fuck is this?"

An ambulance turned the corner, the lights blood-red, and Lucas waved at it. When it came in, he said to the EMT, "Hit by an arrow, he's bleedin' bad," and left her to it, running after the other two men.

He found them zigzagging up the street, still following the blood. "Ten feet at a time," the uniform said. The uniform was sweating with fear and was wet with melting snow. His eyes were too big behind his moisture-dappled spectacles, his breathing labored, but he was functioning. He ran left, and dropped, pointing his shotgun down the blood trail. Stadic went right, dropped. Lucas followed up the middle, dodged and dropped. Stadic went past, and then the uniform cop.

On a patch of loose snow, Lucas saw that they were only following one track.

"What happened to the other two tracks?" he shouted.

"I don't know. They must've turned off back in the street," Stadic shouted back, as the uniform cop leapfrogged past him. Stadic scrambled to his feet, and as he did, he grunted and dropped, and Lucas saw an aluminum arrow sticking out of his chest and just a flicker of movement up the trail. He fired three shots, saw another flicker, and fired two more, the last two low, and then the uniform cop fired a quick shot with his twelve-gauge.

"How bad?" Lucas shouted at Stadic.

"Nothing. Hit the backing plate in the vest," Stadic said, getting to his feet. "He's a good fuckin' shot." He broke the arrow off and they moved forward again, found a puddle of blood, and some blood spatter. "You hit him," the uniform cop said.

"Maybe you," Lucas said.

"Naw, I couldn't see bullshit, was just shooting 'cause I was scared." He looked around and said, "Maybe we ought to wait until daylight. He can't be far. He ain't going anywhere, he was already bleeding before you hit him."

"I want him," Lucas said. He put the handset to his face and told the dispatcher that the three had broken up, two apparently together, the third hurt bad. He gave the location and said, "We're following up."

"There are people coming straight into that block," the dispatcher said. "You're heading right into them. We've got guys with armor coming up, so take it easy . . ."

WHEN THEY SPLIT UP, SANDY HAD RUN ON AHEAD, LaChaise trailing her by fifty feet, with Martin hobbling behind. They ran a block, LaChaise catching Sandy, then a red Ford stopped at an intersection ahead of them. Sirens were coming from all directions: the Ford wasn't moving. Without breaking stride, LaChaise swerved behind it, jerked open the passenger-side door, and pointed his pistol at the driver: "Freeze, motherfucker."

The driver instinctively stepped on the brake, and LaChaise was inside, his gun in the redheaded kid's face. Sandy, when she saw LaChaise turn toward the car, dropped back a few steps. When he jerked open the car door, she turned and ran the other way. When LaChaise turned back, she was gone in the snow.

"Fuck it, fuck it . . ." LaChaise pointed his pistol at the redheaded driver: "Take off. Slow. Go, go . . ."

He slid to his knees in the passenger-side foot well, his head below the level of the dash, the pistol pointed at the kid's chest. They went a block, then the driver said, "No," and swerved, and they hit something, and LaChaise yelled, "Motherfucker," and the driver put his hands up to ward off the bullet.

But LaChaise levered himself up, and the kid babbled, "They almost hit us . . ." and LaChaise saw the two cars— a cop car and a four-by-four—disappearing down the street.

"Go," he said to the kid. "That way. Down toward the dome."

SANDY FOUND AN ALLEY AND STUCK WITH IT, LOPING along behind the apartment buildings. LaChaise had told her, teasing, that if she turned herself into the wrong cop, she was dead. True enough: she had his picture, but not his name.

And he'd be looking for her. Her best option, she thought, was to find a phone and call Davenport.

Now, if she could find someplace open. But what would be open at seven o'clock on a day like this? The city was a wilderness, the snow pelting down in buckets. She stepped out in the open, then back into the dark as a car roared by, then into the open again to look down the street. There was light on the side of the Metrodome. If she could get in there, there'd be lots of phones. She started that way.

LUCAS, STADIC AND THE UNIFORMED COP MOVED slowly up the blood trail, peering into the dark, starting at every shadow; the uniform fired once into a snowblower as it sat beside a house; Lucas nearly nailed a gate, as it trembled in the blowing snow. They shouted back and forth to reassure each other, and to pressure the bleeding man. Keep him moving; don't let him think about it.

MARTIN FIGURED HE WAS DYING, BUT HE WASN'T FEELing much pain. Nor was he feeling much cold. He was reasonably comfortable, for a man who'd torn open a thigh wound and had taken a gunshot hit in the butt. The butt shot had come in from the side, and nearly knocked him down. But he kept moving, feeling the blood running down his legs. He'd have to stop soon, he thought dreamily. He was running out of blood; that's probably why he felt so good. The shock was ganging up on him, and pretty soon, things would start shutting down.

One more shot with the bow, then he'd dump it. And when they came in again, for the last time, he'd go to work with the AR-15. His final little surprise, he thought, and grinned to himself.

LUCAS HIT THE GROUND NEXT TO A BRIDAL-WREATH hedge. A handful of snow splashed up in his face, and he snorted and tried to see past the corner of the apartment building, thrusting his .45 that way. He could feel Bunne's blood on the pistol stock, a tacky patina that'd be hard to get off. "Go," he yelled, and the uniform went past and immediately screamed and went down, and Lucas flopped beside him, thought he saw movement, and fired, and the cop was screaming, "Got me, he got me . . ."

Lucas pulled him back. The arrow was sticking out of the cop's leg, just above the knee: it had apparently hit the bone square on, and was stuck in it. "Gonna be okay," Lucas said, and yelled at Stadic, "Stay back, forget it, just hold your ground." He called for another ambulance on the handset and asked Dispatch, "Where's the help?"

"They oughta be right ahead of you, they're all over that block."

"You can't see the guy," Lucas sputtered. "You can't see him in the snow . . ."

Stadic hunched up beside him. "What do you want to do?"

"Hold it here for a minute. Get the ambulance . . .?"

The uniformed cop picked up on it. "Where's the fuckin' ambulance . . . "

An ambulance swung in behind them, and Stadic turned and ran back to wave it down.

"One more push," Lucas said. He spoke at the downed cop, but he was talking to himself. He got halfway to his knees, then launched into a short dash and dropped behind another hedge. Up ahead, powerful lights were breaking out around the block, and, behind the lights, he sensed moving figures.

"Davenport," he yelled.

"Where are you?"

"Straight ahead; I think he's between us . . ."

And somebody else shouted, "We don't know that's Davenport, watch it, watch it . . ."

Then Lucas saw Martin. He'd been hunkered into the side of a shabby old apartment, next to a line of garbage cans. He broke across toward the next apartment, and Lucas shouted, "There he is," and fired two quick shots, missing.

"He's coming around the apartment, look that way, he's coming around, watch it . . ."

And one second later, the lightning-stutter of the AR-15 lit up the back side of the apartment. Lucas half-ran that way, aware of the slipperiness underfoot, the shotgun already at his shoulder, leading the way. The automatic fire stopped before he was halfway there, then started again with a fresh clip. Glass was breaking, more cops were firing. Lucas reached the corner and peeked.

• • •

MARTIN WAS FIFTEEN FEET AWAY, IN AN ALLEYWAY stairwell. On his right, he was protected by the building. Ahead of him, and to his left, all along the length of a vacant lot, cop cars blocked the route. The cops were returning fire, but they didn't know he was below the level of the stairwell wall. With the snow, they probably couldn't see anything but the muzzle flash.

He crouched for a second, then popped up and fired another burst at one of the cars, aiming low, figuring the cops would be behind it.

LUCAS SAID TO THE HANDSET, "TELL EVERYBODY TO cease fire. Cease fire, for Christ's sakes, you're gonna kill me. I got him if you can make them cease fire."

Three seconds later, he heard yelling on the other side of the street, and the fire diminished. He peeked at the corner again. Martin had reloaded, and was about to pop up again, to hose down the line of cars.

Lucas shouted, "Freeze!"

Martin turned, and his mouth dropped open. He posed like that for an instant, looking at the shotgun, then said, "Fuck you," and the AR came around. Lucas waited for a microsecond longer than he should have, then shot Martin in the head.

TWENTY-SEVEN

———◆———

LUCAS YELLED, "GOT HIM," STEPPED OUT AND WAVED, and a line of cops broke toward him. He stepped through the snow and down the steps to the body. Most of the top of Martin's head was gone, but his face looked almost placid, his eyes closed, his lips turned up in a not-quite smile.

There was little point to it—he was dead—but out of reflex Lucas patted the body, felt the solidity of the body armor under the coat. And something else. A pistol, Lucas thought, but when he touched it, it was rectangular and he slipped it out of Martin's pocket just as Stadic arrived at the top of the stairs.

"He's dead?"

Lucas said, "Yeah," and stood up, a cell phone in his hand. Where'd they get it? Probably a street buy. He frowned at the phone, then stepped up the stairs toward Stadic: "Watch the muzzle," he said. Stadic's shotgun muzzle had drifted toward him as Stadic peered down the stairwell to Martin. "One down, one to go."

"One?" Stadic asked. "What about the woman?"

"She's been talking to us. We're not sure about her status," Lucas said.

"Okay." Stadic nodded, and he thought: *Shit. They're gonna talk with her*.

Lucas brushed past him on the way up the stairs and said, "So let's find them."

The line of cops arrived and Lucas shouted, "There're two more. They're headed up the street toward the dome . . ."

A PATROL LIEUTENANT TROTTED OVER AND THEY BE-gan talking search techniques, and whether they should put it off until light: Lucas wanted to keep the pressure on. Stadic watched them as they talked. Lucas still had the phone in his hand, then unconsciously stuck it in his coat pocket. Had to get it. Stadic stared at the pocket. Had to get it, had to get it, had to get it . . . the chant rang through his mind like a mantra.

"Come on," Lucas called to him. Stadic, jolted back to the present, said, "I'm here," and Lucas clapped him on the back and led the way back behind the building. He was six feet ahead, unsuspecting. Stadic had the shotgun: and there were more cops everywhere. But the temptation . . . an accident.

Nobody would believe it.

Had to get him alone. He had a piece-of-shit Davis .380 in his pocket. A piece of shit but it'd do the job, but he had to have him alone. Alone with either LaChaise or the woman would be best . . . But Christ, who knew what would happen in that chase?

Davenport was electric, animated, and if you didn't know what was going on, you might think *Happy*. Stadic thought about the arrows coming out of the snow, silent razors in the dark, the whack in the chest. If it'd been eight inches higher, it'd have carved a hole right through his throat and he'd be lying in the street with a plastic bag over his face. He shuddered, and followed Davenport.

THE SEARCH GOT UNDER WAY. GROUPS OF COPS SWEPT the streets, parking lots and yards inside a perimeter thrown up in the first few minutes after finding LaChaise's location. Any house that showed fresh tracks was approached, the door banged on, the occupants asked and warned. But there were few of them this early in the day.

Lucas stayed along Eleventh, the billowing top of the dome a few blocks straight ahead, like the Pillsbury Doughboy's butt. Then a uniformed cop who'd lost his hat and gloves, his blond hair soaked with snow, his hands white as ice, ran up and said, "We've f-f-f-found a line of t-t-t-tracks. Small tracks, a woman or a kid, and whoever it was kept stopping behind b-bushes and around c-corners . . ."

"That's her," Lucas said. "Show me the way."

They ran off together, Stadic a few steps behind. Four uniformed guys with flashlights and shotguns were leapfrogging up the track, which wandered through the maze of old houses, apartments, small brick businesses and parking lots. They were moving quickly, but nervously: everybody'd heard about the arrows. They were staying out of the trail, and Lucas stopped, just a moment, to look at it. "Looks the same," he said to Stadic.

"Yeah, gotta be her," Stadic said.

They ran harder, caught up with the uniforms. Lucas said, "Listen up, guys, this woman has been talking to us. She actually called in and left the phone off the hook so we could follow it in to the apartment. We gotta be a little careful, but I don't think she's dangerous."

"G-g-g-good," chattered the bareheaded cop. "I'm f-f-fuckin' freezing."

"Well, Jesus, go get some clothes on," Lucas said. And to the others, "Come on . . ."

They ran along the track, and as they approached a cross street, saw cops ahead. A spotlight beam broke down toward them, and the uniforms waved their flashlights.

"She broke the perimeter before we set up," Lucas said. "That means LaChaise probably did, too."

He fumbled in his pocket, pulled out first the cell phone, then his handset, and said into the handset, "The woman's outside the perimeter . . . we've got to spread it. The woman's outside for sure, LaChaise probably."

He thrust the phone and handset back in his pocket and they ran along again, the cop cars behind them squealing in circles and then heading out to new positions. The larger the square got, the thinner the cops would be: but cops were pouring in from everywhere, from Hennepin County, from St. Paul. No ordinary dog hunt.

As they followed on the trail, Lucas said, "You know what? She's going to the dome."

"You think?" Stadic asked.

"She's trying to find a phone," Lucas said. He took the handset out again, and relayed the idea to Dispatch. "Get her through to me if she calls."

The streets were getting wider as they got closer to downtown, and then they lost the track: she'd turned into a cleared-off street.

"Still bet it's the dome," Lucas said. "Tell you what," he said to Stadic and two of the uniforms, "you guys go that way, we'll go this way, push both sides of that apartment. But I bet she headed for the dome. I'll see you on the other side and we'll go on over."

"All right."

They split up, and Lucas and the other uniform headed off to the left. As they approached the apartment, Lucas thought of the cellular phone, took it out, then the handset and called Dispatch. "Get somebody at the phone company. I need a number I can call where they can trace a cell phone. I'll call them on the cell phone, and I want them to figure out the number, and then give me a list of calls billed from the phone . . . who's at the numbers. Got that?"

"Got it."

They pushed around the apartment, found nothing but pristine snow. Stadic was waiting on the other side, and they all looked over at the dome.

"Let's go," Lucas said, but as he was about to step off the curb, Dispatch called. "That was fast," he said.

"Lucas, Lucas . . ."

"Yeah?"

"LaChaise . . ." The dispatcher was sputtering. "LaChaise is at the University Hospitals."

"Oh, shit."

Lucas look around wildly, spotted a cop car, waved at it, started running toward it, barely heard the dispatcher, "Got your wife . . ."

"What?" he yelled into the handset. And to Stadic: "Stay with her, stay with Darling."

He ran toward the squad car, and as the car stopped and the window came down, Lucas shouted, "Pop the back door, pop the back."

The driver popped the back door and Lucas dove inside and shouted, "University Hospitals, go, go . . ." And to the handset, "What about Weather? What about Weather?"

"They think he might . . . have her."

TWENTY-EIGHT

———◆———

THE KID BEGAN TO CRY AS THEY PASSED THE METRO-
dome, and when LaChaise yelled at him, told him to shut up,
he simply cried harder, holding on to the top of the steering
wheel with both hands, tears pouring down his face.

LaChaise finally pushed himself up into the seat beside him
and pointed the way: down to Washington, right, around a
curve to a lighted sign that said several things, but concluded
with "Jesus Saves," down a ramp and onto a covered bridge.

"Shut up, for Christ's sakes, you do this right, I won't hurt
you."

"I know you," the kid said, "you're gonna kill me."

"I ain't gonna fuckin' kill you if you do right; I got no
quarrel with you."

But the kid started up again and LaChaise said, "Jesus
Christ," in disgust, and they rolled off the bridge past the
beer-can building, up the hill to Harvard Street.

"Turn," LaChaise said. The kid stopped weeping long
enough to get around the corner, and before he could start

again, LaChaise said, "Go straight ahead to that turnaround and then stop."

"You gonna kill me there?"

"I'm not gonna fuckin' kill you, unless you get smart," LaChaise said. "Just stop there and let me out, and go on your way."

There were a half-dozen people on the street, coming and going from the hospital, slip-sliding down the sidewalks. Operations took place early in the morning. LaChaise had had two operations himself, for an appendix and to get a skin patch put over a bad case of road rash, and both times, they'd woken him up at dawn for the trip down to the operating room.

"Right there," he said, "behind that red Chevy."

The kid pulled in behind the Chevy, and LaChaise eased himself out, the backs of his legs on fire. The kid was looking at the gun and LaChaise grinned at him and dug into his jeans, found the remnant of the cash they'd taken from Harp, pulled out the wad of bills and threw it on the passenger seat. A couple of thousand dollars, anyway. "Thanks for the ride," he said, and he stepped away from the car and slammed the door, and walked up to the hospital entrance.

He felt like a cowboy.

He carried his own pistol, the 'dog .44, in his right hand, and pulled Martin's pistol out of his left pocket, and pushed through the doors using his elbows.

An information counter was just inside the doors to the right. A security guard sat behind the desk, watching a portable television. Three more people, two women and a man in a white medical jacket, were scattered around the lobby chairs, the women reading, the man staring sightlessly at the wall, as though he'd made an unforgivable error somewhere.

LaChaise walked over to the guard, who looked up only at the last minute, a smile dying a sudden death. LaChaise pointed the two guns at the guard's chest and said, "Walk me up to the operating rooms or I'll kill you."

The guard looked at the guns, then at LaChaise, and then, slowly, stupidly, at the television: "They're looking for you," he said.

"No shit. Now get out of there and walk me up to the operating rooms. You got five seconds, then I kill you."

"This way," the guard said. He came out from behind the desk, his hands held at shoulder height. He was unarmed. The three people in the lobby were looking at them, but nobody moved from their seats. "There's another guy coming in, in one second," LaChaise said to the room in general. "If anybody's moving, anybody's standing up, he'll kill you. Sit tight and you'll be okay. I'm Dick LaChaise, that you seen on TV, and I'm here on business."

The sound of the line pleased him; it *sounded* cowboy-like. They walked a few feet down a corridor, around a corner to the right, to a bank of elevators. The guard pushed the elevator button and the doors slid open. "Three," he said, as they got inside. "You gonna kill me?"

"Not if you do what I tell you," LaChaise said. "When we get to three, you stay in the car and ride until you get to the top." LaChaise pushed all the buttons higher than three, and a bell rang and the door opened, and LaChaise waved the gun at the guard and said, "I'll stand here until the doors are closed. If you get off before the top, somebody'll shoot your ass. Got that?"

"Yes, sir," the guard said, as the doors closed.

AT THE END OF THE HALL, DOUBLE DOORS LED TO THE operating suite. To his right, an elderly man sat in a chair reading *Modern Maturity*. He looked up, sucked on his teeth, and looked back at the magazine. LaChaise had the odd impression that he hadn't noticed the guns.

Nobody else in sight. LaChaise went to the double doors, pushed through, found himself in a nursing station. Two nurses were looking at a clipboard, and one of them was saying, ". . . must be stealing scrubs again. They're all his size, and it's only the new ones . . ."

They both looked up at the same time. LaChaise was there in his heavy dark coat, dripping water from the melting snow, his eyes dark and two guns in his hand. He said, "Ladies, I need to see Dr. Weather Karkinnen."

The taller and younger of the two nurses said, "Oh, shit," and the older, shorter one shook her head and said, "You can't. She's operating."

"Then let's go down to the operating room and see her."

"You're not authorized," the older woman said.

"If you don't show me, I'm going to kill one of you, and then the other one will show me, I bet. Who do I kill?" He pulled back the hammer on the 'dog, and the catches ratcheted in the silence. The two nurses looked at each other, then the older one began to sniffle, the way the boy in the car had; and the younger one said, finally, "I'll show you."

She led the way through another set of doors, stopped outside of a single wide door, stood on tiptoe to look through a window and then stepped back and said sadly, "In there."

"If she's not, I'll be back," LaChaise said, holding her eyes. The woman looked away, and LaChaise bumped through the door.

WEATHER HAD HER EYES TO THE OPERATING MICRO-scope while her hands made the delicate loops that produced square knots in the nearly invisible suture material. She'd just said, "If you actually listen to The Doors you start to laugh; listen to the words of 'L.A. Woman' sometime and tell me they're not . . ."

The door banged open and she almost jumped, and everybody turned and, without looking up, she said, "Who in the fuck did that?"

"I did," LaChaise said.

Weather finished the knot and then looked up from the scope, blinked and saw him there, with the two pistols.

"Who's Weather Karkinnen?"

"I am," Weather said. He pointed a pistol at her and she closed her eyes.

"Come out of there."

She opened her eyes again and said, "I can't stop now. If I stop now, this little girl will lose her thumb and she'll go through life like that."

LaChaise took a mental step back, confused: "What?"

"I said, if I quit now . . ."

"I heard that," he snapped. "What're you doing?"

"I'm hooking up an artery. She had a benign tumor and we removed it and now we're hooking up the two ends of the artery to get the blood supply going again."

"Well, how long will it take?"

Weather looked back through the operating microscope. "Twenty minutes."

"You've got five," he said. And he said, "You're really short for a doctor."

Weather looked away again, and asked, "Are you going to kill everybody in here?"

"Depends," LaChaise said.

"If I get another doctor in here, he could finish for me."

"Get him."

"Not if you're going to hurt him, or the others."

"I won't hurt him if he doesn't fuck with me."

Weather looked at the circulating nurse and said, "Betty, go down and ask Dr. Feldman to step in here, if he would."

LaChaise looked at the nurse and said, "Go. And if you fuck with me . . ."

Weather went back to the microscope and they all waited, silently, her hands barely moving, for two or three minutes, when a man in an operating gown bumped hip-first into the room, his hands at chest level. "What's going on?"

LaChaise pointed one of the guns at him, and Weather said, "We've got a gentleman with a gun. Two guns, in fact. He wants to talk with me."

"The police are coming," the new doctor said to LaChaise. In the sterile operating theater, LaChaise looked like a rat on a cheesecake.

"They're always coming," LaChaise said.

"However this works out, we've got to finish this," Weather said to Feldman, her voice steady. "Could you take a look?"

The operating scope had two eyepieces, and Feldman, his hands still pressed to his chest, stepped to the operating table opposite Weather and looked into the second eyepiece. "You're almost done."

"I need to put in two more knots, and then it's a matter of closing . . ."

She gave him a quick brief on the operation, and finished one of the two knots. "One more," she said.

"I've got to go down and back off mine," Feldman said.

"How far are you in?" Weather asked.

"Not in," Feldman said. "We were just getting the anesthesia started . . . I'll be back."

He went with such authority that LaChaise let him go without objection. Weather was working in the incision again, and one of the nurses said, "If I stay here, I'll pee my pants."

"Then go," Weather said. "Everybody else okay?"

They were okay. The nurse who thought she might pee her pants decided to stay with them.

Feldman returned: "Where are we?"

"Just finishing," Weather said calmly. "See?"

Feldman looked through the scope and said, "Nice. But I think you might need one more, at . . ."

He was stalling. Weather said, "I think that should be all right." Feldman looked at her and she gave a small shake of the head. "You sure?"

"Better to get him out of here," Weather said.

"What's going on?" LaChaise demanded.

"Trying to figure out what we can do here," Feldman snapped. "We're right in the middle of things."

Weather stepped back from the table. "But I'm done," she said. She looked at LaChaise. "Now what?"

"Outa here. We need a phone. Someplace where they can't get at me."

"There's an office at the end of the hall."

"Let's go," he said, waving the pistol at her.

THE OUTER AREA WAS DESERTED. THE NURSES HAD gone, and the cops hadn't arrived yet. Weather pulled off her mask and peeled off the first of her gloves and said, "What're you going to do?"

"Talk to your old man," LaChaise said.

And kill her, while they were on the phone, she thought. She came to the office and said, "In there. There's a phone."

She gestured and she went through ahead of him, turned. "You have a lot of choices to make," she said.

"Shut up. What's your old man's number?"

"You could probably dial 911 and they could patch you through. He's out there in his car."

"Do it, and hand me the phone . . ."

Weather punched 911 and handed it to him. He listened a minute, the gun muzzle steady on her chest, and said, "This is Dick LaChaise. I want to talk to Lucas Davenport. I'm at the hospital and I'm pointing a gun at his old lady, Dr. Karkinnen."

Weather said, "You don't have much time left: you better start thinking this through."

"I said, shut up."

"Why? Because if I don't you're gonna kill me? You're already planning to kill me."

"You don't want it to come no sooner than it has to . . ." Then he said to the phone, "Well, get him on. Well, when is he gonna be . . . Yeah? You tell him to call . . ." He looked at the phone, but there was no number, and he looked at Weather.

"The surgery suite," Weather said. Lucas wouldn't get on the phone. He knew what LaChaise would do.

"The surgery suite," LaChaise repeated, and he hung up. "He's on foot somewhere. They're getting him."

Weather said, "I've got to sit down," and she dropped in the chair on the other side of the desk. "Look, you're either going to have to shoot me or listen to me, and I think you better listen: My friend Davenport will get here in a few minutes, and if you kill me, he'll kill you. You can forget all about rules and regulations and laws; he'll kill you."

"Like he killed my old lady and my sister."

She bobbed her head. "Yes. He set that up. I talked to him about it, because I couldn't believe he did it. It's caused us some trouble. But when he thinks he's right, he won't turn. And if you kill me . . ." She shrugged. "That's the end for both of us. You won't walk out of here."

"I ain't walking out anyway."

Now he looked at her, and she saw that she was still wearing one glove, and she pulled it off slowly, watching his eyes.

"There's no death penalty either in Wisconsin or Minnesota. You escaped once. You might have to wait for a while, but there's always the chance that you could be free again. One way or another."

"Bullshit, they're gonna kill me."

"No, they won't. Not if you wait a while. They have all kinds of rules. And once you're on television, they won't be able to take you off and shoot you somewhere. Once you're in the system, you'll be safe. My husband, my friend . . ."

"Is he your husband or your friend?"

"We're planning to get married in a couple of months. We live together . . . If you make a deal with him, he won't kill you. But if you shoot me, you can make any kind of deal you want—you can make a deal with the President—and he'll kill you anyway."

He grinned, and said, "Yeah, tough guy," but he was thinking. He thought about Martin, probably dead already, going cold in the snow somewhere, and he said, "They'd stick me in the Black Hole of Calcutta."

"Probably, for a while," she agreed. "Then something bigger and dirtier would come along, and they'll start to forget about you, and they'll give you a little air. Then you'll have a chance. If you die now . . . that's it. No court, no TV time, no interviews, no nothing."

"Well, fuck that," LaChaise said. "Let's see what your old man says."

Weather took a breath: it was a start. "You're bleeding," she said. "We could get a first-aid kit."

TWENTY-NINE

———◆———

THE DRIVER OF THE SQUAD HAD HIS FOOT TO THE floor, his partner, braced for impact, screaming, "Slow it down, slow it down," and they skidded through the first corner and nearly off the street, then they were on Washington headed toward University Hospitals.

Dispatch came back: "We don't know what the situation is, but she's still alive. He's got her on the third floor, in surgery. Wait a minute, wait a minute, he's calling in on 911, he wants to talk to you . . ."

Lucas shouted, "No. I don't want to talk. He wants me to hear him shoot her. Tell him you're trying to get in touch."

"Got that."

He sat clutching the handset, the street reeling by. Then Dispatch again: "You asked for a number at U.S. West."

"Yeah, yeah." He'd almost forgotten, but he took the cellular phone from his pocket and punched the number in as the dispatcher read it.

The phone was answered instantly: "Johnson."

"This is Lucas Davenport. I was supposed to call here to

find out what numbers this phone has been calling.''

"Yeah. We've got the number now, we're reading it now, we'll check the billings and get back to you. You can hang up.''

"Get it quick," Lucas said. "Soon as you can.''

"It'll take a few minutes.''

"Whatever. Call me back at the number," Lucas said, and he hung up, got on the handset, and said, "What's happening?'' and the cop in the passenger seat lifted his hands to ward off an oncoming car, but the driver slipped it to the left and then hooked down a ramp and they were on the bridge.

Dispatch: "He's still in the operating room. Another doctor's going in and out. We've got two cars there, we've got an ERU team a minute away. Listen, the chief wants to talk . . .''

Lucas said, "You're breaking up . . . I'll get back.''

He turned the handset off and said, "Stay off the radio, guys.''

"Why?'' asked the white-faced cop in the passenger seat.

"Because Roux wants to take me off this, and I can't do that.''

THEY FLASHED UP THE HILL ON THE FAR SIDE OF THE river, made the turn and slewed down Harvard toward the hospital's front entrance. As they braked to a stop, Lucas said, "Pop the door," and they popped it, and he climbed out with the cops and said to the driver, "I owe you big time," and they all ran into the building.

A half-dozen security guards were in the lobby, and Lucas held up his ID and said, "What's the deal?''

"They're out of the operating room. They're in an office.''

"Any cops up there?''

"Yeah, but they can't see down through the doors.''

"Let's go up," Lucas said. He'd observed at several of

Weather's operations, trying to learn a little about her life. He knew the operating suite, and most of the adjoining offices and locker rooms. They rode up in the elevator, and when they got off, were met by two uniforms, who saw Lucas and looked relieved.

"He's down there, Chief. He's got her in a back office, and he's asking for you," one of the cops said.

"You got a phone line into him?"

"Yeah, but he says don't call unless it's you."

"All right." He turned to the security guard. "I need an exact floor plan, and all the nurses and doctors who work inside."

"You gonna call?" one of the cops asked.

"Not yet," Lucas said. "And I don't want anyone to tip him off that I'm here. We gotta figure something out."

WEATHER WAS FIGHTING LACHAISE. SHE'D COME OUT from behind the desk, rolling out of the office chair, and she said, "I hope everything goes okay for Betty. I wish you'd come a half hour later."

LaChaise was standing, holding the door open just a crack, peering down the long hall to the double doors. Davenport, when he arrived, should be coming around the corner just in front of the doors, a thirty- or forty-foot shot. But he was half listening to Weather, and he said, "Yeah?"

"She's a farm kid," Weather said. "If she loses that thumb, she'll have a tough time of it. I don't know how you work around a farm without a right thumb. I know I couldn't."

"What do you know about farms?" LaChaise snapped, looking at her now.

"I grew up in northern Wisconsin—I'm a country kid," Weather said. She didn't say, *like your wife and sister*. "Other doctors start out dissecting frogs or something; I started out taking Johnson twenty-fives apart, and putting them back together again."

"I had a Johnson twenty-five once," LaChaise said. "Hell, I guess everybody did, who had a boat up north."

"Just about," she agreed. "My old man . . ."

She went on for a bit, talking about her family. She got LaChaise to talk about Colfax and the UP, and she told him about ski trips to the UP, and it turned out that they both knew some of the same bars in Hurley. "From Hayward to Hurley to Hell," she said.

He laughed abruptly, winced and said, "Ain't that the truth."

"Are you hurt bad?" she asked.

"I got some shit in my legs . . . cop at the other hospital got me with a shotgun."

"Want me to look?"

"No."

She was about to push him on it, when the phone rang. "That's him," LaChaise said. His eyes flicked over to her.

Not yet, she thought. *Please, not yet.* She had him going . . .

LUCAS MUTTERED TO THE COP, "REMEMBER ABOUT Martin . . ."

"Yeah, yeah."

He dialed and LaChaise picked it up.

"Chief Davenport is on the way. He was in the ambulance with your friend, the Martin guy."

"Martin's alive?"

"Yeah, but he's hurt," the cop said. "He got hit in the legs and he surrendered. He'll be okay."

"Martin?" There was wonderment in LaChaise's voice. "You gotta be shittin' me."

"You got a radio or TV? They'll be carrying him into the hospital."

"Ain't got no TV," LaChaise said, looking around the office. "What about Sandy?"

"Who?"

"Sandy Darling, she was with us."

"Oh. Yeah. I guess they can't find her," the cop said. Then, "Anyway, Chief Davenport wants you to know that he's coming. He'll be here in five minutes."

"Don't call back until he gets here," LaChaise said.

LACHAISE TURNED TO WEATHER AND SAID, "THEY SAY Martin made it."

"Good."

"I don't believe them."

"You can't tell what a person'll do when he's hurt bad enough. I've had all kinds of weird confessions when I was working in an emergency room. A person thinks he's going to die in the next couple of minutes . . . something changes," Weather said. She looked at his gun. "I wish you wouldn't keep that pointed at me. I'm not going to beat you up."

He shifted the muzzle of the gun, just slightly, and she said, "Thanks," and thought, *Maybe.*

THE ERU TEAM INCLUDED A YOUNG BLOND IOWAN WHO was carrying a Sako Classic .243 with a fat black Leupold scope. Lucas stepped away from the medical people, who were working out a floor plan, and said, "How good are you?"

"Very," he said.

"You ever shoot anyone?"

"Nope, but I got no problem with it," the Iowan said, and his flat blue eyes suggested that he was telling the truth.

"You'll be shooting just about sixty feet, close as we can tell."

"At sixty feet I won't be more than a quarter-inch off my aim-point."

"You're sure?"

The kid nodded. "Absolutely."

"We need him turned off. He may be pointing a gun at Weather or me."

"I got a low-power, wide-view scope. I'll be able to see his move—if he's got the gun right at her head, if the hammer's down, I can take him, and your wife's okay. If the hammer's cocked . . . then it's not so good, maybe fifty-fifty. If he's got the gun at her head, if you can get him to take it away, I'll be able to see it and I'll take him. You need to get him to take it away just a second, just an inch."

"He can't have any time to recover—not even a millionth of a second."

The kid shook his head. "I'm shooting Nosler ballistic tips—I didn't want anything that'd go through and ricochet around the halls. So all the energy'll get dumped inside his skull. If I hit him anywhere on the face—and I will—he'll be gone like somebody turned off a switch. That fast."

Lucas looked at him for another long moment, and said, "I hope you can do it right."

"No problem," the kid said, and he stroked the rifle like he might stroke his girlfriend's cheek.

Lucas nodded and went back to the medics and to look at the floor plan. Basically, the suite was one long hall with double doors in the middle, dividing the operating rooms from the support offices. He'd put the sniper at the far end of the hall, open the doors himself and talk to LaChaise, who was in one of the offices at the other end of the hall.

"We'll put the gun on a gurney," Lucas said. "We're gonna need an office chair . . . and then I'll call, and go through the doors. . . . Will the doors stay open?"

"You've got to push them back hard," one of the doctors said.

A cop said, "Lucas, the chief . . ."

"Tell her to call back," Lucas said. He looked back at the sniper and said, "Let's do it."

". . . PEOPLE DON'T UNDERSTAND THAT," LACHAISE SAID. "People don't understand how country folks get ripped around by the government. Christ, you start out just trying to get ahead . . ."

Weather was quietly amused at her own reaction: in some way, she liked the guy. He was like two dozen high school classmates back in Wisconsin, kids who didn't have much to do if they stayed around home. You'd see them trying to put together lives with part-time jobs in the resorts, out in the woods, trying to guide . . . willing to work, but without much hope, afraid of the cities.

LaChaise was like that, but gone down some darker, more twisting trail. He hated his father; didn't much like his mother. Idolized his younger sister, and even his wife.

"Candy sounds like trouble, though," Weather said. "Sometimes people push too hard."

"Yeah, I guess. But she was so damn lively . . ."

LUCAS GOT THREE BIG STACKS OF SURGEON'S SCRUB suits, all green, from the laundry. The sniper took off his jacket and pulled one of the scrubs on, and tied a pair of pants around his head. They put one stack of scrubs in the middle of a low stainless-steel instrument gurney. The sniper sat in an office chair behind the gurney, and dropped the rifle across the top of the stack, and put a couple more scrubs on top of it. The other two stacks went on either side of the center pile.

Lucas walked down the hall toward the double doors and looked back. He could see the glass of the scope and the rifle barrel, but they made no visual sense. He couldn't tell exactly what they were, and LaChaise would be twice as far away. The sniper himself was invisible with the green scrub pants tied around his head.

"Good," Lucas said, hustling back. "If we can drop one more suit right here . . ." He spread one across the barrel.

Lucas and another member of the ERU walked down the length of the hall again, and looked back a second time. The other cop said, "This scares the shit outa me."

"Me, too," Lucas said. He nodded at the sniper. "But can you see him?"

"I can only see him because I know he's there. LaChaise . . . no chance."

Lucas walked back. "All right," he said to the Iowan. "I hope to God you haven't been bullshitting me."

The kid said, "You wanta quit fuckin' around and get the show on the road? And stay to the right side of the corridor. The slug'll be coming right past your ear."

THE PHONE RANG AGAIN, AND LACHAISE BENT OVER to pick it up: pain shot down his leg and he grunted, almost stumbled, caught himself, and lifted the phone.

Lucas said, "I'm right down the hall from you. If you look out, I'll open the double doors, and you'll see me."

He was that close? LaChaise put his eye to the door crack and looked at the double doors. "Let's see you."

The first of the two doors opened, slowly at first, and then quickly, pushed against the wall; it stayed open. The man who'd pushed it open was standing behind the other door. He peeked out at LaChaise.

"All right, here I am," Lucas said. "We got a lot to talk about."

"You killed my goddamn wife and sister," LaChaise said. "And I say, 'Eye for an eye.' "

"When your sister was killed, she was firing a gun at us," Lucas said. "She went down shooting. We didn't just shoot her out of hand: we gave her a choice to give up."

"Bullshit, everybody says it was over in one second, I saw the TV . . ."

"Doesn't take long to have a gunfight," Lucas said. "Anyway, what're we going to do here?"

"Well, we've been talking about that, your old lady and me," LaChaise said.

THE SNIPER COULD FEEL JUST THE LIGHTEST SWEAT start on his forehead, just a patina. Through the scope, he could see the crack in the door, and even, from time to time, LaChaise's eye. He thought about taking the shot, but he didn't know what Weather's situation was. He'd seen training films where the crook's gun was taped to the hostage's head, the hammer held back on the gun with thumb tension. Shoot the crook, the hammer falls, and the hostage is gone.

He wouldn't take it, yet. Not yet. He moved his eye a bit farther from the scope: he didn't want the glass to steam up.

"I DON'T WANT TO TALK ON THE PHONE ANYMORE," Lucas said. "I want to talk face-to-face. I want to see if Weather's okay, what you've done to her . . ."

"I haven't done nothin' yet," LaChaise growled.

"I'm gonna push open this other door. I won't have any cover. I'm gonna keep my gun in my hand. You shoot her, you're a dead man. But come on out here—talk to me."

Lucas pushed the second door open, and stood in the center of the hall, his gun by his side, the phone still by his face.

"Trick of some kind," LaChaise called down the hall.

"No. We're just trying to get everybody out of here alive," Lucas said. "Your friend Martin would probably tell you to give it up. He went down shooting, but he seemed happy enough to be alive on the way to the hospital.''

"You swear that's true—man to man," LaChaise said.

"Yeah, I do," Lucas said. "Now let me see your face."

After a moment of silence, LaChaise said, ''We'll come out to talk. Your old lady'll be in front of me and the gun'll be pointing right at her head. Anybody tries any shit . . .''

"Nobody's gonna try any shit," Lucas said.

LaChaise looked at Weather. "He *is* a tough guy," LaChaise said. "Let's go out there. You just stay right ahead of me."

"Don't hurt me," Weather said.

"Let's see what happens. Maybe this'll work out."

She touched him with her fingertips. "You should give yourself a chance. You're a smart man. Give it a chance."

Then she stepped in front of him, and felt the cold steel of LaChaise's gun muzzle touch her scalp just behind her ear. They edged into the hall together, and LaChaise nervously looked behind him—nothing but a blank wall—and then down at Davenport, who loomed large and dark standing in the double doors. He held the gun at his side and LaChaise again thought, "Cowboys."

If he got out of this—he was thinking that way, now—if he got out of this, it'd be a long time before he played any cowboy games again.

"I'm here by myself," Davenport said from the doors. "And I'm pleading with you. Weather takes care of little kids . . . that's what she's doing. For Christ's sake, if you gotta shoot somebody, go for me; let her go."

"You killed my Georgie . . ." But now Georgie was a bargaining chip.

"We didn't want to. Look, for Christ's sake, don't shoot her by accident, huh? Look, here is my gun."

Weather could feel the muzzle on the bone just behind her ear. But she wasn't thinking about it. She was listening to

Lucas's tone of voice, and she thought, *Oh, no, something's going on.* She opened her mouth to say something, but LaChaise, behind her, said, "This one time, I'm going to take your word for it . . ."

Now there was a pleading tone in LaChaise's voice, and Weather felt the pressure from the gun muzzle move away from her ear.

THE SNIPER COULD SEE WEATHER FROM THE SHOULDER up, and all of LaChaise's head, and the muzzle of the pistol. He could hear what LaChaise was saying, but was mentally processing it in the background. Everything else was focused on the muzzle. He saw it start to move, mentally processed the words, *going to take your word for it,* realized that the muzzle was about to come away from Weather's head, and then the muzzle lifted out of Weather's hair and the sniper let out just a tiny puff of breath and squeezed . . .

THE DISTANCE WAS SIXTY-TWO FEET. IN TWO ONE-hundredths of a second, the slug exploded from the barrel and through LaChaise's head, his skull blowing up like a blood-filled pumpkin.

LaChaise never sensed, never knew death was on the way. He was there one instant, moving the muzzle, ready to quit, even thinking about jail life; in the next instant, he was gone, turned off, falling.

WEATHER FELT THE MUZZLE MOVE, AND THE NEXT IN-stant, she was on the floor, blind. She couldn't see, she couldn't hear, she was covered with something—she was covered with blood, flesh, brains. She tried to get to her feet but slipped and fell heavily, tried to get up, then Lucas was there, picking her up, and she began to scream . . .

And to push him away.

THIRTY

THREE DOCTORS, PHYSICIANS AND FRIENDS, BENT OVER Weather, trying to talk with her. She was disoriented, physically and psychologically. The explosion of blood, bone and brain had done something to her. The doctors were talking about sedatives.

"Shock," one of the cops said to Lucas. The doctors had pushed Lucas away—his presence seemed to make her worse. "We'll get her cleaned up, get her calmed down, then you can see her," they said.

He went reluctantly, watching from the back of the room. Roux showed up, looked at the body, talked to the kid from Iowa, then came over to see Lucas.

"So it's done," she said. "Is Weather all right?"

"She's shook up," Lucas said. "She freaked when we shot LaChaise."

"Well, look at her," Roux said quietly. "She looks like she was literally in a blood bath. A bath of blood."

"Yeah, I just . . . I don't know. I did right, I think."

Roux nodded: "You did right." She asked, "Did you talk to Dewey?"

Dewey was the shooter. Lucas looked across the room at the Iowa kid, who had the rifle cradled in his left arm, like a pheasant hunter with a shotgun. He was chatting pleasantly with the team leader. "Never had a chance," Lucas said. "I need to thank him."

Roux said, "He scares the shit out of me. He seems to think the whole thing is very interesting. Can't wait to tell his folks. But he doesn't seem to feel a thing about actually killing somebody."

Lucas nodded, shrugged, turned back toward Weather. "Jesus, I hope . . ." He shook his head. "She acts like she hates me."

THE PHONE IN HIS POCKET RANG AND LUCAS FUMBLED for it. Roux said, "What about Darling?"

"We've got some guys trying to find her over at the dome." Lucas got the phone out—his own phone. The ringing continued in his pocket. "Uh-oh," he said, as he dug out the second phone. "This could be bad news."

He turned the phone on and said, "Yes?"

"This is Johnson, over at U.S. West."

"What'd you get?"

"The phone was registered to a Sybil Guhl, she's a real-estate broker in Arden Hills. There were forty-two calls in the last few days, both businesses and private phones . . ."

"Private phones," Lucas said.

"There were calls to a Daymon Harp residence in Minneapolis," Johnson said in his fussy corporate voice. "To an Andrew Stadic residence . . ."

"Oh, shit," Lucas said.

"Beg pardon?"

"How many calls to Stadic?"

"Uh . . . nine. That was the most frequently called personal phone—actually, it's another cellular."

"Who else?"

There were other calls, but they could be discounted. Lucas said "Thanks," hung up and looked at Roux. "Andy Stadic," he said. "He's the guy."

"Damnit." She brushed her hand across her eyes, as though that would make it go away. "Let's get a team out to his house."

"He's not at his house," Lucas said, backing away, heading toward the elevators. He looked one last time at Weather, sitting head down on the cart, the doctors crouched around her. He should stay; but he'd go. "He's leading the hunt for Sandy Darling."

SANDY HEARD THE KNOT OF COPS COMING UP BEHIND her. She needed to talk to somebody on a phone before she turned herself in. One of the cops—maybe one of those behind her, maybe not—would have a face that matched the photos in her pocket.

If he was behind her, she might not get a chance to talk. When she heard the cops calling back and forth, she thought about running over to the dome, but the street was too wide, too open, and they were too close. She'd been leaving tracks, but there'd been no way to avoid that. Now she ran a few feet into the street, through fresh snow, heading toward the dome. As she got into the street, onto snow compacted by traffic, she swerved left.

An old house, with four or five mailboxes mounted next to the door, was only a few dozen feet away, and behind it, a ramshackle garage. All the windows in the house were dark, but somebody had left it not long ago. A set of tire tracks came out of the garage, into the street.

Sandy hurried to the drive, tiptoed up the car track,

crouched, looked around, then lifted the garage door. The door rolled up easily. The garage was empty, except for three garbage cans and a pile of worn-out tires stacked on one side. She dropped the door, and in the pitch-blackness, felt her way across to the stack of tires and sat down.

She felt as though she'd been physically beaten, but there was hope now. If she could get to a phone . . .

Through the walls of the garage, as if from a distance, she could hear the cops calling back and forth, and then more sirens. She sat and waited.

STADIC AND TWO UNIFORMED COPS CROSSED THE street to the Metrodome. A ramp led up from the street to the concourse level, and they climbed it, spread out in a skirmish line. Four cars were parked in the tiny parking area above the ramp. Footprints led from the ramp area to the doors at the base of the dome. They couldn't tell if anyone else had walked up the ramp.

"Protect yourself, boys," Stadic said to the others. "Davenport might be right that she's helping out, but he don't know everything. If you come up on her, be ready."

The uniforms nodded, and as they approached the line of doors, they saw that one was propped open with a plastic wastebasket. "Five'll get you ten that she came in here," one of the cops muttered. They eased through the first set of doors, then went through a revolving door onto the circular concourse.

Nobody in sight. The concourse was only dimly lit, but somewhere, somebody was running a machine that sounded like an oversized vacuum. Stadic said, "You guys go that way. Holler if you see anything. She could be anywhere."

At that instant, one of the cops saw movement over Stadic's shoulder. He yelled, "Hold it . . . You! Hold it."

Stadic spun, and saw a figure in the dim light. The figure

had stopped in the center of the concourse, and then the other uniform yelled, "Minneapolis police, hold it." All three of them trotted toward the figure. A man; a janitor.

"What happened?" the man asked. He was holding a hot TV dinner in one hand, a plastic fork in the other.

"Sorry," the first cop said. He put his pistol away. "You work here?"

"Uh, yeah . . ."

"Did you see a woman come through here? Hiding out?"

"Haven't seen anybody but the guys down working on the rug," the man said.

"The rug?"

"Yeah, you know, the Astroturf."

"All right: we're looking for a woman. If you see anybody, you let us know. We'll be walking around the concourse."

"What'd she do?" the janitor asked.

"She's that woman with the guys killing the cops," Stadic said.

"Yeah?" This was something different. "Is she, like . . . armed?"

"We don't know," Stadic said. "Don't take any chances. If you see her or any of your guys see her, get to a phone." He waved over his shoulder. There were phones all along the concourse. He scribbled a number on a business card. "Call this number. It'll ring me, right here, and we'll come running."

The janitor took the card. "I'll tell the other guys. We don't try to take her?"

"No. Don't go near her," Stadic said. "We know her sister used to shoot people for sport."

"I'll tell you what I can do—I can go up on top and look down," the janitor said. "We can get up there, see almost everything inside."

"Good. Give me a call," Stadic said. To the uniforms he

said, "You guys go that way. Check all the stairwells, go up and down, look in the women's cans. I'll meet you on the other side."

"Got it."

"And I'll go up on top," the janitor said.

CARS WENT BY EVERY FEW MINUTES, SOME FAST, SOME slow. Sandy could hear nothing else, except the whisper of the falling snow. Finally she stood up and edged back to the door, lifted it two feet, squatted and looked out. Nobody. She pushed it up another foot, duckwalked out into the snow. She looked at the house, the windows still dark, then across the street at the dome. She could knock on the door of the house, maybe get somebody up, get a phone.

But there had to be a phone right there, across the street. No cars coming.

She ran across the street and up the approach ramp. A number of car and foot tracks went up the ramp. As she followed them, she brushed past a green pole set into the concrete. The pole was a modernistic phone kiosk, with a phone hanging on the other side—dial 911, no charge—but she never saw it.

Instead, she went on to the door, opened it, stepped through into the dead space between the inner and outer doors, then pushed through the revolving door onto the concourse. Nobody in sight, just a bunch of wet foot tracks. But she could hear rock music coming from somewhere. Tom Petty, she thought.

Down the hall she saw a sign: rest rooms and phones. She went that way and found a bank of phones. She picked up a phone, listened, got a dial tone, punched in 911. The call was answered instantly.

"This is Sandy Darling . . ."

"Ms. Darling, where are you?"

"I'm at the Metrodome, I'm inside."

"Okay. We'll put you through to Chief Davenport. He's on his way there."

A moment later they clicked through. "Ms. Darling? This is Lucas Davenport. The policeman working with LaChaise— his name was Andy Stadic?"

"I don't know," Sandy said. "They wouldn't tell me. They said if I turned them in, the cop was paid to come kill me. I've got some pictures of him. I took them out of Dick's pocket."

"Okay. I'm two minutes away and we've . . ."

"Listen, I think Dick is going to the hospital where your wife works. You've got to get over there first."

"Dick LaChaise was killed at the hospital," Lucas said.

"He's dead?"

"Yes."

"Thank God . . ." She said it half to herself, but Lucas picked it up.

"I'm just about there and we've got more people on the way," Lucas said. "Stadic is in the dome with you, so you've got to stay out of sight."

"He's in the dome?" She could hear voices and footsteps.

"Yes."

"Oh, God," she whispered. "Somebody's coming."

"Run," Lucas said. "Run and hide."

Sandy dropped the phone and ran across the hall. Two doors and a stairway led down to the first tier of seats: she pulled on a door, not expecting it to open. It did. She went through, down the stairs to the field of blue plastic seats, and turned left. Below her, on the football field, a half-dozen people were doing something to the dark green carpet. Stretching it? She couldn't tell.

She went down six rows, apparently unseen by the people on the field, slid halfway down the row of seats, and lay on her back. They'd have to look down every single row to see her, and she only had two minutes to go. Two minutes, Davenport had said. She thought she saw movement at the peak of the roof, but when she focused on the spot, there was nothing.

Less than two minutes, she thought.

STADIC'S PHONE RANG.

"This is the building engineer, I talked to you . . ."

"Yeah, yeah."

"She's hiding third row down, lower tier, right behind the goalposts."

He had her. "Which end?"

"South."

"What the fuck end is that?" Stadic snarled. North, south, he couldn't tell anything in this place.

"The, uh, hmm, I know: she's on the opposite end from where they're working on the rug."

Stadic said, "Go on back up there and watch in case she moves," then turned the phone off and started running. If he could get her. If he could get the phone away from Davenport. Christ, if LaChaise had Davenport's old lady, they could be there all day. He was still alive, if he could get the girl.

Stadic rounded the end of the concourse and saw people milling around. One of them yelled, "Sandra Darling. Sandra Darling, where are you?"

Who was that? That couldn't be Davenport . . .

He dodged left, went down the stairs to the first tier. He was halfway around. He went down three rows and started running sideways. He was on the thirty-yard line, the twenty, the ten, but still a way to go.

A uniformed cop came out of one of the staircases, saw him and yelled, "Andy Stadic. Stadic. Stop there, Andy."

They had him.

No doubt. But he kept going, he was almost to the woman: he could do that, anyway. He could say that he didn't hear, that he was about to arrest her. He had the .380 in his pocket, if he could drop it, if they found her with the gun . . .

Sandy heard the cops shouting, heard somebody banging toward the seats. She peeked: the man in the photos was a hundred feet away, running right toward her. He *knew* where she was. She began to crawl down the space between the seats, got to the stairs, scrambled up them, hands and feet churning.

"Sandy Darling, stop," Stadic screamed. He brought the shotgun up, centered it on the back of her head and jerked the trigger. The shot boomed inside the stadium and he saw her go down. Had she gone down before the shot? Had he hit her?

Somebody shouted and he turned, dizzy, and a cop fired a pistol and a chair splintered behind him.

Then he saw the woman, scrambling, disappearing into a stairwell. He ran that way, and somebody fired another shot at him, but Stadic had lost it.

The woman, he thought. If he could just get the woman. He forgot about the phone: he thought about the small figure disappearing into the stairwell.

There was his problem. *The woman.*

DAVENPORT APPEARED, LARGE, HAIR STANDING OUT from his head as though somebody had deliberately mussed it, his long black coat dangling down his legs. He was a quarter of the way around the stadium, a pistol in his hand. "Stadic, goddamnit . . ."

But Andy Stadic, too many days with no sleep, one inch from having pulled it off—Stadic was locked into a loop. Find the woman. He jerked the shotgun toward Davenport and pulled the trigger, once, twice, three times, four, and then the gun was empty. Lucas dropped and the shotgun blasts rattled harmlessly off the seats twenty yards away. Not even close. The cops farther up the dome fired three more shots, missing.

Stadic ignored them, dropped the shotgun, drew his pistol, a Glock nine-millimeter, and ran up the stairs, into the stair-well, going after the woman.

And he found blood.

A SMEAR ON THE CONCRETE, THEN A DRIBBLE. HE'D HIT her with his quick shot. He followed the blood around the corner and up. She'd moved to the next tier. Somebody was screaming at him: "Stadic. Stadic . . ."

Not Davenport, one of the other cops.

He was so close.

SANDY WAS HURT. SHE DIDN'T KNOW WHETHER SHE'D been hit with shotgun pellets, or pieces of the plastic chairs, but she was bleeding from the right hip, thigh and calf, and maybe from her back. Her back hurt, anyway, a scratching pain, like a cut.

She emerged on the second level, saw a TV booth to her left. *Try to hide*. She ran to the booth. The door was locked. She went back down the stairs, thinking she might hide in the seats again—and noticed that the booth window was open. She stood on the back of a seat, and pulled herself in.

Not a broadcast booth, but a camera position. Empty, ex-cept for a heavy camera stand. No playoff games this year. She crouched below the window and listened to the cops yell-ing out in the stadium.

●

THE THOUGHTS WERE MAKING A LITTLE TUNE IN Stadic's head: get the woman, fuckin' Davenport; get the woman soon as you can . . .

He ran up the stairs, paused, looked for blood. Heard the

cops calling behind him: "Where'd he go? Get out in the goddamn concourse . . . I think he went up."

More blood. Yes. Going up.

He followed, poked his head out of the stairwell, and a cop at the far end shouted, "There he is. He's up on top."

LUCAS RAN UP A STAIRWELL, PAUSED AT THE TOP, AND peeked. Stadic was in the next well, with a pistol. Lucas poked his head around the corner and yelled, "Andy. Give it up, man."

"Fuck you, Davenport." Stadic swiveled and fired. "You caused this shit."

Somebody shouted, "He's gone, he went back down."

STADIC JUMPED BACK INTO THE STAIRWELL, PAUSED A second, then came back out: and caught him. Lucas, hearing the other cops yelling, had come out of his stairwell and was headed down the aisle toward him. Stadic had his gun up: Lucas's gun was out to his side, as he balanced himself trying to run down the too-narrow row of seats. Stadic fired and Davenport flipped over, went down between the chairs.

WHEN SANDY HEARD LUCAS SHOUT, SHE STUCK HER head up and peeked. Stadic was twenty feet away, Davenport beyond him: she recognized him from TV, the funny shock when you realized that the TV image actually represented a person. Then Stadic fired and Davenport flipped over the chairs, going down.

Sandy looked wildly around the booth, saw the TV stand. The camera mounting-head was fixed to the end of a steel cylinder, which disappeared into a heavy steel base, fixed with two collars held by wing nuts. She loosened the wing nuts and pulled the cylinder out of the base. The cylinder was a chromed-steel pipe four feet long, an inch and a half in diameter. She grabbed it like a baseball bat, hefted it.

STADIC FROZE AFTER FIRING AT DAVENPORT: STUNNED. He'd just killed a cop, for Christ's sake. He stood for a second, looking at his pistol. Maybe he could tell them Davenport was the one, that Davenport had set him up.

Glassy-eyed, he turned back to the trail the woman had left. Blood trail . . .

LUCAS'S HEAD CRACKED ONE OF THE BLUE PLASTIC chairs as he went over the side. The bullet had missed—he didn't have time to think about it, but he was whole, dizzy, disoriented, struggling to get up . . .

THE BLOOD TRAIL RAN TOWARD A DOOR ON A TV booth, then away from the door and up toward the window.

"ANDY, ANDY . . ." THE UNIFORMED COPS. STILL HALF A stadium away, were firing at him. Stadic looked up at the window, climbed on the chair back, pulled himself up. A bullet clipped his coat, another the back of his neck, and he fell.

"Andy . . ."

That was Davenport? He popped up, gun in hand, and saw Lucas again, fired quickly, saw Lucas duck, go down.

He looked up. Christ, the window was right there. Blood on his hand, on his neck, blood on everything, slippery . . .

He went straight up, leaping, caught the window and hauled himself up, heard the cops yelling, "Andy, Andy, Andy," a regular football cheer, doing the wave for Andy Stadic.

He hauled himself up, hands slippery with blood . . .

Sandy was there, looking down at him.

• • •

SANDY HEARD HIM SCRABBLING AT THE BOOTH, SAW HIS hand catch the edge, saw him fall. There were more shots, and then he was up again, bullet-headed, like a gorilla, like King Kong, climbing up the outside of the booth.

Back home, Sandy had always been the one who split wood for the wood stove. She liked doing it, feeling the muscles work.

Now here was this blood-covered man coming to kill her. A man she didn't know, with a gun, crawling up the wall . . .

She swung the steel cylinder with everything she had: for Elmore, for the times Martin and LaChaise had knocked her down, for the fear during the ledge walk, for all the blood. She swung the pipe like a wood-splitting maul.

STADIC LOOKED UP. SAW IT COMING. HAD JUST enough time left in the world to let go of the window.

LUCAS WAS ON HIS KNEES, HIS GUN COMING UP, THINK-ing, *Vest; he's wearing a vest* . . .

The gunsight tracked up Stadic's back to his neck, just as Stadic's head went over the lip of the window, and Sandy loomed in front of him. Lucas snapped the barrel upright, afraid to touch off the shot . . .

He saw the steel cylinder come down.

Heard the crack.

Saw Stadic drop like a rag.

THERE WAS NO SOUND IN THE STADIUM. EVERYTHING had stopped: the workmen, the running cops. Lucas. Sandy. Stadic's body upside-down in the blue chairs.

After a long, long beat, the world started again. "You can come down," Lucas said to Sandy as the other cops ran to-ward them. "You'll be all right now."

THIRTY-ONE

———◆◆◆———

SANDY DARLING LAY IN THE HOSPITAL BED, TIRED, dinged up, but not seriously injured. Her most pressing problem was her left foot, which was cuffed to the bed frame. She could sit up, she could move, but she couldn't roll over. The simple presence of the cuff gave her the almost uncontrollable urge to roll, and a powerful sense of claustrophobia when she couldn't.

She'd spoken to a lawyer. He said the Hennepin County District Attorney might come up with a charge, but there wasn't a case if what she said was true. She was a victim, not a perpetrator.

Sandy had told the truth, generally, with a few critical lies. She hadn't seen them, she said, until Butters came to get her, to patch up LaChaise. After Butters showed up, she hadn't been free to leave. She'd tried to get free every way she could.

There remained the problem of LaChaise's fingerprints and other traces in the Airstream trailer: but nobody but Sandy knew he'd been there—nobody alive—and probably not more than five other people in the world were aware of the Airstream. If they *did* find the trailer, and bothered to fingerprint it, she could attribute any cooperation to Elmore. Otherwise, when she got out, she'd wait a few days, and then go out to the trailer with cleaning rags and a bucket of detergent.

And she should get out—in a couple of days, with any luck, the lawyer said.

She turned on her side, felt the tug of the cuff and looked out the window. She had a view of a snow-covered rooftop and a hundred yards of anonymous street.

Elmore. Elmore would be the problem, she thought. The guilt she felt about Elmore was deeper, more intractable than she would have believed. He haunted her thoughts, in death, the way he never had in life.

She'd babbled something about it to a doctor. The doctor told her that grief was natural, would stay, but could be borne and would eventually fade.

Maybe, maybe not.

God, if I can only get out . . .

She needed to be outside, working with the horses. This was a pretty time of year, if you liked the north woods, the white fences of the training rings, the dark trees against the snow.

The horses would be out in it now, running over the hillside, the blankets flowing over their backs, gouts of steam snorting from their nostrils.

Sandy Darling shut her eyes and counted horses.

THE PLAINCLOTHES GUYS GATHERED IN HOMICIDE, where there really wasn't enough space, like mourners at a wake, muttering among themselves. Much of the talk was about the Iowa boy and his rifle.

And Stadic, of course.

Stadic dead was better than Stadic alive, everybody agreed on that. But already, the amateur lawyers were talking: he'd never been found guilty in a court of law. What would happen to his benefits? He had an ex-wife and kid, would they get them?

"Andy was a greedy sonofabitch, he was always bitchin' about not havin' enough, not makin' enough," Loring said. "All the guy ever thought about was money. That's why his old lady split. But I never thought he'd . . ."

Lester came in and cleared his throat and said, "Listen up, everybody. We're all done. Unless you're on the schedule or you're making a statement, go home. Finish your Christmas shopping. And get the goddamn overtime forms in, and anybody who wants comp time instead of money, come see me, and I will personally kiss you on the ass and shake your hand . . ."

"At the same time?"

A little laughter.

A detective from sex said, "What about Stadic?"

"What about him?" Lester asked.

"I mean . . . we were talking . . . what's gonna happen?"

Lester said, "Aw, shit, let's not get into that. We got a long way to go with the county attorney."

"What about Harp?" asked a drug guy.

"We're looking for Mr. Harp," Lester said. "And pay attention here: if anybody except the chief or the mayor talks to the press about Andy Stadic, without checking with us first, well, that's your First Amendment right, but we *will* cut your nuts off with a sharpened screwdriver."

"Hey, are we gonna be on *Cops*? . . ."

SLOAN AND SHERRILL FOUND LUCAS SITTING IN A WAITing room at the University Hospitals, looking at a sheaf of papers in a manila file.

Sherrill stuck her head in and said, "What's happening, dude?"

Lucas closed the file and said, "Just . . . hanging out."

Taking that as permission to come in, they dropped into chairs facing him, and Sloan asked, "Have you seen Weather?"

"She should be waking up," Lucas said. "I'm waiting to go in."

"Has she said anything to anybody?" Sloan asked.

"Yeah, but she's disoriented," Lucas said. "She really seems . . . hurt. I think I really hurt her."

Sloan shook his head: "You didn't hurt her. You did what you had to."

Sherrill, exasperated, said, "C'mon, Sloan, that's not gonna help."

"What?"

"Clichés," Sherrill said. She turned to Lucas. "Maybe you *did* hurt her. You ought to think about that."

"Aw, Jesus," Sloan groaned.

"The problem that's got me is, it's my fault," Lucas said. "I didn't see Stadic—I should have seen him. If I'd seen Stadic, we would've had them all."

Sloan was irritated: "C'mon, Lucas, how could you have seen Stadic? He saved your life with Butters."

Lucas waved him off: "You remember when we were getting ready to raid poor old Arne Palin? We were talking at the door, you and me and Franklin? And Lester was there, and Roux? Stadic came in, and Franklin said something like, he wanted to sneak back to his place to pick up some clothes for his wife. An hour later, he was ambushed."

"Lucas . . ."

"Listen, after he was ambushed, I ran over to the hospital, and I kept thinking, how could they know he was coming? How could they know? They couldn't just hide outside his house twenty-four hours a day, waiting for him to come along. Why would they? We'd had it on TV that everybody was safe in the hotel . . .''

Lucas pointed a finger at Sloan: "The answer was right there in front of me: Stadic told them. He was the only one who could have."

Sherrill shook her head. "Seeing that might seem possible when you're working it out backwards. At the time, nobody would have figured it out."

"I should have," Lucas said.

"You're feeling sorry for yourself," Sloan said. "Get your head out of your ass."

"Since I didn't see it . . . well, I don't know what else I could've done at the hospital," Lucas said. He spread his hands, looked around the waiting room as though an answer might be written on the walls, then back at Sherrill and Sloan. "I sit here thinking about what I could've done, and I can't think of anything better. Not that that'd given her the best chance of staying alive, with what we knew at the time. Everything we knew said that LaChaise was insane."

"That's exactly right," Sloan said.

"The way I hear it, from what Weather told the docs, she spent the whole time with LaChaise working on him, convincing him he ought to stay alive . . . that *she* oughta stay alive. And it worked. They were both getting out of it and then boom! He blows up, and she freaks out," Lucas said.

"That's got to have some kind of effect on you," Sherrill said.

"What kind of effect? He was a giant asshole," Sloan said. "Getting shot was too good for him."

"That might not be the way she sees it," Sherrill said.

"Well." Sloan looked away. "I mean, what're you supposed to do?"

"I don't know," Lucas said. He pushed the conversation away. "Have you seen Del?"

"Yeah, he's gonna hurt for a while," Sloan said. "He's not, you know, *injured* that bad, but he *hurts* like hell."

"His wife is pissed," Sherrill said. "She says we should have had more people up there, besides Del."

"She's right," Lucas said.

"What about Sandy Darling?" Sloan asked Lucas. "I hear she's talking."

"Yeah." Lucas nodded. He'd spent the best part of an hour listening to the interrogation, before leaving Hennepin General for the University Hospitals. "Basically, she was kidnapped."

"Who killed her old man?"

"She doesn't know. She said it wasn't LaChaise or Butters or Martin."

"Stadic?" asked Sherrill, in a hushed voice.

"I think so," Lucas said. "He was trying to get rid of everyone. He got the truck tags, somehow, and figured out where they lived. He probably thought they were hiding up there, and went up to take them out. He had to see everybody dead to get free—and they all *would've* been dead if Sandy Darling hadn't tripped over her goddamn cowboy boots and fallen on her face in the stadium."

"It's a hell of a story," Sloan said. "The question is, how much of it is bullshit?"

"Maybe some," Lucas said. "Maybe not, though. There were a couple of things: she said while they attacked the hospital, they chained her to a post in Harp's garage. There's a chain around the post, and there're two padlocks, just like she said, and there's paint missing from the post and it's on the chain, as if somebody was trying to pull it free. The chain's got latents all over it, so we'll know if she was handling the chain. I think she was. Then she says she tried to climb out a window on Harp's building, walk down a ledge and go down the fire escape, but that the fire escape was jammed. There are fingerprints on the window, and the fire escape *is* jammed—it's actually an illegal latch, but you can't see it. So that's right. And walking that ledge in her bare feet, on snow, you'd have to be pretty desperate. And when she called from the dome, she didn't know it was all over, and she tried to warn me that LaChaise was going after Weather . . .''

''All right, so she walks,'' Sloan said. He stood up, yawned, and said, ''The big thing is, *you* gotta take care of *yourself*.''

''I gotta take care of Weather, is what I gotta do,'' Lucas said.

Sloan shook his head: ''Nope. Nobody can take care of Weather except Weather. You gotta take care of yourself.''

''Jesus, Sloan,'' Sherrill said. She was getting angry. ''You know what he means . . .''

Sloan opened his mouth and shut it again: A few years earlier, Lucas had gone through an episode of clinical depression, and since then, Sloan had thought of his friend as somewhat . . . *delicate* was not quite the right word; dangerously poised, perhaps. He said, ''Well . . .'' and let it go.

A nurse poked her head in, spotted Lucas and said, ''Weather's up.''

Lucas pushed himself out of the chair and said, ''See you guys later,'' and hurried down the hall after the nurse.

Weather had a private room, and when Lucas walked in, she was on her feet, in a hospital gown, digging into a locker-like closet for her clothes. Her face was intent, hurried.

''Weather . . .''

She jumped, turned, saw him and her face softened: ''Oh, God, Lucas.'' She reached toward him.

''How are you?'' He wrapped her up in his arms and her feet came off the floor.

"If you don't smother me, I'll probably be okay," she gasped.

He put her down. "Probably?"

"Well, when they had me sedated, they talked me into this ridiculous hospital gown." She pulled it out to the side, as if she were about to curtsy. "Every doc I know has been down to check on me, and every one has taken a good look at my ass."

"Just like you: bringing light into people's lives."

"I gotta get out of this gown," she said, digging into the locker again. "Shut the door."

Lucas shut the door, and as she tossed the balled-up gown on the bed, he said, "Really now—don't bullshit me. How are you?"

She was pulling on a blouse, and stopped, suddenly, as her hands came through the cuffs. "I'm sorta . . . messed up, I think. It's the weirdest thing." She rubbed her temple, looking up at him. Then her eyes drifted away, focused in the middle distance past his shoulder. "I'll be going along, thinking about something else, and then all of a sudden, there I am again, back in the hall with this man and you're standing there and then . . ."

She shuddered.

"Don't think about it," Lucas said.

"I'm not thinking about it. I refuse to think about it. But it's like . . . like somebody else holds up a picture of it, right in front of my eyes. It just comes, boom!" she said.

"Post-traumatic stress," he said.

"That's what I think," she said. "But in some way, I never really believed in it until now. It's like people who had it were . . . weaklings, or something."

"It'll go away," he repeated. "There in the hall—I didn't know what was happening with you and LaChaise, I couldn't take any chances, there wasn't any way to really know."

"I worked that out," she said. "And God, the whole thing was my fault. What was I doing here? When he came in the OR, I thought I was dead. I thought he'd kill me right there, and all my friends, the people with me. I felt so *stupid* . . ."

"You can't anticipate lunatics," Lucas said. "None of this made any sense."

Weather was rambling on: "Then he made the fatal error. I didn't see it, because we were talking so . . . normally. But I see it now: he'd maneuvered himself, by what he'd done, the way he was acting, into a spot where all the solutions were drastic and narrow. Thinking about it, I'm not sure he would have surrendered. At the time I thought he would: No, I was *sure* of it. But now, I'm not sure. When we were talking, he'd keep changing his mind, like . . . like . . ."

"A child," Lucas said.

"Yes . . . Well, not quite. Like a crazy child," she said.

She was staring out the window when she said that, looking down at the trees along the Mississippi, when suddenly she focused again, and turned to look up at him. "What about you?" she asked. "We heard about the policeman, that he was killed and you were there . . . are you all right?"

"Oh, yeah, I'm fine." He stood back from her, holding on to her shoulders but at arm's length, looking her over. She seemed so bright, so focused, so normal, so *all right*, that he suddenly laughed.

"What?" she asked, trying on a smile.

"Nothing," he said. He wrapped her up again, and her feet came off the floor again. "Everything. Especially the way that gown showed your ass off."

"*Lucas . . .*"

THE BEE WAS IMPATIENT, CHECKING HER WATCH, PEER-
ing down the street, bouncing on her toes. She was waiting
at the corner of Gayley and Le Conte, next to the Shell station, a forest-green JanSport backpack at her feet. Her face
was a pale crescent in the headlights of passing cars, in the
Los Angeles never-dark.

Anna Batory, riding without her seatbelt, her feet braced
on the truck's plastic dashboard, saw the Bee step out to the
curb and pointed: "There she is."

Creek grunted and eased the truck to the curb. Anna rolled
down the passenger-side window and spoke to the mask:
"You're the Bee?"

"You're late."

Anna glanced at the dashboard clock, then back out the
window: "Jason said ten-thirty."

Jason was sitting in the back of the truck on a gray metal
folding chair, next to Louis. He looked up from his Sony
chip-cam and said, "That's what they told me. Ten-thirty."

"It's *now* ten-thirty-*three*," the Bee said. She turned her wrist to show the blue face on a stainless-steel Rolex.

"Sorry," Anna said.

"Around the corner to Westwood, then Westwood to Circle. You know where Circle is?"

"Yeah, we know where everything is," Creek said. They'd been everywhere. "Hold on."

THERE'S A GUY ON THE CORNER," CREEK SAID.

Ahead and to the right, a woman in a ski mask was standing on the corner, making a *hurry-up* windmilling motion with one arm.

"That's Otter," the Bee said. "And that's the corner of Circle. They must be out—turn right."

Creek took the corner, past the waving woman. The street tilted uphill, and a hundred yards up, a cluster of women spilled down a driveway to the street, two of them struggling with a blue plastic municipal garbage can. A security guard was running down from the top of the hill, another one trailing behind.

"Got them coming out," Anna said, over her shoulder. A quick pulse ran through her: not quite excitement but some combination of pleasure and apprehension.

Nobody ever knew for sure what would happen at these things. Nothing much, probably, but any time you had guards with guns. . . . Did the guards have guns? She took a half-second to look but couldn't tell.

As she looked, she reached behind her, lifted the lid on the steel box bolted on the back of her seat, pulled the Nagra tape recorder from its foam nest. Jason was looking past her, through the windshield at the action, and she snapped: "Get ready."

"Yes, Mom," he said. He fitted a headset over the crown of his head, plugged in the earphone. Creek was driving with one hand, pulling on his own headset.

"Everybody hear me?" Anna asked, speaking into her face mike. The radios were one-way: Anna talked, everyone else listened.

Creek said, "Yeah," and took the truck over the curb, one big bounce and a nose-down, squealing, full stop. Jason had braced himself, and Louis had swivelled to let the chair take the jolt. The Bee toppled over and squealed, "Shit."

Ahead of them, the women carrying the garbage can were jerking and twisting down the driveway, doing the media polka—looking for the cameras, running for the lights, trying to stay away from the guards.

The raiders had gone into the back of the building, over a loading dock; the dock was contained inside a fence, with a concrete patio big enough for fifteen or twenty cars. At least a dozen women and a couple of men, all masked, milled around the patio; then a man ran out of the medical building, carrying a small, squealing, black-and-white pig. Then another woman, carrying boxes, or maybe cages.

As the truck settled, as Bee squealed, Anna was out and running, the Nagra banging against her leg. Jason was two steps behind her with the backup Sony, and Creek was out the driver's door, his camera up on his shoulder, off to Anna's left. Bee, a little out of shape, sputtered in their wake.

Then Creek lit up and Anna yelled at the man with the pig, "Bring the pig. Bring the pig this way. . . . Bring the pig." The man saw them coming and walked toward them, and she had the Nagra's mike pointed at the squealing pig and Jason lit up.

The security guards saw the camera lights and the first one turned to the man trailing, yelled something to the other, who ran back up the hill. The first one continued down and shouted at Creek, "Hey, no cameras here, no cameras."

A group of masked women headed toward him, walled him off from the rest of the milling crowd, pushed him toward the ramp. Frustrated, he climbed up the loading dock and hurried to the open door. Just as he was about to go through the door, he jumped back, and a young man in a blue oxford cloth shirt and jeans ran out of the building and headed toward the lights.

Anna said to the microphone, her voice calm, even, "Creek, there's a kid coming in, watch him. Jason, stay with the pig."

Creek back-pedaled. When Anna spoke into his ear, he'd looked up from his eyepiece and spotted the kid in the blue shirt: trouble, maybe. Trouble made good movies. The kid was striding toward them, a dark smear under his nose, one hand cupping his jaw. He seemed to be crying.

"They were gonna kill this pig, for nothing—for soap tests or something, shampoo," the masked pig-man shouted at Jason's camera. The pig was freaking out, long shrieking bleats, like a woman being stabbed. "She's gonna live now," pig-man shouted as the pig struggled against him. "She's gonna live."

The patio was chaos, with the cameras and the pig-man, the women with cages, all swirling around: Blue shirt arrived and Anna saw that he *was* crying, tears running down his cheeks as Creek tracked him with the lens. The dark smear was blood, which streamed from his nose and across his lips and chin.

"Give me that pig," the kid screamed, and he ran at the pig-man. "Gimme that." The animal women blocked him out, not hitting him, just body-blocking. Both Creek and Jason tracked the twirling scrum while Anna tried to stay out of their line; she kept the Nagra pointed, picking up the overall noise, which could be laid back into the tape later, if needed.

The Bee caught Anna's arm: "He's just a flunky, forget him," she shouted over the screams and grunting of the struggle. "But we're gonna do the mice now. Get the mice, in the garbage cans."

The women with the blue garbage cans were waiting their turn with the lights, and Anna spoke into the mike again: "Jason, get out of there. Go over to those blue garbage cans, they're full of mice, they're gonna turn them loose." Jason took a step back, lifted his head, spotted the garbage cans. "Creek, stay with the kid," Anna said. "Stay with the kid."

As Jason came up, the women with the garbage can, who'd been waiting, popped the lid and tipped it, and two or three hundred mice, some black, some white, some tan, scurried down the sides and ran out onto the patio, looked around, and headed for the nearest piece of cover.

Jason hung close and then the kid in the blue shirt went that way, screaming, "Gimme those," and sobbing, tried to corral the mice. They were everywhere, running over his feet, over his hands, avoiding him, making the break. He finally gave up and slumped on the ground, his head in his hands, the mice all around.

Jeez: this was almost too good, Anna thought.

As Creek tracked him, the Bee was back with her nagging voice: "Do you want an on-camera statement?"

And Anna thought, *Who's running this thing?* But she had to smile at the other woman's effective management: "Yeah, but we'd better hurry," Anna said. "The cops'll be coming."

Anna said into the mike, "Jason, get on the Bee, she'll make a statement." She pushed the mike up, raised her voice, shouted, "Rat, where are you?"

The man with the pig turned toward her. "I'm the Rat," he said. His teeth were bared, his face spotted with what looked like mud but could be pig shit.

"We're gonna need you over here: we need a comment," Anna said.

"No problem," he said. He handed the struggling pig to a

woman. "What exactly do you want?" The Rat had a deep,
smooth voice, a singer's baritone, and showed square white
teeth and a California surfer-boy cleft chin beneath the black
mask.

"Just tell us why you did it," Anna said, nodding at Jason's camera.

He leaned forward and stage-whispered, "For the pub-
licity."

Anna grinned back and said, "Tell that to the camera."

Jason yelled, "Hey, Rat: You wanna do this, or what?"

As the Rat and the Bee talked to Jason's camera, Anna
pulled the mike down in front of her face and said, "Creek,
let's talk to the kid. Let me in there first."

Creek hung back a couple of steps so the camera wouldn't
be right in the kid's face. Anna squatted next to him and
patted him on the shoulder. "Are you okay?"

The kid looked up, dazed, a pale teenage child with brown
eyes behind his gold-rimmed glasses. "What?"

"Are you okay?" Anna asked again.

"They're gonna fire me," he said. He looked back at the
building. "I was supposed to watch them. They were my
responsibility, the animals. I was supposed to keep everybody
out, but they came in so fast . . ."

"How'd you get the bloody nose?" Anna asked.

"I tried to hold the door, but they kicked through. Then
about four of them held me and I couldn't get to the phone,
and they tipped everything over in the lab, all the animal
cages, everything." He touched his face. "I think the door
hit me . . ."

"Look, there's gonna be two sides to this," Anna said.
She looked back at Creek, and said, "Creek."

Creek stepped away, spotted a mouse looking at him from
the top of the loading dock and closed in on it. Behind him,
the Bee and the Rat were still talking to Jason's camera; the

pig was still struggling with the woman who'd taken it, but the squealing had stopped, and the scene was almost quiet.

Anna turned back to the kid and continued, "The animal rights guys will be heroes to some people. And some people will be heroes to the scientific community."

She patted his thigh. "Now, go like this. From your nose."

She made an upward rubbing gesture with her hand, on her own face.

The kid gulped. "Why?"

"Want to keep your job?" Anna grinned at him. She was a small woman, dark-haired, with an oval face and flax-blue eyes behind gold-rimmed glasses: she had an effect on young males. "Be a hero. Smear a little blood around your face and we'll put you on camera, telling your side. Believe me, they won't fire you."

"I need the job," the kid said tentatively.

"Smear a little blood and stand up . . . what's your name?"

The kid was no dummy: He'd been born in front of a TV set. He wiped blood up his cheek and said, "Charles McKinley. . . . How do I look?" His cheek looked like a raw sirloin.

"Great."

Her cell phone rang. She unclipped it and stepped away. "Yeah."

Louis, calling from the truck seventy-five feet away, excited: "Jesus, Anna, we got a jumper on Wilshire, he's on a ledge."

"Where?" A basic rule: everything happened at once. Anna looked back at the two interviews, calculating.

"I don't know, somewhere on Wilshire, close, I think. I'm getting the address up."

"Get it now," Anna rapped. Very tense: a jumper would make everything. The networks, CNN, everything—if they got the jump. She could hear Louis tapping on the laptop keys, where he kept the address database. "C'mon, c'mon."

"I'm getting it . . ."

"How're we doing on the cops here?"

"You got a couple-three minutes, I just heard the call."

"Get the address, Louis."

"I'm hurrying."

Anna turned to Creek: "Get ready to wrap it up."

And to the kid, "Cops'll be here to help, minute or two."

Louis came back on the phone: "Jesus, Anna, it's just down the street, we're a half-mile out. And he's still up there."

Anna spoke into the mike, her voice urgent: "Jason, Creek. Back in the truck. Now! Kill the lights. Move it!"

"Hey, what, what?" Jason kept shooting.

"Close down! Get in the truck. Now."

As Anna and Creek came up, Louis jammed it into park and climbed over the seat into the back, and Jason came through the side. Creek slipped into the driver's seat and Louis shouted, "Down Gayley, then left on Wilshire, it's three blocks, it's a place called the Shamrock."

Creek: "I know the place. Jesus, it's two minutes from here."

"Gotta hustle," Anna said. "Gotta hustle, gotta hustle."

Creek spun the truck in a U-turn, headed back toward the Shell station, paused at the red light just long enough to make sure he wouldn't hit anything, then powered on through.

Louis had an earphone clamped over one ear. "The guy's still out there. On a ledge. There's hotel people talking to him. He's from a party, high-school kids."

Creek had the gas pedal on the floor and they just caught the light at Wilshire. As they swept through the intersection, Anna said to Jason, "Give yourself some space on your tape. You gotta be ready, but the first tape is good, too."

"I'm ready," Jason said.

"Creek?"

Creek nodded. Creek was always ready.

"Louis, talk to me," Anna said.

Louis's eyes were closed, and he was leaning away from them, listening hard. "There're cars on the way, we got maybe a minute by ourselves. Maybe two minutes."

Anna said, "Jason, I want you tight on the guy. Creek will pull back a bit, get the full jump, if he goes. But I wanna see his face . . ."

"You got it, sugarbun," Jason said.

Creek showed his teeth: "Sugarbun?"

Jason grinned at him: "Me'n Anna getting intimate."

"Yeah?" Creek glanced at Anna, who rolled her eyes.

"Me'n Anna doing the thing," Jason said. He was almost talking to himself, looked as though he might giggle. He was wound, his eyes big: he liked the movement, maybe too much. He was talented: might go big in Hollywood someday, Anna thought, if he didn't blow his brains out through his nose. "Doin' the thing," he muttered.

"Shamrock," Anna said and pointed. Ahead, a twenty-story green glass-and-steel building showed a bright green neon shamrock at the top. And Jason, who'd crawled between the seats, spotted the jumper: "There he is! He's toward the bottom, like five or six stories up, you can see him . . ."

He pointed, and Anna noticed that his hand had a tremor: not the trembling of excitement, but the jerk of a nerve break-down. She glanced at his stark, underfed face: Christ, she thought, he's back on the crank.

She turned away from the straining face, and looked where he was looking. Five stories, Anna counted. And there he was. The would-be jumper wore dark pants and a white shirt. From a block away, in the lights that bathed the outside of the building, he looked like a fly stuck to a sheet of glass. "Get us there, Creek," Anna said, breathlessly.

They were doing seventy-five, the wheels screaming, right up to the hotel, then Creek hammered the brake and cut sideways and they went over the curb again and Jason spilled out, running toward the hotel with his camera.

The man on the ledge had his back to a sheet of plate glass, his arms spread. The ledge, Anna thought, wasn't more than a foot wide—she could see the tips of his shoes.

"Guys, I'm gonna try to get up there," Anna said into her mike as she dropped from the truck. "You're gonna be on your own for a minute: Jason, I want *face*." She sprinted toward the hotel's front entrance, the Nagra flapping under her arm.

Hotels didn't want to know about media. As far as hotels were concerned, no media was good media. Anna had two options. She could try to sneak in, but that took time. Or she could run. She ran forty miles a week on the beach and if the stairs were placed right, no hotel security man in California could catch her.

She hit the glass doors and went through the lobby like she was on a motorcycle. Two bellman huddled at the reception desk with a couple of clerks, and one of the bellmen saw her and just had time to turn, to open his mouth and shout, "Hey," when she was past him. The elevators were straight ahead, and a brass plaque with an arrow pointing to the right said "Stairs."

She took the stairs. Ran up one flight, two, then a man shouting again, from the bottom, "Hey . . ." Third floor, not even breathing hard. Anna got off at the fourth: there'd be security on the fifth floor, and the desk people might have called them. She ran into the hall on the fourth floor, looked right and left, decided that the right end would be the far end of the hotel. There should be another flight of stairs that way.

She ran down the hall, now aware of her heart pounding in her chest, turned a corner past a niche with Coke, ice and candy machines, to another stairway. She pulled open the door, looked up and down, heard nothing and ran up to five.

She took three seconds, two long breaths, pulled off her headset, shoved it with the Nagra up under her jacket in back, held it with one hand, and sauntered into the hallway.

Halfway down, three older men—security, probably—stood outside an open doorway. A dozen kids were scattered up and down the hall, a few of them talking, most just looking down at the open door. All the kids were dressed up, the boys in suits and ties, the girls in pink and blue party dresses, all with the stark-white look of fear on their faces.

One of the security men looked toward Anna, and even leaned her way—but as he did, a woman shrieked, and the men in suits turned and ran through the open door.

My God, Anna thought, *he jumped*.

The girls in pastel dresses were looking at the door, the boys were looking at each other, all were frozen: Anna knew that this was one of the moments she'd remember: they were like sculpture in some modern wise-cracking installation called *California Kids*.

Then Anna moved, and when she did, a couple of the girls began sobbing, and one of the boys yelled, "Oh, no. No, Jacob . . ."

Anna ran lightly down the hall, found another open door a few rooms closer than the one where the security men had been. She looked inside: a man and woman, both gray-haired, horrified, were standing at their window, looking out. Anna stepped inside.

"Did he jump?"

The woman, white-faced, looked at her, her mouth working, nothing coming out, then: "Oh, my God."

Anna stepped around an open suitcase, walked across the room, and looked out the window. The jumper was facedown, a black and white silhouette on the yellow stone, six feet from the pool. Ten feet from the body, Jason was moving in with his camera. From across the pool, Creek also focused on the body.

Anna took out the recorder, hit the record switch, held it by her side: didn't hide it, just held it like a purse.

"What happened?" she asked.

"I don't know . . . I think it was just kids, having a party. They were making noise, we could hear them running in the hallway. The next thing we know people were screaming and the hotel people came."

Anna could feel the recorder taking up tape: "Did you see him go?" she asked the gray-haired man.

"I think he was coming in," the man said. "He turned and it was like he lost his balance and all of a sudden he jumped, like he was trying to make the pool . . ."

The woman turned to her husband, "Jim, let's get out of here."

Anna stepped back, looked at the luggage tag on the suitcase: James Madson, Tilly, OK. "Are you Mr. and Mrs. Madson?"

The woman turned toward her. "Yes, yes. . . . Are you with the hotel? We'd like to check out."

"You'd have to talk with the people downstairs. Are you all right, ma'am? What is your name?"

"Lucille . . . I'm all right, but the man, the boy, he. . . . Jim, I think I'm going to throw up."

She started toward the bathroom with her husband behind her, one hand in the middle of her back, patting her, and Anna stepped to the door and looked out.

Hotel security was there in force, along with four or five uniformed cops. She stepped back, said, "Madson, M-A-D-S-O-N, Tilly, Oklahoma, T-I-L-L-Y," to the Nagra, then popped the recording tape and slipped it inside the waistband of her pants. She had two spare tapes in a black pouch on the carrying strap: she took out a spare, slipped it into the recorder. Hotel security usually didn't ask if they could have the tape, they simply took it, destroyed it, and apologized later.

Anna stepped into the hall: two of the men who'd been in the room were just coming back out. Hotel security and a manager-type. Before either could say anything, Anna said, "Could somebody help my mother? I think she's gonna be sick."

The manager-type asked, "What's wrong?"

"She saw the man jump, she's in the bathroom . . ."

The manager went by, into the Madsons' room, while the security man ran down the hall toward the elevators. Anna turned the other way and walked back down the hall to the steps.

Into the stairwell, down and around, and around, to the first floor. Pause, listen. Nothing. She stepped into the hallway, saw a sign that said, "PARKING RAMP," and went that way.

CREEK WAS STANDING FIFTY FEET FROM THE BODY. NO blood, no movement, nothing but a hotel clerk and three cops walking reluctantly toward it. Creek saw her coming and made his open-handed "Got anything?" gesture.

She'd pulled the headset back on. "Quick quotes from a witness," she said into the mike. "They said there was some kind of party before he jumped, or fell, or whatever."

"I'm having a little trouble dealing with this," Jason said. He looked at the body.

"With what?" Anna cocked her head, puzzled.

"I'm just . . . my head's fucked up," he said. Then: "Anna, I'm sorry, but I gotta go." He pulled off the headset and handed it to her, shamefaced. "I'm sorry, but I've never seen this before. I've seen bodies, but this was. . . . He was smiling at me."

He turned his knees in, so he was standing on the edges of

his tennis shoes, head down, like an embarrassed little boy. "I gotta go. You gotta couple of bucks I could borrow until we sell this shit? Take it out of my cut?"

Anna stared at him for a second. Concerned, not angry. "Jase, how bad is it?"

"It's not nothing," Jason insisted. "You're probably done for tonight, anyway. You gotta couple of bucks?"

"Yeah, sure," Anna said. She dug in her pants pocket, came up with a short roll of twenties, gave him two.

"Thanks."

And he went, hurrying away across the stone patio, Creek peering after him. In the background, they could hear sirens: fire rescue, too late.

"What was that all about?" Anna asked, watching as Jason went out to the street.

Creek shook his head. "I don't know."

"Well . . ." Anna hoisted the camera, looked through the eyepiece, focused on the group of cops around the body, and ran off fifteen seconds of tape. Then she ran it back, forty-five seconds, and replayed.

The jump was there, in-and-out of focus, but undeniably real, taking her breath away: and at the last second, the man's arms flailing, his face passing through the rectangle of the lens display, then the unyielding stone patio.

"Jeez," she said. She looked at Creek. "This is . . ." She groped for a concept, and found one. "This is *Hollywood*."